To Joanne
K. Vanghen

LOWERTOWN

A Novel

❦

BY KARL VANGHEN

This book is a work of fiction, although certain places, occasions, and occurrences are based on fact.

This book is printed on acid free paper.

Copyright © 2013 By Karl Vanghen

All rights reserved.

ISBN: 1480086363

ISBN 13: 9781480086364

Dedications

This book is dedicated to those who have assisted in its creation, namely, June, the woman who shares my life, my dreams, and my future. Without her at my side this story might never have been written, for it was she who inspired, she who gave of her time that I might write, and she who loved and comforted me unconditionally. Also, the members of my family, my son Jeffrey who has suffered greatly from the ravaging effects of Parkinson's, my son Richard, who assisted unselfishly by answering numerous calls for help, and my daughter, whose presence always encourages. Those learned professionals of my literary club, whose critiques not only improved my work, but inspired this writer to challenge himself. And my cadre of friends whose companionship, humor, and reassurance kept me focused even when the light of creativity dimmed. To name a few, Connie Anderson, my friend and mentor, Meg Corrigan, for her motivating presence in my life, and Charles and Dorothy Hall, a King and Queen in their own right. And to all historians, both previous and present, who preserved, for us, those invaluable records of times long past.

✵ ✵ ✵

Special thanks to the Minnesota Historical Society for use of their archival photo appearing on the front cover of this book entitled, "St. Paul in 1869, Lowertown", taken by Benjamin Franklin Upton,

✯ ✯ ✯

Other books by Karl Vanghen

GRACED WITH A SWORD
READY TO FIRE: MEMOIR OF AN AMERICAN ARTILLERYMAN IN THE KOREAN WAR, Written for Richard B. Holmsten, published by McFarland and Company Publishers
MY ENEMY, MY BELOVED

LOWERTOWN

Epilogue

Following the collapse of Lord Selkirk's ill-fated Red River Colony in Canada, members of the surviving clan moved south to the protective stronghold of Fort Snelling, the stone bastion situated above the confluence of the Minnesota and Mississippi Rivers. The settlers remained there undisturbed until Major Joseph Plympton assumed command of the fort in 1837. Concerned by so many squatters on a military post, Plympton had the entire area mapped, and later, with map in hand, and with force enough to back up his words, he ordered the intruders to leave. Disgruntled, the settlers obeyed and trudged three miles east to a place near Fountain Cave, where Pierre Parrant, known as Pig's Eye, conducted a brisk whiskey trade. There, they settled down, confident they would never move again. But as the whiskey trade flourished, Major Plympton became outraged at the frequent drunkenness among his soldiers, and so he drew up a new map, placing Fountain Cave within fort limits. In 1840 he ordered the squatter cabins destroyed. Once again, angry and homeless, but undaunted, the settlers salvaged what they could and moved downriver to carve out a small village on the north bank of the Mississippi where the water bent south along the high bluffs. They named their village Pig's Eye, in recognition of Pierre Parrant. The name prevailed until people began flooding into the new territory acquired from France as part of the Louisiana Purchase. Not weather, or danger, or hardship could stop the flow of immigrants that came by the thousands.

In 1841 the Chapel of Saint Paul was built, and as the population increased, those who had brought religion to the city decided to change Pig's Eye to a more respectable name. Soon afterwards the site became known as Saint Paul.

Thus, in the spring of 1849, when April thaws opened the river for steamboat traffic, the citizens of Saint Paul huddled on the bank of the Mississippi to receive long delayed mail. Late in the day on April 9, during a violent thunderstorm, they heard a steamer's shrill whistle, and as lightening flashed, they saw the *Dr. Franklin No. 2* headed toward the levee. They boarded the boat before it was tied to its moorings, and learned that the mail included important news from Washington, D.C. When the town's leaders announced, that on March 3, the bill clearing Minnesota Territory for statehood had been passed a cheer went up, loud enough to be heard atop the bluffs. The news spread rapidly from Saint Paul to Fort Snelling and Mendota and from there to Saint Anthony. In Winona a hundred guns were fired. However, Minnesota was not admitted to the union until May 11, 1858, at which time it became the thirty-second state with Saint Paul as its capitol.

During that same year Fort Snelling was sold to Mr. Franklin Steele for the sum of ninety-thousand dollars. The Bill of Sale also included eight-thousand acres of land that would eventually become part of the city of Minneapolis.

By 1861 a stage line carried mail and passengers between Saint Paul and Minneapolis. In Saint Paul the many business establishments included auctioneers, attorneys, architects, builders, bakers, banks, sixteen boarding houses, butchers, brewers, many saloons, carriage and wagon establishments, engineers, clothiers, five daguerreotype artists, six druggists, two gunsmiths, a police force, a fire department, and a right fine capitol building.

The city was growing up, and like a young lad eager to reach manhood, nothing would stop it.

CHAPTER ONE

Departure

"C'mon . . . we're almost there." Randolph Finch's persistent voice surged back over his shoulder, straight at his younger brother, Devon.

The two boys were running on the dirt road near their home, pouring every ounce of energy into their legs. Sweat saturated them. The sun burned away at their endurance as their feet pounded on the hard-pan like stallions on a chase.

"I'll catch ya," Devon shouted. His words heaved out with each of his breaths.

"There's . . . the fence," Randolph shouted. "You better . . . hurry!"

Randolph Finch always challenged Devon no matter what the circumstance, be it running, or throwing, or fishing, or climbing, to make him better than he was, to make him the best. They were much alike, although Randolph was stronger and faster, more physical, and three years older. Devon, on the other hand, just turned fourteen, considered challenge more like a test, a building of character, and whenever he surpassed Randolph, he felt pride so overwhelming as to nearly burst his heart with glory.

Devon's voice devoured the distance. "I'm gainin' . . . on ya."

A touch of laughter emphasized Randolph's shout. "You gotta . . . go faster, or else . . . I'll beat ya."

"I'm comin'."

Devon squeezed every bit of endurance into the remaining twenty yards. Only ten feet separated him from Randolph, ten feet before he could claim victory. His teeth clenched as his legs pumped harder, straining for a final burst of speed. Seconds later he reached out and touched Randolph's arm.

"You ain't . . . gonna make it, Dev."

"Sure . . . am."

Just before they reached the fence their dash slowed, lest they crash into the wooden rails. Devon plunged forward as Randolph's arm raised slightly ahead of his own. With one final, desperate lunge, Devon's shoulder bumped against Randolph's, and together they met the rail, their breaths surging, their faces red with effort. With their struggle ended, they slumped down, panting, their arms encircling one another as they breathed the scent of tall grass.

"I did it," Devon panted.

"By God, you did for sure." Randolph wrapped Devon in his arms, accepting his perspiration like a balm, as pride swelled his chest.

They lay there, breathing slower, each relishing the moment of glory, that undeniable element of pride. As the sun warmed them, a slow summer breeze carried away their body heat.

When their breathing returned to normal, Randolph wiped a bead of sweat from Devon's forehead, gazed directly into his eyes, and said. "You're the best brother a boy could ever have."

Randolph's words moved through Devon's heart, unleashing tears. No, he thought, it was he who had the best brother. Randolph was . . . he was . . . was . . . words could not define his love, not then, not ever. Reaching up, he scrubbed his tears away. "Dang it, Randolph," he said. "I ran so hard, even my eyes are sweating."

As their laughter subsided, they laid together, wrapped in camaraderie so intense as to be overwhelming.

✫ ✫ ✫

Departure

The day of that run, three year earlier, was strong in Devon Finch's mind as he brushed aside the white cotton curtains of his bedroom window to a day he prayed would never come, for it would be a sad day. Before the morning ended, Randolph would go off to war, leaving only his memory behind.

The day was April 27, 1861, and as the morning sunlight awakened a sense of sorrow, Devon thought about Randolph's impending march into a world of fire and death, into a war between the North and South, a war beyond comprehension. Outside, the morning sky seemed almost profane. The thin, gray fog sheathing the hillsides opposite the river deadened the city beneath its pallor. Randolph stood just inside the fence, gazing out across the scene he'd not see again for months, or perhaps never, if the war went badly. Quickly, Devon opened the window. He had things to say, and his brother's voice to hear, and time would not stand still.

"Hey, big brother, what are you looking at?"

Randolph turned, raising an arm in greeting. "I'm just trying to memorize what I'll be leaving behind. It could be a while before I see it again."

Devon hurried his reply. "I'm coming down. Wait there for me."

Devon turned and glanced at his brother's bed. As always, it was neat to a fault, its blanket tucked, its pillow smoothed. Randolph was a most perfect son, who Devon had been unable to emulate despite all his attempts to do so. He was the first son, his mother's joy, his father's pride, but regardless of Randolph's superiority, Devon loved him deeply. For sure, Randolph's bed would remain empty for a while. The thought of his impending absence made Devon move faster.

As Devon descended the narrow stairway into the small kitchen, his father looked up from his place at the table, his face sullen, his mood intensified by the hardness of his thoughts. At thirty-seven, Harold's thin hair had already turned partially gray. His eyes, deeply set, were fixed with a gaze intense enough to censure most everything with a keen, penetrating stare. He was a tough man, developed by long days in the sun and the sweat of the prairie. Now, he was respected as being quiet but firm, diligent and trustworthy, to all who knew him. As Devon approached, he said, "Good morning. If you're looking for Randolph, he's outside in front."

His mother turned sadly toward him. Immediately, Devon saw her eyes, red from crying. Casually, she wiped her cheek while turning her attention to the stove where bacon was frying.

"Good morning, Mother," Devon said, pausing to touch her hand.

Her head wagged slightly. "Not a good day," she said, clearing her throat. "Today is not a good day."

Devon felt the sting of their sadness as he passed through the parlor and out the front door. As the door closed, Randolph turned. He didn't speak. He just looked at Devon with an expression that conveyed a sense of disillusion. Devon walked up alongside him and leaned into the fence, intentionally touching his arm in doing so. Ahead of them the city stretched away toward the river where ragged bluffs descended sharply to the water's edge. Off to their left the scars of a big fire that had consumed thirty-four structures the year before still darkened the landscape.

"It's a bit cold today," Randolph remarked.

Devon shrugged. "Tis' that, disagreeable at best, but better than earlier this month, when I thought we'd be washed into the river."

April had been wet and cold. Heavy rains had finally moved the ice out of Lake Pepin to the south, unleashing a most damaging flood, sending the Mississippi out of its banks, three miles wide in places. The steamboat *Itaska* rode so high at Winona that it cut the only telegraph line strung to Saint Paul in 1860, severing communications for a time.

Randolph broke the silence. "Most all of the police force is going, near three-quarters of 'em. Won't be many left to watch the city. They'll need volunteers, especially for night duty."

"I've been thinking about it," Devon replied.

"We'll need about two hundred men, four companies, one for each section of the city. Without police this city won't be a fit place to live, given all the troublemakers comin' up-river."

"I said I been thinking about it."

Departure

"As soon as I leave you better get on down to city hall and sign up."

"I'd rather go with you."

Randolph nudged him. "You're stayin' here. When the governor said he'd send a thousand men to help the cause, Pa knew I'd go, but not you. Besides, you ain't old enough. You gotta be eighteen, or no older than forty-five."

"I'm seventeen."

"And I'm twenty. That makes me your senior. It's my job to go and fight."

"Maybe I'll go next year."

"War might be over by then. Those Rebs ain't got a chance against the Union Army. Besides, when they see Randolph Finch comin' at 'em, they might just turn tail and run. Why, I might just be home for Christmas."

Devon wiped his nose. "Certainly hope so. But they whooped us already."

"That's cuz we weren't prepared. It'll be different once we get our forces built up. Right now the Union army is only sixteen-thousand strong, and most of them are spread out on the western frontier, and the state militia is ill-equipped at present. At least that's what we were told. That's why we're so badly needed."

The raw river wind chilled their faces, chasing away the sun's warmth. Devon turned his head to the sound of geese, a flight of near a hundred cutting wind above the steeple of the Presbyterian Church to his left. "Were you with Pricilla last night," he asked. Pricilla was Randolph's girlfriend.

"We walked a spell."

"Was she sad?"

Randolph nodded. "She's got a right to be. But she said she'd wait for me, no matter how long." He patted the pocket of his trousers. "I got a hank of her hair to go with me."

Devon leaned into the fence. "What made you go and sign up?"

"Told you once, all my friends rushed in to sign. I wasn't going to just stand there and look like a coward. Strong men rise to the occasion."

"I wish the Rebs had never attacked us."

5

"Well, they did, and now it's gonna cost 'em."

Devon hunched over, and in a moment of deep concentration, he heard the imagined sound of cannon and the rattle of musketry and the cries of men as they charged through a blizzard of lead toward victory or death. He shivered, imagining that one of them might soon be Randolph. Tears formed in his eyes. "I'll be praying for you, Randolph," he muttered.

Randolph's arm came up to rest across Devon's shoulder, and in that moment of unspoken affection, the bond between them strengthened. Devon remembered the times they had fished along the river, and the nights they had laid together and looked at the stars, and the times they had spoken about distant lands hidden beyond the mountains. And he remembered them praying together when their mother had been sick in bed with influenza, when all appeared to be hopeless. The prayers saved her, Randolph had said later.

"I couldn't have a better brother," Randolph's words choked in his throat.

Before Devon could respond, the house door opened and their mother called to them through the wind. "Breakfast is ready. Come on in now."

Turning, the boys glanced briefly at one another, and then headed straight for the kitchen.

The kitchen was small, room enough for the stove and sink and a cupboard next to the ice chest. The table had four chairs, no more. Devon always sat to the left of his father, Randolph to the right, Nona across from Harold so he could see her clearly. A bowl of scrambled eggs was set on the table, along with hot biscuits and strawberry jam. Before anyone reached for food, Harold crossed his hands. His voice was hollow, lacking its usual depth. "Good Lord, accept our thanks for bounty and love, and keep us safe in these difficult times. Today we ask you to follow our son, Randolph, as he goes forth to protect our Union from those who wish to bring it down. Be his constant guide in moments of danger, and return him to us unharmed. Need we say more, except to thank you for the love that surrounds us. Amen."

Nona reached for the platter as a tear trailed down her cheek.

Departure

"The wagon will be coming about ten," Randolph said. "It'll be pickin' us up at the court house."

The court house stood a block away from the Finch home, in Court House Square. The walk would be short, allowing scant time to comprehend the gravity of the day.

"Will Pricilla be there?" Nona asked.

"I expect she will."

Devon grinned "She has to give him one final kiss."

Randolph sliced his bacon and mixed it with the eggs. "It won't be final," he shot back. "I'll be comin' home to marry her."

"I didn't mean it that way," Devon responded.

As Nona rapped a fork against her plate, the conversation silenced. As was her nature, she changed the subject. "The ladies have formed an organization of volunteers to assemble bedding and clothing that will protect the troops from the hot, southern sun. They'll also prepare jellies, preserved tomatoes, and pickles for the boys, and maybe later on, if the need arises, they'll provide some entertainment for fund raising."

Randolph winked at her. "I hope you'll be savin' some of that entertainment for when I come home."

Nona smiled, momentarily replacing her sadness. "We will, Randolph, you can be sure of that."

Randolph kept right on talking. "I expect before the day is over that we'll have our uniforms and an Enfield rifle, maybe even a kepi to keep the sun off our necks."

"We'll be making some kepi caps as well," Nona remarked.

Harold sat still as a rock, his fists wrapped tightly around his tableware, fork in one hand, knife in the other. When Randolph's eyes set on him, he spoke right out. "I'd like to tell you to fall to the ground as soon as you hear the muskets, but I know you won't."

Randolph's jaw tightened. "Frankly, I don't know what will happen if I'm put on the line. That's something I don't want to think about."

Harold's eyes moved away. "I know you'll do what's expected of you."

"That I will."

"I've known a coward of two in my day. They're the lowliest of people."

"I won't be a coward, Father."

"Enough said. Just be the best soldier you can, and look out for yourself. Just get the job done, and come back home."

Again, the tableware clattered against Nona's plate. "Stop it now, I say. No more war talk at this table. We can surely spend the rest of the morning talking about other things. God knows there's much else that can occupy our time as long as Randolph is still here."

"I won't say another word," Harold said.

Randolph picked up a slice of bacon and bit it in half. "There's talk," he said.

"What kind of talk?"

"When we signed up, someone said the government might cut back on the steamers coming up this far. The army might use most of them between Saint Louis and New Orleans, to carry war materials and men."

"Rumors."

"Might be."

Devon interjected. "They can't just cut us off up here. We need supplies to keep this city running."

"It's just what I heard."

"Let's hope it's merely talk. The *Imperial* is due in here tomorrow." The *Imperial* was a side-wheeler, a wooden-hulled packet boat with two smokestacks. She was usually the first steamer to arrive after the ice went out.

"She'll be bringing in supplies for sure." Harold motioned to Devon. "Pass over some more of that bacon."

From that point on, the four were mostly silent, just small talk and remembrances, like when Randolph and Devon had explored Carver's Cave, where the Dakotas once held their ceremonies, and when they hiked to Kaposia on the flats of the south bluffs, where the Dakota's once lived. "Little Crow's village" it was called.

When breakfast ended, the boys went outside. The sun was higher, but the wind still blew cold. They stood by the fence again and gazed down the street where workmen were laboring to complete the new jail. The old jail, a log structure with only three cells and a single window, wasn't fit to hold animals, much less humans.

Departure

The new jail was constructed of stone. Randolph had told his family that it might fill up within a week, given the nature of the city, with all the drunks, hooligans, and loose women that prowled the city streets and bars.

Randolph spoke straight out. "The army told us we'd be earning thirteen dollars a month. What's even better, they promised us, that when we got out, we'd receive a bounty of one-hundred dollars, and a land warrant for a hundred-and-sixty acres. How's that for getting' rich? They said I'll be part of the First Minnesota Infantry Regiment. It's gonna be a proud unit."

"I expect it will be, since you'll be in it. Are you scared?"

Randolph shrugged. "A mite, I guess. It's gonna be like facing a big, angry bear with only a knife in your hand. I don't know what to expect, 'cept we'll be facing a lot of wrathful men who'll have a score to settle. I've never been in a fight like this before. Biggest fight I ever had is when I took town that drunken Irishman last year after he'd beaten up on three others."

"Quite a fight, I hear."

"Well, he was all tuckered out by the time I got to him, bleedin' from the mouth, just about ready to fall. Takin' him down was easy."

"The war won't be easy."

"I expect it won't, be it guns instead of fists."

"Will you be writing to us?"

"As much as I can."

"Who'll be heading up the Vigilance Committee?"

"Well, old man H. H. Western, for sure."

"What's he like?"

Randolph scratched the side of his arm, while shivering a bit. "He's a big guy with a voice like the roar of a lion, and tough to the core. You'll be seein' him when it comes time to join up."

"I'm going in on Monday."

"Good luck. But I gotta tell ya, the streets look a lot different at night than during the day, especially when they're loaded with drunks and whores. You'll have yourself a time of it, especially if you draw duty here in Lowertown."

They talked until the cold wind sent them back inside. About nine-thirty the family left for the short walk to the court house, an imposing stone structure with four columns in front, and a peaked roof.

Pricilla was there, clothed in a fine dress with lace collar, waiting for Randolph. Devon thought her to be a most perfect girl. After greeting the family, she took Randolph's arm and together they walked a short distance away where they stood talking to one another, her head on his shoulder.

"She's going to miss him," Harold said.

Soon some of Randolph's police friends arrived. Out of courtesy, they left Randolph alone with Pricilla, while giving off loud talk and laughter to ease their apprehensions. Meanwhile, the women tried to overcome their grief.

Moments later the buckboard arrived, and afterwards, the mayor came out and spoke a few words meant to encourage and sustain, some of which were carried away by the wind. The Finch's heard little of what was said. Randolph stood erect, his hand tight in Pricilla's, as tears rolled down her eyes. Suddenly, it was over.

"Guess it's time," Randolph said, trying to mask his sadness, trying to be man enough to hide his anxiety, without displaying a hint of fear.

"Take care of yourself now," Harold said, folding his strong hand into Randolph's, the two of them embracing, their emotions obvious.

Randolph embraced his mother as she spoke. "Write to us now and again." She held him close as if to never let him go.

Devon was last, and when they stood eye to eye they were filled with emotions too strong to conceal. As tears rolled down Devon's cheek, he muttered, "Go and get 'em,"

Randolph pulled Devon forward and held him tight for a moment, his hands thumping against his back. When they separated, Randolph said, "You take care, now. You got a town to protect."

With the farewells spoken, Randolph took Pricilla's hand and walked a distance away, where they could be alone for a while. They looked into one another's eyes with a fondness built on love.

"Don't worry about me," Randolph said to her. "I'll be just fine."

Departure

"I will worry," she replied, as her tears rushed out.

"This is my calling," he said. "Our country needs me, all of us. If we don't stop them we won't have a country any more. We'll all suffer under the Confederate flag."

Words came through her sobs. "It's just talk."

"True talk."

"Hold me. Just hold me."

They embraced until the word was given. Quickly, the men separated from their loved ones and stepped into the wagon, and with a wave and shouts of goodbye, the horses guided the wagon away down Wabasha Street, turning right at Walker's Hat and Cap Shop on Third.

In the wagon, Randolph watched the distance lengthen until the figures of those he loved grew smaller, until tears blurred his vision. Then his glance fell to the floorboards, and he didn't hear the sound of hoofs on the dirt road, or the swish of harness, or the shouts from those on the side of the road who waved and called, waved and called. He heard only his heartbeat.

They passed the American House on Third where the Red Coach Line stopped. There, Randolph raised his head and took a deep breath, realizing that the city would soon be out of sight.

Thoughts came on. No longer would he breathe the scent of home again, or smell the richness of the air, or the scent of the city, or the aroma of wet grass and pine when the wind came from the north. Nor would he see the city's hard dirt streets or the tint of its fires against the sky, or the drift of smoke from Lambert's Landing when the steamers came in, or the richness of a winter snow, or frost on the windows. Nor would he detect the perfume on Pricilla's neck where his lips had pressed, or breathe the scent of her skin when they embraced.

Randolph didn't look up, nor was there much talk in the wagon.

For the first time since he had penned his name on the register, he felt alone and fearful of what might lay ahead for him.

Randolph Finch was going off to war, and the thought of it scared him.

CHAPTER TWO

Carolyn Jean Page

Caroline Jean Page arrived in Minnesota in 1852 at the age of nine with her parents and her sister Bethany. Her only brother had died of influenza when she was seven. Her scant memory of him was limited to visions of his face, red and burning, his breath coming in short gasps. The family buried him in Indiana on a hilltop overlooking a nameless stream. Her mother and father had cried that day.

They arrived in Minnesota with the first great wave of settlers, in a wagon burdened down with all their worldly possessions, shortly after the Dakota Indians had ceded millions of acres over to the new territory. They settled in the city of Saint Paul, which was a major gateway for those seeking property on recently acquired land to the west.

By 1861, Saint Paul was platted with no apparent reason behind its growth. The continual blasting, grading, and draining of its well-watered terrain made the city appear like a volcano after eruption, with ditches, ponderous piles of earth, dangerous precipices, and heaps of rock visible wherever one looked. Its streets were narrow, crooked, some steep enough to challenge a horse, all of it conforming to the hills and river frontage that rested on bedrock comprised of shale, limestone and sandstone.

But growth offered change, and when the city became the seat of government it was quickly ornamented with public buildings, a territorial capital, county courthouse, city hall and jail. Even so, law enforcement struggled to control common offenses like violence, drunkenness, prostitution and disorderly conduct brought on by gamblers, thieves and loose women who thronged the hotels and bars. Eventually, to the dislike of those who thought better of it, the city became recognized as the bawdiest town on the river.

Caroline Page and her family settled right in the middle of it. With money he had saved, Kenneth Page built a right fine home up on Seventh Street within view of the capitol building. By then the city had taken on a look of refinement, and in 1857, as if to mock its bad reputation, the Saint Paul Gas and Light Company, was contracted to furnish the municipality with street lights. After that, before every sunset, lamplighters became a familiar sight; giving people reason enough to walk after dark.

Soon after Caroline settled into her new home, and new school, she met a young boy named Devon Finch, and from then on, her life, and her vision for the future, took on a new and significant meaning.

✫ ✫ ✫

Caroline Page was attracted to Devon when they were fourteen. She first set eyes on him during a rainy day when the spark in his eyes seemed to her like sunshine. She quickly learned that he was a spirited boy with a spunky attitude, and a voice that captivated her whenever he spoke. Her feelings for him were immediate, brought on by the way he moved, by the way he touched her, and by his manliness, as if he had come from another time and place.

As they grew older she became brave enough to hold his hand, even when others were present, and she nearly fainted once when he put his arms around her and drew her tight, to kiss her on the cheek. She felt love then, and when they were fifteen, her hand was in his most of the time.

By sixteen they had shared their first intimate kiss. She was, then, a most beautiful woman. Her playfulness had matured to charm, her voice to a more convincing tone, and her smile to the warmth of sunshine. When they were together he felt as if they were alone in the world, especially when they were on the hillside behind the capitol building, from where they could look north across land filled with pines and oaks; a sweep of nature so broad as to give them a feeling of wonder.

At seventeen, Caroline had acquired the figure of a woman, and a tenderness that claimed her every feature. By then, she was in love, and a future with Devon seemed assured, if only he could make something of himself when he finished school, if only the army didn't take him. She wanted to give Devon the things a man needed, beyond just the goodness of her being.

On the Sunday following Randolph's departure, Carolyn left home immediately after dinner and walked toward the Market House, a large, wooden structure that stood near their homes. Carolyn had said she would meet him there, and she always remained true to her word. Her steps were anxious for she had not seen him alone since the Friday before. As she approached the building she saw him standing outside, looking anxious as always. Her shoulders rose with the glint of her smile.

Devon stepped toward her as she approached, and held out his hands. "I hope the cold didn't get to you," he said, wrapping an arm across her shoulders.

"Thoughts of you kept me warm," she replied. A smile lit her face, and a small hank of hair that often drifted down above her right eye made an appearance from beneath her bonnet. Casually, she brushed it away.

"Did you see Randolph off?" she asked.

"Yes. His parting was sad. My mother took it badly."

"I expected she would."

"There's nothing worse than seeing a brother go away. It must be more heartsick for a mother, to see a son go off to war. I can't think of anything worse, except seeing him dead."

"Don't think on it. Not tonight."

Devon sighed, eager to change the subject. "Shall we walk?" he asked.

"Yes."

"Shall we go up on the hill?"

"I would like that."

The hill behind the capitol was a high point of land. From its summit, one could look north over the forest toward the lakes, however unseen. It had become their preferred place away from the city, a location unlike any other. He took her hand, proud to be at her side.

Caroline was attired in a long, green dress that brushed her ankles. The knee-length coat she wore was suitable protection against the cold wind. She walked with a good stride to keep pace with him. She was magical, he thought, speaking each word like the lilt of a song, with a smile on her face, her teeth as white as the feathers of a snow goose.

On the way up, they talked about their intentions for the summer months, the places they would go, the things they planned to accomplish. He concealed most of what was on his mind, because it bothered him. On this day he had things to say, and a need to express them as best he could, hoping she would accept his words without reservation. Soon they were atop the hill, and as the sun turned orange, they sat and gazed out across the darkening land. Most of the snow had melted, leaving only bare, brown forests and the blue sky above to meet their gaze.

"I have something to tell you," Devon said, as his hand tightened on hers.

Her smile drifted away. As she turned toward him, her eyes acquired a sensitive expression. "What is it?" she asked.

Devon cleared his throat, and then waited a moment, hesitant to speak. The words were all caught up inside him, and he couldn't seem to bring them out. Then, when seeing her anxious expression, he said, "I'm going to join the Alliance Committee."

Caroline nodded. Her gaze drifted away, over the barren hillsides, as if to find solace there. His statement went unanswered.

"Did you hear me?" he asked.

"Yes."

Devon cleared his throat. "Most of the police are gone. The city will need volunteers to keep the peace. If I can't go to war, the least I can do is guard the streets, to keep people safe, to keep you safe. I asked my father. He said it was alright. I didn't want to tell you, lest you get angry."

Caroline smiled, easing his discomfort. "Is that all you want to tell me?" she asked.

"Isn't it enough? With recruiting stations going in, and me being unable to join, I want to prove my worth, to my parents, and to you."

"You don't have to prove anything to me, Devon Finch."

He rocked back and forth, feeling nervous. Then he took her hand and held it tight and looked into her brown eyes with a passion seldom displayed. "I want you to approve," he said.

She nodded. "I need not approve of anything. You are your own man, and whatever you do is perfectly acceptable to me. All I ask is that you go into it with force and meaning, to accomplish your goal, and that you're honest enough to tell me about the troubles, whenever they happen."

Devon's body trembled, expressing relief. "That is what I hoped you would say. I don't want you to disapprove of me."

"I would never disapprove of you."

He looked skyward, tracking a distant cloud formation. "I want to make something of myself," he said. "I don't want to take you for a wife unless I can be assured of a future. I don't want you living in a sordid house with hardly any income to get us through. I want to be successful, to give you a fine home where our children will be happy, where you need not suffer the indignity of poorness."

She placed her head against his shoulder. "I will follow you wherever you go, Devon Finch. If you want to go all the way west, I will be at your side. You already have my love, and I yours. We don't need anything more."

"But I need experience, and this is one way to obtain it. Sure, I can get work at the newspaper, or on the levee, or maybe work up to owning a store someday. But that's not what I want. I know how much Randolph admired the police, and what he gained from it. I want to at least give it a try, to learn as much as I can. If I work hard as a volunteer, and am diligent, perhaps I can earn a position when the war is over."

"It is dangerous work," she said.

"Not if I'm careful."

"Someone was murdered last week, down by the levee."

"There will always be trouble of one kind or another. No one is safe from it. But with training and awareness, I can protect you and others."

She nodded. "You've thought this all out, haven't you?"

"All I need is your blessing."

She sat up straight then and turned toward him, her face strengthened with resolve. The words she spoke were punctuated by emotion. "If you don't know me by now, Devon Finch, then you never will. I am in love with you, and I can see the day when we'll be married, and I will care for you whether we're in a rich home or a soddy. Love is not simply for the wealthy. Love is for those who put the world aside and care deeply for what remains."

A swell of emotion crossed his shoulders. The pride he felt for her was overwhelming. He took her in his arms and held her for a long time. He felt like the most blessed man on earth to have someone like her, to have her speak of them together, through whatever difficulties came their way.

"I'll be a good man," he said. "I'll work hard and do what I must, and I'll be recognized as an achiever. I don't have the stomach for war, like Randolph has. I don't think I could shoot another man, or look into the barrel of a musket and not be scared."

"I know."

"I don't want you to think I am a coward."

"I would never think that of you."

"When Randolph went off, he was so brave looking. All the boys were laughing like they were going to a party or something, but I know it's not going to be anything like a party."

She hugged his arm. "You stay right here with me."

He shrugged. "Sometimes I think I should go. They'll soon be taking men like me, anyone who can carry a gun. I think . . . "

"That's quite enough. You've got your mind made up to join the Alliance Committee, and I agree. You can fulfill your duty right here at home."

He breathed deeply, satisfied that the ordeal was over. He was comforted by her smile. "Thank you, Caroline."

"You needn't thank me. I know you will see your way through life, for the benefit of our future."

He kissed her then, full on the lips, with an eagerness withheld far too long. Her lips were soft against his. When he pulled away he sat still for a moment. Then her smile returned and he thought she was like a cameo he had once seen. He felt fortunate to have a woman like her.

"We are privileged to be here at this time," he said. "By the time we are thirty, this city will be something grand. It's growing so fast. The population is over ten-thousand now. Soon it will be like some of the cities in the east, like Philadelphia perhaps."

"Do you really think so?"

His eyes turned to view the countryside. "Yes," he replied. "Someday this city will spread out behind those hills, perhaps all the way to the lakes. We can put up a fine home there. Why, at Saint Anthony they already have power enough to build factories, to make sashes and doors, flour and ironware. We'll follow, you'll see. I'll make something of myself. Every shoemaker, workhand, maid and stable-boy, who has ever saved up money, dreams about owning property outside the city. I want to be one of them."

That hank of hair drifted down over her eye again. Her voice was gleeful. "We will face the future together."

"Yes, together."

They sat quietly for a while, gazing northward. The sky had darkened in the east, while on the western horizon, the sun was a mere glow as it settled behind the forest's darkening rim. Wind rustled through the naked branches nearby, and out and away, a single bird flew alone across the sky.

He eased her tight against him. "It's late," he said. "We don't have much time."

"Let's just stay a while longer."

"It will turn colder soon."

"Then warm me, before the sun goes down."

The wind swept across the hills like a cold breath, penetrating their clothing. They remained huddled together, their hands locked, their cheeks touching, their eyes on the dark forest. They kissed once more, finding contentment in the press of their bodies. Moments later they arose and began their walk down the slope. Below, on the darkening streets, the lamplighters were busy. Lights winked like fireflies in the darkness, all the way to the bluffs, and to the river beyond.

When they arrived at her door they stood for a while, his body tight to hers. His face settled into the soft curve of her neck as he spoke. "Tomorrow I'll go to the city hall and seek an appointment with the Alliance Committee. I hope they'll accept me."

"They will accept you. You will talk your way in."

"I will try my best."

"Goodnight, Devon," she replied. "Take my love home with you."

"As always."

"I will see you tomorrow, and dream of you tonight."

He kissed her softly, and then turned as she entered the house.

Alone, with only the moonlight to guide him, he trudged up the dirt road creased by wagon wheels, toward Wabasha Street, past the remains of a woodpile that had survived the winter. He paused for a while at the corner, not wanting to distance himself from her. But then he realized that tomorrow the sun would rise, and he would be with her again.

He went on, and then home, and into bed where his visions became dreams, and his dreams reality, and his future one of great promise.

CHAPTER THREE

~⊗~ Signing Up ~⊗~

Because of its character, the Finch house stood out from others amid a community comprised of dirt streets and shacks, wood piles and bleak buildings, piles of excavated soil, and items discarded in yards and empty spaces. The fence surrounding the Finch house had been painted white because Harold Finch thought the color white would give it dignity. During the summer months, Nona Finch planted flowers along the front of the place, adding color and character, setting it apart from others that appeared to have been built without purpose. The house was noticeable, if for no other reason than its charm. When its doors were open it caught the river breeze, and when they were closed the house was warm and comforting, even during winters when the raw north winds screamed down from the wilderness, icing the river to its shores.

Harold Finch had built the house good and stout, the way he was, the way he expected everything to be. Following the teachings of his immigrant parents, he had struggled across endless miles to the northern forests where he helped perpetuate the city named by Father Lucien Galtier after his chosen Saint.

Unfortunately, in 1861, the city was far from saintly. Saint Paul was still a bawdy river town filled with gamblers and river-men, bootleggers and half-breeds, voyagers, lumbermen, fur traders and foreigners, prostitutes and pioneers, all fierce and bold, all grabbing for a fistful of luck. Fortunately, there were also businessmen, statesmen, and clergymen with enough vision to foresee the town's potential.

On Monday afternoon Devon stepped from the house into a strong wind laced with rain. Hunched down inside his slicker, he tugged his wide-brimmed hat tight to his head as he slogged across Wabasha Street and past the Court House toward the jail, a new structure that would replace the dilapidated log and weatherboard lockup. The infernal rain came near every day, except for the few when Randolph had left. The clay beneath Devon's feet had turned to mud, and he realized he would slip and fall if his steps were improperly placed. Within the first block his boots were caked and he paused to stomp the mud away before going farther. Dang, he hated rain, more than snow. Snow you could at least brush off and leave most of it where it belonged. Rain, that infernal wetness, never let go of you.

Ever since the snowmelt, the days had been miserable. As usual the sky west of the city was piling up with high clouds, coming on across the hills like some avenging monster with rain in its belly, dark and gorged with water, and needing to be relieved. The temperatures had already matched those of '42, and if the cold persisted, crops would be slow in coming or would be drowned out by rain. He thought of Randolph, stomping through the mud, freezing and wet, hoping a train would come and take them south, to where the sun shone most of the time.

Two groups of men were already at city hall when he arrived, young men mostly, some in pairs, friends he guessed. He recognized a few, but didn't offer a greeting. Most of them just wanted to get through the rain before it soaked them. As he approached the entrance, someone sloshed up alongside, nudging his arm. "I thought I'd see you here today."

Logan Miller was a friend, the same age as Devon, a husky lad with deep convictions formed through years of trial in the east.

Signing Up

He had trudged to the new territory with an ox train, but unlike Devon, he yearned to join the Union Army despite his parents' firm demand to remain in school until he received a proper education.

Logan spoke eagerly. "You gonna sign up today?" he asked.

Devon nodded. "You know I am. I told you in school last week."

"I'm excited. Can't wait."

"There's much to think about."

"Sure is. Been thinkin' about it all night."

"Let's sit together."

"Best we do."

Logan's voice was by nature high-toned and womanlike, not deep like most boys of seventeen. Even so, he was known to be a tough kid, given to fighting when others goaded him. Good with his fists and hard to bring down, he often won when the odds were against him. Few had beaten him, though many had tried. Logan was a scrapper. He'd make a good volunteer.

After entering the building and hanging their wet slickers on hooks, they were routed to a room where about two dozen others waited. As they sat down, Devon recognized several other men, a neighbor, another from school, an older man who worked in the brickyard, another who worked in the LeDuc bookstore. Unannounced, a uniformed officer came in, emptied a small jar containing bits of paper onto a tabletop, then turned and said, "Chief Western will be here shortly. Keep your places."

Logan shifted in his chair. "Have you ever met Chief Western?"

"No," Devon replied. "Saw him twice though, once leading a gambler by the scruff of his neck, another time down on the levee looking over immigrants coming off the steamer *Minnesota*. He's a frightful sort."

The Saint Paul Common Council tried to cut off the diseased and destitute at the levee by making steamboat captains and others who brought them to the city, choose between returning the dependents to the place they came from, or caring for them. The practice kept most undesirables from living off the welfare of others.

"Some say he's got the blood of a wildcat."

"He needs it for sure."

"Maybe we're gonna need the same kind of blood, and soon."

Devon thought about the job ahead of them, wondering if he'd made the right decision. The city was a fearsome place, given its nature. Caroline might certainly get angry if something happened to him in the course of duty. Come to think about it, he'd never seen her angry. He gripped his hands together as Chief H. H. Western entered the room.

Western was not a big man, but his presence all but made up for his lack of size. His shoulders, huge and muscular, were large enough to tighten his uniform. He came in like a bear on the hunt, his face tightly drawn, his eyes fixed on the small gathering while sighting each man with a hard stare. He didn't say anything, just looked at them as if to decide whether or not they were capable of the task ahead. He took a deep breath before speaking.

"So, there's twenty-three of you today, many less than we'll need. But it's a start. We'll take the best of you for sure, and go from there."

He scanned the assembly again while nodding at those he recognized. "The truth is, we got about six square miles to take care of in a city that ain't as saintly as she sounds. You've all lived here long enough to know what this town is all about. We ain't exactly sinless, but we're here to give this city an appearance of law and order so's our citizens can sleep well at night."

Western paced two steps to his left before pausing. "Right now there's two wars going on, one with the renegades to the south, and another right here. As citizens, you'll be contributing to law enforcement as home guards until our rightful policemen and thirty-nine fireman return, if providence smiles on 'em. If it weren't for the southern uprising at Fort Sumter, and if Abraham Lincoln hadn't put out the call for men, none of you would be here today. But so be it. Now we still got the La Belle, and about two dozen other bars full of gamblers and drinkers, a levee full of sporting men, and riffraff that come up regularly to this city. We got 'em all. Our Mayor John Prince dismissed the entire lot of policemen and firemen so's they could sign up to fight, and now he's got to form a volunteer patrol to look after things. That's where you come in, if you're willin' to take a beating now and then, or spend some of

Signing Up

your precious hours lookin' after rogues who are lookin' for trouble, or money, or women to do their biddin'."

He retraced his steps, pausing for effect. "But don't let me send you running. Most things are better now than they were. We got a new jail replacing the old one, with six cells large enough for a crowd in each. And we got Oakland Cemetery about two miles up from the river if we ever want to plant a few far enough away from the city. Our city fathers put it there because they never expected the city to grow that far, but we all know that it will. Good thing is, we'll probably never fill it up, not in our lifetimes anyway."

Western pinched the edge of his mustache. The silence was punctuated only by the clearing of a throat or the movement of a leg.

Western spoke again. "Now, we're going to have two-hundred men doing the job here. They'll be divided into four companies, fifty to each company for those who don't know your arithmetic." His statement brought a tinkle of laughter. "You're going to be known as the first, second and third ward companies, and . . . The Lowertown Guard. Now William Langly will be captain of the First Ward. Harvey Briggs, one of our best known lawyers will head up the Second, and Ferdinand Wilhelm, a prominent German citizen and banker, will be Captain of the Third. As for the Lower Town Guard, well, you're lookin' at him."

Laughter sprinkled the room.

"Now, takin' up this task will be voluntary. You'll receive no wages. Instead you'll be deferred from signing up with the army, and you'll be relieved of any road work. You all know that road work is a tiring job come rain, cold, and whatever else nature can throw at us. Now if workin' a section of the city without pay is beneath your dignity, then put on you slicker and be out of here."

No one moved. Heads turned, silently questioning, but not a single man arose from his seat.

"Good," Western said. "Good men all."

He turned then, paced a few steps, and stood silently for a moment, hands tucked behind his back. "Now for you in the Lowertown Guard, it'll be the toughest of the four districts. You'll be meeting up with riffraff comin' in from clear down the river, all types, whores, beggars, slickers, and those lookin' for a better life out on the prairie. You'll be seein' all the terrors of a river town that gets so far out of hand sometimes that we can't cope with it. I'm warning you now, it won't be a Sunday outing, no sir. It'll be a daunting challenge. Most of you know that we got only one police wagon. Actually it's a grocer's wagon that's always positioned on the corner of Seventh and Wabasha each evening, just in case we need it. Sometimes we fill it. Sometimes we don't."

"Now you all remember Andrew Belanski, the man who was murdered up in Phalen Creek just about two years past, poisoned by arsenic in coffee given to him by his wife, Annie. And you probability know that Annie was the first woman to be hung in the Court House yard, just last year. I don't expect we'll see anything like that again, but we might. So if you don't like lookin' death in the face, or seein' someone walk up the gallows steps, then I suggest you back out now."

Again, the room silenced. No one moved. Devon wondered what Caroline would think if she heard Western's words.

"There's gonna be fires for sure, so if you hear bells-a-soundin' run like a wildcat to the station house. We got two hook-and-ladder wagons and enough rope for eight men to pull it, one located right here in this building, another over by the Temperance House, both loaded with hoses, buckets, axes, and a four-man pump. We need twelve men to take them on a run. I'm sure you can all remember as far back as last year when we lost thirty-four structures not far from here. We thought the entire city would burn. Worst fire we ever had. You'll soon learn that fire-fighting is more than just marchin' around town in brightly colored uniforms, or competing in water throwin' contests. It's life-savin' work and life-takin' danger wrapped into one horrible blaze. But for those of you who think you'll be going into those blazes with blind eyes, think again. You'll all receive the training you need."

Western paused to stroke the ends of his mustache. "As for those of you who'll be patrolling the streets, you'll be given two things, a whistle and a nightstick. The whistle will be used for calling your partners, and the nightstick, well I guess you know what

Signing Up

that's for, protection or punishment. You'll be the judge of which when the time comes."

Devon clasped his hands together in a prayer-like attitude as his thoughts settled on the many tomorrow's that lay ahead, on the streets where anything could happen. What was he getting into? Would the streets be that bad? He was a schoolboy who avoided the streets at night, except for the occasional walks Caroline and he took to their usual place on the hill. Nearly every citizen had heard commotions at night from the direction of Lambert's Landing. Most had seen the women of the night during daylight hours when they came outside all gussied up in their fine clothes, their breasts barely covered, their faces painted with rouge and lipstick, trying to act refined when they were obviously immoral. What were those women really like? His parents had always depicted them as evil creatures that prayed on the minds of men, who captured them in webs of debauchery. The best duty would be on the north side of the city, away from the river. Life down on Water Street was of another kind, where cheaters and drunks and sometimes the insane found refuge in the dark houses, bars, and alleyways. Logan's elbow jabbed at his side. "Listen," he prompted.

Devon heard Western's voice again. "You'll begin your training as soon as we fill our roster of two-hundred. You'll train all at once so we don't have to go through it over and over. Then we'll settle your hours and hope you'll be ready to take on the task."

Western moved to the table near the wall, where the bits of paper were scattered.

"Now there are twenty-three papers here, all folded the same. Each one has a number on it, a one, two, three, or four. The numbers represent the four sections of the city. Now come on up, take one, and open it. If you don't want your number then trade it with someone, if they're willing. If no one wants to trade, then keep it, or return it to me and go on back home. Now form a line, and take your paper."

Chairs scraped. The men stood up, forming a single line. They moved quickly to the table, each man taking a paper.

"What if we don't get the same number?" Logan mumbled.

"Then we don't work together."

"If we don't, maybe one of us can work a trade."

"Maybe."

When they reached the table Devon took the paper nearest him. Logan selected another. Returning to their chairs, they sat down. Nervously, Devon unfolded his paper. His hands trembled when he saw the number 4 . . . the Lowertown Guard. Logan unfolded his, revealing the number 2.

"We got different sections," Logan said.

"I'll trade, "Devon insisted. "I'll find a number Two."

"Hell no, I will. All the fun's gonna be down there in Lowertown."

"I don't want all the action. Caroline won't want me patrolling the levee."

"What's she got to say about it anyway? Ain't you got a mind of your own?"

Devon wanted to tell him to mind his own business. But then he remembered what Caroline had said up on the hill the night before, that he'd never be a coward. Well, maybe he should prove her right. Maybe the Lowertown Guard might be a proper place for him to build a good reputation. He could make something of himself if he took on a difficult task. He was strong. He could lift close to his own weight. He'd been in brawls. He knew what fighting was all about. But his brawls had been with those his own age, not with men who'd been cutting wood and moving stone and working like a dog on the river. Those men were near animals. Some even carried skinning knives and wouldn't hesitate to use them. Decisions would have to be made in seconds. He was about to stand, when something inside held him back. Then he heard Western's voice.

"Well, which of you wants to trade now?'

"I will," Logan said, leaping to his feet. "I got a number 2. I want to trade it for a number 4."

There had to be four or five number 4's in the room, but no one arose to accept his offer.

"Come on," Logan prompted. "Give it up."

"Sit down, Logan," someone said.

Western's voice came hard, but with humor in it, and at that point Devon decided not to humiliate himself. He'd never want to be branded as a coward. "Guess you gotta sleep with that number," Western said.

"Dang," Logan said, dropping back into his seat."

"Okay now," Western continued. "I got four logbooks up here, one for each section. Come on up and sign your name in the appropriate one, name and address. We need men day and night, no one between the hours of six in the morning and noontime, except for the firemen. Those of you in Lowertown will stagger between afternoon, evening and night. We'll work out the details later. Upon signing you'll be respected for sure because you'll be doing this city a favour, protecting its citizens while our regulars are off fighting a war. Now put your name on the line, and be proud that you did."

All twenty-three men stood up and shuffled forward. When Devon arrived at the table he penned his name without hesitation, so's not to be called a laggard. He felt new blood in his veins, certain that Caroline would approve of his decision. When they were finished signing, Western grouped them.

"That's all for today," he said. "We'll be signing many more before the week is over. As for next Monday, at four o'clock, you'll all be here to begin your training. Some of you are still in school, so that's the reason for the late hour. If any of you fail to show up, then you're out. Now get on back to your homes. And thanks to you all for doing your duty."

That was it. Amid the loud talk, the raillery, and the jesting, Devon retrieved his slicker and went outside. The rain had stopped, leaving the clouds low to the hills. By the looks of the sky, more rain was likely to come later. As Devon and Logan trudged on through the mud, Logan spoke first.

"It's not going to be the same, us not being together."

"We had no control over it."

"Maybe I can make a change later, soon as someone gets their belly full of Lowertown."

Devon didn't reply, he just stuffed his hands into his pockets and leaned into the wind. His thoughts were on Caroline. She would not be pleased with him being in Lowertown, yet he felt compelled to obey his draw. He had always thought fate had a way of moving a man through life for one reason or another. Fate had sent his family west, to where they had wanted to go, and fate had brought him to Caroline. His father had always said that fate was the working of God, and that if a man believed in God, fate would be good to him. Well, here he was, in the Alliance, and so he'd have to trust in God to steer him straight and true.

"Why ain't you talkin'?" Logan asked.

Devon kicked at a small stone with the toe of his boot. "I was just thinking of what Caroline will say."

"Why, she's gonna be proud of you."

"Think so?"

"Why, hell, Devon, she's not gonna say anything that'll make you regret your decision. From what you've told me, she'll support you all the way."

Devon nodded. "That's the way I look at it."

"Same as my Pa woulda done. Why he'd have slapped my back and said, go get 'em Logan. Hell, if that ain't the best."

Devon laughed. "Didn't you study English in school?"

"Sure, why?"

"Because you talk like a river man."

"Always will, I expect. I talk like my Pa. He never had no schoolin'. What's the difference anyway, as long as the message is clear?"

"No difference."

"That's what I say."

Devon thought his mother might not like his choice either. With Randolph off to war she'd surely be worried about him every third night, putting in with people she classified as undesirable human beings. She said she'd met better Indians than some of the people that got off the steamers. Pa wouldn't take it much better. He read the news each day. He knew what deviltry went on down there at night, though he never talked about it. Devon expected a tongue-lashing, just as sure as the wind blew. His stomach knotted just thinking about it.

"Let me know how they take the news," Logan said.

"I will."

When they arrived at the white fence surrounding his home, Devon paused. Logan kept walking up Wabasha Street, toward where Caroline lived.

Signing Up

You have to be straight on, Devon thought, and not let anyone think you're unfit for the task. Why, if Randolph could sign up and fight the Rebels without as much as a what for, why couldn't he walk the streets of a city and feel comfortable in his roll. He had sense enough to make his own decisions in life. He didn't need approval from anyone. Surely they'd see pride in serving the city when so many of its men were gone. They'd be proud of his patriotism, even though he wasn't carrying a weapon.

Start being confident, he thought. No one else is going to fill in for you. Put your chin up and walk like you know exactly where you're going.

As for Caroline, well, he expected she'd just love him a little bit more.

CHAPTER FOUR

The Announcement

Devon knocked on the door of the Page house at eight o'clock, just as the rain ended. Caroline's mother, Lillian, greeted him warmly. "It's a frightful evening," she said. Carefully, she shook the water off his wet slicker and hung it on a hook.

"I think the rain will never stop." Devon remarked as he removed his muddied shoes. He examined his stockings to make sure they were presentable, and then stepped into the slippers Lillian kept for him.

Lillian's smile brightened. "Caroline is in the parlor with her father and Bethany."

Caroline's sister, Bethany, was thirteen, a girl who tried to emulate her in both appearance and manner. As Devon entered the parlor, all three occupants arose from their chairs, Edmund with his hand outstretched, Caroline with a winsome smile, and Bethany with palm down, as if to accept a kiss in greeting. Devon never disappointed her. He took her hand, kissed it lightly, and then accepted Caroline's hand before reaching out to Edmund.

"Welcome on a night when no man should be out," Edmund said.

Devon nodded. "I think Seventh Street will become a river before it is over."

"Aye, and I heard those poor souls in the Hollow lost two homes today. The hills there are like a waterfall. I've never seen the river so high, or the rain so fierce."

Devon sat down in the chair usually reserved for him, a soft-cushioned seat embroidered with roses, firmly backed with arms that curved down in front. Before he settled in, Lillian came with a tray supporting a coffee decanter and four cups. The room remained silent as she poured the coffee and placed the cups on two small tables, one between Edmund and Devon, the other between the two girls. Bethany had yet to acquire a taste for the dark brew, preferring strawberry-flavored water instead.

As they sipped their coffee, Lillian returned to the kitchen, only to reappear with a plate of cookies. "You have to try my Rye-happies," she said. "I made them today. We are fortunate to have some left, because a certain person in this house had wandering hands." She glanced at Bethany, who snickered. Each of them took a cookie. Lillian placed the remainder on the table between Devon and Edmund.

Lillian sat near the window, balancing a small cup on a saucer. A daguerreotype photograph of her mother and father adorned the wall beside her. The miracle of photography had always fascinated Devon. The image of a scene captured on a highly polished copper plate within a camera obscura, and developed in mercury vapors, was, to him, a marvel of human ingenuity.

Edmund opened the conversation. "Well, Devon, Caroline has informed us that you have signed up to become part of the newly formed Alliance Committee, a rather admirable gesture of civil duty, I must admit. What inspired you to put your name in for such a thing?"

"I felt it was my duty, Mr. Page. If Randolph could sign up to serve our country, the least I could do was to protect what he left behind."

"Ah, yes, duty is a noble calling."

Devon placed his coffee cup on the saucer and cleared his throat. He glanced first at Caroline, searching for a nod of approval, and then turned to face her father.

The Announcement

Edmund Page was a common man, but one of strong, moral virtue. He wore a beard extending from sideburns to chin, where it greyed slightly. Narrow-eyed and intently alert, he retained an expression that demanded immediate attention. His smile, when displayed, was quick but pronounced. He always sat straight up in a chair, never slouched, his manner remaining unchanged.

Devon cleared his throat, and then continued. "I, and twenty-two others met Captain Western this morning when we signed on for service."

Edmund nodded. "Impressive," he said stoically.

Devon glanced quickly at Caroline, whose eyes were intent on him. "We will be two hundred strong when the roster is complete."

"Two-hundred?"

Devon swallowed. Come right out with it, he thought. No sense in delaying the inevitable. "We'll be divided into four divisions, one for each section of the city. I happened to draw a number that placed me in the Lowertown Guard."

The room hushed then. Devon looked quickly at Caroline's expressionless face.

Her smile had faded, and her lips appeared to tremble a bit.

"The Lowertown Guard," Edmund exclaimed. "That's a rather challenging choice."

"The choice was not mine. I obtained it by draw."

"By draw, of course."

As Edmund sipped coffee, Caroline drew a breath. "Is that not a dangerous place at night?" she asked.

"At times, there is commotion for sure, especially when the riverboats are docked. But I will not be alone. I will have others with me."

"Strength in numbers," Edmund said.

"One could say so, yes."

"Your assignment might have been better had you drawn a different number."

"Perhaps, but I have always been of the opinion that things happen for a reason."

Edmund ignored the statement, saying instead, "I know Captain Western personally, perhaps a word from me . . . "

"No!" Devon interrupted. "I have made my decision."

Edmund nodded, stroking his beard. "Well, then, you have my utmost respect for accepting a most challenging position. I hope you will find it helpful to your future."

"I am sure it will serve me well, Mr. Page."

"I am proud of you also," Caroline said. "It is not often one gets to protect those who cannot protect themselves. I, for one, admire your decision."

Devon swallowed hard. "Thank you, Caroline."

"More coffee, gentlemen?" Lillian asked, rising from her chair. Attired in a long dark green dress decorated with a bodice of cross-stitched flowers, she moved gracefully to where the men were seated and poured from the decanter.

"I always thought you were a spirited young man," she said while filling Devon's cup. "I know you have given much thought to your decision, and this family respects you for it."

"I appreciate that, Mrs. Page."

Mr. Page spoke again. "Tell me, Devon. Have you heard from Randolph?"

"We have. Just yesterday a letter was delivered from Fort Snelling. He is fine and in good spirits, despite the weather and the constant drilling. They keep him busy for sure, and they're bringing in more men each day."

"Your brother is a brave man."

"Yes, sir, that he is."

"And you'll be doing a soldier's job right here at home."

"I expect so, sir, but without the same risk."

"Your parents are well, I assume."

"They are, sir."

The conversation continued, and soon all joined in. The news of his assignment with the Lowertown Guard soon gave way to laughter. At one point, Edmund said. "What are your ambitions when you finish school?'

Unprepared for the question, Devon shrugged. A moment later, he replied. "I am uncertain, sir."

"Well, perhaps you might study law. We need good lawyers here. I could introduce you to those who might lend a hand to your future."

"If you're suggesting that I go to college, sir, my grades are insufficient. I am only average."

"And so were some of those now practicing law. If nothing else, determination will see you through. Determination, dedication, and hard work are the factors that lead to success."

Devon nodded. "I am determined, Mr. Page, of that I am sure. If that's what it takes, then I will surely succeed."

Just then, Caroline interjected. "Don't let him fool you, father. He is a good and proper student."

"Of course he is. I only want him to know that I am willing to guide him onward when the proper time comes. This city is only getting started. Why, I remember back in 1858 when hundreds of steamboats docked here after the newspapers carried stories of new lands and new opportunities and millions of acres open to population. Why, the people came off the steamers so thick we didn't know where to put them. Soon afterwards, the city lost its French character. We built churches, businesses, and now we've got fresh beef in the city market, and ice carts and milkmen making regular rounds. The city is growing and it's going to need stout and determined people to carry it along. Surely, there's a place for you Devon, sure as God made us."

"I'll be ready when the time comes," Devon replied.

"There's much to be done, for sure. You know as well as I, that little attention has been given to the quality of our water supply being drawn from river springs and wells or from water drainage, even though our officials are aware of the link between sanitation and health. Some have urged strong, remedial action to prevent epidemics, and have established quarantines and pest houses for times of contagion. And now, community residents are demanding further change, demanding something be done about our pestilential air that's filled with noxious smells from reeking yards and privy vaults. And hasn't each of us had to leap over mud holes in poorly drained streets? It's time we cleaned it up. So, if you're the planning type, why there's a challenge for you. There are a hundred different opportunities in this city, and a place for you. We need planners. God knows there are enough workers. I can get you into city planning whenever you're ready. Why, didn't William

Seward tell us that the last seat of power on this great continent will be found within a radius, here, at the head of navigation on the Mississippi, and on the great land-locked spread of lakes? I'll never forget those words, Devon, and neither should you. Opportunity is greater here than at any other place in this land."

"Yes, thank you, Mister Page," Devon replied.

"Right now with patriotism so intense and with fathers and sons going off to war, now's the chance to seize the future, when the sound of fife and drum are so prevalent. When you finish schooling, then you must take the future by hand and let it lead you on. And I'll be there to help you."

A moment of silence followed, during which eyes shifted above the coffee cups. Devon felt uneasy when in the presence of mister Page, because he knew that Edmund was being considered for political office. Still, he didn't want to ask favors of him, even though Caroline had urged him in that direction. He wanted to strike out on his own, to find his own place in life, to build what he could with his own talent and strength.

Edmund's voice came slowly. "There will be one thing on your side down there in Lowertown. They say that steamboat traffic will diminish. The war is going to need boats to carry military supplies and men, south not north. Not many immigrants will be coming our way."

"That's encouraging."

"And that means less hustlers will be coming in, if you know what I mean."

"I know," Devon nodded.

They went on to talk about other things, including reports of Indians becoming restless in the southern counties because of a food scarcity. But soon the conversation waned, and the gaps between words lengthened. Then, when the coffee was gone, Edmund asked Bethany to stand and sing. She had a beautiful, lilting voice, and was not bashful to present proof of her talent. To please her father, she took a place in the middle of the room, curtsied, cupped her hands, and as her eyes mellowed in lamplight, she sang.

Beautiful dreamer, wake unto me. Starlight and dewdrops are waiting for thee; Sounds of the rude world, heard in the day! Lulled by the

The Announcement

moonlight have all pass'd away! Beautiful Dreamer, queen of my song, list while I woo thee in soft melody;

Gone are the cares of life's busy throng, Beautiful Dreamer, awake unto me! Beautiful Dreamer, awake unto me.

She curtsied amid a flutter of applause and then returned to her chair.

Caroline stirred and glanced expectantly at Devon as her smile bloomed.

Devon looked at her with an all too apparent longing. "I must go now," he said. "The hour is getting late."

Caroline arose immediately. "Then I will see you to the door."

Devon nodded to each of them. "Thank you for your hospitality, and for the coffee, Mrs. Page."

"You are welcome any time, Devon."

"Come," Caroline said, taking his arm.

They went to the door. Devon stepped into his shoes, tied them, and together they went outside. The rain had ceased, leaving the night wind soft, but chilly. Devon placed his arm around Caroline and drew her inside his long coat, holding her tight.

"You surprised me with the news," she said.

"I didn't intend to alarm you."

"I am not alarmed. I know you won't be foolish."

"I will not," he replied firmly.

She moved tighter against him. "Promise me one thing. Walk away from danger when it comes."

"I may not be able to turn my back on trouble."

"Then be careful."

"There will be others to help me."

"I don't want you injured."

"I'll be sensible. I'll avoid commotions as best I can."

"Then kiss me, and hold me for a moment."

Her face, solemn and wistful, mellowed in the moon's soft light. He drew her in as her breathing increased, easing the long coat around her, guiding his body to hers. Her breasts pressed softly against his chest as he touched his lips to hers.

"I love you so," she breathed. "Promise you'll never leave me."

The desire for her flared like fire in his veins. He had felt rapture only twice before when holding her close. He wanted to love her fully, like husband and wife, but they had pledged to wait until after the wedding. As she eased away, a tear in her eye glistened in the wan moonlight.

"What is wrong?" he asked.

"I don't want you bloodied," she replied.

"I will always be careful."

"I don't want to walk beside your casket all the way to Oakland."

"Hush," he whispered. "Now you are exaggerating."

She pressed her cheek against his chest. "When you are caught up in fear, just think of me, knowing that I am waiting for you."

"Don't talk like that."

"I must. Life is unpredictable at times."

"Then pray for me if you must."

"I will."

He drew her tight, felt the beating of her heart against his chest. "I will see you tomorrow."

"Goodnight, my love."

He kissed her again, softer this time. Then she eased away and touched his face with her fingertips. The moonlight on her face appeared to be satin. Then she turned and entered the house, leaving him alone in the night.

Deep in the west, thunder rolled again. He felt ashamed for having worried her. Turning away from the house, he began his walk home, sighting on the far hills. The thunder had a cruel sound to it, like a beast about to pounce.

Everything would be alright, he told himself. He'd take whatever came his way and react to it sensibly. He would never be a coward. Caroline knew that as well. She knew he would never shirk his duty. She knew him better than he knew himself.

He walked slowly, immersed in the uncertain days that lay ahead. He stood hesitantly on the corner, wanting to go back, wanting to hold her again, but when the moon disappeared into the clouds, and as thunder approached, he said a small prayer.

As raindrops fell, he headed for home

CHAPTER FIVE

First Day

Following his week of training, Devon arose early, when the sky was still dark. He ate breakfast alone; warm oatmeal with bread and preserves. Then, with whistle and nightstick, he walked down Wabasha Street amid muted sounds; the barking of a dog, voices leaking from doorways, the clop of a horse a block away. His spirits were high. He breathed deeply of the air. He had no visions of the day ahead, only hope that it might be fulfilling and that he would return home at noon without having spent a breath in anger or fear.

  He paused at the river bluff. The sun had risen into a clear, azure sky warming with morning. He looked east to the hills above the river, where two eagles circled, their wings rigid in the breeze, heads poised downward searching for fish. The hillside trees were scarcely beginning to green because of a miserable cold spell that had persisted through half of May when it had rained for fourteen straight days, making rivers of streets, lakes of excavations, mud of soil, and despair of hope.

  He glanced at the Wabasha Bridge. The structure had replaced an old wooden ferry that had been nearly impossible to operate whenever the wind blew hard, causing delays and irritations and foul language, often heard atop the bluff. The flatland beyond the river remained partially flooded from the snowmelt, and as sunlight stroked the water it rippled like jewels cast on velvet. As the sun stroked his face, he breathed deeply of the fresh air. Down on the levee, men were busy moving freight barrels and boxes, making way for new goods coming in sometime between ten and noon.

He looked down Water Street, and then Bench, to where the road began its decline toward Jackson, where the taller buildings stood, those of two or three stories in height, businesses mostly, and rooming houses. His destination was clear. He would pay his respect to the proprietors, and present himself as one involved with the Alliance, an act of goodwill suggested by Western. On this first day, he had chosen to be alone, unimpeded by companions, to make him known in his own way. He twirled his nightstick by its leather strap, and touched the whistle slung around his neck.

As he approached the Palmer Apothecary shop, the owner came out to sweep the wooden sidewalk. Palmer was a short man, slightly bent, with hair gone gray. He wore thick glasses, and had an irritating habit of licking his lips when talking. Palmer turned as Devon approached.

"Good morning, Mr. Palmer," Devon said. "Is it not a fine day?"

The storekeeper nodded. "And who are you, I might ask?"

"I am Devon Finch, a member of the newly formed Alliance Committee, here to help keep the peace."

"Finch? I know a Nona Finch."

"She would be my mother."

Palmer grinned. "You look much like her."

"Thank you for the compliment, Mr. Palmer."

The storekeeper straightened. "So, you're here to protect us."

Devon nodded. "At least I will try, sir."

"Well, you look fit enough to take on a ruffian or two."

"That certainly is not my wish."

Palmer cocked his head. "Aye, there's a few around who'll like to try you out, to see what you're made of."

Devon puffed his chest, pretentiously. "Why, I'm made of lightening, and I'm fast as a lynx and strong as a bull ox."

Palmer laughed. "Now you're exaggerating."

"It's just conversation, sir."

Palmer swept the last of the dirt away from the boards. "Your mother will be around this afternoon, I expect. I've got a panacea ready for her, some of my celebrated female pills."

Devon knew nothing about pills, so he ignored the statement in favor of a question. "Are you stocked for the summer months?"

"I am, thanks to the *Jeanette Roberts*. That workhorse of a boat just brought me some Dr. McLane's Liver Pills, some Perry Davis Vegetable Pain Killer, Cephalic pills Salt Rheum Syrup, Plmonic Wafers and Pesiguagomik."

"What is Pesiguagomik?'

"It's a preparation made from our own Minnesota plants, a cure recommended for cholera, dysentery, diarrhea, and morbus, for those who dwell on gruesome matters, an unhealthy disease of the mind."

"I guess you have to be extremely educated to be in your kind of business."

Palmer nodded. "Education does help."

Devon looked down the street and saw a horse drawn wagon headed toward the levee. He, like the horse, had distance to travel, so he thought to move on.

"Well, good morning to you, Mr. Palmer."

"Too you also, Mr. Finch."

Devon walked downhill toward the American Fur Company, a stone trading post on the corner of Bench and Robert. From what he could see, an ox cart in front was loaded with pelts, both beaver and muskrat. The men appeared to be French, with stocking caps, dark brown pantaloons, one with bear claws around his neck, a pipe in his mouth, and the look of wilderness in his eyes. Devon paid the proprietor a visit, just as he had with Mr. Palmer, but quickly left to attend his duty.

He walked down toward the levee where the La Belle saloon was located. The La Belle attracted every kind of humanity that came ashore, or out of the woods; gamblers, traders, scouts, soldiers, merchants, whiskey sellers, river men, immigrants, farmers and drifters looking for a place to settle or to start a business. They got drunk, and fought and loved. Their fights often sent the losers to either St. Joseph's or St. Luke's hospitals where they were patched up, or to the Cemetery where the dead found rest beneath the oak trees. The women of the place, so he had heard, were as hard as bedrock, as tender as a lamb, or as fierce as a wildcat, given the circumstances.

Devon had never been inside the LaBelle, nor had his father. Men of respect went to the Fuller House, a suitable location for gentlemen who accepted Christianity as their guide. The La Belle was tolerated for its indecency, because if the ruffians didn't have such a place they'd be right up in town with those who appreciated gracious living.

Devon stood outside for a while, imagining what went on inside during the dark hours. The place appeared much like its neighboring buildings from the outside. Its single door was made of heavy oak. Its windows, high enough to prevent peering, had claimed a layer of dust, and its boardwalk appeared to be firm, although surfaced with dirt. A single sign, lettered in red, said only, La Belle Saloon. Windows on the second floor identified the rooms where the women worked.

Devon was nervous while standing alone, spinning his nightstick at the end of its hide lacing. He swallowed hard as fear skittered down his back. He had never been in a saloon before, and this was the worst of them. But he had to make an appearance, to let the proprietor know he was ready for anything that came along. He took the first step forward just as someone came through the door, a man whose forward progress was uneven and hesitant. The man looked at him through squinted eyes, and then puffed his lips with an annoyance of laughter. Without a word, he stepped away, walking unsteadily toward the levee. He was a boatman, for sure.

Devon shouldered his resolve, went to the door, eased it open, and stepped inside. The bar-room was near dark, lit only by several lamps above the poker tables and behind a wooden bar extensive enough to hold about twenty men standing. At this time of day, only eight men stood at the bar, none looking his way. To the left,

First Day

poker tables and chairs stood clustered in no apparent order. At the rear, a staircase led to the upper level. The place held a lingering scent of perspiration, whiskey and smoke which gave him a moment of pause.

A solitary man sat at one of the tables, his hands ruffling a deck of cards, shuffling them over and over as if to wear them out. He looked up as Devon approached, as did two of the bar occupants, each silently questioning the nightstick he carried.

Devon walked straight to the bar, maintaining a safe distance between himself and the drinkers. The bartender, a stout man with a full beard and mystifying eyes, came his way. He placed his hands on the bar and leaned forward, sucking at something inside his mouth.

"I think you're in the wrong place," he said.

Devon cleared his throat. "Is the manager here?" he asked.

"The manager? Now what would you want with the manager?"

"I am Devon Finch, a member of the newly formed Alliance Committee. I wish to talk to him."

The bartender straightened, and then laughed. He glanced down the bar at the other men and said, "So now they're sendin' children to watch over us."

"Is he in," Devon asked amid a sprinkling of laughter.

"Is he in? Why, hell lad, you're lookin' at him."

Devon relaxed, extending his hand over the bar in an attempt to shake hands. The bartender took a step backwards.

"I have come to introduce myself, sir," Devon said. "I am Devon Finch, and I have become a part of a new watch that will try to keep peace and order in this city."

"Peace and order is it?"

More laughter came from the bar.

"We will try, sir," Devon responded.

The bartender winked at a nearby customer. "Well, then, be at it, unless you want a whiskey at this hour, or the pleasure of a woman."

The customers laughed again. Devon felt inferior and humiliated by their apparent scoffing. Then he said, in a manageable voice, "I am here only to introduce myself, and to let you know that I am available if you need my services. I don't drink, nor am I desirous of flesh, but I will be here from time to time, to help in any way I can. For now, I bid you good day."

He turned to leave just as the proprietor replied. "You are welcome here, Mr. Finch. Forgive my crudeness. This place is a destroyer of courtesy."

"I'll drink to that," one of the patrons said, hosting his glass.

"To be sure," another replied.

Devon stepped away from the bar. The wooden floor creaked beneath his feet. As he passed the man shuffling cards, the stranger said, "Mr. Finch. I could not help but overhear your words. Be seated with me for a while and learn what you can about this place."

Devon paused, examined the man's animated smile, and then said, "Your name, sir?"

"I am Simeon Flynn, an artist and a gentleman."

"An artist?"

"Aye, an artist with these cards. With them I create tomorrows, for without them I would be penniless. Come and sit with me. I am lonely at an empty table."

Devon paused momentarily. Perhaps Mr. Flynn could be of help to him later on.

He was well dressed, had a proper approach, and a calm voice. He wore a small cravat at his neck. The glass in front of him was empty. He continued to shuffle the cards with mechanical ease.

"For only a moment, sir," Devon said. He pulled out a chair and sat, trying not to appear nervous.

"You have a rather daunting responsibility, young man." Simeon remarked.

"One that I shoulder with pride, sir."

"Of course, civic duty is commendable."

"The police have gone to war, and now we civilians must do what we can."

"Admirable. Yes, extremely admirable."

Flynn continued shuffling the cards. His manner was stoic, as if indifferent to emotion. He wore no beard. His hair was trimmed shorter than normal. His vest, a dark crimson color, was accentuated with brass buttons. His body scent denoted cleanliness, and he occupied the chair as if it had been crafted especially for him. His deep, dark eyes were sure to conceal secrets.

"Soon you will wear those cards out," Devon said, smiling.

"Ah yes. Indeed, they are a bit worn, but still capable of magic. See." He stopped shuffling, spread the cards in a fan shape face down on the table, and then selected a single one. Smiling, he flipped it over, the Ace of Hearts.

"It is magical," Devon said.

"Magical in a sense, but still a trick. To me these cards have voices. They speak silently, as does the wind to a bird. These cards are my profession."

"Then you must win most of the time."

Flynn winked. "Winning is essential to survival, no matter what the game."

Devon settled into his chair and placed his nightstick across his lap. "Where are you from, Mr. Flynn?"

"From just about everywhere. I am Irish, to be sure. I came to this country with my father when I was just a lad of twelve. My father died at the hands of a ruffian, leaving me with only the will to survive. I worked every job known to man until I found a discarded deck of cards, my one and only treasure. They came to be my friend, and my provider."

He paused, breathed deeply and then grinned, revealing yellowed teeth, one missing at the edge of his smile. "I came up here with the free-traders, wandered the Red River for a while, lived with the Assiniboines, had the pleasure of an Indian woman, and then went south to Saint Louis where I perfected my talent. Now here I am, takin' what I can from those who think they can win. I came up on the *Time and Tide* near a year ago."

"You are a man of the world, Mr. Flynn."

"No. I am a man of the saloons and whorehouses, river crates and tables, wherever I can apply my trade, wherever someone waits for me."

"Is it a lonely life?"

"No. I have plenty of companionship, male and female. But in days past, life was a burden to me, until I found the method of winning at cards, a most rewarding faculty, I must say." His gaze turned toward Devon. His eyes narrowed as his lips formed a straight, dark line. Then he said, "Will you join me in a game?"

Devon shifted in his chair. "Me? No! I know nothing about gambling."

"Ah, but you do. Life itself is a gamble."

"Not in the same way. I can decide what each day will become."

"And what then will happen to you this afternoon?"

"I have no idea."

"Of course you don't. Fate will decide your destiny. As for me, these cards decide my tomorrows."

"But you could lose tomorrow, and the next day, and the next. And by the time the month is over you could be down to your underwear."

Laughter again, sparking glee in his eyes. "You put it so well, Mr. Finch." Leaning forward, he whispered across the table. His dark eyes flickered with wisdom. "But I am confident of my skill. These cards are my rainbow, and the pot of gold at its end. So there be it, Mr. Finch."

Devon liked his wit, his gentlemanly manner. He admired a man who could look at life with respect, and an unwavering drive for success. He wanted to hear more from Simeon Flynn.

"Tell me about this place. Will I have trouble here?"

Flynn nodded. "Here more than any other place in Saint Paul. They named this city after a Saint, but this place is no refuge for the weary. There's trouble here for sure, each man wanting to test another. Stabbings are frequent. Everyone wears a knife and knows how to use it. That man there, for instance." He pointed toward the bar at a tall, heavy-set man with massive shoulders. "He's a wild one. His name is Willius Kane, born in the wilderness and raised with roustabouts. He's got a sense of self that's broader than this fair river. He loves to fight, to prove his superiority, to impress the ladies, like a stud horse would impress a mare. Watch him, but don't get in his way. He'll pound you to dust before you have a chance to bring him in. And if his fists aren't working right, he's got a twelve inch Indian scalping knife on his left hip. Just stay out of his way. The only one who gets near him is Ingrid Lorgren. She's a whore that lives upstairs. He's her protector, and no one stands in his way."

First Day

"I'll stay clear of him."

"Best you do. He's a hater with a long habit of violence. He'll cut you down in the twinkling of an eye."

Devon shivered as he studied Willis Kane. Thankfully, he couldn't see his face, or the hatred settled therein. He hoped he would never come in contact with him.

"There's a few French Canadians who come in here from time to time, rugged men of the wilderness. Few men can equal the voyagers. If you know the fur trade then you know that it's an exclusive possession of the Scottish Merchants in Montreal, the bourgeois. Aye, men strong and hearty, who can easily carry two hundred pounds like you and I carry a bucket of water. They can live on a crust of bread and a swallow of water, and still overwhelm their foe. Stay away from them as well, for they don't like interference."

"You make my task seem dangerous."

"Just keep your distance. This is no place for grown men, surely no place for a lad like you. You'd best remain in the streets and clean up what's left when the night is over. In time you'll determine who the trouble-makers are."

Flynn's gaze drifted past him as a frown creased his forehead. "Well, here she comes, as pretty in the morning as she is in the evening. It's Ingrid for sure, looking over what's left of the night."

Devon turned as the woman descended the stairs. As she stepped onto the floor, she immediately turned her attention toward the bar where Willis Kane stood, and without pause sashayed over to him, placed a hand on his arm and leaned onto his shoulder. Evidently, Kane wasn't in the mood for affection because he eased her away and continued peering into his glass. She stepped back, and then looked toward Devon just as Flynn pulled out a chair. Without pause, she began walking toward them.

Devon took a deep breath as Flynn spoke. "She's a woman with a disputable reputation. I suggest you treat her kindly, lest Kane should get wind of your disrespect."

He glanced quickly at Flynn, who had placed his cards to one side. Flynn's grin widened as Ingrid Lorgren sat down in the chair he had provided. She immediately took Devon's hand into her own and pressed it fondly. "And who is this young pup?" she asked.

Flynn answered for him. "This is Devon Finch, a young man appointed to serve this good city as part of the Alliance Committee."

"And what is that?"

"It is a civilian force, ma'am, organized to keep the peace." Devon could hardly believe that he had spoken.

"But you are so young."

"I am seventeen, ma'm."

She smiled as if to conceal her next question. Devon's curiosity led him to examine her further. Her hair, the shade of fall wheat, had been carefully arranged, each curl a masterpiece. Her eyes, dark amber, were filled with an element of melancholy. She wore a long green dress trimmed with lace at the neck that flowed downward to reveal the whiteness of her half-revealed breasts. Her voice had obviously been formed by years of hard times.

"This is your first visit here," she said, as if to answer her own question.

"It is."

"I am Ingrid. I work here."

"I know, ma'm. Mr Flynn explained your presence."

She giggled while touching his hand. "You have an interesting way of expressing yourself."

Devon felt like removing his hand but he didn't want to seem churlish. Her hand was soft, her fingers delicately placed. Her closeness brought a new aroma to the room, lavender, he thought, or something similar. Her hair, like carved marble, caught the lamplight. Then, just as she breathed, he was drawn to the swell of her breasts.

"The name, Finch," she remarked. "I believe your brother has been here."

"My brother?"

"Yes. His name is Randolph, is it not?"

"It is."

"And he is a policeman."

"Yes."

"He comes here from time to time, looks around, asks questions, and helps out when there is a disturbance. He looks much like you."

"He is older than I am."

"But not as sensitive."

"We share the same values."

She laughed aloud. "Don't worry. He has never followed me upstairs. He has values for sure, the likes of which are not respected here. "

Her eyes brightened with a cat-like stare. She leaned toward him, her eyes afire. She spoke in a low, almost purring voice. "Would you like to come upstairs?" she asked.

His breath quickened. "I cannot, nor would not. I am pledged to be married soon."

"Ah," she sighed. "Then perhaps as yet you have not experienced life's sweetest joy."

"And what is that?" he asked.

"Why, fornication of course."

He blushed as her eyes danced over his features. Her hand, like a leaf in a pond, rested soft and smooth against his. He swallowed his reply as he slipped his hand away.

"Come," she said. "You will enjoy it. I am good at what I do."

A hum of voices came from the bar, low but distinct. Devon had no choice but to be friendly toward her. "Thank you," he said. "But I have to resume my duties."

She withdrew her hand, and then turned to Flynn. "He is pure," she said.

Flynn nodded. "I believe he is."

"Then I shall not tempt him further."

Devon eased the chair back. "I have to go now."

"I am always here," Ingrid said. "Any time you wish to ease life's pressures, I will take you away to another world."

She shifted, bending toward him so her breasts nearly strained out of the bodice.

"I wish you a good day," he said.

"Do you have a dollar?" she asked, before he had a chance to move.

"Yes."

"For just a dollar I will show you what you have missed. There is a whole new world of adventure beneath this dress."

Devon backed away from the table as a curl slanted across Ingrid's eye. Deftly, she tucked it back to where it belonged. The gesture reminded him instantly of Caroline. He was surprised by her outright boldness, and by the manner in which she had approached him, and for an instant he thought she would laugh, so gleeful was her expression.

He turned to Flynn, who had resumed shuffling his cards. "Good day to you as well, Mr. Flynn, I will see you again, I am sure. Perhaps then we can talk a while longer."

Flynn merely nodded.

"And I will also wait for you," Ingrid remarked. "The next time we meet, I will tell you my secrets."

"I will look forward to our meeting," Devon replied, not wanting to be rude.

"Watch your back," Flynn said.

"Goodbye."

Devon took one last look around, then turned and walked away. Immediately, he saw Willius Kane looking at him, his eyes tight, his teeth together as if to hiss. He trembled as he walked toward the door, opened it, and stepped outside. The morning sun struck him full in the face as he issued a sigh of relief. When his knees ceased trembling, he drew a deep breath. So that was the LaBelle, a world apart from his own. In just twenty minutes he had met a gambler, a whore who had frightened him with voice alone, and a ruffian who would not hesitate to beat him senseless if provoked. One thing was certain; he would avoid the LaBelle as much as possible, and would remember this day only as an experience.

He walked down toward the levee, to where the *Jeannette Roberts* was moored. By three o'clock the boat would be empty and passengers would board, and she would back off with black smoke rolling from her stacks and the flag flying full at her jack staff.

He was about to move when a shout brought him up short.

"Devon, hold up!"

He turned. The two men approaching him were Jimmy Hasset, a neighbor, and Clayton Fornier, whom he had met during training. Fournier was near thirty, a man who walked with a limp. Hasset was slender, scarcely older than him, but with a beard already full.

"Where have you been?" Jimmy asked.
"There." Devon pointed at the LaBelle."
"You went inside?"
"Of course."
"Why didn't you wait for us?"
"Because I wanted to go in alone."
Fornier snickered. "You were curious, weren't you?"
"Somewhat."
"Tell me. Who did you meet?"
Devon tried to appear indifferent. "I met a gambler named Simeon Flynn and a woman named Ingrid."
"I know her," Clayton said immediately. " I mean, everyone in town knows about her. Why she's famous here, especially with the river men."
"I've never heard her name before."
"That's because you lead a sheltered life. She's probably the best known whore in Minnesota, or in the territory for that matter."
"You're lying."
"Hell, no. Am I lyin', Jimmy?"
"No. I've seen her, too, up near the American House one day, on the arm of a riverboat captain."
"How did you know it was her?"
"I was with my father. When he saw me lookin' at her he kicked me in the behind and said I shouldn't be looking at trash. She looked right beautiful to me. I asked him what her name was, and he told me it was Ingrid. I never forgot that name, or how she looked for that matter."
Devon gestured toward the LaBelle. "Well, she's in there now, and if you want to meet her, now's the time. She's seated with Simeon Flynn. Least she was before I left. Now she might be with Willius Kane."
Jimmy's face blanked. "You met him also?"
"I just saw him. He's a horrible looking man."
"I heard he's sweet on Ingrid."
Clayton explained. "He's her protector. If anyone gets rough with her, he beats 'em to a pulp. He's sent more than one man to the hospital."

"We're goin' in." Jimmy said impatiently.

"Just remember what Western said about communicating. We either rap our night sticks together, or we blow our whistle. In case of fire, three raps or three whistles in quick succession. At noon we head for home."

"I remember," Clayton said.

"Okay, now go and meet Ingrid. She's waiting for you."

"Whooeee!" Jimmy shouted. "Halleluiah, here we come."

Devon watched as they entered the LaBelle. He snickered, knowing they'd be just as petrified as he was in the company of such beauty. He hoped they each had a dollar in their pocket.

He walked the streets until noon, up past the Central House on Second and Minnesota, and "The Inns of Court" on Cedar. He stopped in at Cheritree and Farwell's Hardware store in the Ingersoll Block, and McCloud and Brothers hardware just to pay them a visit. Then he headed for home. He was anxious to see Caroline again, to tell her about his first day.

One thing was certain, however. He would not tell her about Ingrid Lorgren.

CHAPTER SIX

Looking ahead

Following his first day of duty, Devon walked hand in hand with Carolyn that evening. The balmy weather carried a soft wind, and with it the unmistakable scent of spring. Shadows lengthened in the low sunlight, adding stillness to the city. They talked about school ending, and what they would do during the long summer days following graduation, and other matters concerning the future.

"I've been thinking," Devon said. "I might want to become a surveyor."

"A surveyor? Why?"

"I studied it in school this year, learned all about the tripod telescope with cross hairs and a spirit level, about elevation, and how to use a surveyor's chain. With all the new land being developed, surveying might offer a good living."

Caroline didn't reply at first, she just thought about what he had said. Then she replied, "It would be outside work, rain and snow, summer and winter."

He shrugged. "I was just speculating."

"Father still wants you to get involved in our local government. He has influence with many people, some in high station."

"It would require more schooling."
"Perhaps."
"I don't think my folks could afford to send me to college."
"You might not need college. Father could get you started in a low job, and with hard work and dedication you could advance to something greater."

Devon shrugged. "I don't know."

"I know you've got spunk. Why, you could do anything if you put your mind to it. I'm sure by autumn you'll know if this Alliance Committee will eventually get you into a new police force."

"Maybe sooner. I've still got three months before the leaves start turning."

"You studied political economy, didn't you?"
"Yes, but with some difficulty."
"But you received a good grade."
"If you call a C a good grade."
"It's better than failing."

He sighed. "I guess I could get used to being stuck behind a desk, but it's not something interesting, like surveying, or police work, or . . ."

"Or what?"
"Something besides working with details all day long."

Her hand tightened. "Well, whatever you decide is alright with me, just as long as it doesn't keep you away for days at a time. I want you home with me and the young ones as much as possible."

He liked it when she spoke of young ones, the family to come, a boy for him, a girl for her. Still, it was worrisome in a way, knowing he would have to support them, to put food on the table, to clothe them and educate them and hope that his training would provide them with a good and proper life. Being a father would certainly bring him responsibility of a new kind, to teach them right from wrong in a city filled with an abundance of temptation.

"My father will be after you to make a decision," she said, interrupting his thought.

"I know. I just want to do the right thing for us, even though I know his intention for me is appropriate."

"He thinks highly of you."

"For that I am thankful."

"Sometimes he talks about you as if you were his son."

"I admire him for that."

He could smell the river, like dampness in the air, as the sun settled behind the hills, luring darkness. He put his arm around her shoulder, drawing her in.

"I want what's right for us," he said.

"I know."

"I learned some Latin and bookkeeping in school. But what good is Latin?"

"You might need it in college."

"I thought about that. I didn't especially like learning Latin, except for 'ego, diligo vos'."

She looked up at him, her eyes soft and expressive. "I know its meaning. Thank you for telling me that you love me."

He wanted to kiss her then, but they were in public, and so he suppressed his emotions.

"I promise you one thing," he said. "No matter what I decide, I'll be successful. I couldn't imagine being like that gambler, sitting at a table, wondering when my next dollar would come walking by. It would be a life of monotonous repetition, and I don't want to live a life like that."

She tugged at his arm. "You won't. I know you'll be successful at whatever work you choose. I don't expect you to become the governor, but you could if you put your mind to it."

"I guess I could be. Devon Finch, Governor. Now that sounds respectable."

The sound of her laugher replaced the stillness of the city.

"I don't know why I get like this sometimes," he mumbled.

"Like what?"

"Like thinking about the future as if it's a far-away land, when I know all along that it's right in front of me, so close I can reach out and touch it."

She giggled. "I think you should be a writer."

"A what?"

"A writer. If you could sit down long enough to put all your thoughts on paper, maybe you could write a book. My mother has magazines like Harper's Monthly, and Godey's Lady Book that are tucked full of stories. And that book by David Copperfield that's been passed around school, why it's just about worn to rags because so many people are reading it."

"I couldn't be a writer."

"Why not?"

"Because it's confining, just sitting at a desk all day. It would be no different than that gambler just waiting for someone to come by. With words being my only companion during the day, why, it would saturate my soul with boredom."

She laughed again. "Whatever your occupation, Devon Finch, at least you'll never be boring."

"Please, no more talk about my ability."

"Fair enough. Then I'll tell you that mother made a sour cream raisin pie today."

He licked his lips. "I'll have a slice."

"And the dandelions will be blossoming soon. Remember when we picked them last year?"

"Of course, we made wine."

"Want to do it again?"

"For your father?"

"Yes. After all, it was his suggestion."

Devon recalled the day they had walked north to Phalen Creek, where the fields were bursting with yellow dandelions. They picked several pails of blossoms and brought them back to the house where they were checked for bees and blemishes before covering them with water. They stirred them twice daily for five days and then pressed out the blossoms by hand, straining the water through a cloth. To that they added five pounds of sugar and two slices of unpeeled orange to each gallon of juice. They had allowed it to work in a warm place, skimming it daily. Two months later the brew stopped working. After pouring it into bottles, mister Page had boasted of its flavor.

They turned and retraced their steps as the sky darkened. Lamps had been lit inside and out. They stood together for a while, neither wanting to separate. He feared he had acted a bit vague about his future, and he hoped she was not upset by his true line of talk. He kissed her lightly, whispering. "I love you, Carolyn Jean Page."

"And I you, Devon Finch."

"Someday I will not have to say goodnight to you in front of your house."

"In our own bedroom then?"

"Yes."

She pressed her cheek against his shoulder, pulling him tight to her body. "Everything will come to us as God has planned," she said.

"I will pray that it does."

"You be careful down there in Lowertown."

"It's not as frightful as people think it is."

"That's your impression."

He kissed her again, and then she said to him, "Come in now, for that piece of raisin pie."

CHAPTER SEVEN

Ingrid Lorgren

The first half of June was favored with mild temperatures and the absence of high winds. Clear, warm weather brought out the strawberry crop with surprising rapidity, and by the eighteenth, berries were in the market.

Devon had worked through all his assigned times and had encountered no disturbances other than a few drunkards who found it difficult to stand upright, and a brief scuffle outside the LaBelle that resulted in black eyes and a bit of blood, neither of them his. Most often during the long hours of darkness he just listened to music coming from inside the saloon, songs like *The Boatman's Dance,* or *Jim Along Josie,* or *Old Dan Tucker,* foot pounding music led by a violin and laughter for a final verse. Inevitably someone would sing *Lorena,* and the words would drift out into the night.

The years creep slowly by, Lorena,
The snow is on the grass again;
The sun's low down the sky, Lorena,
The frost gleams where the flowers have been;

But the heart throbs on as lovely now,
As when the summer days were nigh;
Oh, the sun can never dip so low,
Adown affection's cloudless sky.

The music and the voices were nostalgic, filled with longings so tender, as to make the sky weep, soft words from coarse men, sung with a breath of loneliness, away from their homes and the women they loved, wherever they were. Devon liked those moments, the stillness of night, the breath of dawn just hours away, the mood of men disturbed by a loneliness that could only be drowned in drink and song.

He learned soon enough that the men were rude and uneducated, brave and coarse. They enjoyed drinking and fighting and were reckless to a fault, foul-witted and profane. The prodigious braggarts among them were fond of the women and their finery, and for the love they could receive in an hour with the likes of Ingrid Lorgren, or with any of the other four who thought nothing of giving a poke to a stranger bent on satisfaction.

On nights when his duty was finished, Devon walked home and crawled into his warm bed and slept until mid-afternoon. Then, awake again, he thought of Caroline and ate a quick meal. The remainder of the day was spent with her, if she was available. When it came time for rotation he had to adjust all over again. He hated rotation. Just when he became accustomed to one time period, he had to change to another.

The *Ben Campbell,* an elegant steamboat with fifty grand staterooms, came in earlier than expected. The *Milwaukee,* came up behind it, one of the crack boats of the Minnesota Packet Company. Devon loved being on the levee when the boats came in, when the town was drowsing in sunshine, and when the draymen shouted, "Steamboat a'comin'." The drays came then, those sturdy carts with detachable sides, built for carrying heavy loads, hell bent for the wharf, carts and men and boys hurrying toward the oncoming steamer to accept whatever cargo she discharged.

Then the steamboat arrived, her two tall stacks belching black smoke, the flag whipping on her jack staff, her decks teeming with passengers, her wheels churning water while members of her crew clustered on the forecastle. When she came closer one could see the imposing pilot house, its glass and gingerbread designs clearly visible, its paddle box elegantly decorated with river scenes, her name displayed below the white railings of Boiler, Hurricane and Texas decks that shined jewel-like in the sun.

The steamer came in grandly, with people shouting and waving, her flags going limp as she reduced speed in mid-current, as pent up steam shrieked through her gauge-cocks, her stern-wheel stopping at the sound of the bell, then reversing, allowing her to glide into the dock like a gigantic seabird. A deckhand stood atop the stage plank with a coil of rope in hand, and as the steamer nudged the landing he flung it away to a dockhand who secured it tight to a cleat. Nothing stopped those boats except fog.

They were beautiful and grand and majestic in size.

The steamer appeared to sigh as she settled in at the dock, the last of her noise expelled, her journey complete. Then the passengers began coming off in a thin line, first the gentlemen in polished silk hats and shirts with elaborate fronts adorned with diamond breast pins. They wore kid gloves of fine leather, and patent leather shoes, and their beards were trimmed to refined elegance. Their eyes moved carefully over their surroundings, as if putting on airs. Only a few were hasty in their movements, anxious to find transportation. Behind those men of accomplishment came those of common lineage.

Independent merchants came next, those of lesser station, dressed in buckskin coats hung with fringes, and wrist bands of leather, slouch hats, picturesque and magnanimous in their haste to get ashore. They were fine to a point, but many had the look of miles on their faces, weather beaten from traveling on the prairies or the rivers or the long roads. Some had watches with extensive brass chains. A few wore suspenders. Some were silver-haired, while others wore tall, felt hats. Still more had blistered skin from too much sun. One carried a jug in his hand, another, a ledger.

The immigrants came last, some still eating the remains of their breakfast, a piece of bread or a slice of bacon. Disoriented and confused, most looked bewildered while gazing at the city above. A few were picked up by wagons; kinfolk or friends come to take them away. On the boat, the deckhands and roustabouts began unloading heaps of belongings, furniture, small machinery, hand-crafted trunks, mysterious boxes containing items precious to the passengers. The women carried carpet sacks and crying babies. Children who could walk on their own paraded behind them, eyes fixed on their mysterious surroundings, their words silenced by nervousness. All had eyes deepened by being in a strange, new place. Some of the children cried. Most of the fathers were immune to the bleating. The families mustered in groups, looking into the bright blue sky as if asking it to bless them. Others peered up to the sandstone bluffs, to where the buildings stood. Some of the children huddled together, or sat on nearby barrels, to study their unfamiliar surroundings. Some of those who were unaccompanied, carried handmade wooden satchels reinforced with metal straps covered with oil-impregnated cloth some called leatherette. Others carried satchels scarcely large enough to hold a change of clothing, which was just about all a man needed on the prairie. Half-breeds followed, wearing pantaloons and breech clouts; Indians who had left their past behind.

The climate lured many people north because Minnesota was known to have an atmosphere more pleasant and healthful than most eastern cities. Some said they never breathed better air. Others attributed the healthy condition to the forests and lakes.

For that reason the steamboats would keep on coming, and Devon would do his part to help, to give directions, to recommend lodging, to offer assistance, and to inform the urgent where the nearest facilities were.

At eleven o'clock, only one hour of duty remained, minutes filled with nothing but observation and alertness. The steamship had discharged all its passengers. Freight was still being offloaded amid a hive of activity, men moving barrels and crates, with drays and baggage vans coming and going, passengers working their way into the city. The racket continued to punctuate an otherwise calm waterfront.

He sauntered up toward the LaBelle, where silence was less disturbed. The dock would be noisy for a while, until the work

Ingrid Lorgren

was over and done with. Then the river men would come to the saloon, and later in the day the Pilot might lift a glass or two, to spend some of the two-hundred and plus dollars he earned for a month's work, enough money to pay a preacher for a year.

Devon had intended to walk right past the LaBelle without as much as a glance, but as he passed the saloon, a voice called out to him.

"Devon Finch."

He turned, to take a quick look before moving on. Two women were there, sitting in chairs propped against the wood siding. Dressed casually in ordinary clothing, they appeared out of place. He waved when recognizing one of them as Ingrid Lorgren. He shouted, "I don't have a dollar."

Ingrid spoke rapidly to the other woman who then arose from her chair and entered the saloon, leaving Ingrid alone. "Devon," she called again. "Come and talk to me. I am lonely."

"But you just had a companion."

"She could not stay. I will be on my best behavior, I promise. I will not be the woman I was when we first met. You will see that there is another side of me, one less ill-mannered and crude."

"But I . . ."

"No one of any importance will see you here. Those who live on the hill have better places to go. Please, come and talk. Remember, I told you the next time we met I would tell you my secrets."

He stood in the middle of the street as his thoughts began a silent scuffle. What if someone saw him with her? What if someone . . . . ? But he could see no harm in just talking. She had promised to be on her best behavior . . . but still, his reputation could be tarnished . . .

"Only for a few minutes," she called.

He looked at the dirt street, as if it held answers, then turned and looked at her. He wanted to go on toward the high bluff, but his feet failed to move. Then the sudden nervous chill he had experienced left him, and before he took a step forward he turned and faced her.

"I'm short on time," he said loudly, for she was about forty feet away.

"There's enough of it," she replied.

He stepped off, hesitantly. Something told him it would be alright. Mere conversation was not improper. On the other hand she had been impolitely coarse when they first met, using saloon talk while seeking him as a customer. He walked forward, stopping several steps away. She smiled, leaning back in the chair. "It's only two more steps," she said humorously.

"It's just . . ."

"I know. I know. I'm an improper lady and you don't want to be seen with me."

"It's not that."

"Come on. Come on." She patted the empty chair beside her. "I want you to know that I'm not as crude as I presume to be. There are two Ingrid Lorgren's inside this body."

He shrugged, took the steps quickly and went directly to the chair. But even as he sat down, a nagging uncertainty continued to rile him. "I'm a bit nervous," he said.

"I expect you are. But you needn't be. I saw you walking past, and I knew I had to apologize for being so forward when we first met. I was that other woman, the one everyone expects me to be, that blistering maid of sexual indulgence. I want you to see the other side of me."

"You needn't apologize."

She seemed at ease, her face common-like, not all made up with powders and lipstick, her eyes clear and soft in the daylight. She was quite unlike the lady of the night who had sat with him and Mr. Flynn. Her features were soft and delicate, her hair free falling, without curl, as if she had just used a comb.

She turned toward him and gazed at his face, as if to see him for the first time. Then she said, "That woman you met the other day was someone I'd rather you not know."

Devon leaned forward, nervously. "Then who was she?" he asked.

"I was crude with you, as others would expect me to be. It's my job to be crude. If I were the woman I want to be, in there, no one would . . . well, they would go elsewhere."

He relaxed, wondering where the conversation would take him. She appeared different than the first time they had met, more lithesome, more common. So, with his curiosity heightened, and his apprehensions easing, he promised silently, that if she reverted to that of a bar-room whore, he would simply get up and leave.

"I want to change your opinion of me," she said.

"Why?"

"Because when we first met, I sensed something good in you. You're different than others. I think you're a man of character, like your brother."

"That's just a guess. You don't know me."

"Oh, I think otherwise. I would wager my life on it."

He grinned. "That's a mighty large wager."

She shrugged. "I'm not worth much."

He turned toward her, and saw her eyes tight to the sky. She was pensive, as if looking at a likeness she did not quite recognize. "You are worth as much as anyone," he replied.

She reached over and lightly touched his arm. "See what I mean. That sort of reply could only come from a man of character."

The brief silence was broken by shouts down on the levee, and the clang of a bell somewhere in the distance.

"Where are you from?" Devon asked.

"Before I tell you, I want you to know that you can leave at any time. I will not pressure you to stay. I realize how delicate this is for you."

Devon nodded. "I'm not that sensitive."

"Then I'll go on." She turned away from him and gazed at the sky. A frown creased her forehead. She drew a deep breath, nodded, and then glanced quickly toward him to capture his attention. Then she began. "When I was a little girl, we lived in a small Pennsylvania town. My father was a farmer."

"Why did you leave?"

"If I reveal my past, you must keep it in confidence."

"If you have trust enough to tell me, then, yes, I will."

She raised her knees and held them in an elevated position while maintaining a contemplative pose. She had things to say to him, things she had kept secret for many years, private things she could only reveal to someone trustworthy.

Suddenly Devon felt inadequate. He had no purpose in wanting to know the background of someone who was looked down upon by men and women alike, as someone who could leave this earth and never be missed? He would have left then, had she not spoken.

"My birth name was Mildred Klein."

"Then you are German."

"Yes. I was born aboard ship, and was nearly lost in childbirth. I'm a daughter of the sea."

She giggled, as would a schoolgirl, and for a moment she appeared like everyone else. Then, as if to unearth visions of the past, she closed her eyes, and sadness came over her.

"I was ten years old when my mother died giving birth to my third brother. We buried her beneath a tree near our cabin. After that my father was not the same."

He was surprised at her calmness and the way she spoke, unlike her crude manner in the saloon when men were present.

"After my mother's death, my father began drinking. Soon afterwards he started beating me with a broom, and whenever he did, my brothers would laugh. They had no sympathy, none of them. My hate grew quickly. I couldn't love them even though I tried."

"You don't have to go on," Devon said.

"But I must. I want you to know who I really am. I don't have courage enough to tell others. Besides, if I did, they would just laugh. I'm telling you, because I know you'll listen and understand."

"But I'm a stranger, and only seventeen."

"Not to me. I saw decency in you the first time we met, which I can't say about the men who favor me. They make me feel lonely. Most men who come here are pirates of the river. They wouldn't understand a word I said, even if I told them a thousand times. If anything, they'd laugh at me. I'm just a woman who's passed around for everyone to use, until discarded for someone more attractive, or more ravenous with their body. Only one other knows my story."

"Is it Willius Kane?"

She looked at him blankly. Her bottom lip trembled. "Flynn told you about him, didn't he?"

"He told me only that he has a yearning for you."

"Kane has a bad reputation, but he is not a bad man."

"How does he make a living?'

"I don't know. He never told me. He gives me money for no reason at all, and watches over me when others get too demanding or brutal with their fists. He has broken a few bones to keep me safe from harm."

"He's your protector then?"

"Yes, my protector."

She stood and stretched a bit, then leaned against the wall while looking over the river to higher ground festooned with trees. Then she sat back down, facing him. "When I had enough of my brothers' fists and broom stick, I tried to run away, but they caught me and brought me back, screaming and kicking. A month later my father indentured me to a farmer who said he would take care of me."

"Rather fortunate, I would say."

"Not so. When he picked me up in his buckboard, the first thing he said to me was, my what a wild creature. I have just what it takes to tame you."

She swallowed hard, wiped a stray tear away from her eyes and then went on.

"For a week I was happy to be away from my father and brothers, but I learned quickly that my new caretaker was no better. He clothed me in rags and treated me like a slave. He worked me to exhaustion and put little food on the table. When I was about thirteen, and growing into a woman, he took me to his bed and began poking me. I didn't like it, but he was big and strong, and he held me in a grip so tight I couldn't move. He did everything to me, everything a man could do to a woman, and he expected the same in return. He was a good teacher. He taught me the rawness of life, and how to accept men at their worst."

"It's a frightful story," Devon said.

"I feared for my life at times, afraid that if I didn't please him just right he would kill me. He had that look about him sometimes, like a snarling wolf. He didn't teach me anything, except which he could say by mouth. He kept me away from school."

"Couldn't you turn him in?"

"The possibility occurred to me, but I was frightened so much I couldn't begin to act on it. When I was fourteen, I took what I had and ran away."

She hung her head momentarily, as if the memory pained her.

"I ran all day and all night, until I was exhausted. Then, with breath near out of me, I slept and did the same the next day and the next night, until I came to a town deep in the mountains. A church lady found me and took me in, and before long, when they couldn't handle my anger, they put me in an orphanage. I went to school for four years, where I learned to write and read a bit. One of the teachers spent time teaching me to be a lady. She said if I didn't learn I'd end up dead. So I learned. At least no one abused me. The other kids kept away from me. They said I was a bitter child, and I was, no denying that. When I was done with school I took off through Ohio and into Illinois where I took shelter in a church again. Only this time I behaved myself and got to know some people, one of whom was a church-going madam. She'd go halfway across town to church, where few people knew her, and after she had her sins relieved she'd go back to the brothel and do it all over again 'till the following Sunday. Edna wore two faces, but she was a good woman who treated me fairly. It wasn't long before I took up with her and became what I am. I learned to associate with some genteel folks, until they'd had enough of me."

"Did you find any comfort in religion?"

"None that I remember. I prayed and sang the halleluiahs, and knelt and bowed until my knees was sore. It all didn't make much sense to me, getting morally healed by someone I couldn't see."

"You're a non-believer then?"

"Guess so. What god would ever put up with someone like me?"

Devon pointed skyward. "He would."

"Jesus?"

"You're just the kind of person He's looking for."

"To cleanse my soul, and put me on the straight and narrow? Why he'd take one look at me and cast me into perdition."

"No He wouldn't."

"I'm too far gone, Devon."

"No one is ever that far gone."

She snickered. "Well, maybe someday when I get too old to get into bed with strangers, maybe then I'll get cleansed."

"Where does Willius Kane fit into all this?"

She laughed. "Kane? You want to know about Kane?"

"Only, if you want to tell me."

She breathed deeply, and then grinned. "Well, I met him quite by accident down in Cairo. He near saved my life one day when a stranger got rough with me. After that we were close. We had our times, and he came to liking me for more than I was. He became my guardian so to speak. He thought I needed a new name, so he called me Ingrid Lorgren. I don't know how he came up with the name, but it fancied me a bit. We came up here in fifty-eight, and he got me a room here at the LaBelle. I provide services for the men, and he protects me. Nobody gets out of hand with Ingrid. Kane's rough, but not with me. With me he's gentle as a mother with a new baby. He's scarred up a few men though with that big knife of his. I don't know what he does for a living, but he's always got money. Sometimes, when my take isn't good, he gives me some. I've got a bit stashed away, just in case something happens to him." She touched an object at her neck, a necklace made of a single pearl set on a disc of silver. "He gave this to me. It's got my initials cut in on the back of it. M.K., so I'd never forget where I came from. He said remembering our past was just as important as planning our future."

"Then, he's different than he appears to be."

"Much so. Kane's got a soul somewhere deep down inside him, even though he's rough on the outside."

Devon watched the eagles again, gliding above the river, carefree and unhurried. They seemed content in the air with nothing to disturb them except an appetite and a yearning for fish in their talons.

"Well, Devon, what's your opinion of Ingrid Lorgren now?"

He shook his head slowly. "It's a wonder. Here I am, just a stranger, and now I know the story of your life. Why did you tell me your secrets?"

"Because I saw a tenderness in you."

"And now you speak so differently, not like . . . ."

"I know what you meant to say. I read some. Crudeness and profanity are not found in books."

"Caroline says I'm affectionate."

"Who's Caroline?"

"The girl I'll marry, as soon as I can provide for her."

"Caroline is a lucky woman."

"No. I am the lucky one. She's the finest."

"You have your whole future planned, don't you?"

"Not entirely."

Ingrid breathed into her hands, and then brushed them across her cheeks. "I'd like to find a man, someone who doesn't know my sins. Every time I look into the mirror, I see the woman I want to be."

Devon gestured to the hills across the river. "Believe me, there's a man out there somewhere, just lookin' for a woman like you."

She gazed pensively at the hillsides. "Sometimes I look over there, trying to see what's beyond, but all I see is more of the same, and I think, maybe this is how it's meant to be. But I don't reflect on it much. I don't have many more tears to shed, even though the past still haunts me."

"Why don't you just leave?"

She sat up straight and extended her legs, then took a deep breath. "The world out there is frightful. I get nervous just thinking about it."

"There's new lands opening up west of here, endless lands filled with opportunity for anyone strong and determined enough to want a new future."

"Not me. But I've thought about leaving more than once."

He shrugged. "My brother would say, just gather up your courage and go. God knows, you're pretty, just the way you are now, without the fancy clothing and face paint and curled hair. You're better this way. I'd bet there's a thousand men out there who'd like to team up with a woman like you. They needn't know about your past. You can become Mildred Klein again, and go down to Saint Louis and find a wagon train. Why you'd be snatched up sooner than you could say Hurrah for Oregon."

She turned toward him, her face tinged with hope. "You really think that could happen to me?"

"Darn right. Anything is possible. All it would take is a little courage, and I know you've got that, considering all you've been through."

She sighed deeply. "For the past year I've had a strong desire to move on, but I'm afraid my past will follow me wherever I go." She gazed at him momentarily, allowing him to see the sensitivity she harbored. "I'm telling you this to remind myself of the woman I want to become."

His reply was resolute. "Then become Mildred Klein again. You'd be her just as soon as you made up your mind to do so."

"I'd never be brave enough to do something like that."

"Huh, you're probably the bravest woman I've ever met."

"Are you sure of that?"

"Sure as I see those two eagles up there."

The door opened then, and a large woman stepped onto the porch. She took one look at Ingrid and snapped, "So there you are. Get in here. I got a gentleman who needs a poke. Work's a callin'."

As the woman went back into the saloon, Ingrid stood up, stretched her arms, and sighed indifferently. "Trying to please the worst in men is what my life is all about. Thanks for listening to a worn out harlot who sometimes doesn't want to see tomorrow. Guess I'll just have to go and see who's waiting."

Devon looked kindly into her eyes. "Remember what I said. There's a new life for you out there on the frontier. You don't have to cheapen yourself any more, if only you've got the gumption."

She reached over and touched his hand. "I hope I didn't embarrass you."

"No ma'm."

"Then, I'll see you again Devon Finch."

"To be sure, good day ma'm."

She left him then, and went back inside the LaBelle.

He stood for a while on the porch, and watched the eagles fly downstream. So that was Ingrid Lorgren, not the same coarse women he had first met, but someone of a different character who might just become a new person someday. Although surprised at her frankness, he still couldn't determine why she had told him about her past. Come to think about it, it defied all reason. She was just a woman intent on changing her life, but hesitant to do so, and he, just an innocent fellow who happened to sit at a table with a gambler one night. Fate was always there to take a hand in things. Fate was beginning to rearrange his life for sure.

With the sun near noon, he went home and ate. Afterwards, he went over to Caroline's house, but was told she had gone shopping. So he wandered back down toward the river and sat on the bluff and watched the final cargo being loaded aboard the *Ben Campbell*. At near four o'clock the crew hauled in the stage planks. Then the steamer cast off her lines, and with all the turmoil and racket spent, and with her wheel turning slowly, she eased back into the river. Then she straightened out as black smoke rolled from her twin stacks, and with her flags flying she began her trip downriver into a peacefulness that reached as far as he could see. He knew, just as sure as the *Ben Campbell* pushed south, that someday a woman with a new name would be aboard a similar craft, heading toward a new life.

He sat there for a while, until the steamer was out of sight, leaving behind the smoke of her passing. He had never been so concerned about another person as he was about Ingrid Lorgren. She meant nothing to him, yet, in a strange way, their lives had knotted into something meaningful. He, talking with a harlot? What a strange alliance. What would Randolph think?

Perhaps Ingrid was crying deep tears inside right at that moment, while pretending to be satisfied with a man who meant nothing to her. What a terrible life she led.

Dang, he thought . . . if only I could help her.

Or then, in hindsight, perhaps he already had.

CHAPTER EIGHT

Final farewell

On June twenty-second, the steamers *War Eagle* and *Northern Belle*, tied up to the landing at Fort Snelling to embark the soldiers of the First Minnesota Regiment led by Colonel Willis A. Gorman. Then, with blasts of steam shrieking from their whistles, and with the turn of their mighty wheels, the boats pushed off toward Saint Paul where the soldiers would parade through the streets before heading off to war.

In Saint Paul, the entire Finch family waited impatiently for the arrival of the steamers, to bid goodbye to Randolph. They stood on Minnesota Street just south of Sixth, knowing the soldiers would parade up Minnesota to the capitol building where the Governor would speak grand words about duty and country and sacrifice. Then the troops would retrace their route to the levee where they would board again for the voyage south.

Hundreds had gathered that day for a glimpse of their soldiers, many of whom had just graduated from school, others who were young fathers, still others who were from outlying farms and communities as far away as Stillwater and Saint Anthony. Caroline was there with Devon, as was Pricilla Udahl, Randolph's girlfriend.

Nona was nervous. Her hands flexed steadily while her eyes sought something afar off in the sky. Father stood calmly. He didn't say much, just filled his mind with thoughts enough to last forever. Pricilla stood quietly, contemplating Randolph's arrival with silent anticipation.

On that bright and beautiful day, they could hear the steamers' whistles as they pulled into the landing, and it wasn't long before the shrill call of fife and the rattle of drums drifted toward them. Patriotism was intense. The street lamps were draped with red, white and blue. Flags flew from nearly every building and home. The people were hushed as the Regiment came closer. Then the troops appeared, marching in grand order, their feet pounding on the dust, their heads high. The sight of their uniforms and the burnishing of new arms added magnificence to their ranks. Then cheers erupted, followed by shouts and tears of joy, as the troops marched past.

"There he is," Devon shouted when sighting Randolph in the middle of the ranks. "There! There!" Pricilla jumped up and down as tears streaked her face. Nona placed her head on Harold's strong shoulder and waved a piece of red cloth high above her head; sadness on her face instead of happiness.

Devon called. "Randolph! Randolph! Here! Here!"

Upon hearing the call, Randolph turned his head and grinned proudly. His eyes settled on all of them at once. Then, in a moment, he was past, and music led the soldiers onward toward the capitol.

The crowd dispersed then. Some went uphill to listen to the Governor while others walked slowly down toward the levee to gather there, to say goodbye to loved ones about to venture into Hell. Sadness masked their faces; men going off to war, homes broken by the departure of fathers and sons. The chill of separation lay heavy on the city.

As the Finch's walked those long six blocks to the levee, they each remarked in their own way. Nona said, "He looked so grand. And now my first son will be gone, to satisfy his duty to country. I pray God will return him to me."

Harold remarked, "Many a man has gone to fight at one time or another. He'll do his best I'm sure, and he'll come back to us, just you wait and see."

Final farewell

Pricilla wept while standing behind them. She spoke only when arriving at the levee. "Now I'll have only his picture, and the memories he'll leave behind."

"I will miss him also," Devon tried his best to conceal his sadness.

They huddled together and embraced one another, and said a common prayer, imploring God to watch over him. Afterwards Devon thought of the horror awaiting Randolph; the hail of bullets and shell, the cut of swords, the crying and death. The horrible thoughts persisted until the troops came back down Minnesota an hour later, dispersing into the huge crowd to find their kin, to say their final words before boarding the steamers.

Randolph found them quickly. He sank into Nona's arms and held her close for a long while, whispering words he had practiced over and over, to give her assurance of his return. Then he went to Pricilla and took her aside, and together they talked in low tones as he wiped tears from her face and embraced her longingly. He shook his father's hand stoutly. Harold suppressed his emotions like a true man as Randolph spoke grandly of the Regiment.

Then he came to Devon and Caroline, and after greeting them as one, he took Devon aside, and with his back to the others he spoke words from his soul.

"I'm taking a pebble from the shore of the river, and that old coin you gave me, and also a lock of Pricilla's hair and a piece of wood from the house. They'll be my talisman, all of them together."

Devon felt his tears rising. "I feel guilty not going with you."

Randolph squeezed his shoulders. "You'll be doing your duty here, and I'm proud of you for that. We'll clean up this mess, and soon I'll be home to take your job back."

The two of them stood eye to eye. Devon tried hard to prevent his lips from trembling.

Then Randolph spoke again. "I'll always remember when we caught snakes and kept them in the back shed, and when I cut my foot on a piece of glass. You padded it up tight with your own shirt and carried me home."

Devon replied. "I remember when we swam naked in the river, and the snow forts we built in the winter, and the butterflies we chased, and the rain coming down on our sand castles. Those were good days, brother."

Then Randolph's eyes turned aside and he looked into the sky, and Devon saw something in him he never seen before. Then Randolph spoke, and Devon knew what it was.

"The sun gets us up each morning at five-and-a-half, and afterwards we drill for an hour. Then we eat breakfast and have recreation for a half-hour. Then we drill for five more hours before eating again. Then after another recreation, we drill for another five hours. Every day is the same. We went to bed one night because we dared not touch the food it was so bad. But it's not bad all the time. We got blankets from the ladies in Stillwater. The clothing is poor, and the rations are slow in coming."

Randolph went on. "The nights seem so much darker now. From time to time I see things in the shadows, moving toward me. I don't know what they are, or what it means, but something always takes them away." He paused and then added. "There's a guidance that calms my fears."

Devon was about to reply when Randolph shook his head. "Listen to me now. We shared a lot of secrets, so keep this one firm in your mind. If I don't come home, I'll be clothed in a new spirit, because someday this life will have to let me go. I'm ready for that should it come to pass. Ready as I'll ever be."

"Randolph, don't . . ."

"Listen to me now. I already know that fear has a taste all its own, and sometimes it actually burns in my throat as if I'd swallowed poison. But even so, I hope to die without pain, the Lord willing. In the end, it doesn't matter where we fall."

Tears came to Devon's eyes. He tried brushing them away before Randolph saw them. He ached inside; a hardness in his chest, a trembling in his arms, a sorrow deep enough to be all-engulfing. He hardly heard Randolph's words.

"We sing a song around the campfires. You know the one. *Soon we'll reach the shining river. Soon our pilgrimage will cease. Soon our happy hearts will quiver with the melody of peace.* Don't worry. The Lord will march with me."

Final farewell

Devon went into Randolph's arms then, weeping on his shoulder until Randolph eased him away. Then, arm in arm, they rejoined the family. For a while there was small talk, and quivering embraces, and a moment or two of forced laughter. Then the whistle of the *War Eagle* shrieked, deadening all voices. Someone with a megaphone shouted. "Men of the First Minnesota Regiment, board your boats."

The farewell was swift and sorrowful as the soldiers moved straight onto the vessels. Then, with flags waving, and fifes sounding, the steamers eased away from the landing and turned bow forward into the long river, and with shouts ringing from all the decks, the men of Minnesota drifted away beneath a beautiful sky from where God looked down on them.

Soon they were out of sight, and the mass of people on the levee turned and walked sadly back into the city, and all was as it was before their leaving.

That night, Devon Finch cried until he could cry no more, until his pillow was wet with tears.

CHAPTER NINE

The Comet

Comets had appeared above Saint Paul before, one in 1845, another in 1858, but none as bright or as vivid as the one on June 30th in 1861. When the sun went down that day, it was as if the sky had given birth to a miracle, for it beamed in the sky like a gigantic white fan, its nucleus burning bright and luminous. Majestic in size, it brought people into the streets where they watched it for hours, as it remained nearly motionless in the sky. Because it appeared on a Sunday night, some thought it was a message from God, meant to show the world His majesty.

Devon had worked the boring afternoon hours that day, and when finished he rushed home to eat his evening meal, then dashed to Caroline's house. When Bethany answered the door her voice was ecstatic with wonder. "Have you seen it?"

"I have. It is wonderful."

Bethany called then. "Caroline, Devon is here."

Caroline dashed in from the adjoining room and welcomed him with a warm but modest embrace, then took him into the parlor. "Let's go to the hillside," she said breathlessly. "Many are already walking that way. I have never seen such a grand sight."

Edmund sat in his chair by the fireplace, dressed in a brocaded vest and a shirt with ruffled collar. He arose as Devon entered the room and extended his hand. His broad smile expressed the excitement of the hour. "We are privileged this day with a display of God's grand design," he said. "In my lifetime I have never seen such a sight in the sky."

"It is huge," Devon remarked. "I cannot believe the size of it. Come with us to the hillside."

"No, you two go ahead."

"Can I come along?" Bethany asked, her face seeking an affirmative reply.

"Yes, the three of us will go. It's a fine evening."

"It exceeds all belief," Edmund said. "Why its tail alone obscures some of the sunlight during daylight hours. Had you noticed how hazy the sky appeared today?"

"Yes, although for a moment I didn't know what it was. Down on the levee the men talked less than usual. Everyone was looking up. Some were afraid, I think. I heard one man say that it was the end of the world, but no one believed him."

"Viewing should be good from the hillside. Go now, and bear witness to a wonder of the universe, for you'll probably not see another again during your lifetime."

The three of them left and walked uphill to the green stretch of land behind the capitol where hundreds of others sat and stood and gasped at the wondrous sight on display.

The comet's position was near the Big Dipper, the constellation of the Great Bear, between it and the North Star. The nucleus was poised about ten degrees below the lowest star of the constellation, on a line with the handle of the Dipper. Its tail stretched in a massive V formation of nearly ninety degrees, all of it perceptible to the eye. Its nucleus was more brilliant than Venus at its most favorable time, its tail luminous and radiant. Every eye was trained on it, every voice silenced by its majesty.

The three found a place near the top of the hill, stretched out their blanket, and laid down.

"Do you know much about comets?" Bethany asked.

Devon replied. "I know only that they come and go, and that they are prevalent in the universe."

The Comet

"What would happen if one of them struck us?"

"It would be terrible. But I don't think something like that will happen. The universe goes well beyond anything we can see. It is deeper than deep."

"We learned some about the universe in school," Caroline said.

"The universe doesn't matter to me," Bethany added. "I want to be a singer."

Bethany's idol was Sallie St. Clair, who, with Bernard Couldock, delighted audiences at Market Hall as part of the Hough Dramatic Company. Sallie was not only an actress, but also a singer with a sweet, soulful voice. She was the reason for Bethany's willingness to stand up and sing before anyone. Devon had no doubt that she would one day be in the theatre, perhaps singing with Sallie St. Clair or someone just as talented.

"Someday I want to hear you sing in the Concert Hall," Devon said'

"I will. I'm certain I will." Bethany left no doubt as to where she was headed.

Devon fanned his arm out wide across the assembly of people. "Here is an audience. Stand up and give them a song."

Bethany's expression was unassuming. "They are too busy with the comet. I would only disturb them."

"But with the right song you could heighten the experience."

"Devon," Carolyn interrupted. "Don't tease,"

"But I . . ."

"I said, don't tease."

He replied humbly, "Yes, my darling."

To that, Bethany snickered.

They stayed on the hill until near ten o'clock. The comet was still bright in the sky when they walked home beneath its light. When they arrived at the house, Bethany went inside, leaving the two of them alone. Carolyn slipped easily into Devon's arms and held him tight. He could feel every curve of her body beneath the dress she wore.

"I worry about you," she whispered.

"Why?"

"Because of your mingling with that horrible riff-raff."

Her hair moved softly against his face. "You needn't be worried. The task is easy, and without risk. I have had no altercations, and practically no excitement. If it were not for moments of casual conversation with strangers, I would be bored."

She eased away. The moonlight softened the gentle curve of her cheek. "It is not always as peaceful as you say. I've heard stories."

"And so have I, many of which are exaggerated."

"You're saying that just to appease me."

"No. I speak the truth. For the most part it is unexciting."

"People have been killed down there."

"As they have in the best of places. Death is no stranger to the upstanding."

She shrugged. "I guess you're right. But still . . . I worry."

"Then come and hold me." He drew her into a soft embrace, shielding her in his strong arms.

He wanted to lay her down beneath a bower of trees, or inside the house, where they could be alone and undisturbed. His passion was aroused, and he felt compelled to kiss her, and not let go of her for hours. He had almost loved her completely when they were alone in the house, when her parents and Bethany had gone to the Athenaeum to see a stage performance. On that night he had unbuttoned her dress and had slipped it down over her shoulders, to take her breasts in hand. They had nearly succumbed to lust when she whispered, Devon, we mustn't. So they had parted, although reluctantly. She had told him once that they would have to wait for mating until after marriage, and he had pledged to obey her request.

"You are warm tonight," he whispered.

"Yes, though it is not the comet or the night that warms me. It is you."

He pressed his lips to her forehead. "Sometimes I feel that I cannot wait for marriage, to love you fully."

"But we must wait."

He breathed deeply, burying his face into the curve of her neck.

"Go now," she whispered.

"So soon?"

"You would stay all night if I didn't send you home."

"I would, for sure."

"Then go. Tomorrow will come the sooner you get to bed."

"But . . ."

She shook her finger at him. "Now listen to me, Devon Finch. Go now, and take my memory with you."

He eased her body forward one last time and rocked momentarily on the edge of ecstasy. Then he stepped away. "Goodnight, Caroline," he said.

"Goodnight, my love."

Stepping back, he released her. They smiled at one another momentarily, as if their separation would be long and agonizing, then he turned.

When he looked back she had already entered the house.

CHAPTER TEN

The deserter

"Devon Finch."

The call came from Western's office at the moment Devon was about to leave the building to begin his morning duty. He turned at the sound of his name and saw Western standing just inside the office door.

"You called, sir?"

"Yes, yes. Come in. I have a specific job for you today. I'm glad you're here. Now I don't have to round someone off the street. Sit down. Sit down."

Devon eased into one of the chairs facing Western's desk. "What is it, sir?"

Western stroked his beard. "We've got a deserter in the cell. We found him last night at his woman's home. He ran off from Fort Snelling three days ago. His woman's father turned him in."

"A deserter?"

"The first of his kind. There'll be a lot more when they begin hearing cannons."

"Who is he?"

"Fella named Carson, Bradley Carson. Do you know him?"

"No sir."

"I didn't think you would. He lives in Uppertown. He's a young fella with a grieving woman and child. It's a sad sort of predicament. I want you to come with me. We're takin' him back to the fort and turnin' him over to his officers."

"What will happen to him?"

"Don't know right off. It's the army's decision. Sometimes desertion requires the penalty of death. Sometimes they choose just one man in order to set an example for others. Bradley Carson might just become an example."

"But he's got a child."

"Don't matter. He's government property. Chances are, they might grant him a public appeal, and maybe promise to give him a pardon if he voluntarily returns to his unit, which I hope he does. I'd hate to see him hang for just being homesick for his woman and child."

"Is that why he came back home?"

"Indeed. Truth of the matter is, he cried like a baby when they dragged him out of his woman's house, with her father screamin' bloody retribution. Now we got to take him back. Damn sad duty, that's what it is."

"And you want me to help."

"Yes. The wagon's ready. Earl will drive the team. You'll sit back with Carson, just to make sure he doesn't jump out. Don't think that'll be possible though. We'll have him tied to the wagon. And don't think of beggin' off this detail. You're the only man I've got right now, so let's get on with it."

They brought Bradley Carson outside, tied wrist to wrist with a tight, knotted rope. Another rope at his ankles gave him only about a one-foot stride. He wouldn't be able to run far even if he tried. Devon wondered what was going on in that mind of his. Bradley's eyes were swollen from crying. His beard, a scattering of untended hair, covered half his face. His sorrowful eyes were fixed with a far-away stare, as if gazing into a less-troubling place. When he looked at Devon, he didn't appear to see him. He simply obeyed when they helped him up into the back of the wagon. He sat down promptly on the base-boards and turned his head away

The deserter

from everyone, trying to place his mind elsewhere, probably back home with those he loved.

Devon climbed onto the wagon and sat opposite him while Western drew another rope around his waist and tethered it to the side-boards. Devon wondered why he had been selected to go along. Bradley Carson couldn't escape the wagon even if he tried.

Western was up front with Earl when Devon and Bradley first gazed at one another, eye to eye. Bradley seemed to look right through Devon; a deep and profound expression of loss, like the stare of a dead man. Just then, before either could say a word, the wagon lurched and started off toward Fort Snelling. Devon settled in, to get as comfortable as possible.

They hadn't cleared the end of the block when Bradley said, "What's your name?"

Devon looked straight at him. "I'm Devon Finch."

"I 'spect you already know who I am."

"They told me your name was Bradley Carson."

"Tis that."

They jiggled with each turn of the wheels, and bounced whenever they struck a depression or a slight mound of dirt.

Devon didn't know what to say. What could a person say to a deserter, a man who might be headed to the gallows? Carson certainly didn't look like someone who had broken the law. Given the sight of him, he wasn't much older than Randolph, and he appeared to be empty of meanness.

"How old are you?" Devon asked.

"I turned nineteen just last week."

Devon looked away to free himself from the need to talk, but then decided to keeping the conversation going. "They told me you ran off from the army."

"I did so."

"My brother's in the First Minnesota Regiment. We sent him off on a steamer this past week. He's probably on a train right now headed east. Being from Fort Snelling, maybe you know him. His name is Randolph Finch."

"Don't know anybody by that name."

Silence again, punctuated only by the sound of the wagon, the clop of the horses' hoofs, and the creak of the wheels.

Devon had never seen an expression as forlorn as the one on Bradley's face. The man was downcast, deep in a pit of despair because he was headed for some sort of retribution for what he had done. He was curious about the man, wondering why he had fled the army, taking a chance on never having a future if the military court decided to hang him. He wondered what Bradley's thoughts were, being all tied up and bound for justice. The only way to find out was to ask him.

"Must have been a powerful lure to make you leave the army," he said.

Bradley jounced a bit as the wagon hit some ruts. His eyes shifted, heavy with remorse. "I had to see my boy again. He's just one month old."

Devon shuddered with emotion. "Are you married?"

"Naw. My woman and me just got careless one night. Her father near killed me when he found out. He wanted no part of me. Told me he never wanted to see me again. Told me I was never welcome in his home again. After Kenneth was born, I thought I'd never see him. Kenneth is my boys' name."

"How come you joined up?"

Bradley snickered. "That's the strange part. When I came around the house to see Kenneth, her father didn't send me packin'. He said that if I joined up with the Union army he'd probably have a change of heart when the fighting was over. If I survived, and performed my duty, I'd be welcomed back to help raise my son. Then he took me into his shed and tied me up. Next thing I knew, I was in the jail house."

"So you joined up voluntarily."

"Did so, lest I'd never see my boy again. I signed up and went off to Fort Snelling."

"Then how come you deserted?"

Bradley looked into the sky as his lips twitched. Devon thought he had asked too many questions, the last being the most personal. But then Bradley reached up with his tied hands and brushed his eyes some. His voice was hoarse when he spoke.

The deserter

"I took a chance and lost." Bradley sighed. "I thought I could take my woman and my boy and head out west, to make something of myself. But her father caught me. Knowing what I'd done, he tied me up in the shed again and went to get the police. I never did get to see Kenneth. So here I am, headed back to take my punishment."

"What'll they do to you?"

Bradley shrugged, and then drew his legs up tight to his chest. He rocked forward and backward for a while as he spoke. "They might hang me, I guess."

"For wanting to see your boy?"

"They don't care. I guess they figure if I don't want to fight for them, then I ain't worth keeping alive."

"Isn't there someone who can help you?"

"In the army? Hell, all those lawyers in uniform aren't about to care for me. To them I'm just about the lowest of the low, like dirt under their shoes."

"Don't seem right."

Bradley straightened his legs, and then rapped at them with his fists. "Nothin's right anymore," he said, as his eyes filled with tears. "I might just as well be dead."

"Chief Western says that if you make an appeal, and promise to join back up, they might not press charges. I guess that's better than hanging."

Bradley shrugged. "I'm not so sure. There'd be scorn heaped on me."

Devon recalled the discussion he had with Ingrid that day outside the LaBelle, on her desire to go west. Might the same advice work for Bradley? He felt the need to say something that might give Bradley hope. "If you survive the war, you could take Kenneth and your woman out west, to start a new life."

Bradley looked long and hard at Devon, their eyes forming a silent union. Devon could practically sense Bradley's thoughts. Then Bradley said, "Could you say something on my behalf when we get to the fort?"

"I'm just nothin' to them."

"They might listen."

Devon nodded. "I could try."

"I'd be obliged. Right now there's nobody on my side except the devil."

Devon nodded. "I'll think on it."

They continued down the long road to the river ferry. When they arrived, they tied the team and wagon to a post. Then Western told Devon to walk Bradley to the barge, and to accompany him to the fort, while he stayed behind. Devon imagined the assignment to be some kind of training, so he took Bradley to the ferry and sat him down on the planks. Devon helped draw the flatboat across.

Fort Snelling sat high on a bluff denuded of trees. From the landing, a trail led upward, causing Bradley some difficulty in shuffling to the plateau on which the fort was situated. When they arrived at the gate, two sentries took one look at Bradley and laughed. One of them said, "I guess you'll be headin' to the Promised Land." Then they led him away.

Devon's mood sorrowed, seeing Bradley being led away like a cow, maybe to be hung before the day was out, just to set an example. He was about to leave when he remembered what he had said to Bradley. He turned to one of the remaining guards, and said. "Can I see your commanding officer?"

"Might I ask what for?"

"I had a brother stationed here with the First Minnesota Regiment. I have a question to ask him."

The sentry led him inside the compound, and pointed across the field where near two-hundred men were drilling. "See that building there? You'll find him inside."

Devon walked alongside the parade ground, past the long row of enlisted men's quarters and the blacksmith shop. The sound of discharging cannon caused him to halt as a squad of men passed him at a full run.

This was foolhardy, he thought. Bradley had broken a military law. Why would they listen to a plea from a greenhorn? For sure, they'd probably turn him around and kick him out of the fort head first. He questioned why he was doing a favor for a deserter. Bradley was a soldier who had to account for his own error. Still, he couldn't dismiss the forlorn look in Bradley's eyes when he

The deserter

had spoken about his son, and so he continued on. When he came to the officers' quarters he asked a guard if he could see the commandant.

The guard motioned to where three officers stood. "He's the one with his back turned," the guard said.

Devon took a deep breath and walked toward them. Here goes, he thought. Might just as well get it over with and get back to town where I belong. Danged if my foolish persistence might get me into trouble someday.

One of the officers saw him approaching and motioned to the commanding officer who turned as Devon approached.

"Sir," Devon said, pulling up short. "Can I have a word with you?"

The officer scanned the other two men as if annoyed. He was young for an officer, a man with thin eyes that sparked when looked into. His beard was peat black, neatly trimmed. He turned to Devon, and then stiffened as if annoyed. "Quickly," he snapped. "I don't have all day."

"I am Devon Finch, sir, of the Saint Paul Alliance Committee. I have just returned one Bradley Carson to your command."

The officer huffed. "The deserter."

"Yes sir. I would like to say a word on his behalf, sir."

The officer chuckled. "On his behalf?"

The other two officers grinned.

Devon remained unruffled. "I would like to recommend that you hear his plea, sir. He will be asking for a public appeal, so he can return to duty."

The officer uttered a slight laugh before he spoke. "So he wants to return to duty, does he?"

"Yes sir."

"Well, your request is unconventional, to say the least. Certainly, this is not a civilian matter."

"I realize that, sir, but he has a young child, a new born that he was yearning to see. Absence from him pulled at his heart, sir."

"He has a child?"

"Yes sir, a boy only one month old."

The officer looked at the other two men, one of whom nodded. They said nothing between them. A moment later the commander returned his attention to Devon.

"Why are you speaking on his behalf?"

"Someone has to, sir. He is a good man. He'll do his duty."

The officer nodded. His expression was ambiguous. "Well, son, now that you've spoken for him, I suggest you be on your way back to Saint Paul. We will discuss this with him. But I offer no promises."

"I understand, sir."

"What is your name."

"It is Finch, sir. Devon Finch."

"Finch?"

"Yes sir. My brother is part of the First Minnesota Regiment."

The officer nodded. A grin came through his beard. "Well, then. I will convey your sentiments to those who will determine his fate. This matter is now in the hands of our army."

"Thank you, sir."

Without saying another word, the officer turned his back on Devon and walked away with the others.

Devon left the fort feeling good about offering a plea on Bradley's behalf. He had spoken up, which might, or might not, save Bradley's life. Randolph would have done the same. Randolph had always looked out for others.

He rode the police wagon back into the city. He didn't tell Western what he had done. That afternoon he continued his daily duties.

He never found out what happened to Bradley Carlson.

CHAPTER ELEVEN

Willius Kane

Devon couldn't have been more tired, had he just eluded a fox. Questions still burned in his mind, allowing him only four hours of uninterrupted sleep. Before he left the house he ate some rye cake and a piece of baked pickerel left over from the evening meal, and by the time he walked into the hot, humid night air he felt somewhat awake, though he lacked the needed attitude to confront Lowertown. A side-wheeler had arrived late and was still being unloaded when nightfall came. By now the crew would be drinking and whoring in both the LaBelle and Pig's Eye saloons, and at other bars scattered throughout the city. Devon would have his hands full if any of the river men turned nasty.

He whistled a short tune with no apparent melody, something to keep him company on the rather long walk. He turned west that night, for no reason but to delay his arrival. The levee could wait for him. His indirect route took him past the People's Theatre on Saint Peter Street, the only frame theatrical building in the city, a theatre that boasted a colored gallery whose patrons paid as much for admission as did the nabobs, the rich and well-dressed who sat in the parquet area behind the orchestra pit. The night breeze tickled his hair, and soon the scent of the river reached him. One could just about taste it during the night hours when everything was still and senses were searching. The moonlight delineated the hillsides on the opposite bank, outlining a scalloped stretch of trees atop the bluffs; moonlight of a pale kind from a sky thick with stars. He thought of Caroline, asleep now, alone in her bed, where he wanted to be. There, above the river, he could nigh on feel her presence.

Later, as silence began reclaiming the city, he walked down toward the LaBelle. He began hearing music some distance away, a piano and violin combined. The tune was *Blue Tail Fly*, rousing and imperfect, but gay in sound. Some of the men, stirred up by liquor, would be dancing, their boots pounding on the wood floor, reckless men who had abandoned the weariness of labor for a moment of merriment.

He paused and looked down at Lambert's Landing where a dim row of lights glinted along the rail of the steamer. Beyond it, a path of moonlight sparked across the black water. When he came to the LaBelle he heard the tone of raucous voices, like a grumble of beasts within a cave. He would go in, look around, ask if he could be of service, and then, amid catcalls and ridicule, he would leave and settle in somewhere on the street where he could hear the night sounds, and wait there with his nightstick and whistle should they be needed.

He entered, head high, his stride slowed by the smoke of cigars and the smell of unwashed bodies scattered amid the taint of alcohol. Heads turned, casting sneers and disinterested glances. Someone said, "Here comes the law." The words were followed by laughter. He strode in, took notice of the men packed against the bar with hardly a gap between them. Simeon Flynn was at one of the tables, his back to the wall. Four men sat with him, crowded together with hardly room between them. Flynn had just dealt. The others looked at their cards with silent expressions, most locked in a grim mood, as if the cards were talking to them, telling them how to play. Three were river men dressed in thin shirts, their skin darkened by sunlight, blistered in places. Simeon had most of the money, but another was close behind. Devon didn't wait to see the ante, he just moved on, glancing everywhere. He nodded at one of the bartenders, the portly one who spoke to him on occasion. The crowd appeared to be orderly, no one overly drunk, no one headed for the stairs.

Back in the corner one of the women in a red dress was leaning over a table, displaying her wares. She had one hand on a man, caressing his long hair, hoping to lure him upstairs. Devon recognized her as Mildred Polshki, the one whose mere presence caused others concern. By the looks of her, she was a tender woman, but Devon knew she was just the opposite, sharp-tongued and bitter, a harlot without a heart, a woman with the disposition of a wildcat. Devon had heard she had a scar or two, from men who got out of hand, although not many came away from her room dissatisfied. She glanced his way as he approached. No smile, just a downright undeviating glimpse that sent a chill through his body.

He stood by the back stairs for a while and then started toward the front door. As he approached the end of the bar a man stepped out, stopping him short. The man was Willius Kane.

He had never met Kane, had seen him only from a distance when his face was suspended over a whiskey glass, or looking straight at the back-bar where a large painting revealed the figure of a long-legged nude on a bearskin rug, her body facing outward exposing all her womanly particulars. Most of the men looked at her while drinking, to become aroused when the time came to go upstairs to view the real thing.

"Mr. Finch." Kane said.

Kane's sudden appearance stopped Devon instantly. He had only to look at the man to recognize danger. Kane was a head taller, and a whole lot meaner than anyone he had ever met. Devon automatically touched his nightstick, a move that brought a grin to Kane's face. During the few moments of indecision, Devon had an opportunity to study his face.

Kane's dark skin had the appearance of old wood. One of his cheeks bore a ragged scar from just below his eye to his chin, an old scar partially hidden beneath his tangled whiskers. His eyes, deep set and dusky, had a wolfish appearance. He stood erect, his hands fisted at his waist. Devon took a step backwards.

"Can I buy you a drink?" Kane asked, motioning toward the bar.

Devon shook his head. Some of the other men looked at him with obvious curiosity, expecting a brawl. "I don't drink whiskey," he replied.

"Sarsaparilla, perhaps?"

Devon shook his head as his throat constricted, stalling his words. "I have rounds to make."

"You have no rounds. I know you're free-roaming, like a prairie steer." Kane wiped a hand across his mouth. His eyes glinted in the lamplight.

Devon stood like a stone statue, facing one of the most feared men in town, without any why or wherefore. Panic coursed through his body. His hands trembled. The tightness in his throat caused a sudden loss of breath. He didn't know what to say, so he said the only thing that came to mind. "To be truthful, Mr. Kane, your reputation causes me concern."

Kane's grinned as he suppressed a laugh. Then his eyes widened, softening his frightening appearance. "And right it should. But I'm not here to threaten you. There's an unoccupied table in the far corner. I'd like to talk to you there." He motioned to a table just inside the door, a place in shadow.

"About what, if I may ask?"

"About a common interest."

"Well, I . . . "

Kane's eyes narrowed. "There's no refusing me."

They walked to the empty table and sat down facing one another. The remainder of the patrons returned to what they had been doing, convinced there wouldn't be a conflict, nothing to holler over, nothing to arouse their animal instincts.

Kane sat back, easy like, and folded his arms. His menacing expression softened. He kept his voice low so no one would hear him. "You're too young a'man to be in this sort of place."

Devon felt a bit more at ease. "It is my duty to be here."

"Ah, duty. Sometimes it rings like a chime, and sometimes it rings like a death knell."

Devon's shifted uneasily. "What do you mean by that?'

"Just what I said. Duty is a two-sided coin."

"I know a bit about duty. My brother joined the First Minnesota Regiment."

"A fighting man?"

"No. He's just someone who wanted to fulfill his patriotic responsibility, same as me."

Kane laughed slightly, but loud enough to be heard. He leaned forward, his arms crossed in front of him. He stared intently at Devon, to capture his attention. "Enough about duty. I said we had a common interest. Her name is Ingrid."

Devon gasped as his skin crawled. Here it comes, he thought. Kane knew about the time he had spent with her. Now he would want to know why. He might be told to keep his distance. Or perhaps questioning would begin. He felt powerless against the weight of Kane's words. Without further thought, he spoke.

"Wait now, Mr. Kane. I have no interest in Miss Lorgren other than having met her on my first night of duty, and again out front when passing. We have no connection."

Kane's expression mellowed as he eased back in his chair. Light from the nearest lamp slanted across his face, accentuating his scar. "I am aware that the two of you met, and talked. Ingrid confides in me."

Devon held his hands tightly together. "Yes, she told me about you."

Kane's eyes narrowed. "Then she told you how she came to be here."

"Yes, that as well."

"And how she wishes to leave here someday?"

"Again, yes."

Kane sat back and fumbled with a shirt button. "She wants to talk to you again, Mr. Finch, now, tonight, as soon as possible, at a time when she is alone."

"About what?"

"That is for her to say."

Devon's uneasiness returned. Perhaps someone who knew Mr. Page was here. Eyes might follow him. How would he explain if he were seen going upstairs? He remained silent while constructing a prudent reply. "Mr. Kane, I have no . . ."

Kane cut him short. "I said she wants to talk to you, tonight. She knew you would be here."

"I . . . I . . ."

"Don't stammer."

"I am confused."

Kane leaned forward again, close enough for Devon to smell the whiskey on his breath, close enough to see the true depth of his eyes. "She has had a terrible life with a cruel father, and brothers who tormented her, then with a farmer who abused her, 'till she went into an orphanage. She had a bitter existence, until she fell in with me at a most unlikely place, on a wharf in Cairo."

Devon nodded. "She told me all that."

Kane's lips curled, revealing yellowed teeth, one of which was missing. His eyes narrowed again. "I am not the kindest person, Mr. Finch." His finger touched the side of his face. "See this scar? It's a constant reminder of my violent days. I received it from an Indian who slashed me with this knife I carry, and though I may have lost my ability to smile, he lost much more."

"His knife?"

"No, his life. And he was not the only one. I was a bitter man those days. I fought, killed, drank, and whored aplenty, until Ingrid came along. But then her name wasn't Ingrid."

"Names don't matter much."

"Huh! She was a sight back then. We were two lives with nowhere to go, escaping demons of our own, wondering why life was so goddam brutal, wondering if we'd ever learn what honest humanity was all about. We got our scars for sure, I got 'em on my body, and she's got 'em on her soul."

Kane sat back, relaxing somewhat, his features frozen in thought. His thoughts reached into the past, where bad times were still fixed in his memory. Devon saw him as younger then, when he was tough and heaped with anger so intense that it erupted at the slightest grievance. The frontier held many men like him, those who could take a life without hesitation, without a moment of regret. That sort of man didn't seem to fit Willius Kane at that particular moment.

"You've been good to her," Devon said. "She told me so."

Kane relaxed somewhat. "Good as I could be, although I couldn't give her anything but much of the same, a room in a saloon, sellin' herself to strangers. I would never marry the girl. She wouldn't want to bed permanently with a man like me, not a man who could turn on her when he was full of whiskey. All I can do is watch over her. These people here know I'd kill 'em if they harmed but a hair on her head."

"So why does she want to see me?"

"I'll let her tell you herself."

Devon glanced back over his shoulder at the stairs leading to the rooms. He shivered thinking that he might have to climb them in full view of the saloon. He balked at the thought. "I'm not going to walk up those steps back there, not where everyone could see me. If word of that got out to Mr. Western, or to my woman, why I'd be out on the street for sure."

Kane motioned with a tilt of his head. "There's stairs on the outside goin' up to the second level. You go out the front door, and I'll go up inside and clear the way for you, and to unlatch the outside door. Ingrid's room is the first one to the left. She'll be alone. Just rap on the door and she'll let you in."

Kane made no effort to move, so Devon didn't know if he should stand or remain seated. Then their eyes met in an extended stare as if to seal the agreement, and Devon stood up. He didn't reach out to shake hands. Instead he simply scratched an itch on his chin, and said, "Thank you, Mr. Kane. I had a whole other opinion of what you were like."

"I expect everyone does. People ain't always what they appear to be. Now take that gambler over there." He pointed at the table where cards were being dealt. "Flynn's got that forever grin on his face, like it would last forever, but down inside he's not the man he appears to be. I've seen his anger, seen him bring down men with a devil viciousness he can't control. Why he nearly killed a man last week when you weren't here because he caught him cheating. He was afire as any man I've ever seen, much like I used to be before Ingrid came along. We pulled him off just in time, 'fore he squeezed the life out of him."

Devon nodded as if to agree. "I'll go now, Mr. Kane."

"And I'll go upstairs and open the door."

"Thank you."

"T'was nothin'."

Devon went to the door as Kane worked his way through the bar and past the fiddle player. Most of the occupants were watching Kane, so Devin slipped out the door and into the hot night unnoticed. He felt a bit relieved as he stood in the darkness. Confused and nervous, he paused momentarily and looked toward the river. The water was as quiet as he had ever seen it, the silence punctuated only by the merriment inside the LaBelle.

He walked to the side of the building, glanced to his right. With the westerly moon already low in the sky, the stairs ascending to the second level were deep in shadow. He hesitated. Something told him not to go up, but he had made a promise, which had indirectly put his honor at stake. Placing one foot on the bottom step, he eased up to the second. Eight more steps remained until he reached the landing, eight more steps to another page of his life he didn't want to turn. He felt as if a dozen people were watching him from somewhere in the shadows. His legs trembled. He swallowed dryly, took a deep breath, and mounted two more steps. Then the door above him opened. Kane motioned. "Come on."

Devon took the remaining steps quickly, and entered the narrow hallway, lit by only one lamp. The walls were covered with flowered wallpaper. Four or five doors lined the way. Kane pointed to the first one on the left. "She's by herself," he said.

Kane stepped out the door, leaving him alone. Nervous and short of breath, he turned quickly to Ingrid's door and rapped. He would have laughed had he not been so danged scared. What if someone saw him now, anyone? What would he say? How would he explain his presence? A second later the door opened and Ingrid motioned him inside.

She was dressed plainly, in ordinary street clothes, not in a flowered, low-cut gown that made her appear cheap. Her uncurled hair tumbled like a golden waterfall across her shoulders and down her back. Her face was absent of rouge, lipstick and powder, and invitingly warm to the eye, as was her smile. "Hello," she said. "Come in, please. Take a seat on the chair."

She directed him to a small, wooden chair at the foot of a simple narrow bed covered with white and yellow blankets and two large pillows of a flowery design. He could only imagine the many times she had lain there with men, to satisfy their need, to take money from their pockets.

She sat opposite him on a small bench adjacent to a nightstand complete with mirror and ornaments and small drawers where female possessions were kept. A chamber pot was positioned in one corner. Two pictures on the wall denoted scenes of a city resembling Paris. The faded room was enlightened only by the tint of its wallpaper, the bedding, and the warmness of Ingrid's smile.

They looked at one another for a moment, she with a rather disturbed expression, he with one of nervousness because of where he was, and who he was with. His clenched fingers shifted uneasily.

She smiled, to place him at ease, and then said outright. "I'm leaving, Devon." Her glance led him to a small, leather-strapped case, and a small carpetbag and parasol resting alongside it. A bonnet crowned the carpetbag, its tie strings flowing to the floor.

He sat up straight, his eyes wide with surprise. "What do you mean?"

"I'm leaving on the steamer tomorrow. I'm boarding it tonight. Kane has booked my passage. He'll carry my belongings down soon after you leave. Then he'll go and I'll head out on my own."

Devon stared at her in disbelief as his forehead creased. He unfolded his hands. "So sudden?" he remarked.

She nodded as her soft, full lips formed a smile. "Not sudden at all. I just had to get up my nerve. You helped me make my decision when we talked outside. I wanted to express my gratitude before leaving."

"But won't Kane be angry?"

"No, he understands my need. He knows what I've been through, and what I'm searching for. He gave me money to ensure my passage." She rubbed her hands together, and then glanced at him in a way that clearly expressed her intentions. "I'll find a wagon train in Saint Louis and head out for Oregon. There are good people going west. I'll find someone, I know I will. As for these past years of my life, well, I'll just leave them behind and forget they ever existed."

He reached out to take her hand, but hesitated, offering her only a smile. "You're a brave woman, Ingrid."

"No, not brave. I've just got this feeling inside me that's all churned up, ever since the day we talked. As you know, many of my days past have been horrible. I grew to hate the places I've been, except here. But I'm a grown woman now, with gumption, and I can face whatever comes my way, be it good or bad."

"What about Kane?"

"He's has his own interests."

"How does he earn his money?"

"I believe he has a claim somewhere."

"He's never told you?"

"He never has."

Devon looked beyond her at the only window in the room, darkened by night, as if everything outside had vanished. "I expect you'll feel uneasy with him not at your side."

"Some."

Devon leaned back, trying to sort out everything that had been said. He thought it strange that she had listened so carefully to the words he had spoken on the front landing, and then accepting a suggestion from a young boy she had known for less than an hour. He looked at her again. The smile on her face remained as beautiful as ever. "I guess all I can say, Miss Lorgren, is Huzzah to Oregon."

She laughed slightly, glee on her face. She looked extremely pretty then, different from the woman she was when down in the saloon, different from the woman he had sat with outside on the chair. She was of a new mind now, her purpose well set, her direction clear-cut. She was neither nervous nor anxious, just herself, with a destination firmly in mind, and anxious to get there.

"You have been a good friend for a short while," she said.

He blushed. "I was sort of forced into it."

She leaned forward and took his hand and pressed it to her cheek. "I won't forget you, Devon Finch."

"Nor will I forget you."

Her touch was soft and tender, that of a common woman with a face toward the future, with hope and new life present in her eyes. "Now I have to say goodbye, and leave this room for good, to see what's out there beyond these walls."

He looked at the dim light, at the straight white curtains, the nightstand, the water bowl and pitcher, at the common soap made from fat and Lewis Lye, Ammonia, Kerosene and Borax, at the single extinguished candle, at the mirror so carefully positioned so as to reflect the bed. His exploratory glance ended at her face. "You won't miss this room, will you?" he asked.

"No I won't. Nor will I miss the men and their foul breath, and their animal ways, and the low-down disrespect most of them carry for a woman. I've seen all kinds here. I know the sort of man I want. With luck, I'll find him on the trail."

He touched her hand then, felt her skin soft against his fingertips, felt a connection between them, stronger than ever. "There'll be hundreds of men out there lookin' for a woman like you, to be their wife, and a mother to their children."

"I'll be a good mother."

"I know you will."

Her face settled downward. "I never knew my own mother. But I'll know how to love a child."

He wanted to embrace her then, but he knew he shouldn't. Instead, he said, "Well, goodbye then, Mildred Klein."

She chuckled. "You remembered my name."

"I will never forget it."

They stood at the same time. Then she stepped back and gave him a smile so bright and likeable that he thought he would weep. "Keep your head high," she said.

"You do the same."

She went to the door, opened it, peered down the hallway to see if it was empty, and then ushered him to the outside door. When they reached the door she took his hand again and kissed the back of it.

"Be happy in life, Devon Finch."

"I will be, for sure."

Then, before he knew it, he was outside and the door closed behind him. He stood alone on the landing for a while, gazing at the stars to ease his sadness. Then he descended the stairs and crossed over to the edge of the bluff and looked upstream to where the stars reflected in the water.

"Goodbye," he muttered. "I hope you find happiness."

He walked away, wanting no more of the night, up Bridge Street, past the darkened buildings, onto higher ground where the sky met the land afar off, where the night sky was illuminated above the woodlands. He seemed at a loss, but he didn't know why. Surely, Ingrid was just another person passing through his life on a journey of her own, into a future unknown.

Refreshed by a wind that carried the scent of the land and not the city, he strode slowly along, far enough away from the saloon so as not to hear its sound, to wait in the shadows until he heard the call of a whistle being blown in the low streets, or until he met one of his counterparts.

Finally, he would go home, to sleep, while trying to forget the evening, for it was now part of his past.

CHAPTER TWELVE

Murder

"Devon."

The woman's voice was soft in tone, tender of sound. He thought at first that he was dreaming, but then a hand gripped his shoulder and shook it gently. He opened his eyes and saw the wall of his room just inches away. The hand shook him again and he accepted the awakening.

"Devon, there's someone downstairs to see you."

He turned, and looked into his mother's face. She peered down on him with a rather concerned expression. He could tell immediately that the sun had risen. The light coming through the window rested on the backside of her body as she leaned over him.

"Who is it?" he asked.

She backed away, allowing the sun to strike him full in the face. He closed his eyes momentarily against the glare as she spoke. "It's Mister Western, from the Alliance."

Devon squinted, shielding the light. He shifted uneasily beneath the single cover as questions formed in his mind. "Mr. Western? What does he want?"

"He wants to speak with you. He said I'm to get you on your feet, and get you dressed. So come downstairs as quickly as possible, so as not to keep the man waiting."

"Is it that urgent?"

"I expect it is. He's impatient."

"Tell him I'll be right along."

As Nona left the room, Devon eased out of bed and stood on the small rug his mother had woven from an old blanket. He yawned, stretched, and then stumbled half asleep to the water basin, the one he and Randolph had shared. The soap was still damp since he went to bed not more than an hour before. Given the slant of the sun, he judged it was near seven o'clock. He washed, ran his fingers through his hair, pulled on his trousers and shoes, and tried his best to be alert as he descended the narrow stairs into the kitchen. His father glanced at him with concern in his eyes, as his mother said, "Mr. Western is in the parlor."

Western was there alright, dressed in full uniform, his face fixed with a dour expression. He stiffened as Devon approached him. His greeting was curt. "Good morning, Devon. You'll come with me, please."

"Why?"

"I'll tell you as we go." Then he called into the kitchen. "I'm sorry to have disturbed you, Mrs. Finch."

The two went outside into the bright morning. The sun had already risen above the eastern bluff and the day was beginning to heat. Devon wondered where were they going at such an early hour? Western appeared to be impatient. His pace was quick even though the distance was short. They boarded the carriage and sat side by side as the driver whipped the reins. The horses jolted forward. The sound of clopping hoofs carried over the houses. Devon squinted into the sun. "What is this about, if I may ask?"

Western's face was marble-like, fixed with a stern expression, his thoughts nearly visible above his furrowed brow. "We have a problem down at the LaBelle. There's been a murder."

Devon gasped. "A murder?"

"Aye, last night. You were on duty down there. Were there any commotions, anything that might lead you to suspect a disorder?"

Western's eyes emitted only a sliver of sight. Sternly serious, he turned his attention toward Devon. "Well, did you hear anything, or see anything, that may have caused you concern?"

Devon shivered from the sudden, unexpected tension that gripped his entire body. He remained speechless for a moment while trying to comprehend the gravity of Western's statement. His hands fisted as he spoke. "No, I heard nothing. It was a quiet night. Who, may I ask, was murdered?'

Western turned away. "A woman resident named Ingrid."

His words struck Devon like a hammer blow. He sat back, bewildered, as confusion raked his thoughts. Words locked in his throat. He gasped. "Oh my Lord."

Western faced him again with a hard, undeviating stare. "Did you know her?"

Now the questioning would begin. Devon knew he would be forced to reveal everything he knew about Ingrid, their initial meeting, their discussions, and the facts as he knew them. He was in for it now, with no way of escape. He would have to convey the truth, no matter how much it involved him. He covered his mouth, as he always did when troubled, when words were nearly impossible to speak. He glanced at the outline of the city, hastening to find an answer.

"I asked if you knew her," Western said.

"Yes," Devon blurted. "I met her on three occasions."

"When?"

"Once inside the saloon on my first visit there, when I was talking with a gambler named Simeon Flynn, and another time outside the saloon, when she called me over to talk. We had a discussion."

"And the third?"

"Last night, when I was in her room." Devon realized it was time to reveal everything, in spite of the results.

Western's reply was instantaneous, his voice coarse. "Why were you in her room?"

"I knew she was about to leave town, because Kane told me so."

"What did she say? And be specific about it. This ain't about standard conversation. It's about a brutal murder."

Devon was direct. "We talked about her leaving to go west, to start a new life, the same as we discussed the day we talked outside the LaBelle."

"Why would she want to go west?"

"To escape her miserable life and to start over."

During a moment of silence, Devon heard other sounds, the clatter of wagon a block or so away, the rumble of something moving, then a barking dog. Sweat formed across his upper back, bringing with it a sinking feeling. The sun glared down on him as if he was guilty of a great crime. The scent of wheat cakes and bacon whirled in the wind. For a moment he couldn't make sense of what had happened to Ingrid, or what might lie ahead for him during the hours and days to follow.

Western's words were like a knife thrust to his body. "Why would she want to talk to you?"

"I don't know. I first met her when in the company of Mr. Flynn, again one afternoon outside the bar, when she needed a listening ear."

"Didn't you think that strange, for a whore to talk to a young man she barely knew? Or were you interested in favors of a sinful kind?"

Devon shook his head rapidly. "No. My interest in her was innocent. You must believe me, sir. Our association was one of friendship only. Mr. Flynn introduced me to her as a courtesy."

Western looked straight ahead as if unaffected by Devon's answer. "Those whores are devious. They'll prey on just about anyone, young men like you being no exception. I still cannot believe that she'd talk to you alone, especially about something as personal as going west to start a new life. It sounds contrived, Devon."

Devon felt the trap of involvement closing, without a means of escape. His mouth went dry. His hands began trembling. "She was not what you think. She was a woman with a terrible past, and in desperate need of friends. Only one man helped her. His name is Willius Kane."

"I know of him."

"He's her protector."

Western nodded as a groan rumbled in his throat. "I have met him only by chance. He's been in our jail once or twice for reckless behavior. He's a knife man, you know."

"Yes, I know."

Western tapped him on the knee as the carriage turned onto Jackson Street. His reply was reasonably convincing. "Rest assured, I believe what you've told me. But if what you've said proves to be a lie, then you'll answer to me in another way. Not even a trusted member of the Alliance Committee will escape the law's wrath if involved in something as heinous as a murder, not even you, Devon Finch."

"Believe me, sir, I am telling the truth."

"Then we'll leave it at that."

The horse plodded on, its head bobbing, its harness jangling noisily along the length of its body. A building in front of them emerged from the sunlight, casting shadow across the street. Beyond, the river appeared motionless, as if its water had ceased to flow. Devon could make out the bow of the *City of St. Paul,* the steamer Ingrid had intended to take south. He felt a sudden sorrow deep in his body, a leaden, soul-shaking sorrow that almost made him cry. The question he wanted to ask was lodged in his throat, until he was unable to withhold it any longer.

"How was Miss Lorgren killed?" he asked.

"Someone slit her throat ear to ear."

Devon shivered. "Oh, my God," he muttered, as tears formed behind his eyes. He could still hear her voice. Her final word had been, *"Be happy in life, Devon."* And now she was dead, killed by some unknown assailant.

"It's a frightful sight," Western said. "I've seen a lot in my days, but this one is, well . . . it's horrible, to say the least."

Devon tried not to envision the scene. He closed his mind to it as best he could while trying to appear unnerved. "Do you know who might have done this?"

Western nodded. "We can only suppose that it was Willius Kane."

"But he was close to her. He wouldn't have ... "

"Anyone is capable of murder when things go against them. Kane might have been her friend, true, but seeing her away might have tripped his mind. I've seen people killed merely because their assailants were grieved with sorrow. Man against wife, lover against lover. The mind is weak when it comes to sorrow or hatred."

"But I was with Kane just before I talked to Miss Lorgren. He was not sorrowful. His intention was only to help her."

"If what you are saying is truthful, then he either hid his intentions well, or was angered at the final moment. We can only guess what went through his mind when he bid her goodbye. Early this morning he had brought her belongings, a carpetbag and other essentials, to the steamer. She was booked for passage to Kansas City. But why would he do that if he had just killed her? It was he who booked passage for her, and now he has disappeared. No one has seen him since last night . . . when he was talking to you." Western turned then, and looked directly into Devon's eyes. "Why were you talking to Willius Kane?"

"Because he pulled me aside in the saloon, saying that he wanted to talk to me."

"About what?"

"About her leaving."

"Why?"

"Because he said she wanted to talk to me before she left, to tell me how much she appreciated my help in providing encouragement for her decision."

"What interest was that of yours in the first place?"

"None sir, until she revealed the story about her youth, the troubles she had with her family, and with those who led her in wrong directions, until she met up with Kane."

They conversation began closing in on Devon, giving him pause. Pressure tightened his body, and for a moment he felt trapped. "You don't think I had . . ."

"No! Just answer my questions. What interest was she to you?"

Devon replied as fast as thought permitted. "Our friendship was kindled that first night when I was seated with Simeon Flynn. We were talking when Miss Lorgren came over. Our discussion was brief, but friendly. I saw her again several days later, at which time she revealed her desire to go west. She spoke of Willius Kane in endearing ways. It was he who helped her settle here following a frightful childhood of beatings, loneliness and destitution. We had no other connection but that."

"That's all of it?"

"Yes sir."

Western turned toward Devon again. His expression was stern and authoritative. "If there's anything else, tell me now, or I'll hold you liable for concealing vital information concerning her murder."

Sweat burned in Devon's armpits. "I know nothing else but what I've told you."

As the carriage pulled up in front of the LaBelle, several men were standing there, including one who had trained with Devon.

Western spoke quickly. "I've emptied the saloon of all parties except those we need to question. If you were in her room last night I want you to return there and look for evidence. So if you're prepared to face the crime scene, then wait here. I'll go inside and come for you when I'm ready."

They stepped out of the carriage onto the street. Western went immediately inside, leaving Devon alone with two others of the Alliance Committee who were on morning duty. One of them asked, "What are you doing here, Devon?"

"I'm going upstairs with Western."

"Why?"

"Because I was the last one to see Ingrid Lorgren alive."

The man drew a sigh. "You were in her room?"

"Yes, but not in the way you think. I was there to say goodbye. She was leaving town, never to return."

The man giggled while stroking his short beard. "You're in it for sure," he said, snickering.

Devon resented the comment. "No, I'm not in it. I'm just someone who last saw her, nothing else. I already told Western everything I know. Now, I'm asking you to keep quiet about this."

Before the man could answer, Western appeared at the door, motioning rapidly.

"Come on in, Finch. We're going upstairs."

The two of them entered the bar, Western leading. The place was empty except for the owner who stood behind the bar. Only two lanterns blazed above him, giving off little light, most of which illuminated the painting on the back wall. The bartender looked at them with an expression of annoyance as they walked through, sullen in the fact that the investigation would mean a loss of business until the body was removed, until Western completed his investigation.

They headed upstairs. The steps creaked beneath Devon's feet, as if condemning him for a crime he didn't commit. At the top of the stairs, Western turned to his left and proceeded down the narrow hallway. Pausing outside Ingrid's room, he turned to Devon. "She's not a pretty sight," he said. "But I want you to see the way she died?"

"Must I?"

"You were here last night. I need you to remember."

Devon exhaled nervously, imagining what he would see on the other side of the door. He had never seen a dead body, not one murdered; only those prepared nice and proper for funerals, all dressed up and fixed with a look of grimness. Viewing dead bodies made him skittish. The dead, he felt, were better left alone. Western reached for the door and turned the knob.

As the door opened, Devon sensed the smell of death, that putrid beast that had already begun to reclaim her body. As he went inside, he saw Ingrid's arm dangling from the edge of the bed, her fingers barely touching the floor, her hand relaxed, as if she were sleeping. The bed board hid the rest of her, until he saw her, full view.

He stiffened as his stomach churned, rendering him unable to move a step further. His eyes fixed immediately on the terrible dark slash across her neck that looked at first like a dirty, red scarf. Reeling, he caught his breath; saw Western looking at him to judge his reactions, to determine if perhaps he had already seen the dead woman the moment after he had killed her. Devon gazed at the whole of her, at her face so calm looking, at her eyes, closed as if sleeping, at the death of her just inches below her chin, where the knife had cut her dreams short. Tears filled his eyes. Emotion

Murder

swelled hard in his chest as he looked at the rest of her, trying not to see the blood path that had dripped from the bed and onto the floor where it had pooled.

"Do you see any signs of a struggle? Western asked.

Devon looked away from the corpse to examine the room. Everything appeared to be in order, just as he had seen it only hours before. One thing, however, caught his eye, a broken mirror on the floor near the head of the bed.

"That is all," he said, pointing to the mirror.

"There appears to have been a slight struggle," Western said. "I believe the intruder struck her first and then laid her on the bed before he slashed her. There's hardly a hair out of place on her head. I don't think she knew that death was on its way."

"All her luggage is gone," Devon remarked.

"It's on the steamer. We've already looked through it. If she had money, it's missing . . . along with the murder weapon, of course. Whoever killed her took it along."

"Devon's voice hushed. "Might she have been robbed for the money Kane gave her?"

"How much money had he given her?"

"I don't know. Enough I expect."

"Strange," Western replied. "Why would he give her money, and then take it back after he killed her?"

Devon looked toward the door, unable to gaze at Ingrid's body again. He wanted to remember her as she had been, clean and determined and smiling. He glanced at her only long enough to scan her neck. He gasped.

"Something is missing," he said.

"What?'

"She was wearing a necklace. It's gone."

"What kind of necklace?"

A small gold chain and pendant with an inset pearl."

"Are you sure?"

"Yes. I saw it more than once. She wore it regularly. Kane had given it to her. The initials of her real name, M.K., were etched on the back. Her birth name was Mildred Kline."

"Interesting." Western nodded. "It's something Kane might have wanted."

Devon didn't reply. He thought, perhaps Kane wasn't as innocent as he appeared to be. Perhaps Kane had been angered by her planned departure, and had used him to place the guilt elsewhere. He looked at Western who was deep in concentration.

"Can I go now?" Devon asked.

Western nodded. "You can go, yes. The photographer will be here shortly, as soon as he opens his shop. We've already summoned him. After he photographs her we'll remove her to the hospital so the doctors can examine her. A statement of death is required by law."

"Shall I wait downstairs?"

"Yes, in the saloon. We'll talk to Mildred Polshki next. Do you know who she is?"

"Yes, she is the madam in charge."

"Have you met her as yet?"

"No, I've just seen her."

Western appeared confused for only a moment. "I'm sorry," he said. "It disturbed me to bring you here, but you are involved whether you like it or not. The worst is over. Now we'll concentrate on the facts as we know them, while trying to piece this murder together, until we find the man, or woman, responsible. Are you with me, Devon?"

Devon nodded. "Of course, I'm just nervous."

"You should be. It's a frightful thing, murder, especially when a woman has died so violently. But you're all I've got, the only one who was here. If you have any feelings left for poor Ingrid Lorgren, then you'll stay with me on this."

"I will give it my best, sir."

"I am sure you will."

Devon shuddered as they left the room, thankful that the ordeal was over. They returned to the bar and sat at a table near one of the lamps. The bar was eerily quiet, as if Ingrid's ghost had taken up residence. As they waited for Mildred Polshki, Devon tried to appear calm, although his throat was dry as desert sand, and his hands nervous with unintended motion. Western, however, appeared unaffected. He sat straight up with his eyes fixed on the ceiling, until he heard the sound of a creaking step. Devon sat up, fully alert, as Western said, "Here she comes."

Devon glanced toward the stairs just as Mildred Polshki's feet struck the floor.

She was a large woman, plump but not fat, her breasts being her main attraction. Her arms and face were powdered, emphasizing her eyes and lips. The dress she wore was ruffled at the sleeves, a dark purple gown tied at the waist, open at the neck to reveal a single heart-shaped pendent. She appeared stiff and unfriendly as she walked toward them, the type of woman who had authority on her side. She halted before the two men and looked at them with a gaze built by years of observation. "Here I am," she stated, her eyes shifting back and forth between them.

"We have an unfortunate circumstance," Western said.

"Seen it before," Mildred huffed. "With the likes these girls associate with, it's a wonder this doesn't happen more often."

Western sat back, looking at her with a steady eye, and then said. "When did you last see Ingrid Lorgren alive?"

"That's easy," she said, motioning to the back of the room. "Just before Mr. Kane went up those steps. He was going up when I was coming down."

"Did he speak with you?"

"No, he didn't even look at me. He's got eyes for only one woman."

"And who is that?"

"Ingrid, and none other."

She shifted her weight to one leg while folding her arms loosely beneath her breasts, awaiting the next question. She didn't look at Devon.

Western squinted. "Did you speak with Ingrid last night, before she was murdered?"

Mildred turned her gaze directly to Devon before she replied. "Saw her only once, during the day. She wasn't workin'. This was her time of the month. My girls don't work when they got the curse."

"Did she tell you she was leaving?"

"She never told me anything, lest she was asked. I didn't know she was going anywhere until I learned that her luggage was aboard the steamer."

"Then you didn't know she was killed?"

"Not until one of the other girls went into her room and found her dead. Not until I heard screamin'."

"Do you know Devon Finch, here, a member of the Alliance Committee?"

Mildred turned. Her shrug was hardly noticeable. "I've seen him in here."

"Apparently he was the last one to see Ingrid alive."

Mildred raised her chin, and then looked down her nose at Devon. "What were you doing in Ingrid's room? I don't allow anyone upstairs unless they're customers. How'd you get up there?"

Devon glanced at Western, and then responded, nodding. "Mr. Kane let me in through the side door."

"What for?"

"So I could say goodbye to Ingrid."

"You knew she was leavin'?"

"Yes, Kane told me she wanted to see me before she left."

"Where was she goin'?"

Devon looked again at Western. Although he felt at ease with Mildred, he hesitated answering her question. When Western nodded his approval, Devon continued. "She was going to Kansas City and then on to Saint Louis to get on a wagon train bound for Oregon."

"Why didn't she tell me that?" Mildred blurted.

Just then Western raised his hand, silencing the conversation, as if to infer that Mildred's questioning had nothing to do with the circumstances at hand. When silence returned, he continued the questioning.

"Was Ingrid having any problems with men, or a certain man?"

Mildred shrugged. "Don't know. The girls usually tell me if someone gets unruly, so we can expel 'em. We don't want 'em here. Besides, Mr. Kane has let it be known that any man who abused Ingrid was gonna get battered up something awful. Mr. Kane would do it too, you bet he would."

"Has Kane ever mistreated her?"

Mildred shook her head sharply. "No, absolutely not. He's her protector. He's like a father to her. Why, he wouldn't let a fly land on her if he thought it would harm her. No sir, he's always been good to her, better than any other man. He wouldn't do this, no sir, never."

"Are you sure?"

She looked at Western offensively. I'm tellin' you truthfully. Why, don't you believe me?"

Ignoring the question, Western settled back and picked at the table with his fingernail. "Maybe he got mad because she was leaving."

"No sir! I doubt that he would. I never saw him lay a hand on her, never heard his voice rise when speakin' to her. He was a gentleman to her, completely opposite of his reputation. No! He'd wish her the best of luck, he would."

"Is there anyone else who might have had problems with her?"

"None that I know of, unless there's a man out there who didn't receive enough of her for the money he spent."

"Were you on good terms with her?"

"I expect so. I treated her as fair as the other girls. I have a reputation for fairness and honesty. Every whore in this town would work for me if they had the chance."

Western's gaze shifted to Devon, then back to Mildred. "Have you seen Mr. Kane since last night?"

"No sir, he just vanished."

Devon interrupted. "He must have left town immediately after he took her belongings to the steamer."

Western nodded. "Where might he have gone?"

"He made mention of Stillwater, the lumber camps up river."

Western's eyebrows lifted. "He'd be hard to find up there in the pineries. You could hide an army up there. Besides, they're about done for the winter."

With one quick motion, Mildred slammed her hand onto the table top. "This was not the work of Willius Kane," she said emphatically.

Western's voice was sharp. "Then who might have done it?'

"Coulda been one of them river hogs from a steamer. They's rough boys."

"Were any of them upstairs with Ingrid last night?"

"I told ya. Ingrid was flowing. Besides, the girls take care of themselves. No one heard any disturbances."

Western turned his attention to Devon. "What time did you last see her?"

"About four o'clock, shortly before the sun started rising."

"Then she was killed only an hour or so before she was found." Mildred muttered. "Poor thing."

Western spoke again. "Is there anyone else who might have been aware of her movements last night?"

"Maybe Flynn. He's got an eye for people."

Western nodded. "He's the gambler."

"Yea, he keeps his eyes on everything."

"We'll see him. Where does he live?"

"Don't know. But he'll be here later on. He always comes in near midday."

Western shifted to find a more comfortable position, and then looked directly at Mildred. "Then we'll see him this afternoon. In the meantime, this saloon is closed. Your patrons will have to go elsewhere until this investigation is over."

Devon spoke up. "What about the luggage, sir?"

"Mildred's luggage?"

"Yes."

"We're moving it uptown to the jail, as evidence."

"Was there any money in her handbag?"

"I said before, no money was found. If she had some, it's gone."

"She said she had over a hundred dollars."

"She had nothing in her handbag but female things."

Mildred offered her opinion. "Could have been anybody killed her. Why would Kane giver her money and then kill her to get it back. Don't make sense to me."

"Change of heart, maybe."

"No, sir," Mildred replied.

Western stood up, stretching his arms wide, then looked at Mildred who hadn't moved. He spoke slowly and distinctly. "Now we're going to take Miss Ingrid out of here and move her to the hospital morgue. After we fix her up, she'll be going out to Oakland, probably to a potter's grave. We can't do much else for her lest somebody pays for a stone."

Mildred thought a moment. "I think this saloon can pay for a simple stone, just one big enough for her name."

"Any marker will be sufficient."

Western placed his hand on Devon's shoulder. "Devon, go home now and get some sleep. I want you back here at midnight, on your regular duty hours, so's we can question Mr. Flynn, to learn if he saw anything unusual last night. I'll be here about that same time."

"Good day, gentlemen," Mildred said. Immediately she turned, walked through the saloon, climbed the stairs, and was gone.

"I don't think I'll sleep much," Devon said.

"This is part of what police work is all about, son. You don't have to like it. You just need a strong stomach and a powerful desire to do what's right. Now go home, and get some rest. There's already a man outside from the Minnesota Pioneer. You can read about yourself in the paper tonight if we make today's issue."

Devon left the LaBelle and began walking home. He didn't notice much on the way except the street beneath his feet. He thought: so he'd be in the newspaper. Caroline and her family would read it for sure. He would have to brace himself for questions. His own parents would insist that he drop out of the Alliance and seek work elsewhere. They would be adamant in their persuasion. And what would Caroline say? Much of the same, he expected. He would be like someone battered by a storm, accepting the worst of it.

So what would he do? Strangely enough, he didn't know.

He walked on, wondering why his good deed of helping the Alliance had turned to something ominous. Why couldn't it have happened to someone else? Why had he chosen Lowertown for his section? Why hadn't he backed out when the opportunity had presented itself? Why hadn't he traded with Logan when the offer was given? He kicked a stone and sent it scudding, then kicked it again part of the way until it tumbled into a ditch. He dodged a horse and wagon, only to pause for a while to review the happenings of the morning. He was disturbed way down in his stomach by a beast intent on eating him alive from the inside. He hoped Caroline wouldn't confront him angrily. He didn't know if he could take her displeasure on top of what had happened. Finally, he tried to dismiss the image of Ingrid lying on the bed, her throat ripped opened like a rabbit's belly, before it was gutted. He gagged a bit, swallowed it down, and then moved on until the white fence appeared. Clearly, nothing could turn time around. He would have to face whatever criticism came his way and hope it would not cause him further harm. Breathing deeply, he stepped off toward the house where he would face his first test.

Upon entering, he went directly to the kitchen. His mother was alone, his father having already left for work. He pulled out one of the chairs and sat down.

His mother spoke to him over her shoulder while washing the morning dishes. "What did Mr. Western want?"

He lowered his head, hesitant to reveal the news. "A woman was killed down at the LaBelle last night just after I left for home."

She turned, wiped her hands on her apron. Her expression was one of shock. "That's horrible," she said. "Who was the victim?"

"Her name was Ingrid. She was . . . one of the ladies who worked there."

"I understand what you're saying."

Devon scrubbed his face with his hands. "Western has begun an investigation."

Nona nodded, eased a chair out from beneath the table and sat down opposite him. She took one of his hands. "And you're right in the middle of it, I expect."

"I'll be working with Western to figure it out."

Her eyes mellowed softly as she attempted to console him. "I expect the paper will have one of their newsmen down there to get the story."

Devon nodded. "A reporter is already there. It'll be in the Pioneer for sure, probably with my name right there on the front page."

She appeared not to have heard him, or was she pretending in order to avoid further concern for the both of them.

"Just like the Pioneer, on top of everything." She hesitated as anguish soured his face. She probed for an answer. "Is there anything else you want to tell me?"

He sighed. "No. I'm tired. I need sleep."

"Of course you do. This sort of thing can strain a person."

"It has."

She smiled, displaying her often seen affection that had put him and Randolph at ease during difficult times. She had a way with men, a gentleness that subdued their demons, and a love that penetrated any difficulty. "I know," she said. "Now go upstairs and get some sleep. You'll need a keen sense to get through this."

He took her hand. "We'll be questioning a gambler tonight."

She nodded as if to understand. "Stay as clear of this as you can. No need to get bogged down in such a horrid situation if you don't have to. Leave that to the authorities."

He looked straight into his mother's eyes. "I'll want to see Caroline tonight, before my duty time."

"Of course. We'll have supper right on time. I made some liver stew and bread pudding."

He nodded. "Don't know if I'll sleep much. This has got me frazzled."

"I'll keep the house quiet."

"I didn't know this job would be so agonizing."

"Maybe this will be the worst of it."

"I surely hope so."

He went upstairs, stripped to his under-shorts and crawled in beneath the single cotton coverlet. He pressed the pillow around his head and tried to clear his mind of turmoil, but the vision of Ingrid could not be dismissed. Within five minutes tears came and he sobbed into the pillow to muffle the sound. His sobs lasted for some time before they ceased. Then, relieved of his anguish, he looked over at Randolph's bed.

He remembered one of the days he and Randolph had fished together down on the flats where the fish grew to be as long as his forearm, the larger ones from fingertip to shoulder. And he recalled with great clarity, the day they had carried home a catch of five, only to be caught in a drenching downpour, causing them to slip and fall into the mud, laughing. They had lain on a weed-soaked hillside in the midst of the deluge to wash the mud away while looking skyward at the thunderclouds, allowing the rain to fill their open mouths. Afterwards, they had walked home, sloshing wet, with the fish dangling on the stringer, getting muddied again, finding comfort in their closeness. God, those were good days. Why did Randolph have to go away?

He turned in bed and laid out full length, his eyes closed. He tried to revive other memories, but found it difficult, until recalling the day Randolph and he had found a lost puppy trembling beside a fence . . . and without a moment of pause he fell asleep.

CHAPTER THIRTEEN

Objections

Devon arrived at Caroline's house shortly after the dinner hour. He knocked, waited for a moment, and then saw Bethany's face through the small glass window at the top of the door. Without opening the door, Bethany turned and left, leaving him with concern on his face.

Moments later Caroline came out, and without saying a word she walked straight past him to the edge of the street. He followed her, anticipating a cold reception. As she turned toward him, her eyes flared with concern. "We read the newspaper, Devon. Why, I can't imagine that you're involved in something so . . . so . . . evil."

"Neither can I," he replied outright.

"What angers me most is that you were associating with a . . . woman of disrespect." She turned away, as if the words had dirtied her somewhat.

"I can explain."

She swung around, her eyes narrowing, her mouth stern and straight. Her voice was sharp and distinct, as if flung at him. "Well, I hope you can. Everyone's asking me why the man I'm intending to marry was in the company of . . . a harlot."

"I was not in her company."

"The paper says you were."

He grasped for an explanation. "Let me explain, please. So you can understand."

"Yes, so I can understand!" Her chin quivered. She took a half step back, her eyes levelled as if peering through a rifle sight. Devin knew he was in for a good tongue lashing if he failed to convince her of his innocence. Her voice snapped at him. "Now look me straight in the eye and tell me the truth."

He breathed deeply, knowing what he had to say. He told her about the day he and Ingrid had first met, and about their innocent conversation outside the Labelle, then about her wanting to leave, and the unexpected conversation with Kane and finally about the morning he and Western stood in the room where the body lay.

Caroline listened without any hint of satisfaction. Then she turned and gazed over the city. A full minute passed. Finally she said, "Now listen to me clearly, Devin. I want you to quit this Alliance Committee. It's done nothing but worry me, and now a murder, of all things."

Her demand shocked him. He had not expected an ultimatum. "I can't get out now."

"Why not?'

"Because Western needs my help. I'm the only one who knows the people who might be involved. We're going to question one of them tonight."

She turned on him, scowling. "You're not hearing me. I want you to quit this sordid business."

He jolted. She had never objected to anything with such resentment. She was like a different person just then, clearly touched by the circumstances. His immediate intent was to disagree, and so he said, "I expect I will, just as soon as I can."

"Don't you have a will of your own? If you stay on this . . . this, investigation, I don't know what I'll do."

He tightened his stance. "What exactly does that mean?"

She hesitated briefly, and then said scornfully, "It's about reputation, Devon. What are people to think?"

He straightened, rising to the challenge. "Let them think what they want. I've done nothing wrong, or indecent. I just happened to know the woman who was killed. She told tell me she was leaving St. Paul for Oregon. She wanted to start a new life. My God, Caroline, don't let something as innocent as this come between us."

Her eyes slanted away. "I expect it might."

Devon stiffened against the onslaught. "You're wronging me, but why, I don't know. Don't you trust me? You know me inside and out. You know I wouldn't put myself in a situation like this on purpose."

"I don't know what to think."

He felt compelled to meet her hostility head on. He hadn't done anything wrong, and he resented her thinking otherwise. She should be offering support, not confronting him like a stern-headed court attorney. He had never seen this side of her before. Even so, he would not yield to her stubbornness. If she was to become his wife, then she'd have to support his decisions and not point fingers at him. He stood erect, confronting her staunchly. "Well," he said straight out. "First of all, the Devon Finch you know wouldn't consort with whores, nor would he kill anybody."

Her face paled instantly. "I'm not saying you killed anybody."

"Nor have I done anything immoral. Now, you're either with me, or you're not. So which is it?"

Her words softened. "I was just using a for instance."

"I took on a job Caroline, for the good of the city, and I intend to keep it whether you approve or not. I won't be a weasel, nor will I try to wiggle out of my responsibility."

The bite of his words mellowed her. "Devon, all I'm saying is, lay this business aside, and come to work for my father. He still wants you follow a career in law, and he'll see that you get the right schooling."

"You know I don't have money for schooling."

"He'll help you rise up through the ranks."

He remained adamant. "I can't, Caroline. Not until this is over. I'm in it to the end, can't you see that?"

She sighed. "When will that come?"

"As soon we find the killer."

"That could be forever."

"Not with Western on his trail. He's a top-notch policeman."

She took his hand and squeezed it. "Can't you see? I'm embarrassed. Some people look at me as if I don't have a sensible thought in my head."

"What does your father say about all this?"

"He's going to talk to Mr. Western tomorrow."

Devon eyes squinted. His nostrils flared. "Good. Western will set things clear."

She took him into her arms then and held him. She spoke with a muffled sob. "Oh, Devon, I'm so scared. What if the killer comes after you? All you have for protection is a wooden nightstick? What good is that against a knife?"

He shielded her in his embrace. "He won't come after me."

"How can you be sure?"

"Coming after me would be utter foolishness."

"That's not a suitable answer, and you know it."

He eased away and peered calmly into her eyes, trying to be responsible enough to handle the situation. He spoke softly. "Please, Caroline. Calm down. Get hold of yourself. Everyone is excited and curious about it now, but within a day the shock of it will be gone. People will go back to their normal way of life, and forget about a dead woman who had few friends."

She nodded, and then kissed him on the neck. "Give me some time to shed this terrible fright. I can hardly eat. And I know I won't sleep, knowing you're down in Lowertown in the midst of all that turmoil."

"I'll ask Western to put me on days only. Will that help calm you down?"

"It might help. Days are better than nights."

"I'll ask him tonight, when we question the gambler. I'm sure he'll approve, especially if I appear to be frightened."

She looked into his eyes. "Are you frightened?"

"No. The experience was horrible, but I've adjusted. It's not as frightful down there as you think it is. Whenever something happens, stories get expanded to something bigger than they are.

Objections

The men and women are rough, but they aren't stupid. Fights are usually settled over a shot of whiskey. C'mon, Caroline. Let go of your fear."

She nodded. "I'll try. Right now I'm trembling, just thinking about it."

He eased her into his strong and comforting arms, saying, "I don't feel any trembling?"

"My fear is way down inside," she sobbed. "Oh, Devon, I love you so. I don't want this Alliance work to come between us."

"It won't." He looked up toward the hill where they went sometimes, where they enjoyed perfect contentment. "Shall we walk up behind the capitol?" he asked.

"Not tonight."

"Soon then?"

"As soon as you do what's best for us."

He thought back on the night they had talked about the future. "You said once that you wouldn't stand in my way no matter what I did."

"I remember. But this is different. This is dangerous."

"So is logging. So is mining. So is trapping. So is newspaper printing, if you get caught up in one of the presses. So is just walking down the street and getting struck by a team of runaway horses."

"Hold me," she implored

He drew her tight to his body. She appeared to be comforted, having said her piece. He hoped she understood the meaning of honor. Why, what sort of man would he be if he shrugged responsibility? No different than if Randolph turned tail and ran when the Rebels started firing at him. Deep down inside, he knew Randolph wouldn't run, therefore neither would he. No one he knew would shirk their duty in the face of danger. Her father wouldn't either, if it came right down to it.

His emotions eased as he looked into her eyes. "I have to meet Western now. I hope we can talk more, later."

"Have him put you on days then."

"We'll see, Caroline."

"Goodnight Devon."

"Bless you, Caroline, for being patient. I love you for caring about me."

He kissed her forehead, then turned and left her standing alone.

Two hours remained before he would meet Western outside the LaBelle. He would wander a bit in the darkness, and look for answers in the sky, and perhaps talk to God, away from city.

The moon was quartered above the forestland.

Up river, in the darkness, a fire was lit.

CHAPTER FOURTEEN

The Gambler's story

Flynn entered the saloon at near ten o'clock. He crossed the room at a slow pace, his boots rapping on the hardwood floor. He was dressed in dark trousers, a red vest, and a stiff-collared shirt. Pausing short of the table where Western and Devon were seated, he grinned and then sat down without saying a word.

Western reached over, offering his hand. "I am Captain of Police, H. H. Western. I believe you already know Mr. Finch."

Flynn glanced at Devon, nodding. "I know him."

Western sat back, rapping his fingertips on the table top while looking directly at Flynn. He spoke without delay. "You know why we're here, of course, to delve into Miss Ingrid Lorgren's murder."

Flynn wasn't the least bit flustered. He just nodded. "Continue."

Western and Devon exchanged glances. Devon felt out of place, he being the youngest and least experienced of the two.

Western's expression hardened as he spoke. "Mr. Flynn, did you notice anything unusual during the activity here last night, anything out of place, anything odd?"

Flynn scratched his head, and then worked something away from his teeth with a fingernail. He stretched a bit. "Nothing but much of the same." He spoke low and unhurried so Western could get every word. "The night was quiet save for some off-key music and a stream of cussing comin' from the river-men. I was active at the game of poker with several others, one of them being a man of renown, a Mr. Arlin Dermott, from Agony Hall. Have you heard of him, Mr. Western?"

"I know him."

"He's a fine gentleman."

Western continued. "Where were you seated?"

"Right here at my table. I'm situated here early every evening with my back to the wall."

"Do you gamble every night?"

"During the spring and summer months only. When cold weather sets in I often go elsewhere."

Western scratched at his beard. "Then last night you had an ample view of the staircase."

"I did."

"And did you see Mildred Lorgren last night?"

Flynn thought momentarily, his brow wrinkling. He dampened his lips. "No. She did not make an appearance."

"Did you see any other activity on the staircase?"

"Some. A few men went upstairs. One went up thrice."

"Who might that be?"

"Willius Kane. I saw him once shortly before midnight, again at about four o'clock, again near a half-hour later. Never saw him after that."

"Are you sure about the times?"

"Sure as I can be. I'm usually pretty close on time."

Western leaned back in his chair as if he had completed his questioning. He stretched to ease himself, then reached into his pocket, removed a small cheroot, examined it, and then dampened its tip while probing into his top pocket for a match. He grinned as he struck a flame. He lit the cigar, puffed twice until its tip glowed red, and then exhaled the smoke in one great puff. He leaned forward again, his eyes levelling straight at Flynn. "Mr. Kane and Miss Lorgren were friends, were they not?"

"Friends? I guess you could call it that."

The Gambler's story

"How would you call it, Mr. Flynn?"

Flynn attacked an itch at the side of his nose. "She was beholden to him. He is, or was, her protector."

"Did you know him well?"

"Few knew him well. We talked on occasion." He snickered. "He played poker with me once . . . and lost."

Western blew a long stream of smoke away from the table. "What is your opinion of him?"

"He's a rough man with a reputation for aggressive behavior. He carries a Sioux scalping knife, and he's been known to use it."

"Have you ever seen him angry?"

Flynn's eyes narrowed. "Huh! Once was enough. He took a man down right here, with his scalpin' knife touching skin. Was about to slash him when several others pulled him off. His opponent got away with his life that night."

"Did you ever see him angry with Ingrid Lorgren?"

"Once, He would have struck her had she not turned quickly away. He had fire in his eyes that night. She said something that went against his grain, but I don't know what it was. He was up close to her, saying something right into her ear when she turned and huffed off."

Western flicked some ashes onto the floor. "How long have you known Mr. Kane?"

"I've been coming here close onto three years. Ingrid and I talk once in a while, like the night Devon came in. Ha! She teased him a bit that night. Those that knew Kane before he met Miss Lorgren, say that he was a vicious man. I heard once that he used to wear a string of beads made out of the leg bones of a bird, and that he often carried a scalp on his belt, taken from the Indian that cut his face. I heard he found an Indian mound once, opened and defiled, then went into a fit about how heinous the white man was. The Indians were special to him. Liquor was no friend of his when he had too much of it. He lived with the Sioux for a time, had a squaw once."

"Did he ever mistreat Miss Lorgren?"

"I saw him hit her only once, late one night. She said something he didn't like and so he gave her a blow across the face that nearly knocked her down."

"How did she react?"

"She just turned around and went upstairs. I never saw her cry."

Western examined his cigar. He glanced around the empty saloon, and then turned his attention to Devon. "Do you have anything to add?" he asked.

Devon shook his head negatively.

Western leaned into the table and looked directly at Flynn. "Are you sure about everything you've told me?"

"In this business one must have an exceptional memory."

"Have you heard how Miss Lorgren was killed?"

"Mildred told me her throat was cut."

Silence settled over the table. Eyes turned. Neither man looked at the other. Devon was unsettled, as if Ingrid was standing right there watching them.

Western broke the silence. "Willius Kane carried her luggage down to the steamer just before sunup. Did you know she was about to leave town?"

"No."

"We think whoever killed her came and went by the side stairs."

"Likely it was him, then."

"The only other person with her last night, near as we can tell, was Mr. Finch here."

Flynn snickered. "Well, maybe it was Mr. Finch who killed her."

Devon stood out of his chair, his face reddening. "What are you talkin' about?" he bawled. "I was just there sayin' goodbye to her. She was still alive when I left her. You just hold that mouth of yours."

Flynn waved him down. "Hold your fire, lad. Sit down. I was only speculating."

Western nodded Devon back to his chair. "We know Devon is innocent."

"Why" Flynn asked.

"Because whoever killed her did so after Devon had left."

Flynn's eyes narrowed. "Kane could have done it just before leaving her room, before he took her luggage away."

No one answered. Western nodded, accepting the statement with nary a move.

The Gambler's story

Flynn went on. "For what it's worth, I saw Devon and Kane talking earlier. Then Devon left and Kane went upstairs. I thought it was odd that Devon was talking to him. They ain't exactly compatible, you know." Then his sight leveled at Devon. "Why did you go up to see her?"

Western leaned forward. "The answer to that question has no bearing here, only in a court of law."

Flynn fumbled with his fingers, uneasy without cards to shuffle. "Looks like Willius Kane's in a heap of trouble. I think you've got your man if he shows up here again."

"Do you know where he went."

"Possibly to the pineries."

Western eased his chair back and stood up, stretching a bit. "Well, Mr. Flynn, if you've nothing more to offer us, then we'll go."

Flynn remained seated. Devon stood and backed away, still angered by Flynn's insinuation. "Hope you catch him." Flynn said. "Miss Lorgren was a fine woman even though she whored. She was respected by most everybody."

"Goodnight, Mr. Flynn. We're going to allow the LaBelle to reopen now, so you can start shuffling your cards."

"Thank you. I've been away from 'em too long."

Devon and Western went outside and stood for a moment looking at the steamer. A small crowd had gathered some distance away, most of them from the boat. Western waved them forward. "The place is open. Go on in." The crowd of about seven moved forward as one, clomped up the steps and went inside. Silence came on again.

Devon turned. A worried look crossed his face. "I didn't like what Flynn said about me."

"He was just talking."

"I can't imagine anyone thinking I was involved."

"They won't. It appears certain that Kane is the killer."

Devon felt instantly relieved. "Do you believe he actually did it?"

He's a suspect for sure. But sometimes coming to the truth of the matter isn't as easy as it looks. Sometimes the longer you stay on a case, the more confusing it becomes."

"This one doesn't appear to be confusing."

"Well, we have a suspect named Kane, but he's gone, maybe to Stillwater, maybe to the Dakotas. We may never see him again."

"What if he does return?"

"Then we'll start over. As for you, Mr. Finch, you go home now and try to scatter those demons. I know this has been trying to you."

"I have only one question, sir."

"And what is that?"

"Am I to remain down here in Lowertown?"

"Are you uneasy here?"

"Not as much as before."

"Then I'd like you to stay. You can recognize Kane, whereas someone else may not. If he shows up I want you to report it to me at once. Will you honor my request?"

Devon hesitated. But then he saw Western's eyes boring in on him, with his demand clearly visible, and so he said, "Yes, sir."

"Good, then it's settled. If you see, or hear of anything connected with this profane deed, no matter how slight, get to me at once."

"I will, sir."

"Now I'm going back in and look around a bit, and perhaps question a few of those roustabouts."

Devon stood straight up. "Thank you, Mr. Western."

"For what?"

"For trusting in me."

Western nudged him with his elbow. "You're a good man, Devon Finch. Now go home and get some rest. You still have some responsibility in this god-forsaken place."

As Devon walked slowly toward the buildings looming dark and mysterious in the near absent moonlight, he felt better about his role in the investigation. So what would Caroline say now, about his staying in Lowertown? He expected she would be sorrowful. He hoped she wouldn't be angry. And what would folks say about his being mixed up in a killing? He hoped the newspaper would get the details right so as not to point fingers at him. Furthermore,

The Gambler's story

his father might insist that he abandon his commitment. My Lord, he thought, what if Kane does show his face again?

Devon was ruffled to say the least; nervous inside, with fate leading him on again, and he following like a blind man with a short cane. Sooner or later he'd arrive at that fork in the road. He hoped he'd follow the right path, if given a choice.

He also hoped his mother had set out a piece of raisin cake, for he was a bit hungry.

CHAPTER FIFTEEN

Dangerous Encounter

Devon had accompanied his father to a place near the fence where Nona could not hear them. Harold had heard much about the murder. The news had described Devon as just an innocent bystander caught up in the misery. But like most fathers, Harold had something to say, so when he stood with Devon, eye to eye, Devon listened.

"I'm afraid for you sometimes," Harold said, his voice clear and direct. "Every time you go into that bar I quiver a bit."

"It's not what you think. There are fights for sure, but they don't last long, drunk as the men are. Most of the time when it's over, they belly up and drink together. They're a strange bunch, for sure."

"Mother and I have been talking." Harold paused, as if hesitant to continue. "We've got some money saved up. We thought maybe now's the time to send you away to college."

Devon looked directly at his father. The subject of schooling had never been discussed before, at least not when pertaining to him. Randolph used to talk about college, because he was the oldest, and the wisest. Devon shrugged in answer to the question. "I'm not smart enough for college."

"You are. You just have to apply yourself, like you're doing now."

"Even if I could, where would I go?"

"We thought you'd be best suited for Hamline University in Red Wing. It's the most prestigious school in the state. I hear they're going to close the new University of Minnesota because most college age men have gone away to fight. It's a shame; a new school like that lying mostly empty."

Devon shook his head. The subject of advanced education brought his thoughts to a complete standstill. He was unsure of what to say, or how to say it. "What would I study? I don't know what I'm suited for."

Harold stared at him, his eyes direct and insistent. "You could figure it out by studying the curriculum. Journalism would be a fine trade. Learn to be a reporter, or a writer. You always liked writing."

Devon felt uneasy, as he always did when faced with a decision. He knew deep down that he should honor his father's request, but that danged uncertainty came again, disturbing his thoughts.

"It costs a lot to go to college," he said.

"Surely it does. But we've got some money saved up. We were going to send Randolph off, but then the war came, and, well, he's gone now."

"But he'll be coming home again when it's over."

"God willing."

"Besides, the army might take me as soon as I quit."

"That's unlikely. Mr. Page will intervene on your behalf."

"Have you spoken to him?"

Harold grinned. "Some days I do more than just work on a newspaper."

Devon looked at the sky, blue from horizon to horizon, except for a scant layer of gray clouds that ranged out beyond the Kaposia hills. One thing was certain. Caroline would be delighted if he accepted his father's suggestion. Her fears would end. The tension would disappear. She wouldn't worry any more, about Lowertown.

If he agreed, and started planning, he would be relieved of further harangue. Still, he felt uneasy about using money that had been put aside for Randolph. Sort of like stealing, he thought. Moreover, Mr. Western had placed a good deal of trust in him. He couldn't back out while he still had an unfinished commitment. Damnation, why had he ever taken that slip of paper from Western's desk, and why had that slip of paper sent him down into Lowertown, when he could be up on the hill patrolling peaceful streets with Logan Miller.

Going on to college seemed like a simple decision. Just a nod on his part, and the standoff would end. But then the inevitable questions arose. Why was he so tied to commitment? Why was he afraid to make a life changing decision, even though it might improve his future? What was he afraid of? Perhaps, in the end, he was just afraid of himself. So he said, "Mr. Western wants me to continue on for a while. He's depending on me."

Harold's voice strengthened. "He can depend on someone else."

"I suppose he could."

"Then let me talk to him. I can end your obligation within the hour."

Devon stiffened. "I can't let you do that, Pa."

"Why not?"

"I've got to see it through. I told myself I would. What kind of man would I be if I walked away from responsibility?"

Harold stroked his chin. He remained silent for a while, and then he said, "You're just like your grandfather. He was so set on keeping his word that it nearly cost him his life once. He'd have walked into the fire of Hell before losing face. Strong man, he was."

Devon had never known his grandfather, but he had heard stories about his courage, about his steadfast willpower, about his strength of mind. He thought perhaps his Grandfather's stubbornness was the reason behind his own bull-headedness.

"I'll know when the time is right to quit," Devon said.

"I could get you into the newspaper tomorrow," Harold said.

"Doing what?"

"Start at the bottom. Work your way up."

"I don't know if I could handle that day after day."

"It's good, honest work."

"But not for me. It would become a chain around my neck. I'll know soon enough what I want to do with my life. Right now I'm undecided."

Harold took a deep breath and then nodded. "So I guess this conversation is over. I might just as well talk to the wind. So there it goes. Let me know when you get your craw full of this adventuring, and we'll talk again."

"I will."

"Okay. So get on now. Your saloon is waiting. Be careful. That's all your mother and I ask of you right now. She may appear to be unconcerned most of the times, but inside she's upset. She don't like you consorting with the worst of men . . . and women."

"I'll be okay, don't you worry."

"Take it on, then."

With that Harold turned and walked back into the house.

Devon stood alone for a while, trying to understand why he had refused his father's offer, when he could have taken a new road. The answer came slowly through a cloud of confusion. He had to honor his commitment, lest he'd be thought of as a quitter, a person neither he, nor his father, or Caroline would want him to be. A moment later he opened the gate and started off toward the levee.

He walked down Wabasha toward Cramsie's Blacksmith and Wagon Shop into a slight breeze drifting up from the river. Sunlight glazed the trees atop the bluff. He whistled, knowing he would be with Caroline that night, maybe up on the hill in the warmth of evening.

As he approached Water Street he heard the shrill sound of a whistle, one blast followed by another, and another and another, as if they would never stop.

Something was wrong. His body tensed, sending a chill across his back. Up ahead, a crowd of men had gathered in the street. Instinctively, he ran toward them.

He estimated the crowd at near one-hundred, mostly older men with some boys crowded in around them, their attention

Dangerous Encounter

fixed on something within the ring. They were shouting. Near to one side he saw Clayton Fornier blowing his whistle, one blast after another, with little effect. As he ran up, Fornier swung to face him.

"They're deaf for sure," Fornier groaned. "They won't listen to me."

"What's going on here?"

"It's a dog fight. They got two animals in there, one looks like a wolf, the other like an Alaskan husky. I can't break it up, so I sent Jim Hasset runnin' to get Mr. Western. You're the first one came along to help."

The crowd roared. Devin could hear the dogs now, growling, gnashing inside the circle. Dog fighting had been banned for its cruelty. Western didn't tolerate abuse to animals. It had to stop, preferably before Western arrived. He wouldn't approve of the two of them just standing there doing nothing.

Devon looked directly at Fornier. "We're going to stop them now," he said.

"How?"

"Get your nightstick up, and follow me."

Fornier didn't move. He stood flat-footed, his face tightened in fear. Devon scanned the packed crowd. Most were concentrating on the battle inside the ring. Devon figured if he and Fornier moved quickly they could push through the crowd unaided. Once inside they could demand a stop to the fight. Just then a great cheer went up from the crowd.

"Get in behind me," Devon commanded, lifting his nightstick. Together they pushed through the onlookers, blowing their whistles.

Devon voice came loud and commanding. "This is illegal. No dog fighting here. Go now. Disperse. Take your dogs and be off."

Angered by the interruption, the dog owners drew the animals back by the scruff of their necks. The dogs panted profusely, jowls curling back over their teeth, hatred burning in their eyes.

"Get away from us, boy," one of the spectators yelled.

"We're having us a fight here," someone else added.

One of the dog owners shouted. "Get the hell away. We got a contest of animals going on here, and not you, nor anyone is gonna stop us."

"I'm stopping you," Devon shouted. Immediately he looked around at the ring of men. All eyes were on him. Silence covered the crowd like a blanket. One of the dogs sat down on its haunches. Blood stained the edge of its mouth.

"You got no right stoppin' this," the dog owner shouted.

"I have every right. We're part of the Alliance Committee, and we say that dog fighting is illegal. Mr. Western is on his way right now. If you don't disperse now, you'll be arrested."

"Who's going to arrest a hundred men?" someone shouted.

"Not a hundred, just those owning the dogs."

"He ain't taking me," the dog owner shouted. His anger was up, heated like something about to explode. His bull chest heaved with every breath. He was a short man with hair the color of lead. His eyes blazed hatefully.

Devon faced him squarely. "He will. And you'll spend some time in his fine new jail. Now get going if you want to keep your dogs."

"Who are you to tell us what we can or can't do? If I had my way, I'd turn my dog on you. Nightstick or not, you'd be bloody in less than a minute."

Devon looked at the Husky. Its eyes were like cold steel drenched with hate, its teeth like ivory studs, and its growl clear and threatening. Blood stained its jowls. Fear heated Devon's body as he raised his nightstick, as if the act itself would settle everything.

He was in it now. He couldn't back down. Backing down would ruin his reputation, and cause him personal disgrace. He turned to scan the faces in the crowd. None were familiar to him. Most of the onlookers were river men, and locals, by the looks of them, and a few attired in business clothes.

"Now pack up and go," he shouted. "This fight is over."

The dog owner who had confronted him slipped a rope muzzle around his dog's mouth. "You'll hear from me," he said.

To Devon's surprise, the crowd began dispersing, most of them toward the buildings facing Water Street. The man with the wolf walked away without saying a word. The one with the Husky came up close to Devon.

"I lost some good money here," he sneered.

Dangerous Encounter

"I don't care," Devon said. "This gathering is against the law. Now take your dog and go, and don't come back thinking you'll fight him again."

The dog owner raised his fist to Devon's nose. "We better not meet sometime soon. I don't forget those that stand in my path."

"Just take your dog away. He's done fighting in this city."

The dog owner pulled on the leash, and then turned away. As he was leaving, he said over his shoulder. "You're a bastard, who's wronged a hating man."

A minute later just he and Fornier stood alone on the hill, as the last of them disappeared between the buildings.

"You did it, by golly," Fornier said.

"I didn't think they'd resist. Most were just citizens wanting to see a good fight."

"You're a brave man, Devon, braver than I'll ever be."

Just then Western and two others came running toward them. When Western pulled up, Fornier was the first to speak. "Devon sent 'em all a'runnin'."

Western seemed somewhat surprised. "Was it a dog fight?"

"Yes, sir, it was."

Western pointed to Jimmy Hasset. "Jim here says they were an unruly bunch. How did you break it up?"

Fornier spoke up first. "Devon just plowed right in, told them it was against the law, and they went their own ways, most of 'em without sayin' a word."

Western smiled. He nodded at Devon with an expression of thanks. "I think you're a magnet that attracts trouble, Devon."

"No sir. I just happened to be coming this way."

"Well, this is another feather in your cap. Good job. Good job. Now get along, all of you. The day's but half over."

"I think the dog owner is out to get him." Fornier said.

Western looked at Devon. Concern shadowed his expression. "Is he?" he asked.

"Well, that's what he said. But I won't put much thought to it. He was just angry, I expect."

"Well, anyway, watch your back."

"I will, sir."

Western nodded, apparently satisfied. As a parting statement, he said. "Now you all know what the whistle is for. Use it when you must. I think the three of you had better stick together today, just in case the owner of that dog intends trouble. Three is better than one when it comes to a showdown."

All of them grinned as Western turned and walked away.

✭ ✭ ✭

At near four o'clock they worked their way down to the LaBelle. They stood outside in the sun, just talking about nothing in particular while enjoying the day's comfort. Not a single steamer was tied up at the dock, just a row of wagons close by, the horses seemingly asleep in their harness, heads hung down, with only their tails swishing to drive away the flies. Freight wagons, by the sight of them, dirty, with half the continent clinging to their wheel braces. Probably came down from the Red. When the wind was right, a person could smell them from a distance. Then Devon saw a dog in one of the far wagons, its head showing just above the sideboards, the same Husky he'd seen at the fight. So that's where they came from.

"There's our troublemakers," Devon said, pointing to the wagons.

"Then they're inside."

"Getting filled up with whiskey before makin' the return trip."

"Guess we better stay well enough outside."

"Best we do."

Devon didn't like the idea of cowardice. Randolph had never backed away from trouble, nor would he. Something told him he had to go inside, to prove his worth.

"I think we should go inside," Devon said.

Fornier stiffened. "Are you crazy? Why that dog man said he's tear you apart next time he saw you."

"He was just bluffing. He had to show off in the face of others."

"Didn't look like a bluff to me," Hasset said.

"It was a bluff. I've seen bluffing before."

"Hell, even if there is three of us, I still don't like the idea of fighting the likes of them. Most are as tough as an old oak."

"We'll just go in and look around, just to let them know that we're not scared of their threats. They aren't going to scuffle with a crowd around."

"I guess you're right."

"Let's go, then."

Braced with courage, the three of them entered the saloon. Immediately heads turned. The line of patrons at the bar appeared to be Red River men, shaggy, unkempt, more like animals than men, burly and muddied up. Their hair hadn't seen water in a year. The man in the middle looked over at them. He was the dog man, the one who had threatened Devon. He sneered, picked up his glass, and tossed down his whiskey.

Devon hitched up his trousers. "We'll make one revolution, just to show ourselves. Then we'll go out."

Devon led the way, walking slowly past the tables. He saw Flynn, his eyes set in stern concentration. Devon noticed something else as well. Sawdust had been spread across the floor. He said to one of the men at the bar. "Where'd you get the sawdust?"

"Stillwater. Hawkins bought fifteen bags of it from one of the saw-mills. Smellin' sawdust is better than smellin' puke." The men nearby laughed. Devon and his partners passed on through without as much as a nod from any of them.

He was abreast of the bar, headed for the door, when the Irishman stepped out, baring his way. Devon pulled up short as a chill curled down his back. "I'd say you was a brave, young hog," the dog owner snapped. His teeth showed yellow behind his lips.

"We're just passing through."

"Looking for trouble?"

Devon shook his head. "No, like I said, we're just passing through."

Fornier and Hasset looked at one another and stepped back. Immediately, two other men grasped their arms. "Hold still," one of them said.

The Irishman glared directly into Devon's eyes. "You done me wrong by stoppin' the fight. My dog was winning."

"I was just doing my job."

"Your job be damned. You were stickin' your snot-nose in where it didn't belong."

He's bluffing, Devon thought, showing his bravery in front of the others. Still, he felt uneasy as fear crawled into his groin.

Devon looked around. All eyes were on them. Flynn had set the cards aside. Devon made an effort to step aside, but the Irishman grasped his shirt, holding him fast.

"I don't think you're going anywhere," he growled.

"Yes, I am."

"Back home to mama?"

Laughter came, then silence. The saloon drained of all sound.

The Irishman snickered. "I got a dog outside wants to chew your balls off for stoppin' the fight."

Devon heard laughter over near the poker table. Some men moved in closer. Others backed away. The inside of the saloon had suddenly taken on a tension all its own. Voices hushed. The piano in back tinkled its final note. Even the bartender turned, looking their way.

"That's enough now," the bartender shouted. "He's just a boy."

The Irishman turned, his eyes reddened. "You keep your ass out of this. I got a score to settle with this little piss-ant."

"Go your way," the bartender replied. "I don't want blood on my floor."

Devon gasped.

The Irishman tightened his grip on Devon's shirt. "I'd say you got a debt to pay." Tension gripped Devon's entire body as the calves of his legs began trembling. Fear snaked down the back of his neck. He thought . . . what have I done?

Instantly, he Irishman shoved him hard against the chest, forcing him backwards. Automatically, Devon raised the nightstick.

The Irishman stood his ground, snickering. "So, it's a fight you want? But it ain't fair that you got a weapon, and I got only my

Dangerous Encounter

fists." He turned to one of his friends. "McCullum, get me something to fight with."

The man, McCullum, moved quickly. He grabbed a nearby chair and smashed it against the table, and then picked up a chair leg and placed it in the Irishman's hand.

"I'd say we were even now," the Irishman sneered.

"I don't want to fight you," Devon said, backing away.

The Irishman laughed. "You got no choice, lad. Now defend yourself, or be forever branded as a coward."

As the others drifted away, the Irishman became a solitary figure in Devon's path, like a hulking, dirty bear waiting to charge. Devon's legs were set like posts on the wooden floor. He shook slightly as he crouched, awaiting the inevitable lunge.

A catlike grin rippled across the Irishman's face, as a demonic glint raged in his eyes, an indication that his thoughts were precisely directed.

Drawing the hide loop of his nightstick over his wrist, Devon paced off to the left observing whether the Irishman favored a certain leg, or if his stride was unbalanced because of the liquor he had taken. Seeing neither, he watched the set of his eyes, and the location of his hands.

The Irishman's head shifted from side to side, on a neck that was no neck at all, just shoulders rising into chin. "I'll show you no mercy, you white-livered skunk," he seethed.

"You are wrong to face me," Devon shouted.

"We'll see who's wrong."

The two men stood apart, four feet between them. Those who were with the Irishman crowded around like vultures. The tension in the room thickened. Shouts began rising. "Get him! Get him! Beat him down McGuffy. Pound him into the fuckin' floor."

So that was his name. McGuffy. At least now he knew his adversary.

The shouts increased to a steady din, some from behind, others ahead of him. The piano player began pounding away at the keys, a lively melody. The notes mingled with the taunts and jeering faces. Everyone in the room awaited the first move, a sudden lunge that would unite them in battle.

"I will not fall to you," Devon shouted. With those final words of invented bravery, he crouched to await the Irishman's first move.

At that moment he was unaware of his surroundings, or the onlookers. He saw only the Irishman and the chair leg, and the burning hatred in his eyes. He knew time was against him. Within seconds they would be joined. Hesitation would only increase his fear. As a thin line of sweat slanted down his nose, he took the first step toward his opponent, and said silently, pray for me, Caroline.

The Irishman swayed like a massive, immoveable rock but in an instant of distraction, his eyes shifted and the chair leg he held slanted toward the floor.

Now! The silent message came like a shout in Devon's head.

Devon lunged forward on lightening feet, his nightstick raised. He had taken only a step when he realized his terrible miscalculation.

The Irishman had drawn him in, and now his black eyes rolled like a violent nerve as he warded off the first thrust of Devon's nightstick with a flick of his arm, stepping aside as Devon churned past him. The Irishman struck out. The chair leg missed Devon's head by inchers, catching the tip of his shoulder, driving him down. As he stumbled forward into the crowd, a thunderous roar went up.

He was going down! Impossible! And the fight only seconds old.

Blind instinct told him to pivot.

Spinning on his heel, Devon scuffed away as the second blow whistled past his ear. Righting himself, he spun, and faced the Irishman like a beast at bay.

No delay! Not a second!

Devon's nightstick flashed like white fire, pressing the attack.

McGuffy skipped away from the swath it cut, manipulating with the grace of a dancer, waiting for the mistake he knew would come.

The Irishman's makeshift weapon stabbed toward Devon's gut in a long, calculated arc.

As the chair leg slanted toward him, Devon drove the nightstick forward, catching McGuffy at the side of his rib-cage, throwing him off balance. The Irishman crashed into the crowd amid

Dangerous Encounter

a howling of voices. Devon rolled away, across the sawdust, and scrambled immediately to his feet.

He regained his footing quickly, but by then the Irishman was up, speeding toward him, his weapon raised. Before Devon could react, the chair leg smashed across his extended arm, raking flesh, bringing blood to the surface. He felt a numbing sensation as his fingers constricted.

Devon didn't pause to consider the damage. Nothing existed but the two of them. Victory or defeat hung on instant decisions. Wounds were unimportant. Randolph's words blared in his ear . . . no more mistakes . . . no more careless moves . . . think, brother, think.

He crouched to meet the Irishman's attack. Sawdust and sour sweat coated his tongue. I am a better man, he thought, repeating it continually as his breath came faster.

Then the Irishman feigned a blow.

The movement had been well calculated to test Devon's reactions, and now the Irishman grinned because Devon had registered a slight flinch when there should have been none. Fire blazed in the Irishman's eyes, a desperation that would propel him forward with blood-lust frenzy.

Devon was not a fighter, but he was smart. He could think clearly, and quickly. McGuffy, on the other hand, was stupid with whiskey and acting only on instinct.

As the Irishman charged him, Devon's mind clicked with the speed of a ferret, and as the chair leg rose to strike him down, he ducked aside and jabbed the nightstick directly into McGuffy's stomach, full force. He knew instantly that his calculation had been correct.

As he wheeled away from the Irishman, Devon heard the breath go out of him as he sprawled face down into the sawdust, into the legs of those crowded around him. Behind the onlookers, the piano filled the room with noise. Devon heard his friends shouting. "Get him now! Get him now!"

The Irishman spun on the floor, spreading sawdust. Immediately he scrambled to his feet. Turning, he regained his balance, wincing to conceal the pain. His mouth tightened. Fire flared in his eyes. Eager for action, the crowd pushed him into the makeshift arena while shouting encouragement. He stood gallantly, facing Devon with determination. Like a menacing bull, he moved forward.

The two crouched, each awaiting the other's onslaught.

I must win, Devon thought. If I lose now I will certainly be crippled. He will have no mercy on me.

Then, swift as a cat, the Irishman lunged toward him.

Devon had scant time to raise his nightstick. Instinctively, the Irishman's blow went beneath it, catching Devon in the stomach, sending him backwards onto the floor with force enough to wheeze the breath out of him. McGuffy was on him in a second.

As the chair leg tightened across his neck, Devon's breath stalled, then gasped as the pressure increased. He heard shouting, distant-like, as if it were coming from across the river. His fingers constricted like claws. Breath was unattainable. Fighting was useless. The pressure on his neck was intense as he yielding to unconsciousness.

Seconds later, the pressure eased. Air raced into his lungs with bellows force. Sound erupted in his ears. Shouts, loud and clear came to him with increasing rapidity.

The voice booming above him sounded like the blast of a ship's horn. "Touch one more hair on his head and you'll lose your manhood."

Devon rolled over as hands lifted him up. Light flashed into his eyes. Staggering, he found footing on the floor. Two men were holding him, Jimmy Hasset and Fornier.

"He near killed you," Hasset said.

Then Fournier's spoke. "We couldn't help. They had us hemmed in."

The scene ahead of him formed quickly. A big man was holding the Irishman by the neck. A huge knife, gripped in the other hand, was poised inches away from his eyes. Devon struggled to make out the man's features as strength pulsed into his legs.

The man with the knife shouted directly into the Irishman's ear. "You lay one more hand on him, and I'll slash you from ear to ear. Do you understand what I'm saying, you miserable clod?"

Dangerous Encounter

The Irishman nodded as best he could. Then, as the man released him and shoved him away, Devon recognized his savior. Willius Kane.

The piano had ceased playing.

Men shuffled back to the bar, or to the tables. Flynn, grinned broadly, and with cards in hand he motioned two players back to their chairs.

Like an apparition in dark clothing, Willius Kane sheathed his knife and turned immediately to face Devon. He grinned without parting his lips. "You near got yourself killed," he said.

Fornier and Hasset led Devon to a nearby chair. Kane drifted in behind them and sat down at his side. Devon rubbed his neck as the pain eased away. His voice was hoarse. "Where did you come from?" he asked.

"Stillwater. I heard about Ingrid. I had to come back."

"But you're a suspect in her death."

"Guess I am. I'm also innocent, which is why I'm here. If I'd been a little bit later, I'd be attending your funeral."

"My thanks, Mr. Kane. What can I say that'll . . . "

Kane interrupted. "You can say that I'm no more guilty of killin' Ingrid than you are. You know how close we were. Why, I couldn't have harmed a hair on her head even if it meant my own death."

Devon swallowed dryly. "I know that."

"Then come with me to see Western. I've got some things to say to him."

"I will."

Hasset sat back in amazement. "Now ain't that something," he muttered. "Mister Kane comin' back just in time to save your life, and . . . holy cow . . . I can't believe my eyes."

Kane glanced over toward the bar where the Irishman stood drinking. "He won't bother you anymore. He got his satisfaction."

As the fiddle began rasping along with the piano, Devon worked his fingers around his neck, trying to ease the pain still centered in his throat. As tears filled his eyes, he looked at Kane. The man he had once feared had just saved his life.

"You're gonna be a bit black and blue for a while," Kane said.

Devon nodded. "It's better than dying."

Kane arose, motioning Devon to remain where he was. "I'm gonna get you some water. Now you just sit there and keep on comin' back."

Devon relaxed as best he could as his tension eased away. Nervously, he wiped his eyes. He had a question or two for Kane, things he had to know. He waited patiently, saying nothing, until the glass of water was set down right in front of him. He drank slowly while Fornier and Hasset moved to a nearby table.

"I owe my life to you." Devon said while looking directly at Kane.

"I was here earlier. I came in about ten o'clock this morning, and then went upstairs to Ingrid's room where I sat for a while, trying to put it all together. I came down here about an hour ago. I saw you walk in, but time wasn't right just then to talk, so I just stood back and watched. When the fighting started I thought I might be needed."

"I would have died . . . if you hadn't . . ."

"He wouldn't have killed ya."

"Why not?"

"Not in front of a crowd. He's a stupid man, but not that stupid."

"When do you want to see Western?"

"Soon as you're up to it."

Devon drank again, and then found some stability in his legs. He grinned. "I'm ready,"

The four men left the saloon, trudged up past the wagons and began the long walk to the jail house.

Devon and Kane walked side by side.

CHAPTER SIXTEEN

Kane's story

When Devon and Willius Kane entered Western's office, the Chief welcomed them straight on and then sat back in his chair as if it were a throne of sorts. He gazed at them unflinchingly, in a way that signified his interest. Then he crossed his arms and said to Devon. "And who might this be?"

Devon stepped forward, and spoke straight out. "This is Mr. Willius Kane, sir."

Western's eyebrows rose a bit. Any direct interest remained hidden. He stared directly at Kane, meeting his gaze as if totally prepared for his presence. A moment passed before he spoke. Then in a strong voice, he said, "Mr. Kane. I thought I'd never see you again, especially under these circumstances. Your presence here is quite surprising."

Kane stepped forward. "I was in Stillwater, sir, when I heard of Ingrid's death. As you know, she and I were the best of friends. You might say she was like a sister to me. When I heard word of my suspected involvement in her murder, I was compelled to return."

"Why?"

"To prove my innocence, and to assist in locating the fiend who took her life."

Western nodded, to confirm the statement. "Then you did not kill Miss Lorgren," he said directly.

"I did not. No reason on earth would compel me to do so. She had money with which to travel, money I had freely given her. She had a destination. We said our farewell. I wished her a safe journey. Then I took her luggage to the steamer and immediately set off on the long walk to Stillwater."

Western seemed surprised. "You walked all the way?"

"I did, to relieve my sorrow. She was dear to me."

"She was a whore." Western spoke in a way that was meant to elicit a true response.

Kane remained unruffled. "Not to me. I found her to be quite ladylike."

"Then who might have killed her, if not you?"

Kane's jaw stiffened. A glint of revenge sparked in his eyes. "If I knew, I would take his goddam life."

Western glanced at the scalping knife attached to Kane's belt. "She was murdered with a knife, you know."

"I know."

"You carry one on your belt."

Kane tapped the knife with his fingers. "For my protection."

"I understand that you have used it to kill."

"I have, but only in defense."

Western rubbed the back of his neck, and then motioned them to the chairs in front of his desk. When they were seated, he began questioning again. His words went directly to Kane. "When did you last see Miss Lorgren?"

"Just before the sun rose, on the morning she died. It was still dark when I removed her luggage from the room."

"And you left the city forthwith?"

"I did."

"Then someone must have gone directly to her room for the purpose of killing her. Why would someone want to take her life?"

"I have no answer to that question. Perhaps it was a disgruntled customer, or someone who knew she had money."

Kane's story

"Might you know of anyone other than Devon who might have known she had money in her possession?"

Kane shook his head. "No. But perhaps someone other than the two of us knew she was traveling. Perhaps she had told Mildred Polshki, or someone else at the La Belle."

"Perhaps, be it man or woman."

Kane was unmoved. "I don't know. I didn't speculate on that."

"Did she have problems with any of the other women?"

"None that I know of. She was respected."

After a brief pause, Western continued. "Whoever killed her had reason enough to go to her room."

"I assume so."

"We found no money on her person, or in her luggage. The killer took whatever money she had."

"It appears to be robbery then."

"So it appears. She probably had the money in her handbag"

The questions stopped coming then, and for a while Western sat silently, as did the others, each posing their questions silently.

Kane eventually broke the silence. "Will you be holding me?"

Western shook his head. "No, I happen to believe you. Your return has given more thought to the case."

"I can be of much help to you."

Western nodded. "For that I will be thankful."

Once again, Kane slapped the knife at his side. "I would use this on whoever took her life. Ingrid was a jewel in disguise."

Western leaned into his desk. "That is a strange way of describing her."

"Not if you knew her as I did."

Western removed a cigar from a wooden box on his desk, lit it, and puffed until its tip glowed red. He expelled the smoke out one side of his mouth, and then looked directly at Kane. "Where will you be staying now that you're back?"

"With a friend."

"Who might that be?"

"Alpheus Fullerton, a merchant."

Western tapped the cigar on the edge of the ashtray. "I know him."

"He and I have done business together. We trust one another."
"Can I contact you there?"
"You can."
"Then go. And thank you, Devon, for bringing Mr. Kane here." He looked keenly at Devon, as if to see him for the first time. "And by the way, what has happened to your neck?"

Devon glanced at Kane, smiling. "I was in a brawl, sir."
"With whom?"
"With the Irishman whose dog fight we interrupted this morning."
"He did this to you?"
"Yes. Luckily, Mr. Kane saved me from further injury."
"Then you are beholden to him now."
"Yes, sir, I am."

Western moved to accompany the two men to the door, and then turned his attention directly to Kane. "Mr. Kane. I would like you to be my eyes and ears, at the LaBelle and around town. If you hear anything that might connect another to Ingrid Lorgren's murder, I want you to report it to me at once. Perhaps together we can catch the scoundrel who took her life."

"I will help. And if we find out who it is, I would like to be the executioner."

"I wouldn't go that far if I were you."
"It's just a craving I have."
"Good day, gentlemen. Thank you again, Devon."

Devon and Kane walked outside and stood in the sun. Shade patterns from a single small tree danced on the ground. For a moment Devon was distracted by a flock of birds sweeping past them overhead. Neither spoke for a moment, each harboring thoughts of their own. Then Kane said, "I'll be going now."

"Thank's for saving me."
"You're a right good man, Devon Finch, a man worth saving."
Devon blushed slightly. "Nice of you to say that."
"Huh. I've seen many bad ones, some who'd kill you just for lookin' at 'em, others who'd take your scalp just for sport. Saw 'em all before I came here with Ingrid."

"She said you met down in Cairo."

"Yea, Cairo, a pitiful place for mankind. She was standin' near the river when I first saw her, alone and saddened by life, a pitiful sight. When I came near her she bolted, lookin' at me as if I was a ferocious animal about to pounce on her. I wasn't much different from an animal then, all bushy haired and bearded, my clothes the color of dirt, my face burned by the sun."

"What made her come to you?"

"Don't know. I saw the hurt in her eyes, a loneliness that couldn't be described, and I just held out my hand."

"She took it?"

"That she did. And then we walked alongside the river in plain sight of everyone, She told me her name was Mildred Klein, and as the day progressed she told me about her life. Even an old rover like me was unprepared for the words. Right then I took a liking to her, and with her permission, I tagged along as she came upriver."

"I know the story. She told me."

"We came to trusting one another. I offered her advice, and protected her from others. We became like brother and sister." Then as Kane looked up the street toward his destination, he pulled on Devon's arm. "Walk with me. It's 'bout time you got to know the real Willius Kane."

They headed down Fifth Street toward the Court House, and for a time neither of them spoke. Then, for no reason at all, Kane began talking.

"I still remember the day I stood with my father near our home in Ohio. It was the first time I'd ever held his rifle, a long gun with a shiny stock. We was going out to shoot us some Passenger Pigeons, for they was in flight, hundreds of thousands of them, so many that they nearly blocked out the sun. Goin' south they were. We went into the field and stood there, just watching 'em fly. I lifted the gun and shot, and down they come, two, three, four at a time. Then Pa loaded for me again, and for some reason I turned to a noise just as I was liftin' the gun, and caught my Pa right in the chest with the shot. He went down. Don't quite remember what happened next, 'cept that when I knelt at his side he said that it was alright, and that I shouldn't be blamed, and that God would forgive me. Then he died, and I was without a father."

Devon didn't reply. He just walked on and listened.

"My mother went into a rage, hit me, slapped me, kicked at me, and ordered me out of the house. Right then and there I was about in the same shoes as Ingrid was when she was a girl. I had nowhere to go, so I just started walking."

"I teamed up with a lone man who had nothin' more than a horse and wagon, neither of which was fit for this world. He told me I could tag along with him, said it was my responsibility to get food, so that became my job, huntin' and trappin' bringing back whatever I could so's he could roast it over a fire. We ate fairly well, begged a bit. I left him soon as we crossed the river. Then I headed west."

"I had the wanderlust by then, and I longed to taste the freedom of a mountain man, to sit beside a fire at night, and just listen to the language of the wild places. I scrounged what I could, stole a bit, found a saddled horse all by itself out on the prairie, and some clothing in an empty wagon tipped on its side, a grave marker beside it. I crossed the Missouri and saw the buffalo, thousands thick, darkening the prairie like a slow movin' sea of mud. I shot one, skinned it, dried its hide, made a right good coat for myself, then lived with the Indians for a spell. I was no threat to them. I made a good friend with a brave named Deep Water. I was near twenty by then."

He looked at Devon and grinned. "Guess I'm borin' you with my chatter."

"Not at all."

"I just want you to know that Ingrid and I was something special, so let me get to it."

"By the time I returned east again I was near thirty years old, lookin' more like forty. Don't know what possessed me to take Ingrid under my wing. I just thought it as a good deed. I got tired of shootin' buffalo. Got remorseful when I seen the pelts stacked up higher than a man at the rail stops. Thousands of 'em. The herds were going faster than seasons, just like the Passenger Pigeons were. It made me sad in a way, seein' all that death, the meat rottin' on the prairie, the Indians beginning to see the demise of their land in much the same way. I came to thinking that life might be better back in civilization."

Kane's story

He looked into the sky, and said nothing for a while. Then he spoke again. "Now you might be thinking that Ingrid and I were more than just friends. Well, we weren't. She became a lady of the night out of need, and I became her protector, simple as that. You see, beneath these clothes, is the body of an animal. From my neck to my feet, I'm covered with hair. I think when God made me he got me mixed up with a buffalo. I never liked myself that way. I smelled like an animal most of the time. But Ingrid never saw me that way. I never undressed in her presence, though she suggested it several times over, until askin' became useless. So when we came to St. Paul and she went to work in the LaBelle saloon, I went up the streets to take my pleasure out with the likes of Long Kate, and Dutch Henrietta, and with Mother Robinson from time to time. I always had money, 'cept I won't tell you where it came from."

"You found gold, didn't you?"

"I ain't sayin'."

When they paused at Wabasha Street, Devon pointed. "That's my house over there, the one with the white fence."

Kane nodded. "A mighty fine place."

"It was, 'till my brother went off with the Union army."

Kane nodded. "It seems at times that all men yearn for the same thing, to kill one another."

"Maybe someday they'll stop doing so."

"I'm thinkin' they won't. We got kindness and hatred intermingled inside us. Sometimes hatred seems to be the most forceful of the two."

Devon nodded agreeably and then thought of Randolph about to face the wrath of southerners who hated northerners. "Well, I have to be going, Mr. Kane."

"As do I."

"Thank you for introducing me to the real Willius Kane."

"My pleasure, boy."

"I always thought you were a ruthless person, given the scalping knife and all. Someone told me you even carried a scalp on your belt."

"I did, for a while." he said. "Truth is, I wanted you to know me as I am, so you'd know for sure that I didn't kill Ingrid."

"Now I know."

Kane looked away, toward the river. "I'll be off then."

Devon spoke before Kane moved. "We forgot to tell you. Whoever took Ingrid's life, also took the necklace you gave her."

Kane paused, turned, and looked at Devon with a blank expression. Thought roved across his forehead, wrinkling his skin. Then he said, "Whoever did, he'll wish he wouldn't have, especially if I get to him."

With that, Kane stepped away, turned his back, and began walking down Wabasha Street. Devon watched him go, his pace slow and relaxed as if he wasn't in a hurry to get anywhere. Before long he disappeared between the buildings down near the river. Devon relaxed momentarily. In his heart he knew Kane could never have killed Ingrid. He was amazed that such a bestial appearing man could be so tender inside. Did the wilderness change people in ways that only God could understand?

So now what? Ingrid's killer still prowled the city, or had gone to world's end. They might never find the person who put a knife to her neck.

Oh well, he had other things to worry about. He'd have to explain to Caroline how his neck got all black and blue. Just the thought of it made him cringe.

CHAPTER SEVENTEEN

The Fourth of July

On July 3, the sun drifted toward darkness on a dry and warm day. The near cloudless sky created a mystical kind of twilight, when one could stand outdoors and feel totally comfortable regardless of the pestering gnats and mosquitoes that always made a perfect place unpleasant.

Devon knocked on Caroline's door early that evening, waiting patiently for her appearance, all the while wondering what she would say about the bruise on his neck. He had prepared his story. He wouldn't tell her about the actual fight, but of something less brutal, a story that would not upset her. His nervousness peaked when the door opened, but then retreated a bit when he saw the pleasant smile on her face, so beautiful to look at.

"Come in," she said. "I'm nearly ready."

They were going up on the hill to lay beneath the stars, to enjoy the peacefulness that usually came with darkness. He went inside and greeted her mother, then Bethany, who was helping with kitchen cleanup.

Mrs. Page said to him. "Would you like some Cracklin' Cookies? I made some fresh today."

"No thank you, Mrs. Page. I just ate."

"What happened to you neck?" Caroline asked,

He raised his hand to touch the black and blue mark. "Oh that. I broke up a dog fight on Wabasha this afternoon, and the man who owned one of the dogs got mad. He swung at me and struck me in the neck. Can you see where he hit me?"

"It's a bit discolored."

Mrs. Page turned. "It's not so bad that you need a wrapping."

"It doesn't hurt," Devon said.

"Black and blue doesn't look good on you," Caroline quipped.

Devon swallowed hard. "It's the color of honor."

"That's your opinion?"

Caroline lifted a blanket from a kitchen chair to use as protection against the mosquitoes and gnats that might be out on such a fine night. They waved their farewell, stepped outside, and began their walk. Without saying a word, she took his arm and held it against her side, tight in so he could feel her breast against his skin.

"I thought you might be angry with me for getting hurt," he said.

Her reply was quick and pointed. "I'm getting accustomed to it."

"It's nothing," he replied.

"Maybe not to you, but it is to me. I don't like seeing you hurt."

"I'm not hurt."

"Not this time, but what about the next, and the next, and the one after that?"

He made light of her comment. "Your fear is unfounded."

"I read the paper, Devon. Last week someone was stabbed, and a body was found across the river, not to mention the brawl on the levee."

"Not during my duty hours."

"Does that matter? Eventually it will come to you. We both know that."

"It'll never happen."

"It will."

Her voice quivered a bit. "And then there's that . . . that scarlet woman who was murdered, the one you were friendly with."

The Fourth of July

"I wasn't friendly with her. We talked one day, that's all."
"I didn't mean you were friendly in the way you were thinking."
"Well, I wasn't."
"With those tarnished women, and a murder besides, what's a girl to think when the man she loves consorts with those type of people? It's enough to give me insomnia for sure."
"They're just people. She was broken and disturbed. Probably no one ever talked to her decent like, except Kane, or me."
"I know about Kane."
"You don't know him well enough. He's not what most people think he is."
"Then what is he?"
"Someone who's led a difficult life. As a boy he accidentally shot his own father, and never lost the guilt."
"I didn't know."
"I might be the only one who knows the story. Perhaps I'm just someone he likes to talk to."

She pouted a bit. "Still, I don't like you associating with those... those, rabble. Whenever you go down there at night I'm unsettled."
"Don't be."
"I can't avoid it, Devon. Worry just comes on to me like a sickness sometimes."

He was about to reply when she laughed, that winsome, joyful sound that made the world seem better than it was. Her voice sounded like the trickle of water in a clear stream. A smile accompanied her words. "Now what kind of woman would I be if I went on about a little black and blue mark on your neck? What kind of wife would I be if I got mad about my husband coming home with a slight injury? Why I wouldn't be a good wife at all, would I?"
"I thought it would initiate concern."
"Concern, yes. But not enough to spoil a good evening like this. I am intelligent enough to know that every day can't be trouble free. Why, I burned my finger on the iron today. Look."

She held up her hand, exposing a blister as red as a cranberry on the side of her middle finger. He laughed. "Now what kind of husband would I be if I didn't say that was the finest-looking blister I ever saw?"

She pressed his arm tighter to her body. "Why, thank you, Devon. Mama bathed it with sweet oil. When the blister breaks she'll wash it with lime water."

"You are a careless young lady."

"Not more than you." She tugged him tighter. "Now no more talk about nasty Lowertown. I said what I had to say, and it's over. I don't want anything to spoil our time together."

Devon was relieved. She had a way of making light of things which might otherwise destroy a fine moment. They walked on. He told her about Kane and him going to see Western, and about the story Kane had revealed about his journeys. And he told her that Kane wasn't a suspect anymore, and how perplexed everyone was about who actually killed Ingrid.

"You really enjoy this, don't you?" she asked.

"Well, it sure is interesting."

"And you aren't going to stop it, are you, no matter what I say?"

"Not just yet. You and I know that things will slow down this winter after the steamers stop coming. The cold weather will keep everyone indoors except for those needing essentials. The fur carts won't come again until spring."

"Just like always."

"Nothin' much changes."

She removed his arm and swung her hands into the air, then danced around in a circle, free as a bird in flight. "Tomorrow is the Fourth of July," she chimed. "And we have three choices as to entertainment. We can go aboard the steamer *Messenger* for a fifty mile excursion to Hudson on Lake Saint Croix, and be back by morning. And while we are there we can enjoy a grand barbeque, and a free dinner and dancing. Or we can take a carriage to White Bear Lake and go boating, or just sit on the swings and look at the moon. Or we can cross the Wabasha Bridge for a picnic at Union Hall. The Great Western Band will be playing. There'll be dancing and shooting at a mark, and bowling on the green, and fireworks in the evening. Now make your choice. Bethany and I have made Pea Salad and Almond Tarts and Cracklin' Cookies. She can come along with us. I'll be fighting angry if you don't invite her. She adores fireworks, and being with you."

The Fourth of July

He didn't have money enough for a steamer excursion, and barely enough for a carriage ride to White Bear Lake. His decision was easy. "It's Union Hall, for sure."

"Just you and I and Bethany."

He laughed. "Now what kind of husband would you be if I didn't allow your sister to come along?"

She eased up to him and squeezed his chin between her thumb and forefinger. "If it were punishment you needed, you'd go hungry for a week, no food, no water, no love. I believe it would be sufficient?"

He swept her up and whirled her around. "I could go without the food or water, but not the love."

"Not the love?"

"Without it I would certainly perish."

Laughing, she took his hand and ran with him toward the top of the hill. There they spread out their blanket and laid down as the first stars appeared in the darkening sky.

He felt good about the way she had accepted his injury, about the way she eased up tight to him and held his hand, and kissed him when he turned toward her. His love for her was strong that night.

Later, when the sun slipped down behind the trees and the sky went dark, he took her in his arms and eased one of his legs between hers, while listening to her quickening breath. He moved gently against her thighs, after insuring that no one was nearby. During those times, when they ventured into forbidden territory, they felt passion strongly, and sometimes it was difficult to separate right from wrong, until an indistinct noise, or the ruffle of leaves, or a bird chirp interrupted their embrace. Then she would ease away and peer into his face, and he would see her love for him in the depth of her eyes, and he would feel proud and selfless just to be alive.

Their physical contact never went further than touching. They had never been alone together, when time was not a factor. They had yet to make love in a thorough way, naked and unrestricted. The total experience would be saved for marriage. Caroline was firm in that regard and he was man enough to honor her commitment to chastity.

They didn't talk much when they sat together on the hillside. Just looking skyward gave them each a sense of wonder, and they knew they could not wait much longer before giving in to passion.

Near ten o'clock they retraced their steps down the hillside. In the shadow of her house, he pulled her close and kissed her hard, and felt her body against him with such pressure he thought he would burst.

"I love you, Devon Finch," she breathed softly.

"And I love you."

"We will marry, you and I."

"Yes."

"Someday soon," she stated.

"I cannot wait that long."

"Nor can I."

The world seemed to disappear as he drew her gently into his arms. Enraptured, he breathed her scented hair, and for a moment he imagined he was in paradise.

✻ ✻ ✻

The following day, on the Fourth of July, a Thursday, Devon, Caroline and Bethany walked over the Wabasha Street Bridge and ascended the broad path onto the heights above the river. There, in a small, shaded park alongside Union Hall, they spread out their blanket and ate Pea Salad, tarts and cookies. Devon tried his luck at shooting, but missed the mark. The girls chided him for his lack of marksmanship, and in mock disappointment he chased them playfully toward the river where they stood and gazed at the city until the Great Western Band began playing.

He danced with the girls well into dusk, amid a gayety filled with delight. For Devon, it was a time of removal from the grim, dirty streets and the daily activity of the city, and the bustle of the levee.

The Fourth of July

The fireworks began at dusk, as the warmth of the day retreated. They sat on the blanket and watched as colorful explosions laced the sky. The band played military marches loud enough to quicken their hearts. Word was passed that the Minnesota State fair had been cancelled due to the war. When the festivities were over they walked back across the bridge, over a river glazed with moonlight.

Devon would remember the day long into the next, and for some time to come.

CHAPTER EIGHTEEN

Discontent

During the second week in July, Devon and Jimmy Hasset began their day at noon. For those of the Alliance Committee, the summer months had proven to be kind and warm because of the pleasurable weather, with little rain to dampen the streets. But lack of rainfall concerned many others, primarily the farmers. Some folks said that if rain didn't come soon, crops would begin to fail, and if crops were scant many people would suffer. A cutworm infestation had already begun chewing away at the corn crops in the Minnesota valley where many of the Sioux Indians lived. It didn't seem right that a little worm could cause people so much misery.

On this particular day the sun was high and the streets were so hard packed they barely raised dust. Even so, everything appeared to be right and proper. Jimmy was whistling, and Devon's thoughts were centered more toward Caroline than on duty. He intended to keep it that way.

When they turned the corner on Third Street, east of the R.O. Walker's Hat and Cap shop, Devon might have missed sight of the couple emerging from a store on the opposite side of the street, had a sound not drawn his attention. He recognized the woman straight off as Pricilla Udahl, Randolph's girlfriend, and she was hanging tight to the arm of a gentleman. At first sight they appeared to be more than just friends. Her manner toward the man appeared romantic in nature. She clung to his arm the way Caroline did whenever they were together. An irritating spark trembled down Devon's back as the couple turned the corner and headed north on Cedar Street.

Devon swung immediately toward Hasset. "You go on ahead. I've just seen my brother's woman friend. I haven't talked to her since Randolph left for war. I've got to see her."

"Well, go on then. I'll join up with you later."

Devon stepped away, having decided his course of action. Certainly, the woman he saw was Pricilla. But confusion clouded his thoughts? Could it have been someone else who closely resembled her? Certainly, Pricilla wouldn't be seen on the streets with another man, especially when she was betrothed to Randolph. Why, that would be downright sinful of her, especially when he was fighting for their future.

If he acted quickly enough, he could sprint through the alley across the street, and wait until they appeared at the end of the block. Then, if they turned his way, he could approach them straight on. Without further thought, he struck out, crossed the street and ran between the buildings. He exited on Bench Street just in time to see them turn toward him. He thought; what I am going to say without appearing impertinent.

Pricilla's attention to the tall gentlemen faded when she looked his way. For a moment she hesitated and drew back as if unsettled. Then, with firm resolve, she came toward him, her face beaming with a smile. As they drew close, Devon stepped into their path.

His eyes were as doleful as his greeting. "Pricilla, imagine meeting you here."

Obviously, she was surprised and confused by his presence. "Devon, you surprised me."

The man accompanying her was neatly dressed in sharply creased trousers, a light tan vest with black buttons, and a short tie. A silver chain curved away from his watch pocket. A black v-shaped

Discontent

beard masked the lower part of his face. His dark brown eyes carried a hint of disfavor.

Devon looked at him directly, even though his words were intended for Pricilla. "And who might this be?" he asked.

Pricilla hesitated, trying to dismiss her nervousness. "Why, this is Mister Brian Mallory, an acquaintance of the family."

Without extending his hand, Devon said, "Good afternoon, Mr. Mallory. I am Devon Finch, the brother of Randolph Finch, Miss Udahl's betrothed."

Before Mr. Mallory could reply, Devon spoke directly to Pricilla. "Have you been receiving letters from Randolph?" Devon asked.

Pricilla's voice trembled slightly. "Yes, I have."

"And what does he have to say?"

Pricilla cleared her throat. "Well, he is in good spirits, getting along as best he can under the circumstances. But you must know that."

Devon nodded. "I do. He also mentions you in each of his letters, in endearing terms."

She stood stiffly alongside Mr. Mallory, her arms tight to her sides. "I am pleased to hear that."

Mallory took a half step forward as if to shield her from further questions. He pointed at Devon's hand. "What are you doing with that nightstick?"

Devon didn't especially like Mr. Mallory, not at first sight, and definitely not then. His stern and overbearing attitude had a hint of authority. Devon's reply was brisk. "I thought it obvious. I am a member of the Alliance Committee."

"Oh, the civilian patrol."

"Yes. I'm one of those who's concerned enough about our city to keep it safe."

Pricilla sensed where the conversation was headed. She reached over and tugged impatiently at Mallory's sleeve.

Devon wanted to know more about the man who had apparently taken Randolph's place in Pricilla's life. After tangling with the likes of Kane and others at the LaBelle, Mr. Mallory didn't frighten him in the least. In fact, he thought him to be a man who lived by the wit of his tongue instead of the strength of his arms. So he said, "Are you a businessman, Mr. Mallory?"

He posed the question to test Mallory's pride, and it did. "I am a banker, to be specific."

"I thought so. You are too well dressed to be from Lowertown."

Pricilla's raised her right arm and extended it in front of Mallory, to provide a wedge between the two. Her voice was sharper and demanding. "How is Caroline?"

He was somewhat hesitant to reply. "She is extremely well. But tell me. Why are you here with Mr. Mallory?"

Her expression changed just then, from one of concern to one of defiance. "I told you. He is a friend of the family. We are shopping."

Devon felt uneasy, the same way his brother might feel if learning of Pricilla's new friend. Disappointment came easily. He tried to relate how Randolph would react if confronting Mr. Mallory.

"You seemed to be more than friends," Devon said spitefully.

Mallory stepped forward, ahead of Pricilla, as if to shield her from insult. Devon had struck a nerve, one that Mallory did not appreciate. Even so, he spoke to Devon in a milder tone. "Look Mr. Finch. Why don't you just go on about your business and let Miss Udahl and I continue on. Frankly, I think you are a bit annoying."

Devon felt the need to explain his feelings in a most exact way. "I am annoyed because Miss Udahl is betrothed, to my brother. She shouldn't be seen on the arm of another man."

Devon saw distress in Pricilla's eyes. She was about to speak when Mallory silenced her. "I am well aware of Pricilla's future plans. She has spoken to me about Randolph, and I respect her for being loyal to a soldier. But our association is no business of yours, and it is certainly not one of romantic inclination. Now, if you'll just let us pass, we'll be out of your sight."

Pricilla's anger surfaced then. Devon saw fire in her eyes. "We are friends, Devon, nothing more."

"I expect so."

"Then do as Mr. Mallory suggests. Go on about your duty. You have no right to question me, or him. We are none of your concern. I can't believe your impertinence. Why, Randolph would be outraged by your behavior."

Discontent

Devon nodded. "I'm sorry if I troubled you."

Pricilla's anger subsided "You are so wrong, Devon. Someday I will explain."

Mallory interjected. "You've overstepped your bounds, Mr. Finch. Now if you'll let us pass, we'll be on our way."

Devon didn't like the way she held onto his arm, in a more than friendly way.

"Randolph loves you, Pricilla. Don't go sending him discouragement."

Mallory responded abruptly. "Stay out of our business."

They walked away then, leaving Devon alone. He thought, just as sure as fire could burn, that Pricilla was being unfaithful. He felt the same as he had when he saw Ingrid's dead body sprawled on the bed.

How would Randolph react if he ever found out? Would he be distraught enough to walk straight into Rebel guns, fearful that if he came home she'd just turn her back on him? He felt sick inside, to think that someone he once admired would spurn the man she had promised to marry. Randolph hadn't been gone for more than three months, and already she was shouldering up to some fancy banker with creased pants and a silver chain.

The sounds of the city interrupted his thoughts and he realized that his mood had become dismal. Instinctively, he thought about Randolph, somewhere in the south. Was he marching now, or fighting, eating or sleeping? How would he react if receiving news that Pricilla was on the arm of another man?

He'd have to forget what he'd seen, lest it wear away at him. Just maybe the fancy Mr. Mallory would move on to someone else. Perhaps he would tire of a Lowertown girl in favor of someone with more grace and beauty and money. Maybe then, Pricilla would see the worth in Randolph, a man who would follow her through Hell if need be. There weren't many men like Randolph.

He walked on, indifferent to his surroundings, until he came to the river. Then, far down on the levee, at a place where only birds could be heard, he sat on the bank and looked out over the far hills, while trying to stifle his discomfort.

CHAPTER NINETEEN

Death of a different kind

During a period of calm in Lowertown, Devon went to the market at his mother's request, to purchase some early-blooming Hellebore. Back home, he rubbed the blossoms with molasses and placed them in every room of the house to kill the invading cockroaches. Also, he applied a spread of arsenic to bread and butter to prevent the ravages of mice and rats. Finally he placed a mixture of cobalt, spirits and sugar onto a shallow plate and positioned it high on a shelf to kill the recent plague of flies. The spirits attracted the flies, and the cobalt poisoned them; necessary work to curtail the summer infestations.

The family had received several letters from Randolph throughout the weeks, welcome letters for sure, those read over and over by every member of the family. He wrote about the friends he had made, and about his marches toward places where battles were being fought. He said he missed them all, and further stated that he had received letters from Pricilla, of which he was truly thankful. Never did Randolph mention sadness or discomfort, or being homesick.

On the evening of July seventeenth Harold brought home an early edition of the *Pioneer and Democrat,* but it wasn't until the meal was concluded and the apple pie eaten that he withdrew it from his pocket. He unfolded it slowly while bringing the family to full attention. Then he said, "There's a report in the paper I thought you should hear." His gaze settled on each of them to assure their full attention.

Nona and Devon exchanged glances, and for a moment Nona appeared flustered. Nervously, she wiped her hands on her apron and fumbled with the tableware. News in the paper was not always good. The Union Army was going through a period of testing, and early battles indicated that the task ahead would be long and wearisome.

"Now, don't get upset when I read this," Harold said. "I promised that I'd keep you informed of the war news, especially where Randolph is concerned, so that's what I'm doing."

Nona nodded, folding her hands. "Go on," she said.

Devon leaned forward, eager to hear Papa's words.

"Well, it's come over the wire that about ten percent of the men in the Minnesota Regiment are unfit for duty. The report says that many of the boys are sick and badly provided for, and that they're eating only hard bread, pork and beans, and sometimes a meager portion of beef and rice. Unsuitable rations, for sure. The report also says that they're the poorest regiment in the entire service. Many of the boys have been out for days because they've no pants to wear. And as if that isn't enough, there's no pay being given. Many are in need of things, but they have no money."

Nona's hand went to her mouth, stifling a sigh. A moment later, a tear trailed down her cheek. "The poor boys," she muttered.

"We're certain not to hear about discomfort from Randolph. He'd never give us bad news, even if he was affected."

Devon touched his mother's hand. "He's probably not one who's sick."

"The news came by wire yesterday," Harold went on. "We printed it this morning. If Randolph is feeling the brunt of this misfortune, and if he's written us about it, his letter won't arrive for another week or so."

Death of a different kind

Devon leaned back in his chair and sat upright. "Randolph's a strong man. He wouldn't . . ."

"Well I know one thing," Nona interjected. "I belong to the St. Paul Volunteer Aid Society, one of the first of its kind in the country, so we're told. We've rolled hundreds of bandages, and made almost nine-hundred emergency cases and twenty-five oilcloth guard bags, and we've supplied the troops with needle books, mosquito face nets, and five hundred Havelock's. And we've done all that amid the dreadful heat in Ingersoll Hall. Well, evidently, we haven't done enough. I guess it's time we sewed the boys some pants. Now those ladies with sewing machines will have new garments to make. Our boys aren't going to run around the battlefield half naked."

Devon laughed as Harold re-folded the paper. Nona had always made light of distressing situations, to place humor where sorrow had bred. She would bear her anguish silently, beneath a heart as shiny as freshly polished sterling. Nona had been through desperate times before, and had always used determination and humor to brighten even the most disheartened soul. Devon remembered several times when she'd taken him aside when he was dispirited, and had told him stories of hardship he could barely comprehend. He had always come away from those stories with a new look at life. Yes, Nona would make trousers for the troops, and more things if necessary. She'd whip that Volunteer Society with words of encouragement so strong and convincing that the pants would roll out of that building on the southeast corner of Bridge Square faster than they could load the wagons. Before long the boys would have so many pants they wouldn't be able to wear them all.

"And something else," Harold said. "The law against killing prairie chickens has expired. Soon there'll be a plentiful supply in the markets. You know how much I like prairie chicken. Too bad we can't send the chickens eastward to the boys."

"The boys will persevere," Nona said.

"And there's something else," he said, looking directly at Devon. "There's a girl missing in the city, a sixteen year old named Wilma Huggins. Might you know her, Devon?

"No, sir, I don't."

"She's from down in the hollow. Been gone since last Friday. Reports are that she's a small child with brown hair and freckles on her face. Last seen she was wearing a dark blue dress with a lace collar. Her mother's frantic. Her father's out scouring the streets. Has Western informed you about this?"

"I haven't seen Western in over a day."

"Then, perhaps you should get to him first thing tomorrow. Maybe you and the Alliance boys could be of some help finding her."

"I expect they already are. Tonight I have duty by the levee. I'll listen to what they have to say down there."

"It's a sad thing when children are missing."

"Maybe she's run away. There were two last year, just up and took off, angry at their parents for some reason or another."

"It happens."

"Still, I'll be on the lookout."

As they were about to leave the table, Nona remarked. "Now, Devon, I've a fine rabbit in wraps. I received it from Sarah Keiter just this afternoon. If you'd skin it we'll have some good rabbit stew tomorrow."

"I'll do anything for rabbit stew." Devon replied.

When the dishes were dry and put away, Devon unwrapped the rabbit. He had cleaned rabbits before when helping Randolph, so he took up the sharp knife and went to work. First, he cut off the fore feet at the first joint, and then cut the skin around the first joint of the hind leg. He loosened the skin and then slit it on the underside of the leg at the tail. Then he turned back the skin and removed it from the hind legs. After tying the legs together, he hung the rabbit to a hook, drew the skin over the head, slipped out the forelegs, cut off the end of the nose, and removed the entire pelt. He then removed the entrails, saving the heart and liver. Then he cleaned and wiped it carefully inside. Finally, he washed it with acidified vinegar water, sprinkled a little pepper over the head, and stored it away in the small wooden ice chest lined with tin. The chest still contained a bit of ice Harold had bought earlier. The ice storage warehouse down near the levee still had ice to last until winter set in, provided people were frugal with its use.

Death of a different kind

He did not see Caroline that night. Instead he read from one of Randolph's books, a treatise by Ralph Waldo Emerson, from his *Conduct of Life*, particularly the part about behavior. Randolph had always thought of Emerson as one who could lay out a right good plan for life. He read by candlelight for nearly two hours, mulling over the lesson of behavior, something he thought every man that ever entered LaBelle's should read and learn from, good behavior being one of their poorest traits.

Just before midnight he stepped out onto the street and began his walk down toward the levee, beneath a fine moon. He walked slowly, enjoying the silence that made the passage of time seem indefinite, while wondering where Wilma Huggins was, for surely she was not within the city. Had she just wandered away? Was she now somewhere north of the city in the vast network of forests and lakes? Or had she been taken by someone intent on harming her? Perhaps he would find out the following day.

He met his two cohorts, Jimmy, who had chosen to patrol the streets up and around the Temperance House, or Moffet's Castle as it was sometimes called, and Clayton, who liked the peace and quiet of the area near Bridge Square. After talking a while they went each their own way.

Unhurried, Devon sidled down toward the levee, then empty of steamers, the last having pulled out at four o'clock the day before. He imagined it would be a quiet night at the saloon with none of the river men in town. The whores would have a night of rest. When he was about a block away he heard music, faint but distinct. He recognized the song, *Alberta, Let Your Hair Hang Low,* and he smiled a bit. Even though the steamers were gone, someone still liked their music.

Only six people occupied the saloon when he entered, several who were singing, one behind the bar, another sitting deep in the shadows, eased back in a chair, apparently dozing, his hat tilted forward on his head. Devon recognized him instantly as Simeon Flynn. Just then, Kane's voice came from the shadows, loud enough for him to hear.

"I was hoping you'd show up tonight. Come here. I got things to say."

As Devon walked to the table, Kane pulled out a chair so Devon could sit down. He pushed his empty glass aside and leaned forward. His voice was like a snarl, his eyes like ice. "I can't control my anger some of the time," he growled. "I keep thinking about Ingrid, and I get deeply hurt. I could kill whoever says a bad word about her. I sit here and see her comin' down those stairs, all prettied up and dusted with beauty, and she's lookin' at me with those dark brown eyes of hers. Damn to Hell whoever laid a hand on her." His fists pounded the table. "Sometimes I think I'm goin' crazy?"

Devon shook his head. "Not crazy. Furious perhaps, knowing how she died."

"For nothin' but money," he seethed.

Kane turned the empty glass around and around. He didn't say another word, just stared at the glass as if her image was there. Devon just sat there looking at him, afraid to enter his confusion. Devon knew that if Kane ever found the man who killed Ingrid, he'd hang him up and skin him just the way he'd skinned the rabbit.

"I've been askin' around," Kane finally said. "Some said a man came off the steamer *Frank Steele,* the day Ingrid was packin' up to leave. I was told that he was upstairs twice that day, once with Ruth Keene, she's the one with dark hair, and with the other whore they call Sissy. Sissy said she saw him talking to Ingrid just an hour before she was killed. He was angry, wanting to lay with her, but she pushed him off, telling him she was going away. Sissy said he just stood there lookin' at her, not sayin' a word, just lookin'. When she turned away to leave, he grabbed her by the arm and twisted her around, and he said, you ain't goin' anywhere until you satisfy my need."

Kane sneered. "Ruth says he left her then, swearing all the way down the steps. His name is Dermott. He's a boiler tender aboard the *Frank Steele*. And guess what, the boat is docking tomorrow morning."

"The *Frank Steele.*"

Kane nodded as cold fire lit up his eyes. "Could be, I'll be talkin' with Mister Dermott."

"Don't be hasty."

"I'm just going to talk to the man."

"I'll be seeing Western first thing in the morning. I'll tell him about Dermott. He'll come down here, so you best keep away lest your temper gets unmanageable."

Kane snickered. "You seem to know me pretty well by now."

"I can see the anger in you."

"Just the surface of it. Down deep it's boiling."

"I knew her as well."

Kane just shook his head. "Not to the depth of her. She was the only one ever listened to me, or cared for me."

The men at the piano had begun singing a new song, *Lorena*. When their voices chimed together, Kane leaned back in his chair and propped his head against the wall, listening. When they came to one verse in particular, he sighed.

Yes, these were words of thine, Lorena
They burn within my memory yet;
They touch some tender chords, Lorena.
Which thrill and tremble with regret;
T'was not thy woman's heart that spoke;
Thy heart was always true to me;
a duty, stern and pressing, broke
The tie which linked my soul to thee.

Kane fell asleep just sitting there, his head against the wall, his eyes closed in sorrow. Devon knew then that Kane could not have taken Ingrid's life. He had loved her too much, had respected her for something far more apparent to him than to anyone else.

Devon left the LaBelle as the final verse of *Lorena* drifted out across the street. He wandered slowly down near the river where the silence of the land lay so peaceful as to make him pause, to take in its silent, darkened beauty, its moonlight across the river, its canopy of stars like a coverlet of diamonds above him, its breath but a soft touch against his face.

He remained there for most of the night, and dozed a bit near dawn. And when the sun came up, and the world around him began to move, he walked slowly up the awakening streets to see Western.

Come seven o'clock, Devon was waiting at his door.

Western entered the building shortly afterwards. He appeared to be tired. His eyes were filled with weariness. His usually hurried gait was slow and plodding. He glanced quickly at Devon, and without saying a word, went directly to his office, leaving Devon alone in the hallway.

Devon sat down on one of the chairs, wondering what had happened during the night to make Western so beaten down. He had his answer within the next five minutes when Western opened the door and waved him inside.

"You got something on your mind?" Western asked bluntly.

"I do."

"Then out with it. I got about two hours sleep last night, due to the fire."

"What fire?"

"Didn't you hear the alarm?"

"No. Part of the time I was inside the LaBelle, talking to Mr. Kane. I heard no alarm."

Western stood up and brushed at his clothing, then looked out a nearby window as if needing sunlight to brighten his appearance. He cleared his throat, and then wiped a hand across his mouth. His voice was brusque. "We had a house on fire, a fast blaze that lasted only a half hour before the place collapsed. A man and his wife were badly burned. She'd thrown a lamp at him in anger, caught him on the arm, set him afire. Then the house started burning. Damn those arguments." He took a deep breath, and then went on. "A man and a woman, they fall in love and get married. Then children come along, and with them problems they never expected. They get testy, angry, and sometimes furious. Bad words come out, and the love they once knew sours like milk in the sun. Before they know it, they's fighting and cursing, and the devil's anger gets the best of 'em. Soon they hate one another, and all the loving they once brought them together gets boiled in the devil's stew."

Western took a deep breath, gathered his composure, and then smiled. "And what did Mr. Kane have to say that brings you to me this morning?"

Devon relaxed as best he could. " Mr. Kane has been asking questions. He's learned that one of the ladies at the LaBelle, a Miss Ruth Keene, had entertained a boiler tender named Dermott, from the *Frank Steele,* the night of the murder, and that he had approached Ingrid for favors. When Ingrid refused him, he got mad. Another woman named Sissy, said the man was angry, bitter angry."

"Interesting."

"The *Frank Steele* will be docking this morning."

"I know."

Western didn't say anything more. His eyes traveled to a far corner of the room where shadows prevailed. "Could be that Kane is just throwing us a new line."

"No, sir, I believe him."

Western grinned. "You are young yet. You haven't seen the whole of life."

"Enough of it"

"I know the women you speak of. One's a hussy, the other is, well, she's a bit more tame. Could be that Kane is paying them to tell a story."

Devon didn't reply for fear of rebuke.

Western busied himself about his desk and then said, quite unexpectedly. "We'll see this boiler tender and listen to what he has to say. I'll go aboard later this morning and seek him out."

"Can I go along, sir?"

Western's grin came slowly. "I can see that Ingrid Lorgren's death has heightened your interest."

"It has, sir. I feel compelled to help in any way I can."

"Splendid, then you can . . . "

The door opened just then, cutting his message short. A thin-faced man with a rather fine mustache entered. His deep, resonant voice cut through the silence. "Pardon the interruption, sir, but there is news."

"What is it?"

"Wilma Huggins, the young girl who's been missing. Well, she's been found, sir."

Western's relief was apparent in his nod. "Good. I'm sure her parents will be most happy."

"She's been found dead, sir."

Western expelled his breath. The initial expression of joy sank beneath the weight of his shoulders. "Oh, dear God in heaven," he muttered.

"Two young boys found her down below the bluff near the base of the bridge. At first they thought it to be a dead dog, but upon a closer look they discovered it to be the girl."

"Where are the boys now?"

"They are here."

"Then show them in. I have questions for them."

"They are with their mother."

"All of them then."

Western motioned Devon to a chair. "You can listen. Perhaps we have a maniac on our streets."

Devon sat down immediately, speechless and somewhat frightened. Another death, a young girl this time. He tried to compose himself before the two boys and their mother were led into the room.

The woman was slight of build, casually dressed, her hair straight down. She appeared to be a bit uneasy because of the way she held the boys, tight to her side. One was about twelve, the other, about nine. All appeared frightened. Western immediately recognized their anxiety, and calmly told them to stand before him.

"What are your names?" he asked.

The woman answered. "We are the Priam's. The older one here is Samuel. The younger one is Ephram." The oldest boy cleared his throat while trying to keep his hands from shaking.

"And where do you live."

"Over in the hollow." She appeared to be more confident as she released her hold on the boys.

"Samuel," Western said, "Where did you find this girl?"

The boy answered straight out. "Below the bluff, sir, alongside the bridge."

"How did you find her?"

"Our dog found her. We was goin' fishing when the dog ran off and started sniffing something. He wouldn't come when we called, so we went up to take his collar. That's when we found her."

"What did you do then?"

The boy appeared nervous. "Well, we ran for home and told our mother."

Western looked toward Devon, whose attention was fixed on the children.

"Tell me what you found."

The younger boy looked up at his brother. Tears came immediately to his eyes.

The older one put an arm around his shoulder and whispered something to him. "My brother is scared," he remarked.

"Clearly, I understand."

The boy breathed deeply. "We no sooner reached the dog when we saw the girl. She was layin' behind a heap of rocks, face down. At first we didn't know what it was, but when we came up close we saw it was a girl. She was dead, no doubt."

"Was she clothed?"

The boy shook his head. "Yes sir."

The smaller boy began sobbing. He plunged his head into his mother's side and wept openly. Remembering was a terrible thing sometimes.

"We got scared and ran home." Samuel said

"Did you see anything else?"

"Nothin 'cept her."

"Was that all?"

"Sir, our hearts was scampering, so we ran away fast as we could."

"Did you see any wounds about her?"

"No, sir, but we saw blood on the rocks."

Western knelt down in front of the boys. He took the youngest one's hands into his own. "Now, you've had a tryin' time. But before you go I want Mr. Parker here to record everything you've told me. Then, when you're done, we'll take you back home. Thank you for bringing them, Mrs. Prium?"

"Won't you need them to show you . . . the place?"

"No m'am, we can find it on our own. We know where it is."

"Thank you. They've been through . . ."

"I know. But it's over now, and they need comforting."

Western stood and nodded toward his orderly. "Write this all down, Parker, and then see that these boys and their mother are delivered home."

He took the boys' hands and shook them heartily. He rubbed the younger one's hair. "You're brave lads, for sure. I hope this won't spoil your dreams."

The boys looked at one another, their sorrow clearly exhibited. Then they turned and followed their mother and Parker out of the room. Western just stood there shaking his head. "And now the parents must be told that their daughter is dead. What a terrible thing. It's the Devil's work."

Devon felt the weight of Western's grief. The stillness of the room cloaked him tightly, and he heard nothing until the ticking of the pendulum clock penetrated the silence.

Western breathed deeply. "I'll be takin' one of my men with me to have a look at the girl. You can go home now and get some sleep."

Devon was on his feet in an instant. "Can I accompany you, sir?"

"Why?"

"Curiosity, I guess, and to help if need be. If I'm to become a policeman I'll have to know about these things."

"Aye, you have curiosity, for sure. I guess as part of the Alliance, you're entitled to see the worst part of life, that of its ending. That talk with the boiler-tender on the *Frank Steele* will just have to be put aside. Obviously he wasn't the one who killed this girl, or Miss Lorgren. So there you have it."

"Thank you, sir."

"Well, this is the worst part of police work, that of pickin' up the dead. I've had my fill of it, but I'm sure there's more to come. Let's be about it then. We'll take a bit of rope, some blankets, and a firearm. Have you ever carried a pistol, Devon?"

"No sir."

"Well, this is not the time to go experimenting. I'll carry one for protection, an Army Sheriff weapon, with a black-powder cap and a ball, both of which are barrel loaded. It's the best we've got. Go out in the hallway and wait. I'll stir up another man to get the wagon ready, and then we'll head out. Until then, I've got a bit of work still remaining, so be patient. I'll not be long."

Devon left the room and closed the door behind him. He found a chair near the window. He wondered about the dead girl, how she had fallen prey to a killer, and what had happened moments before her death, and what kind of person would take her life, if indeed she had been murdered. Like Western had said, the worst part of life was its ending. So here he was, face on into another death. What would Caroline say? What would the outcome be? Was the person who killed Ingrid and Wilma, still walking the streets of the city, or had he fled downriver to some other town where he'd meet up with another woman? Had the same fiend killed this youngster? Or had she fallen on her own?

He was still deep in thought when Western motioned him outside. They climbed aboard the wagon alongside a teamster named Earl. As they departed from the jail house, Western began talking. "Whoever took that little girl's life had to have some kind of sickness. A person in their right mind wouldn't do such a thing. She was no doubt confronted by evil . . . unless she fell of her own accord."

"She could have fallen in the dark."

"Aye, there's loose rock that could trip a person gettin' too close to the edge."

"It couldn't have been Kane."

"We can't rule anyone out. Sometimes it's the one we least expect. People just crack under strain of hate, or jealously, or anger. I've seen men about to kill their children when they go mad in their head."

"Where will you bring the girl?"

"We'll turn her back to her parents for a proper burial. If they're of a certain religion they'll not want the body damaged any more than it is. This is not like a war, where most of the dead is laid down in a pit and sprinkled with lye, or just left to rot on the battlefield. No sir. Sometimes an autopsy can tell us things not visible on the surface."

Devon didn't say a word. He thought about soldiers being dumped into pits, without care for who they were. He thought of

Randolph being dropped into a pit and then sprinkled with lye, or left to . . . . The image shivered him throughout.

"Sorry about the mention of war dead," Western said. "I forgot that your brother was in the army. Short sighted of me, for sure."

The rattle of harness shattered Devon's vision of the battlefield.

"We'll have to be careful takin' the girl out," Western remarked. "There might be some clues about. Don't know yet if she was killed on the bottom or the top of the cliff. Maybe she was dropped over. Maybe she fell on her own. You can follow me and Earl while he does the looking. As an army man, he learned tracking from an Indian scout. He's good at his work." Earl nodded as if to agree.

Devon wondered if he had overburdened Western with his curiosity. "I guess I must bring you more problems than anyone else," he stated.

"Heaven's no! Why I get problems every day, from every part of the city. I've got men like you on every street in Upper and Lowertown. Not a day goes by that I don't get some report of fight, or thievery, or threats, or drunkenness, or husbands and wives fighting, or kids thinking they're immune to punishment. Trouble won't ever stop comin'. If I didn't have men like you helping me I'd go near out of my mind." Western laughed, and then told his driver to speed up the horses.

When they arrived at the spot, Parker reined up and tethered the horses to a tree. When Devon looked toward the pile of rocks the boy had mentioned, he felt a slight chill even though the sun was directly at his back. A small willow tree stood to the right of the rock pile. To the left, the Wabasha Bridge rose up tall and grand between its massive stone support columns. While Earl went ahead to peruse the surrounding area, Western handed the blankets to Devon and told him to carry them. Then they walked toward the cliff face.

Before they cleared the top of the stone pile Devon saw the flutter of her dress, a movement of blue cloth lifted by the wind.

"There she is," Western said. "Just where the boys said she was."

The body was sprawled face to the rocks, one arm extended sideways, the other bent beneath her torso. A trace of dried blood discolored the side of her face. Her hair was all tangled and covered with dirt. Western knelt down and lifted her head, had a look, then lowered it back down. "She's had her neck broke," he said." He lifted her matted hair, revealing a three inch scalp wound, most likely caused by impact.

"She didn't have a chance," he muttered.

He arose and stood silently for a while. Devon thought he was praying because he remained still with his head bowed. When his contemplative moment was over he said simply. "She's a fright, poor thing."

Devon turned away, not wanting to look at her again. Uneasiness rolled in his stomach. He heard Western say, "Cover her up."

Without looking directly at the body, Devon unfolded one of the blankets and fluffed it out, scattering flies. After he had placed it gently over the girl, his moment of uneasiness ended.

Western's voice softened. "We'll carry her down to the wagon. Then we'll see how her folks want to tend her. She's been dropped from up above, for sure. Couldn't have done this much damage just by tumbling off her feet."

They placed the blanket beside her, lifted her up, and wrapped her in cloth. Earl carried her back to the wagon and loaded her carefully into the box. As they were about to cover her, Western noticed something. Reaching over, he lifted a small necklace from around her neck.

The moment Devon saw it he gasped. The necklace was comprised of a single white pearl set on a disc of silver. He gasped. "Miss Lorgren wore a necklace exactly like that one."

"Are you sure?" Western asked.

"She showed it to me. It was a gift from Kane."

"It can't be the same one."

"It is, if it has the initials M.K. carved on the back. "

"Western turned it over, cleared some dried blood off the back of it and said, "There are initials, M.K. But they don't match Ingrid's name."

Devon drew a sudden breath. He remembered the conversation with Ingrid outside the LaBelle on the day she revealed her past. "It's hers," he said quickly. "Her name was Mildred Klein before she changed it."

Western's expression registered surprise. "German by name."

"Yes. She told me about her past as we were talking. When she and Kane came upriver he suggested that she change it to Ingrid Lorgren."

"She told you as much?"

"She did."

"I didn't think you knew her that well."

"She was eager to talk the day she told me about her intention to head west."

Western looked curiously at the necklace. "Then whoever killed Ingrid also killed this woman. But why?"

Earl spoke quickly. "To place the killing on someone else."

Devon drew a sharp breath. "You're thinkin' of Kane, ain't you?"

"Maybe so."

Devon replied boldly. "Well, he wouldn't have left the necklace behind. He'd have taken it."

"He would that." Earl agreed.

"Then whoever did this wanted us to think that it was Kane."

"I think so, sir," Devon said bluntly.

"But who? Does anyone down at LaBelle's have a score to settle with him?"

"No sir. Not that I know of. But Kane has roughed up men from time to time. He's got a reputation for violence."

Western nodded. "I know. I've seen some of 'em all bloodied up."

"But if it's not Kane, then who?"

"Someone who gets pleasure out of killin' women."

"Maybe so."

"The worst kind of human being is a man without a soul or a conscience. Same thing happened down in Keokuk this last winter just before the river thawed. A young girl all cut up."

"How did you learn about her?"

"We get word. Law enforcement has to be open about these things."

They stopped talking then, climbed aboard the wagon and headed back toward the levee.

Before Devon left Western that day, and as several other men carried the body inside, Western pulled Devon aside.

"Now listen closely," he said. "The next time Mr. Kane shows up at the LaBelle, which might be any time now, send one of the boys up to get me. I want to talk to him about the necklace we found on Wilma Huggins' body."

"I won't be working until midnight."

True. I might be sawin' wood by then. Tell me straight, is it a task you can handle by yourself?"

"I can, because I know he's innocent."

"Then disclose to him what happened here, and let me know what he says. Come here tomorrow morning, just as you did today."

"Yes, sir, or I'll bring him along, if he's willing."

Devon went home sorrowful because the death of the young Higgins girl weighed heavy on his mind. He ate a skimpy breakfast, told his mother about the girl, but not in detail. She thought it terrible that he was involved in such matters.

After he had eaten, he went upstairs and took to the bed. He did not sleep well that day, or the next.

✰ ✰ ✰

Willius Kane was nowhere to be found.

During the days that followed, Wilma Huggins' parents claimed her body, without suffering the indignity of an autopsy. To them, even the thought of one was sacrilegious. Instead, they cleaned her up and purchased a wooden coffin, and within three days laid her to rest in Oakland Cemetery at the edge of the woods.

A killer lurked somewhere in Lowertown, and everyone Devin looked at for the next week became suspect. The *Frank Steele* had tied up, but no one bothered to question the boiler-tender named Dermott, unless Kane had done so. Caroline had spoken her mind about him being involved in such a horrible thing, and suggested that he leave the Alliance again, but did not pressure him on the subject. Nevertheless, it became obvious that she was becoming more and more distressed about his involvement. Her mood was not as cheerful as before, nor was her touch as warm.

Rain did not fall for weeks. The Mississippi began losing its water.

Willius Kane returned, unexpectedly, a week later.

CHAPTER TWENTY

Insinuations

Devon had seen the news report about Wilma's death in the newspaper. The report was written exactly as Western had outlined it, with one exception. The necklace had not been mentioned.

On a Saturday morning, one week later, Devon was about to enter the LaBelle for a quick look around when he saw Kane standing beside the flagstaff outside the Central House, two doors away. The sight of him dressed in leggings and a blanket coat, with a beaded bandolier bag hanging from his shoulder, brought him up short, for he resembled a trapper who had just left the woods. Kane had been in the sun for sure. His face was dark and splotched in places where the burn had peeled. His whiskers were longer than usual, and his eyes had rudeness in them. Kane wasted no time talking. "I hear you're lookin' for me?" he asked.

"I am."

"About the girl they found?"

"Yes. Then you've heard about it?"

"Indeed. Even in the wilderness, men get word of things like that."

"I was with Mr. Western when she was found."

"I saw your name in the paper."

"Terrible thing, that."

"So I expect they're lookin' for someone who took pleasure in killin' women."

Devon shook his head. "Perhaps. But there's one bit of evidence that wasn't printed in the newspaper."

"And that is?"

Devon glanced away from him as he spoke. "We found Ingrid's necklace on the dead girl, the one you had given her with her initials etched into the back."

Kane drew a sharp breath as his eyes turned to fire. Anger hissed through his clenched teeth. "The one and only thing I ever gave her."

"Western has it now. He wants to talk to you."

"I expect he does."

"As soon as possible."

Kane's expression changed to a sneer. "Does he think I'd be foolish enough to leave that necklace around her neck if I'd been the one to kill her?"

Devon hurried his words. "We know you're innocent. We know whoever took Ingrid's life also took her necklace. We believe it was planted on her, to cast suspicion on you."

"Seems so. Even an idiot could figure that to be the case."

Devon hesitated while gathering his thoughts. Then he said. "You left town right after the girl was killed. We thought at first you'd run."

"We?"

"Western and me. But I knew you couldn't have done it."

"And why is that?"

"Because I believe you're an honest man."

Kane scratched his beard. His voice hissed. "Then I'll tell you honestly. If I catch the bastard before you do, I'll kill him, sure as I'm standin' here. I'll gut him slow to watch him suffer."

Devon didn't reply. He knew, as sure as the river flowed, that Kane wouldn't hesitate to cut the man up.

"I'll go and see Western now," Kane remarked.

"He's waiting."

"I'll let you know later how our talk went."

"I'll be around."

Kane nodded, and without saying another word, he walked up Bridge Street.

Devon entered the LaBelle as three others came out laughing. One of them, a plucky man with bull-bears and mustache, whose hair hung down over his left eye, was counting money. Their hilarity broke the morning stillness like a rifle shot. Inside, the barroom was so quiet he could have heard a mouse scamper across the floor. Only two men were there, one behind the bar, another at a table. Simeon Flynn sat with his head laid back, his hands resting alongside five cards that showed three queens and two eights. His appearance told Devon that he had played all night.

The only noise came from the sudden rattle of glass behind the bar. The bartender looked over at him, his eyes showing sleep, his expression filled with boredom. He would be going home soon, after another man named Cutter, relieved him. Devon was about to leave when Flynn kicked a chair his way. "C'mon and sit. I need a friendly voice this morning."

Devon drifted over, placed his billy atop the table and sat down. Flynn was just about used up. A quarter-inch of whiskey still occupied his glass. He appeared weary, like someone who'd just walked trail for an entire day and was looking for a place to bed down.

"Looks like you lost," Devon said.

"Can't win 'em all. He took me clean." With that, he scattered the cards across the table and then ran his fingers through his hair, scratching aggressively at his scalp. His wearied eyes closed momentarily.

"So where are you going now?" Devon asked.

"Back to my room where I'll sleep a while, then dig up some cash so I can play again tonight. It's the main virtue of the thing, a continuing certainty."

"Don't you ever get tired of it?"

"Sure. But it's all I got. It's my way of living. Last night I got driven down by old Pig's Eye."

"Parrant?"

"That's him. He was here, right where you're sittin', lookin' at me with that devil eye, while snickering like a madman, his yellow teeth brimmin' with an evil smile. Anyone who looks at him gets flustered now and then."

"I never saw him."

"Good thing you haven't."

Devon leaned forward, his elbows on the table. "What's he like?"

"The devil made him for sure. He's coarse and ill-lookin' with brows that cover half his forehead. He's got one marble-hued eye that's crooked with a sinister white ring around its pupil, giving him a kind of piggish expression. He's sodden and ill-tempered and half mad, still holdin' a grudge because he lost that foot race to Michael le Claire."

"What race?"

"You were just a child when they had a dispute over a claim. They aimed to settle it by having an eight mile foot race. Whoever got to the finish line first won the claim. Well, in the end Claire outdistanced him, and by the time Parrant got there, sick and mad and furious, Claire had already staked the claim. Parrant's been mad ever since. It's a poor ending for a man who was once heralded as the Romulus of our new city. He's got a saloon across the river, down on the flats. If you want to see him up close just walk over across the bridge. The saloon bears his name."

"I'm not that curious.

Flynn collected his cards like someone intent on neatness, shuffled them three times, and placed the stack aside. Devon thought he would get up and leave then, but instead he looked over and grinned. "You're playing a rough game also, one that might eventually get you hurt."

Devon cocked his head. "Explain what you mean."

"Willius Kane's not a whole lot better than old Pig's eye."

Devon sat up straight. "Well, I beg to differ with you. There's a whole lot of gentleman down under that gruff exterior of his."

"You think so?"

"Yes. I've had considerable talks with Mr. Kane, probably more than anyone else in this saloon. He's not what a lot of folks take him for."

Flynn's feet moved nervously beneath the table. "He's got you buffaloed."

Devon rose to Kane's defense without considering options. "No. He and I have talked a lot, ever since Ingrid's death. He's as innocent as I am."

"Maybe he is, and maybe he ain't. But you haven't heard the stories."

"What stories?"

"Those who know him best say he can kill a man and not even be flustered."

Devon remembered what Kane had said outside the LaBelle about wanting to kill and skin the man who killed Ingrid. He expected that Kane had spoken in all honesty.

"I expect he could, given reason."

"I'd say you were best to stay away from him, lest you become the reason."

"Kane and I respect one another."

Flynn laughed. His smile appeared contrived. "Respect, hell! That lasts only long enough to become useless. You'd be better off sleepin' with a grizzly bear, than seeking respect from someone like Kane."

Flynn's sudden discourse about Kane brought Devon to full attention. Up to the present, he had entered into only a few brief conversations with Flynn, none of which were revealing. Maybe Flynn wasn't who he appeared to be. Perhaps Flynn, like Kane, had some hidden characteristic that wasn't noticeable first hand. Maybe he had reason to talk about Kane in a derogatory manner.

"What have you got against Kane?" he asked.

"Nothing, he goes his way. I go mine. I'm just warning you about his tendency to explode. I've seen that knife of his come out faster than a snake can strike. Saw it pressed under a man's chin before he even knew it was there. If you ever see the detestation in Kane's eyes, you'll know what I mean."

"I see it every time he thinks about Ingrid's death."

"Go slow with the man. I'm just warning you."

"I know my limits."

"Best you do. I'd not like to see you caught up on the end of his skinnin' knife."

Devon didn't like the flow of conversation. It was time to get up and leave.

Just then Flynn said. "He cut out a man's heart once."

Flynn looked away from him, but not before his eyes took on a squint, the way a father might look when trying to impress his son, the way his own father looked when he wanted to plant words firmly in his mind.

"I expect he might have," Devon replied. "When?"

"Some time back, up in the woods."

"For what?"

"Can't say. I was told he did."

"That's not proof. Sometimes stories are made up."

Flynn nodded. "Yes, they are, but not that one."

"How can you be certain it wasn't?"

"Because I knew a man who was there when it happened. He said Kane was like a madman, all because of a disagreement between him and a friend."

"A friend?"

"That's what I heard. A partner." Flynn leaned forward and looked directly at the table as if searching for just the right words. "I'd be careful if I were you. Anyone who can kill his friend could maybe kill his girlfriend too."

"You mean Ingrid?"

"I can't say. Stories are what they are. Men are what they are. I'm just warning you to be careful with the man."

Devon was becoming irritated with Flynn's suggestive talk. He'd had just about enough when Flynn picked up his cards, slipped them into his pocket and strode out of the saloon.

So there it was, a finger pointed directly at Kane. At first Devon was a bit confused, but then the suggestion began rooting in his mind. If someone could kill a friend over a disagreement, then perhaps he could kill another he thought highly of. Crazed people could erupt over the smallest of things. When they got caught up in frenzy their minds forgot all reason. But Kane killing Ingrid? No! He didn't think it possible. But still . . . . .

Anger had a way of changing people. Western had told him about husbands and wives, and fathers and sons beating on one another. People exploded. Hate could surely find a way of directing a soul. And when it did, only a sudden surge of reason could turn it around.

Devon looked around the saloon, empty except for the bartender. Then he walked to the door and went outside into the fresh morning. He heard the shout of a drayman, "Steamboat a'coming." Downstream, twin drifts of smoke were visible from two steamers coming up river one behind the other. If they offloaded all the goods and passengers before four o'clock the LaBelle would have another busy night, as would other taverns stretched across Lowertown.

CHAPTER TWENTY-ONE

Warfare far and near

The news of a battle near a place called Bull Run was foremost in the news following that dreadful day of July 21, when the Union army was routed by Confederate troops. Twenty-eight thousand Union troops under the leadership of General McDowell, had met thirty-three thousand southern boys led by General Beauregard at a place north of Manassas. At the beginning of the fight the Union had the enemy on the run, and they would have routed them had not a stubborn brigade led by a General named Jackson, held its ground. His obstinacy and ability gave his men enough courage to hold their positions until nine-thousand more soldiers came up to reinforce their lines near a place called Henry House. The battle had been brutal. The Union troops had fled back toward Washington, leaving near three thousand dead in their wake. The Confederacy was reported to have lost a third less men. The First Minnesota had fought all day. Randolph had been in the midst of it for sure.

Tears were shed at the table that morning, when prayers were spoken. Heartache was felt for the men who would never return home, and for those who mourned their deaths. Casualty reports would come later, when names had been sorted out, when bodies had been identified by the little slips of paper some carried inside their pocket. They prayed that Randolph would not be one of them.

Devon wondered what it must be like, to be thrown into the eruption of cannon and the rattle of musketry, the smoke, the shouting, the fear, the downright horror of it all, the confusion and the death and the dying. He wept openly at the table that morning with his mother and father as his food went cold, and he yearned deep down to rush out and enlist, to teach those grey-bellies a thing or two. Harold had tried to rally their spirits, but even he succumbed to the pressure of grief. Nona moved like a ghost, doing this and that, like someone lost in time.

Afterwards Devon went outside and stood by the fence, at the same place he and Randolph had occupied on the day he went off to war, and he wondered what Pricilla was thinking as she read the paper. Was she sorrowful and in need of holding Randolph in her arms, or was she eager to get into the embrace of the gentleman she had been with that day he saw them together? Her apparent disloyalty made him angry, and he hoped she would hear that Randolph had been in the midst of all that horror.

During their annual vacation time, Caroline, her mother and sister, had taken a steamer down the Minnesota River to Mankato to visit her aunt. Edmund had stayed home, his occupation with state business denying him time off. Devon was lonely in her absence, and news from the war front made his days all the more difficult. He missed her intensely during the dark hours when he was alone in his bed, and during the day, when he would go about his routine with her image firmly fixed in his mind.

At the LaBelle, brawls could erupt on any given day, usually between drunken men from the steamers, who were quick to prove who was the strongest or the toughest or the most proficient with their fists; always something, day or night, to strip his vision of Caroline away. When the fights ended, and interludes of calm prevailed, he would often sit by the river and dream of future days and imagine her beside him.

He had received three letters from her, one of which read: *You are with me always, day upon day, and when your nearness comforts me I can envision us as we build a love strong and secure. I miss you, Devon. I yearn to be by your side.*

When alone with his thoughts he would think of those words and they would bring him comfort.

August came, bringing cooler weather, while down in Mankato the days boiled in near one-hundred degree heat. Because of the drought, the water level of the Mississippi continued to drop. Before long, the citizens began wondering if rain would ever come again.

Devon had afternoon duty during the first week in August, on a day when three steamers lay tied up at the landing. Until three o'clock that Tuesday, everything had been calm. The streets were filled with shoppers. Merchants were busy storing supplies. Well dressed women walked beneath their parasols. Children romped. The streets were crowded with commerce.

When Devon heard the shrill piping of whistles, his senses quickened. The high-pitched sound came from down near the levee, indicating trouble. He started running past a line of wagons near Bridge Square and was on his way down Water Street when he saw the commotion.

Ahead of him, a crowd of twelve boatmen had gathered near the landing. Close by, facing them, were Chief Western and eight members of the Alliance Committee. Shouts came clearly up the street, angry words, mostly from the boatmen gathered near the steamers.

Devon ran full out, nightstick in hand, his thoughts racing as fast as his legs. What was the problem? Why were the boatmen confronting the police? Had there been a fight? Had anyone been hurt? As he neared, the shouts became clearer.

"Get away from us," one of the boatmen bellowed. "We can handle our own fockin' problems."

"There'll be no fighting here!" Western's voice answered, sharp with authority.

The boatman shouted back. "Do us the courtesy of minding your own fockin' business."

Lowertown

More curses erupted from the boatmen, stirring their anger.

Western shouted again, his voice loud and firm. "And I say, disperse."

From the boatmen. "And we say, go home and play with your cock."

Devon ran to Western's side. Jimmy Hasset was there, rigid with fear. Fornier's, lips were tight to his teeth. Several others stood grouped together, facing the river-men, their clubs ready.

"What's this all about?" Devon asked, breathlessly.

Sweat dripped from Western's face. "Two of them were fightin' when we first arrived. Goin' at it strong, they were. Then others from their respective boats came and joined in, creatin' a free for all. When we tried to break it up, instead of quitting they turned against us. Hearty bunch for sure, itchin' for a battle."

"We're outnumbered."

"Aye. But we got our billies. They have only their fists."

One of the boatmen called out. "Tell that new sonny boy to go home to his mama."

"Go back to your duties," one of the Alliance men shouted.

Western spun around and faced the man who had shouted. "No responding to them, you understand?" Western voice was firm and sharp. "I'll do the talkin',"

The boatmen continued to ridicule. "You couldn't break a goddam egg if you sat your fat ass on it," one of them shouted.

Then another shouted, "You city boys is nothin' but shit-eatin' swine?"

Western shouted over their heads. "That'll be the end of it. Go back to your boats. We're disbursing. This standoff is over."

One of the boatmen had a belaying pin in his hand, another, a stock of wood, still another a metal rod. Most were angry and seething; some bruised as a result of the commotion Western had come upon.

Aboard the steamers, the respective Captains stood on the foredecks. One shouted. "Get back aboard, you hooligans. We're pullin' out soon. Tend the boilers now and get up some steam."

From the other boat came three sharp whistles. Only two heads turned.

"Get aboard," Western shouted.

"Not 'till we bring you down," came the answer.

Western thought it might not be settled with words. He turned to the group and laid out his orders. "If they come at us, you'd better fight hard. They's a mean bunch for sure, just craving for a fight. Don't be afraid to swing those billies. They'll crack even the hardest head. You know how to use 'em." He paused and looked quickly at the crowd of boatmen. They continued screaming.

"Your mothers are whores," someone shouted.

And then another. "And I'm a fuckin' wildcat with the meanness of a she bear."

"I'll taste your blood," yelled still another.

The boatmen made a lunge forward, a slight feint. Everyone in Western's ranks stiffened. The boatmen laughed instantly.

"You're shitin' in your goddam pants," one of them yelled.

Three more shrieks from the boat only made them angrier.

One of the Captains shouted. "Get aboard. We got only two hours left here."

As the men of the Alliance awaited Western's instructions, Devon's hand tightened on his club. His heart pounded. Fear grew in Jimmy's eyes. As he wiped his mouth, it appeared that he was praying.

Western voice was firm and commanding. "Now we're gonna walk away and hope they'll go back to their boats. Some of 'em are already battered. Maybe they'll see the futility of it all." He looked at each man in turn, to make sure his words were being heard. "But if they come at us, you've got your training, and I know you've got determination. These men are the scum of the river, but they're tough, and some of 'em don't care much if they see tomorrow. So aim at their heads, which is the weaker part of them. Put your club to them if you must."

Western turned toward the mob. Many were crouched and waiting. He shouted urgently to his men. "We're goin' now, all together."

As the boatmen brandished their makeshift weapons, boards, pieces of pipe, and ropes, the men stepped off. As if answering to a command, the mob surged forward.

Western's voice boomed out over the dock like an officer enabling his troops. "Here we go men," he shouted. "Have at them."

As the crewmen aboard the steamers massed on their respective forecastles, a mighty roar went up among them. At the same moment, pent up steam shrieked through the boats' safety valves.

Devon gripped his nightstick tightly, its hide loop snug around his wrist. He tried to swallow, but had no saliva. His mind screamed silently as the boatmen charged toward him. His thoughts raced . . . he had to fight with a brutish instinct, the way Kane would fight, or the men charging toward him would batter him senseless. They would fight until they won or lost, lived or died. He thought of Randolph facing a billowing cloud of musket fire, and as the boatmen charged toward them, he planted his feet and thrust his stick toward the first man in his vision. An instant later the lines collided.

Devon reeled under the shock of contact. He was thrown back instantly as a blast of breath exploded from the boatman's mouth. As his attacker's full weight drove him backwards, he fell to the ground, into an avalanche of sound.

Devon scrambled to free himself as the boatman grasped his free arm, bending it upward. An immediate rasp of pain rushed into his shoulder. He cried out, squirming as he brought his nightstick down on the boatman's head. The blow had no effect. The man climbed over him, scratching his way toward Devon's neck, his claw-like hands ripping at his clothing.

Devon struck again, at the side of his head, three blows in rapid succession. With the last of them, he felt a release, a letting go. The man sagged onto his left arm, unleashing a flood of pain, his face so close that Devon could smell his breath. The attacker slumped as his eyes rolled back. Devon was about to push him away when another body fell across his legs.

Legs, and bodies and arms pounded around him in a hurricane of noise. Boots thundered hard onto the dirt, inches from his face. He knew he had to get up before they crushed him. He tried desperately to inch out from beneath the bodies, but his left arm was useless, oozing pain. Broken, just above the wrist where the pain was most intense. Movement was impossible. Fearful, and glazed

Warfare far and near

with anger, he turned his head to avoid the seething mass of men around him. His face burned. Dirt peppered his eyes. Someone's boot slammed into his head. He squirmed beneath the weight on him and sank beneath a blaze of sheer panic.

The sound became an avalanche of noise. Someone went down to his left. Another blow to his shoulder unleashed a torrent of pain.

He made one last attempt to free himself, until something crashed against his face. Then, as he drifted into a non-feeling silent world, the noise became muted, except for the cries of men, and the dull pounding of their boots.

Someone had fallen next to him. When he opened his eyes he saw tangled wavelets of black hair, like that of a dead animal. Submerged beneath two bodies, he gasped for air. Something hard pressed against his chest. . . his nightstick.

Orders were being shouted, then curses, and wild screaming. Above it all, came the shrill screech of the steamers' pipes. . WHEE . . .. WHEE . ... WHEE.

Feet pounded around him. The mass of men started to come apart. He heard an anguished cry of pain, then more thuds. His skin felt cold. He turned his head as best he could, saw a body, inches away, a face pressed to another man's leg, his mouth agape, his tongue reddened with blood. A man on his knees was trying to rise.

Then a rally cry went up. Indistinct sounds flowed among the bodies still on the ground, grunts and moans from injured men. A few arose slowly. Curses accompanied their movements. The silence was punctuated by shuffling, and moans of pain.

The man who had fallen on him was lifted away. Someone knelt down beside him. A hand touched his shoulder. "Are you alright, Devon?"

He recognized the voice as Western's. "I'm not sure," he replied.

"Lay still. I'll come back to you. Others are in worse shape."

Devon didn't move, except to relieve the pressure on his chest. His arm was too painful to move. He tasted blood in his mouth, and rawness where his tongue searched. Ahead of him, men began rising.

Western's voice boomed above the silence. "They've gone. They had their pleasure. A five minute fight, boys, but a good one no less. They got their satisfaction. Now they're back aboard their boats, and we got lots of hurtin' to fix."

Devon rolled over on his good arm and attempted to stand. The pain in his left arm surged like fire. The arm was broke, for sure. Someone he didn't know came over to help him, an older man bleeding from a scalp wound. "Be careful," Devon said. "My arm is broke."

"Easy then," the man said. "Can you stand?"

"I think so."

"Then it's up with you. The donnybrook is over."

Devon found his footing. He stood until his dizziness abated. Western was a short distance away, tending some of the other men, most of who were on their feet. Some onlookers who had stood silently nearby, came forward to help wherever they could. Someone shouted. "Get a wagon. We got wounded here."

"They was god-awful fierce," another said nearby.

Jimmy Hasset came over to him, limping. "Devon, you made it through."

Devon blinked as his dizziness abated. "I got a broken arm." He held the arm tight to his chest.

"Some's worse. Jake Wells got his head split open."

"I was never in anything like this before."

"Nor I. It was more fierce than scuffling with friends. They were a brutal bunch, like a pack of wolves, to say the least."

Western made the rounds to check everyone for injury. Most were on their feet. Only one man remained on the ground beneath those attending him. Western came over when he saw Devon holding his arm.

"They busted Devon's arm," Hasset remarked.

Western nodded. "We'll get you to the hospital. A broken arm can be fixed. We'll have you back home before nightfall."

"I didn't get a lick in," Devon said.

"They came on like an avalanche. Most angry bunch of savages I ever saw. But we had our way with a few of them. There's lots of blood still running aboard the steamers. They'll be days healing."

Warfare far and near

He motioned to a wooden crate not far from where they stood. "Go over to that crate and sit down. We got help comin'. I'm scarin' up some water from the LaBelle. Sorry about your arm."

"It's broke just above the wrist, I think."

"Well, keep it stationary. I don't see any bone stickin' out. Clean break. Don't move the arm lest you damage some nerve-tissue in there." Western looked directly into his eyes. "You don't look weak. Your breathing seems normal. We'll forgo a temporary splint. You just hold that arm still. The wagon'll be comin' along soon." He grinned then. "Looks like you just earned yourself some time off."

Devon and Hasset went to the crate and sat down. Dizzy and disoriented by the scuffle, Devon sat quietly and looked at the steamers. Some of the river-men on the steamer's deck made menacing gestures. Others were giddy with their bloody victory. The Captain of one boat came and rousted them below. Several were already bandaged. One man leaned on a makeshift crutch.

"Hey, Devon, here come some of the girls from the LaBelle."

Devon turned and saw Mildred Polshki headed his way, accompanied by another girl, the one called Sissy. They carried water jugs and glasses. When Mildred saw Devon she walked straight toward him, her dress rustling. She spoke at the moment Jimmy nudged his side.

"Why Devon Finch, what are you doing in this fracas?"

"We just tried to settle down some ornery boatmen."

She looked angrily at the steamers. "They're not meant to set foot on dry land. All they know is the river. It's where they ought to stay. Would you like some water?"

"Yes, ma'm. I'm thirsty."

"His arm's broke," Jimmy said.

Mildred snickered. "I hope that's all he broke."

Jimmy's face reddened a bit.

Devon drank while Sissy helped some of the other boys eager enough to take advantage of her presence. She smiled and cajoled, and they did likewise as if her presence made their pain and discomfort less severe.. They did lots of scanning.

211

After Devon drank he returned the glass to Mildred. Without saying a word, she walked away to help others.

"She's a fancy one," Jimmy said.

"She's the madam."

Jimmy's eyes followed her backside. "Do you know all them whores?"

Devon smiled. "I sure do. That other one is named Sissy."

"She don't look like no sissy to me."

"She ain't."

Jimmy rubbed a slight bump just below his hairline "Did you ever think you'd be consorting with the likes of them?" he asked.

"Never, but they're not what you think they are. They're human beings, just like the rest of us. Most of 'em just had a run of bad luck."

"Like the one that got killed?"

"That was the worst of it."

Jimmy nudged him lightly. "Looks like you're gonna be spending more and more time with Caroline."

"She'll be pleased for sure. She's wanted me out of the Alliance ever since the first day. This'll only strengthen her resolve."

"Are you gonna quit?'

"I might."

"This is as good a' time as any. You're not under any obligation."

"Just my word."

"That ain't the same as an obligation."

"To me it is."

The wagon came moments later. Those who were busted up worst were the first to board. One of the men sprawled out on his back because he couldn't stand. Devon sat up front with the driver so nobody would jar his arm. When the wagon was full they started up Jackson Street toward St. Joseph's hospital.

Devon didn't talk to anyone on the way. He just sat still and held his arm, grimacing every time the wagon struck a bump. When the hospital came into sight he settled down a bit, and when it pulled in next to the entrance, he eased himself down and stood in line. When a nurse came up to him, a scanty little girl with a thin face and deep set eyes, he said simply, "I got a broken arm." She told him to follow her. Soon he was in a room with a doctor, a padded wooden table with a white sheet atop it, and a shelf lined with an assortment of cures.

When they reset his arm he nearly passed out. Soon afterwards, as the pain subsided, they applied a wooden splint extending to the palm of his hand and across both sides of his arm, wrapping it with a tight cloth. The doctor called it fracture bracing. The doctor also told him it would take a month or two to heal, during which time he had to return periodically to change the splint, and to receive instructions for increasing his activities in order to restore muscle strength, joint movement and flexibility. The doctor was convinced that the arm would heal nicely. As soon as the muscles, ligaments and soft tissues performed their regular functions, the splint would be removed. Before he was released they put a sling around his neck, propped his arm inside, and ushered him to the door. They offered him a ride home, but he preferred to walk.

Devon started for home shortly after five o'clock. By then the city had settled in from the long, hot day as if to welcome the silence, for hardly a noise was heard, not a hoof-beat, nor a voice, nor the shout of a child, just a stillness that carried the sound of chirping birds and the padding of Devon's feet on the hard-packed clay. Mother would be preparing dinner. Papa would be home near six o'clock. Caroline would be sitting down to write him a letter, or so he hoped.

He walked up Sixth Street, past the Fuller House, and headed for Market Hall. He paused in front of Caroline's house, lingering there a bit, wishing she were home. His loneliness became more intense the longer he remained and so he went on.

Surely, his mother would admonish him when he came home all busted up, his face scratched, and his arm slung? She would have cause for concern. But then, she was used to adversity, given all the bumps and scrapes he and Randolph had received during their growing up years, when scuffling became part of strengthening, and brawling became an ingredient of camaraderie. Maybe now was the time to give up the Alliance. He had reason enough, to be sure. He had fulfilled his commitment with a busted arm. But so had others, some worse than he. What would they think of him if he walked away and they continued to fulfill their duty? How would Randolph react if he was in his shoes? Hell, he would go on, for sure. Randolph wouldn't let anything stand in the way of doing what was right. Randolph would die to honor his pledge, as he might if the war went badly.

Activity on the streets increased as he neared Wabasha, and soon he stood in front of his house, taking stock of his predicament. After assuming a more cheerful appearance, he opened the gate and walked inside to an aroma of corned beef and fresh-baked egg bread.

Nona glanced at him momentarily, with a 'what did you do now' expression. She didn't say a word, just looked at him, knowing he'd been in a scuffle.

"We had a fight down on the levee," he said. "Some boatmen wanted to show us how superior they were. I got my arm broke."

"Thank God it isn't worse," she said as she came toward him. She turned his face so she could better see the scrapes on his cheek. "I've got some salve for that bruise." She shook her head. "This is what I get for raising boys."

"It's nothing, mother."

"Nothing, you say? A broken arm is nothing? Well I say it's something to be taken seriously. My word, the longer you're with that Alliance, the worse it gets. All that scuffling, fighting, and murders, and who knows what else. It ain't a place for a young boy like you."

"I'm not a young boy any more, mother."

She shrugged. "We won't get into that."

She sat him down in a kitchen chair and rubbed his cheek with ointment, careful not to bump his arm, or apply too much pressure to the wound. "Your father will have something to say about this," she admonished. "I'm sure by now he's heard about the ruckus and is wondering if you were mixed up in it."

"We tried to disperse them peacefully, but they were intent on fighting."

"River men. Bah! I think this city would be better off without them."

"But they're the ones that bring us supplies, food, furniture, and clothing. Everything we need and depend on."

Warfare far and near

She slapped him playfully on his good arm. "We all know their worth. Why most everything we own came up here by steamer."

"I was just trying to sooth your feathers."

"My feathers don't need smoothing. I'm just concerned that if you don't end this craving to become a hometown hero, you'll run into something dreadful, as if two murders ain't dreadful. Bless me, I never knew how dangerous this town was until you took up with the Alliance."

"You did, mother. Randolph used to tell us what he went through."

"Maybe I didn't listen carefully enough."

Devon snickered. "You listened. You told him the same thing you're telling me."

"Well, it never hurts to repeat myself. Maybe someday you'll hear me"

"Mother."

"Don't mother me. You come home all busted up, and I'm supposed to act unconcerned. At least Randolph got paid for his work. You're earning nothing."

Devon leaned into the conversation. "But if Western thinks my work is good enough I might have a chance to become a paid police officer when the war is over. Talk is, they'll be paying the regulars four-hundred-and-sixty dollars a year."

"The war might go on for years." She waved her words away. "Let's put talk of war aside."

Nona didn't like war talk. Every time it was mentioned, she thought of Randolph being involved in a horrible battle, which brought her near to tears. Even as she put the salve away, Devon sensed her weariness. Mothers, he thought, had a particular grief to bear. Bringing children into the world, and then giving them up to some horrible war, was enough to wring the joy from anyone.

Devon stood and went to the stove where she stood. He eased back her hair, already turning gray in places, and kissed her gently on the neck.

"I'm going upstairs," he said. "I want to write Caroline a letter. It'll be two weeks yet before she comes back home."

"You go on up. I've got more work ahead of me."

He needed to say more, especially when she was saddened. It affected him when she was downcast. "Thank you, mother," he said. "I love you more than you'll ever know."

She turned and smiled. Her face had mellowed. "I know," she said simply.

Devon kissed her cheek and then ascended the narrow wooden staircase. In his room, he went to the writing table, opened the single drawer and removed a piece of paper, pen and ink. He sat down on his bed and began writing.

My beloved Caroline. First I must say how much I love you. Your return cannot come soon enough for me. Unfortunately, when you return home you'll find my arm in a sling. Now don't be alarmed. It will heal just fine. Within a month or two, with care and exercise, I'll be back to my natural self. Western and some of the Alliance boys, including me, had a confrontation down by the levee with a group of angry boatmen who just wouldn't obey Western's commands. As a result, they chose to show their superiority. Thus, my broken arm. Well, that's over and . . . .

He went on to write lovely words of endearment. He was rather good at putting affections on paper. He wanted to tell her about his decision to leave the Alliance, but he didn't. He would rather tell her when she returned home, when they were alone. It would mean more, coming from his lips. When he finished writing, he sealed the letter for posting. He was about to lie down on the bed for a while when his mother called him to dinner.

The moment Harold saw him, he said. "Got busted up in that fracas, didn't ya?"

Devon took his place at the table. "We couldn't avoid it."

"I heard the details."

As silence settled over the table, Nona said grace. Then, as Harold cut into his corned beef, he said. "Good thing it wasn't your right arm. You'd look kind of strange eating with your left."

Devon and Nona laughed. Nothing further was said about his arm, or about the Alliance, or about his future, or about the war. Instead, Harold talked about his work at the newspaper.

Devon's sleep was slow in coming that night. He laid in the twilight and thought of Caroline far down in Mankato, with thoughts so vivid at times that she seemed to be right next to him. He wanted so much to touch her, to stroke her hair, to feel her skin beneath his fingertips, to taste her lips. He was aroused for a while, and he thought of them together in their own bed, doing what they had never done, and his emotions soared.

He thought about those precious to him, his parents, his brother, Caroline, for sure, and as his thoughts took structure, he realized that the Alliance was something he could give up, right then and there, if he made up his mind to do so. He could just get up the following morning and say, that's the end of it, and he would never have to worry about the dangers and temptations in Lowertown again.

In time he drowsed, even though his arm pained him something awful, and just before sleep overtook him he knew he would make his decision before Caroline returned, to end her concern once and for all.

CHAPTER TWENTY-TWO

Taking the bait

On the day before Caroline was to arrive home, Chief Western summoned Devon to his office.

By then, Devon had made his decision . . . he would leave the Alliance. Caroline would be delighted, as would his parents, and he would be free to plan his future, although still undecided as to its direction. Although peacekeeping was important to him, the brawling, and mingling with riff-raff, didn't fit his vision of the future. So he approached Western's office, determined to act upon his decision, forthright and with strong intent. But on entering the room, he saw Western sitting commandingly behind the big desk, his face fixed in a broad grin, and his decision faltered.

"Sit down. Sit down," Western said, motioning to the chair. "How's that arm?"

"It's healing fine."

"Good. Good. I rarely saw a broken arm that didn't heal right, and I've seen a few more than I need to in my day."

"I expect you have."

Western lifted a cigar from the ashtray and puffed until the flavor came to him, then he blew the smoke toward the ceiling in a pleasing way. "I've been meaning to talk to you, and would have sooner had that disturbance down on the docks not interrupted me. I had my mind set on telling you that you're one of the best men I've got on this Alliance Committee. Your steadfastness with Miss Lorgren's murder, and the way you handled yourself when we returned that deserter, and found that young Huggins girl, convinced me that you're destined for police work."

Devon was about to reply when Western held up his hand. "Now wait a minute. I ain't done yet." He looked straight at Devon, clasped his hands into a ball, and spoke directly. "Last night we brought in a man from the LaBelle, drunk and disorderly. His name is Curtis Weimar. He's a merchant, a man who's known to take too many whiskey's from time to time. Might you know him?"

"No, the name is unfamiliar."

"I thought you might not. He visits the LaBelle infrequently, but when he does, he generally sits back near the stairs. He's been known to go up with the ladies from time to time because he enjoys diversion. Actually, he's got a wife and two children back home."

Western puffed his cigar again, and then rolled it between his fingers. "I've an exceedingly difficult job here, Devon. Why when the economy buckled two years ago, leaving only two banks in operation, over half our citizens moved out. We dang near lost our city. Last year alone we had over two-hundred accidents and ten attempted suicides. We found twelve bodies, some putrefied, not to mention hundreds of lost cattle and horses, six robberies, and over a hundred lost children, most of 'em found, praise God. We're not that far ahead of the frontier, and the job just keeps getting worse. Then the entire force up and signs into the Union army, and I'm stuck with inexperienced men while trying to make the best of things amid chaos."

Devon watched his eyes, studying him, without movement of any kind, as if to peer into his soul.

"But I'm not complaining," he continued. "I'm just telling you how difficult it is to keep my concentration on things. That's why I need men I can trust, men who have been thrust into the fray and have come out stronger."

Devon sat absolutely still as Western's eyes continued their silent analysis. Western was going to ask him to stay on, to continue the work he had started, even though his arm was broke, even though he harbored intentions of leaving the Alliance. Just as sure as he was sitting there, that was Western's objective. Devon squirmed a bit, as if suddenly uncomfortable in the chair. Western's eyes squinted in response. Damn, Devon thought, why did this have to happen just when his expectations had gone to the contrary? He sat still, awaiting Western's next remark.

"I want to get back to the Weimar fellow. He had some interesting things to say when he was under the influence. We didn't pay much attention to all his rambling, until he mentioned a name. Then we tightened up and took notice. The name he spoke was Ingrid Lorgren."

Devon sat up a bit straighter.

"He was babbling on about how fine she was in bed, how she could satisfy a man with certain delicate movements and distinct pleasures not usually associated with intercourse. He mentioned how disturbed he was that a woman of such sexual talent could be killed. The statement nearly brought tears to his eyes. So we listened to him while he went on talking."

Western picked up the cigar again, puffed on it, then looked around the room as if Devon wasn't there. He brushed a bit of ash off his sleeve cuff, formed a small bellows with his lips and blew out a thin, narrow stream of smoke that disappeared in whirls and eddies.

"He told us about how affected the men were about her death, and how they talked among themselves about the pleasures they had received from her. He said most of them were saddened, except one man, a man who never blinked an eye when brought into discussions about her fine, specialized means of comforting a man. And then he spoke a name, one that had us looking at one another in sheer curiosity."

Devon was amazed at how cleverly Western had crafted the story, practically like fishing, dangling the bait in front of him, making it so danged tempting that he, like the fish, would sacrifice his life just to have a taste of it. He wanted to ask Western who the man was, but he was speechless. Instead, he squirmed in the chair and just looked at the bait.

Western continued. "We asked him who the man was, and just like that, he stopped talking as if he'd suddenly realized he'd said the wrong thing. Well, we kept on prodding him but he didn't say another word until we carried him into a cell. Turned out, he'd never been behind bars, and it had a loosening effect on him. He told us he didn't want to go to jail, that his wife was waiting for him back home, that his kids needed him, and that he was sorry for drinking and whoring. On and on, confessing his sins as if he was standing in front of God Almighty. Then we thought maybe we'd scare him a mite."

Again, he waited through the anticipation and the dead-silent suspense. Western had him, and he knew it, sure as hell. Devon leaned forward in his chair, eager to hear more.

"We told Mr. Weimar that we'd had enough of his carousing and that we were going to get his wife to take him home, and that we were obliged to tell her about his whoring. Well, that loosened his tongue. We said we would hold back on charging him with drunk and disorderly conduct if he could tell us the name of the man in question, and then he spoke it."

Sure enough, the bait was there, right in front of him, so close he could see it and smell it and almost taste it. Like a patient fisherman, Western just waited for him to strike, so he could set the hook and yank in his big catch.

"Who was it?" Devon asked.

Western's grin broadened. "I knew we'd get to that. But first . . . I've got to be open and honest with you."

Devon waited, not knowing what to expect.

Western's fingers rapped on the desk, tap, tap, tap, tap while he formed his reply. "When you signed your name on that ledger back in April you became a member of the police force, although no pay was offered, no badge given, or no distinction made. You were a volunteer, a citizen who offered his services. As such you were entitled to direct communications with those of us who were responsible for guiding your efforts. We were authorized to give you all the information and training you would need in order to

Taking the bait

complete your work effectively. You were, then, and are now, a member of the Saint Paul police department."

Now Devon could see where this was going. He would receive an ultimatum, to either continue on with the Alliance, or go home, never again to be privy to police information. Western would, at his word, put him out to pasture, like a horse having run its last race. Firmly convinced of his thought, Devon nodded silently.

"You know what I'm about to say, don't you?" Western said.

"I think so, sir."

"Well, then here it is. You were involved in this case from the start. You knew the woman, Ingrid Lorgren, and the man we thought had taken her life, Willius Kane. We gave you permission to question others, to observe their actions, and to report your findings if suspicions were raised. You proved to be a capable man, in whom we could confide, and our confidence was reciprocated."

"I understand."

"Now, the facts are, we have no eye-witnesses to Ingrid's murder. No one saw anyone go up the stairs. No one saw anyone leave her room. No weapon was found. And now we're wrapped in presumptions, except for a new name, which may, or may not, amount to a pile of cow manure."

Devon shifted in his chair. "You want me to continue on as part of the Alliance, don't you?'

Western looked straight at him. "You're damn right I do. But if you don't, then I must bid you goodbye right here and now. And as a civilian, with no further access to police information, or to any evidence connected with Ingrid Lorgren's death, you'll no longer be privileged to work with us in that regard, except perhaps in a court of law, if and when, her killer is found and put on trial."

There it was, laid out specifically. His involvement would end immediately. All it would take was a word or two, an expression of finality, a quitter's statement, and he would walk out of the room, never again to be associated with the Alliance.

The strain of further involvement had occupied his thoughts for the past two days. His decision to quit had been final, but now this, a chance to perhaps uncover new information about Ingrid's murder. Western had something in mind for him, something definite, but he would never know what it was if he stepped aside. He had only seconds in which to make his final decision, and Western was not a patient man.

"Well," Western demanded.

Devon knew he had to speak right out, without delay. "I was intending to give you my resignation today," he said. "With my injury and all, I thought I might not be able to give my full attention to the Alliance. But now, if I can still be of help, I will change that decision. I know Miss Lorgren would have wanted me to stay on."

"Then it is final?" Western grinned and held out his hand. Devon stood instantly. Reaching over, he gripped the hand firmly. Then Western motioned him to the chair again. "I had a feeling you would. After all these years as a policeman, I have learned to judge people quite accurately."

Devon took a deep breath, expelling it with his decision. "I will remain with the Alliance."

Western's mustache failed to conceal the smile. "Well then. Now I can tell you the name Fullerton gave us. The name was that of Simeon Flynn."

"Oh, my God," Devon whispered.

"That's what we thought. So we took Mr. Fullerton out of the cell and placed him in a chair and told him to speak slowly and carefully while Officer Rankin wrote it all down. And he did."

"What did he tell you?"

"Nothing specific, other than Flynn had a hatred for women who sold themselves to men, even though he occasionally took advantage of their skills. He was known to express his hatred most often when whiskey got to him, or when he was losing at cards, as he was the night Ingrid was murdered."

"What connection does that have to her murder?"

"Nothing at this point, except that he left his chair the night of the murder, to relieve himself. He was gone for about ten minutes. Nothing unusual about that, except that it matches the time frame in which Ingrid was murdered. Perhaps it is nothing, but it is worthy of investigation. So, here's what we'd like you to do."

He began. "If this is a credible lead, then we'll need someone inside LaBelle to bear witness to everything that goes on there. You

Taking the bait

know the people, better than anyone else on the Alliance. You can speak directly to Kane, and to Mr. Flynn, and too many of the others. And you know the ladies. They're comfortable with you, and, I believe, if you give them an ear, they'd be willing to discuss matters they would otherwise conceal. In other words, I want you to be our eyes and our ears inside the LaBelle. My presence would be far too obvious. And the other Alliance men who frequent the saloon on your off hours seldom go into the place, much less talk to anyone. They choose to remain on the streets and answer a call rather than place themselves inside that den of iniquity. So, you see, in that regard, you're invaluable. Will you accept the challenge?"

Devon felt as if he was about to step into a bottomless hole. Being inside LaBelle was one thing, acting secretly while trying to remain innocuous was something quite different. One mistake, one wrong question, and he could be placed in mortal danger. But he could not back out now. He had given his word. He had no recourse but to make the best of the situation.

"I'll do it, sir." he said.

Western nodded. "Good. Good. I was confident that you would. There's a full payin' job for you when this war is over. I'm sure you know what Saint Paul police officers were paid. You'd be respected, for sure. And the higher you go in rank, the more you'll be earning. Being a policeman might be difficult sometimes, but it is rewarding."

"I'll give it my best, sir."

"I know you will. But for now, just be yourself. Nobody is likely to tangle with someone who's got a broken arm. I just want you to sit and observe, and listen. You'll know what's right and what's wrong when it comes your way. Just don't show yourself all the time. Keep your routine same as it is, so as not to gather attention."

"I understand, sir."

Western came out from behind his desk, took Devon's good hand and shook it firmly. "Keep in touch with me. If you hear of anything that might have bearing on Ingrid's death, let me know immediately."

Devon nodded. "I will, sir. Right now I have to go back home,"

"Ha, yes, indeed you will."

"And I will tell my Caroline that I will remain on the force. She will not be happy with me."

"She will learn to accept it."

"I can only hope she will. I told her I would resign. Now I have to go back on my word."

Western nodded. "Then Mr. Weimar came along at just the right time."

"I think fate is beginning to rule my life again."

Western laughed. "Ah, yes, fate, that worrisome little imp that governs our lives. That little scalawag can alter the course of individuals, and, ah, yes, nations too. I have had him in my head more than once."

"I'm pleased to know that I'm not the only one he manipulates."

They walked to the door and then outside into daylight. There, Western bid him goodbye. "Take the remainder of the week off. See your woman. Show her a good time. Tell her what's in your heart. She'll be a willing listener, I'm sure."

"Good day, Mr. Western."

He walked home slowly, filled with thought. He had been challenged again. Past discussions with Randolph about allegiance to a cause had now plunged him into something incredibly dangerous and decisive. Despite his firm objection to remain on the force, he had been easily led to the contrary. Had curiosity changed his mind, or had he been swayed by the danger of the decision itself? Certainly, the possibility of exposing Ingrid's killer had played mightily in his decision, but at what cost? Would his decision offer proof of his steadfast loyalty to a unit he had promised to serve, or would Caroline see it as a setback to their marriage? He would earn no money. He would be unable to save for their future. He would be locked in until the war was over, or until he had gumption enough to see the futility of it all.

But he would see it through, for a while at least. He would observe and report, and if nothing came of it by the end of the year, he would quit for sure, and seek a different means of employment.

Caroline would be home on the following day. She would disembark from the steamer and flow into his arms, and the world would be condensed to just the two of them.

Everything would be alright, he thought.

Everything would be alright.

CHAPTER TWENTY-THREE

The Promise

The days were dry. A fine, gritty dust clung to the air from morning to night. The mosquitoes, thick during July, had ended their plague and now the wind came heavy with a parched smell in its breath, as if everything north of the city had withered and decayed. The prairie fires, even from afar, gave off a stench different from the dryness. Sometimes the smoke dimmed the sunlight, and grasses, what remained of them, wilted and turned brown. By August eleventh the river was so low that the mail boat didn't arrive until after midnight. Some even implied that those living on the western shoreline could go to bed every night without their life preservers. Humor found its way into everything those days, even during drought.

The little steamer *Antelope*, bearing Caroline and her family, was scheduled to dock at approximately ten o'clock in the morning.

Devon was on the landing a full half-hour before the steamer's arrival, gazing upriver toward the point where it would come into view. He was nervous. He stood with his hands clasped. His mood had improved since breakfast, when the thought of telling Caroline about his intentions were at their height. He had obviously appeared uneasy at the table because his father had asked him what was wrong. Of course, he had answered, 'nothing at all', to which his father uttered a barely audible grunt. His parents knew that Caroline would be sensitive about his decision to remain on the Alliance, and they expected, that if her response was harsh, Devon would swim in a lake of misery for days to come.

Devon looked across the river at the shanties tucked away beneath the Wabasha Bridge, their sordid structures no better for the light of day. The lowland was a terrible place to live, flooded in the spring, snowed up in the winter, relieved from seasonal misery for only four months of the year. He was glad to be up on the hill where the river never reached them.

Shortly before the steamer came into view, Edmund Page arrived in a carriage drawn by a beautiful black horse, indicating that he would not allow the women to walk through town. He saw Devon straight-away, and after a hailed greeting he walked over to him and held out his hand.

"It's a grand day," Edmund said. "The ladies are coming home."

Mr. Page was attired in a three piece ditto suit and waistcoat, a linen shirt with a turnover collar, and a wide necktie tied in a bow. Devon felt somewhat inferior standing next to him, wearing a loose white shirt with billowed sleeves and wide-legged trousers.

"You have been injured," Edmund remarked.

"My arm was broken . . . right over there." Devon pointed to the approximate location where the fight between the Alliance boys and the boat men had occurred.

"Ah, so you were in that terrible scuffle."

"Yes sir."

Edmund nodded, glancing upriver. "My daughter will obviously have something to say about that."

"I am sure she will, sir."

He studied Devon with a rather pompous curiosity. "We haven't seen you for a while."

"I have been busy with the Alliance."

"Of course you have. And with Caroline gone, well . . . it's understandable." Then his face lit up. "Ah, here she comes."

The Promise

Devon glanced westward to where the river curved. There, emerging from the greenery, the *Antelope* appeared like an apparition, its white prow catching the morning sun, a spark of light glinting from her pipes. Its steam cock blew just then, two short blasts, and someone behind them shouted. "Steamboat a'coming." Then the commotion began.

"Caroline will be glad to see you," Edmund said. "Her letters indicated that she's been homesick. She misses you."

"Yes, I know."

"Well then. I expect we'll be seeing more of you now."

"With your permission, sir."

Edmund motioned to the carriage as the horse swished flies away. "You're invited to ride back with us. I'm sure Caroline will have a hundred things to say. She has been busy in Mankato. Not a day went by that she didn't have something interesting to do, with her cousins of course, the two girls and the boy, Samuel."

"Caroline told me about them."

"They're fine children. She is fortunate to have them as relatives."

As the boat moved slowly toward them, Devon began searching through the individual passengers lining the upper deck. It didn't take long to identify Caroline. She stood tall and straight, her arm waving in excited animation. A sudden longing sent quivers down his back. She wore a small hat with ribbon streamers, and a red, long-sleeved, bell-shaped dress. As the boat came nearer, her beaming smile appeared as broad as the river, as bright as the sun. Then, as the ship curved toward the landing, she waved her last and headed for the gangway, intent on being one of the first to disembark.

"Ah, it will be good to have them home again," Edmund said.

"No more making your own meals," Devon joked.

Edmund shook his head. "No. It is them. They can make a man feel like a king."

They waited patiently side by side as the steamer docked. Devon stood back a bit, to give Edmund the first opportunity to greet his family. He knew his ranking.

The landing had been a place of tension and pause only moments before, but now it clattered with sounds of horses and wagons and fleets of men as they surged toward the steamer. The ramp had been lowered. Passengers of all kinds, the tall and short, the gaunt and deep-tanned, those of hard muscles and those of simplicity had gathered on the deck in one great mass. Devon was sure he saw Caroline's red dress fluttering amid the throng. Then she came into view, and he felt the need for her like a craving for food. He would have run forward had Edmund not been standing next to him.

As the fleet of passengers shuffled forward, Caroline began her descent down the swing ramp, taking her eyes off him only long enough to observe her footing. Once ashore, the three women moved anxiously forward to greet the men they had left four weeks earlier. Bethany, in her haste, darted ahead of the others, her arms wide-spread like an eagle in flight. Edmund whisked her up and swung her around, and as they embraced, Caroline and Lillian came up behind her. Caroline's gaze was fastened on Devon even as she hugged her father. Then, at the appropriate moment, after the family had greeted one another, Devon moved forward to intercept the woman he loved. Immediately, Caroline drew him aside.

"I have missed you so," she said, taking his good hand in her own. She did not mention the cast on his arm.

Devon looked at the others a short distance away. "I want to kiss you," he said, maintaining a proper distance between them.

"As do I." Her eyes were cloudy with emotion, but reserved.

"It has been so long since I've seen you, a year perhaps, maybe two."

"I feel the same way. How long can a month be?"

"At times it seemed like an eternity."

Devon stood apart from her, at a respectable distance. Her father and mother would not approve of an emotional display in public. Even Edmund and Lillian refrained from displaying any sort of emotion with others nearby. They merely touched cheeks and exchanged smiles. Withholding emotion in public was a custom that Devon Finch would just as soon abolish.

"Is it sore?" she asked, touching his arm.

"Somewhat."

The Promise

Her lips stiffened, then relaxed. "You are a bad boy, Devin Finch, for getting into fights like that. I should have you flogged."

He laughed, answering the simulated pout on her lips. "Then go about it. I will accept your punishment."

Her face gleamed as she whispered. "I have something else in mind, later, when we are alone."

As the others approached, Caroline turned to greet them. "Can Devon can ride home with us," she asked.

Edmund grasped Devon's good shoulder and shook it gently. "I have already asked him. You three can ride in back. Mother and I will ride in front. Come, let's get the trunks. You can carry the smaller ones with your good arm."

When the trunks were loaded onto the back of the carriage, and strapped down securely, the four of them boarded. Immediately, Devon found Caroline's hand beneath the edge of her dress, and during the ride back to the Page house they could not keep their eyes off one another.

At the house, Devon helped carry the trunks inside, one to each bedroom. Devon had never been in Caroline's bedroom and he hesitated momentarily to glimpse the surroundings, the bedspread ruffled with lace, pictures on the wall, one of the family, another a country scene, white curtains, a varied-colored oval rug on the floor, woven with thick wool braids. A small table held a basin, a water urn, a collection of scents, a comb and a brush. He would remember the room that evening when he laid down on his own bed, wishing he were there beneath the ruffled bedspread.

While drinking hot tea in the living room, Caroline spoke about their time in Mankato, when they had ridden horses, and had picnicked on a sandbank near the Minnesota River, swimming in the shallow waters. The family dogs, Duke and Earl, whom they assumed were of royal lineage, romped with them throughout the day. They had taken long walks on the prairie above the hillsides, and had attended church, a wooden structure having only ten rows of benches on which to sit. They drank lemonade and warm milk, and ate enough at each meal to nourish them through the days. During one afternoon of the second week, soldiers from the Union army came and launched a hot air balloon from the middle of town as a means of enticing locals to join the newly formed balloon corps. The "grand bubble", powered by heated air, rose to a height of five-thousand feet amid the raucous cheers of the town folks. They had seen Indians on the prairie not far from town. Word had it that the Indians were in a terrible plight because of the drought. At night the girls reclined on a blanket and peered into the sky, wondering what was out there. The eldest of the family, a thirty-year old man named Kenneth, told them that someday man would venture into the void to find other worlds. No one believed him, not even his parents. A prairie fire gave them concern during the third week. They had watched the smoke for nearly a day, fearing it might come their way, but it never approached Mankato. It blew itself out on the third day.

There were more stories, but Devon didn't hear them all. His attention was on Caroline, and whenever their eyes met he felt a longing so strong that he wanted to leap up and take her into his arms. Her eyes sent a similar message, warming his silent passion. He remained at the Page house through noon lunch, until two o'clock in the afternoon when Caroline walked with him outside, hand in hand. Before they parted, she said, "Daddy has given us a present." Her face beamed with the announcement.

"What sort of present?"

"He has purchased a day trip to the Indian Mounds, a picnic for the two of us. The carriage will leave Bridge Square at nine o'clock tomorrow morning and will pick us up at four o'clock in the afternoon. We will have the entire day together. I will bring lunch. Isn't that wonderful?"

Devon beamed. "It is the best of news."

"Come for me early."

"I will be here at seven."

She scribed an invisible design on the back of his hand with her finger. "Have you ever been there?"

"Never."

"I know of a place where we can be alone, within a shelter of trees, with a beautiful view of the river."

He laughed a bit. "I will not sleep now, thinking of it."

"Tomorrow, then," she replied, touching his cheek.

"Yes, tomorrow."

✫ ✫ ✫

Devon and Caroline arrived at Bridge Square ahead of the other four passengers. The day trip would take them through Lowertown and up the steep hill to Dayton's Bluff, the majestic overlook above Carver's Cave. The morning sun had already lost its golden glow, replacing the night coolness with a breeze warm and comforting. The four-horse carriage arrived right on time. They boarded amid the company of two sisters from Uppertown, and a husband and wife recently arrived by steamer from Keokuk on their way west to stake a claim in the Dakotas. Devon and Caroline sat side by side. None of the passengers spoke much on the way, except to comment on the marvelous weather. All had food baskets and blankets with them. Dayton's Bluff drew good crowds on weekends, but this was a Tuesday, when most everyone was working. Devon and Caroline looked forward to peace and solitude, at a spot she had occupied twice before with her family, a site she considered to be a bit of heaven on earth.

The ride took about twenty-five minutes. When they arrived, Caroline was the first to step out. She grasped Devon's hand while hurrying to secure the location she had in mind. "Come," she said. "Before the others acquire our place."

They walked quickly between stands of oaks and maples, and through fields of wildflowers that beautified the ground with colors, red, and yellow, purple and orange.

"We're almost there," Caroline said, near breathless in her haste.

He held on to her hand, eager to be guided. His heart raced at the thought of being with her for several hours, just the two of them on this tree-decked hilltop where the ancient Indians had buried their dead in a series of mounds extending clear back to a point above the cave, thirty-nine mounds in all, many of which had been opened and plundered. The Sioux Indians had named the place, *Mni-za Ska dan,* meaning Little White Rock.

Caroline found the desired location soon enough, a huge oak tree whose roots flowed like wooden rivulets across a grassy knoll overlooking the river. There, away from others, they spread their blanket. Caroline snuggled quickly into his arms, and for a while they laid silently while looking at the broad river drifting south between the hillsides and isles, at the cloud-tufts suspended above the Kaposia bluffs, and at the unbroken land, seemingly untouched by man.

Devon had propped his back against the tree, allowing his broken arm to rest comfortably against his chest. Caroline lay at his right side, her head on his shoulder. They said little at first while enjoying the fresh breeze, allowing the sun to both warm and shadow them as the clouds drifted eastward with the gentle wind. He kissed her several times on the cheek when certain no one was watching. She purred, as would a kitten, while settling into his arms.

"I love it here," she said at length. "Isn't it a beautiful place?"

"It is."

"It will always be our place."

"Forever."

"I wish you could have been with me in Mankato. The days were so long without you. I missed you so much."

"As I missed you."

They watched the sky, the relentless movement of the clouds, a solitary steamer plying its way upriver, and the birds overhead. The wind off the land brought a distinct scent of woodland and water, the fragrance of summer. He had never felt so wholly content, or as fortunate, to have her at his side.

Sometime later they arose and walked the path alongside the mounds, to where they had been defiled. There, disturbed by the apparent destruction of such a sacred place, they retraced their steps, pausing to pick wildflowers, a small bouquet of yellow Lady

Slippers and Black Eyed Susan, two Wild Roses and Little Bursts of Sunshine. Their conversation was casual, and they avoided looking down at the city whose scar defiled the land, as if a beast had taken a bite out of nature. Grasshoppers greeted them, springing up from the grass, to land on their clothes and their arms, evoking laughter and scorn.

They paused to inspect a giant spider-web laced between tall weeds, marveling at its design, while wondering how a small, insignificant creature could create such a delicate device for trapping its prey.

"It is a work of art," Caroline remarked.

"No, it is a fiendish device intended to snare a victim."

"It has two purposes then, one to amaze, another to trap. I would rather see it as beautiful."

They lunched in the shade. Opening the picnic basket, Caroline brought forth napkins, good silver and cups, and when she placed them on the blanket it appeared to be a finely set table. They ate wine biscuits with wild plum jelly, grapes and blackberries, with a delicious tea served cold, some dried apples and molasses cookies. After they had finished eating, she packed the remains back into the basket. Devon couldn't have been happier, just the two of them together without a care in the world. He wished that the moment would last a lifetime. After lunch they sat by the tree again, and as the sunlight dimmed behind the clouds they reminisced about past events and school, and their times together, until the conversation acquired a different tone.

The topic had been on Caroline's mind throughout the day, and when she thought the time was right, she spoke directly, "How long are going to remain on the Alliance?"

The question took Devon by surprise. "I spoke to Chief Western, just yesterday. He will be offering me a place on the force if all goes well."

"What does that mean . . . if all goes well?"

"After the war, the boys will be coming home. There will be opportunity then. But I'll have to wait."

"The war could go on for years."

"Perhaps. We're not exactly winning the fight."

"I don't know if I can wait that long, Devon."

The statement rattled him. She was on the attack, for sure, and prepared for a fight. His first thought was to create a diversion. "I can't see into the future. No one can. If the war goes badly maybe the army might even come to get me."

"Would you go?"

"I might not have a choice. Right now they're counting on volunteers, but if the battles continue to favor the Confederates, who knows what might happen."

She snuggled tighter against him. "I hate to think of that. It would cause so much pain for either of us."

"Surely it would. But duty must be served."

She took his hand, pressed it tightly. "I hate that word, duty. Look what it's done to you, got you all broken up and beaten down, working those dreadful streets at night, consorting with the worst of humanity. You don't know how many nights I've laid awake wondering if you're safe down there in . . . in . . ."

"It's not as bad as you think."

"Oh, isn't it! I know what you're going through. I see the black and blue wounds, and the broken arm, and who knows what else beneath the clothing."

He sensed the subtle change in her voice, and in her abrupt words, each spoken with firmness, each one increasingly more desperate.

"I want you to promise me something," she said brusquely.

He followed the flight of a hawk as it soared above the river, and for a moment he felt like the bird, alone and without direction. "What is it?" he asked.

"I want you to promise me that you'll leave the Alliance come Christmas. I want nothing more than that, no present, no token, nothing of value, just your word."

He breathed deeply as she shifted her position. She looked directly at him. Her eyes glowed with a deep intensity, conveying a silent demand.

He spoke quickly. "Yesterday I told Western I intended to quit. Then he told me about some new information that might unlock the mystery surrounding Ingrid Lorgren's death. He asked me to stay on, to see if we could complete the puzzle. I said I would. I have made a commitment to him."

"What about your commitment to me?"

He drew her toward him but felt a slight resistance. "Hear me now. This I promise. I'll remain on the force until Christmas. Then I'll give you the present you want. I will leave the Alliance."

She shuddered, releasing her emotion. "I know what values mean to you. I realize that honoring your pledge is important, and I am nearly heartbroken to ask this favor of you. But I love you, Devon, and it hurts me time in and time out, to have you in such a dangerous place. I hear what happens down on the landing, from others, things you don't tell me."

"I don't want to upset you."

"I know."

"Christmas it is, then," he whispered. "Perhaps Western will allow me a proper position."

Caroline stiffened. "No! No policing."

"If not policing, then suggest something else?"

Her voice became more urgent. "My father will put you to work, or you will find employment with the newspaper, at your father's request. I cannot, and will not, put up with this . . . this . . . fright I carry."

"We'll see."

She eased away from him, putting distance between them, and then gazed at him as if he were a stranger. "You will find something proper," she stated emphatically.

He didn't want to argue, not in this peaceful place, nor anywhere. The thought of an outright quarrel disturbed him greatly. He replied, with a sense of defeat. "The promise will hold. I will find something proper."

She leaned into him again. "I don't want to complicate your life, Devon. I just want assurance that you'll be safe when I send you off to work, so I needn't worry about you for the entire day. Is that being selfish?"

"I know how you would feel. It would not be selfish."

"Aren't you fearful on the streets, in the saloons, near to those who don't care a whisker about you?"

"I am, sometimes."

She embraced him hungrily. "I love you. But I don't want to worry about you throughout our lives. I just have this dreadful feeling that someday your luck will run out, and you will be . . . ."

A tear came to her eye as he eased her forward. She nestled easily into his embrace, into a place of ultimate comfort. She cried silently for a while.

"I don't want to be the sort of woman that runs your life, or tells you which way to go, or what to do when you get there. It's just that this danger you're in has me worried sick that something dreadful will happen."

"It won't."

"I saw a man just the other day with only one leg. He could hardly get around. And last year, when that horrible fire destroyed so many structures, four policemen were terribly disfigured. Why, they weren't even firemen, Devon, just men who wanted to do their duty. I don't want something like that happening to you."

"I'll hold to my promise. I'll leave come Christmas."

"Christmas will be the deadline, then."

"Yes."

"Thank you."

He sighed "Then what?"

"I know something will come along that we can agree on. I want you out of the Alliance. I want you in a respectable job, one that is safe."

"What is safe? Men get hurt wherever they work, surveying, constructing, logging, anywhere. Life is unpredictable."

"Don't try to change my mind. We have set a date, and that's firm."

"And you'll lead me around like a horse?"

She stiffened defiantly. "No, Devon. I will not lead you. You can make your own choices in life. But if you stay with the Alliance, well . . . well, I might let go of the reins."

"Then we'll be through?"

"I did not say that."

"But you leave me no choice."

"On the contrary, the decision is yours."

She embraced him then, careful so as not to disturb his bad arm.

Devon didn't like the ultimatum, but he loved her so for caring about him. He was not concerned about quitting the force, only about finding suitable work that would not tie him to a desk, or have him listening to the clatter of presses throughout the day, or setting type endlessly hour after hour in a depressingly noisy room. Actually, he didn't know what he wanted, anything besides going to war, if war could be avoided. He knew the hardships one could encounter on a farmstead when depending on the weather, be it heat, or snow, or rain, or violent wind. Too much of anything could spoil a crop. He had heard of cattle dying for no reason at all. He had seen sodbusters in worn out clothes, and worn out wagons, and worn out wives, and sad-faced children who looked like walking dead. No. He wanted none of that. He wanted to be dependent on his own skill; at whatever profession he would chose, one that would include a good home for his family, and an income he could depend upon.

His depth of duty went deep, but not so deep that he would die for it. He wanted to marry Caroline and live out his days with her, and not fight for a cause that someone else deemed worthy. Randolph had different passions than he did. Randolph would follow the crowd, would take up the shout, and would lead the charge to whatever the end. Randolph had always been a leader. Devon wanted only to live a good life and watch his children grow into fine young men and women, and feel pride in his heart as they overcame their difficulties.

He eased Caroline into his arms as her body stirred with silent sobs. He kissed her cheek, content with the pressure of her body against him, content with her honesty and devotion. He would want it no other way.

They spent another hour in each other's arms, drifting into sleep at times while embracing beneath the huge tree that sheltered them from sunlight. Then they ate the remainder of the food, and drank the last of the tea, and watched the butterflies, the Monarchs and the Swallow-tails and the Mourning-Cloaks as they glided among the flowers.

When the wagon came at four, they climbed aboard and took the long downhill road back into the city, and walked hand in hand to the house where he said goodbye.

Her scent remained with him, and when he went to bed that night he could still detect it, there in the room, where the moonlight lay soft against him.

Four months remained until the holidays.

What would happen in four months? Would they find the person who killed Ingrid, or would the months pass without closure? The winter would be long and silent, cold and dreary, as always. He could not remember a winter being otherwise. Steamers would be unable to come upriver. Near March, the woodpiles would run low, as would food and medical supplies, and sometime during the bitter cold, a house or two might burn down, or someone would freeze to death, or influenza would arrive with a fury no one would be capable of stopping. The river would remain closed until April. Furthermore, sometime after December he would have to find suitable work to occupy his future, lest Caroline give up hope of his ever being man enough to support her.

Later, before his dreary thoughts led him into sleep, he prayed he would find a solution before year's end.

Until then, he would gamble his life, while awaiting a decision that only fate would decide.

CHAPTER TWENTY-FOUR

Sissy

Devon returned to the LaBelle saloon the following week. He arrived late on another rainless afternoon, shortly after one of the steamers had run aground downriver due to the low water. Upon entering, he received side glances and shrugs from those at the bar, a wave from several others. He took a table near where Flynn usually sat and waited near an hour before he showed up. Attired somewhat shabbily, Flynn walked right past Devon, giving him only a shrug, then sat down and began shuffling his cards while scanning the crowd for someone who might wish to challenge him. Devon remained seated, careful not to pay him much attention. Flynn sat patiently, smoking a cheroot, and whenever the door opened, he glanced to see who was entering. Before long he had two others at the table and the poker game began.

Devon felt strangely out of place. He didn't drink anything but sarsaparilla, and that sparingly. He felt conspicuous, sitting by himself, doing nothing. Soon he became restless and went outside as the red sun settled into the trees. He was just about to walk away from the place when a familiar figure turned the corner. Willius Kane held out his hand as he approached.

"Well, look at you," Kane remarked. "Who busted you up?"

"I got in a fracas right down there." Devon pointed toward the levee. "A river man broke my arm."

"I heard about it. Didn't know you was mixed up in that."

Devon snickered. "Fate has a way of dealing bad hands now and then."

"It surely does. Are you going inside?"

"I was already there."

"If you're willing to listen, I got something to say."

Devon pointed to the door. "I'll listen, if you talk."

"Let's go."

They went into LaBelle's and sat down at a table near the door. The piano player was hammering out *Rowdy Soul*, but no one appeared to be listening. Kane walked to the bar and ordered a whiskey, then returned to the table, tipped the glass to his lips and swallowed all of it in one gulp without as much as a grimace. Then he sat back and looked at Devon for a long while, as if silently questioning him.

"I went to see Western, that day we talked on the street." Kane looked straight down at the table. "We had a good talk, and I came away convinced that he didn't suspect me as having anything to do with Ingrid's death. I think he recognized me as an honest man, despite my reputation to the contrary."

"I'm pleased to hear that."

"He's more a man than I thought he was. He's the type who'll listen."

"That he does."

"He also told me that he has the name of another person who might know something about her murder. Might you know who that is, Devon?"

Devon tried to remain unruffled. His facial expression didn't change, nor did his posture, or the breaths he took. "No," he said. "He didn't tell me anything of the kind."

Kane snickered. "I think he was afraid that if he told me I'd kill the man, which I might, if he had anything to do with Ingrid's demise."

Kane would, without thought, without remorse, so the stories went.

"Are you gonna be spending time here?" Kane asked.

"Some. I've streets to patrol as well. But I'll be here."

"Then you might want to talk to Sissy. She's been as skittish as a hen near a wolf. She won't say a word to me. She might to you."

"Sissy?"

"You know who she is, the thin one with the long curls, and a forced smile. She hears everything, forgets nothing. Must have a thousand stories tucked away in that head of hers. Maybe you can force one of them out. You're not a threat to her."

"Huh, I ain't a threat to nobody."

Kane lifted the empty glass and peered into it. "I'll be gone for a time."

"Where to"

"Stillwater. The lumberjacks will soon be fellin' trees. Did you ever cross a river on foot and not get your feet wet?"

"I can't say that I have."

"Next spring you'll be able to walk across the Saint Croix without a drop of water gettin' on your boots."

"You'd do that?'

"Have before."

"Lumbering is dangerous work."

"Not more than anything else. Got your arm busted right down on the landing, didn't ya? It could have been worse. You coulda' been killed."

"Guess you're right."

Kane leaned back. "There's fresh air on the river. Pine smell so strong it can stay with you for an entire week, like perfume in your clothes. Besides, bringin' down trees builds strength in your legs and arms. It's better than standin' at a bar."

"I wish you luck then."

"Might need that, considering the men I'll be with. Bear strong, all of 'em."

"You'll hold your own."

"I always do."

Kane sat back in his chair just then and looked toward the staircase in the back. "Here comes Sissy."

Devon turned, just as the woman's shoe met the sawdust floor. She was dressed quite casually in a dark dress and a shawl of brighter color around her neck. Her arms were bare from the shoulders down. She glanced around the room, disinterested in what she saw. Instinctively, she walked toward the bar while gazing at the customers, her face solemn, her lips tight together. Then Kane gave her a slight wave of his hand and she came slowly toward them, her arms tight to her sides, her shoes scuffing through the sawdust.

She came up to the table and placed her hands on a chair back, then leaned forward to display her breasts, hardly contained within the dress. "Well, look who's here," she said. Her voice was soft, without a hint of emotion.

"Hello, Sissy," Kane replied.

She looked briefly at Devon. He grinned and nodded. She turned back to Kane. "Can I offer you boys anything today?"

"Just companionship." Kane replied.

She straightened, placing her hands to her waistline. "A girl can't make ends meet by just talking. I had more in mind, like a meeting with my sweet tuft."

"Not today, Sissy. Tell you what. Why don't you just sit down here and have a talk with Devon. He's a bit broken up, with his bad arm and all. He could use a voice other than my own. I'm going to the bar for another whiskey."

Sissy turned toward Devon. Her expression was one of indifference. She reached up and stroked a curl away from her forehead, and then eased onto the chair, making sure that her cleavage was properly exposed.

"You're the one got busted up down on the dock the other day. I remember you. You were Ingrid's friend."

"I am, and I was."

"She told me about you. She said you were a proper boy. So, what is a woman like me doin' in the presence of someone who won't accept my invitation?'

Kane laughed, got up, winked at Devon and then walked toward the bar.

Devon's concentration was difficult because of Sissy's closeness. Her breasts kept tugging at his eyes while the scent of fresh powder engulfed him with sweetness. He had to admit, she was quit a lure. He remained silent while gathering his thoughts. He didn't want to say anything that would send her packing. He had to draw her in careful like.

"I'm in quite of a fix," he began. "My arm's in a sling, and I'm as useless as a one armed juggler. I don't know what to do, except sit here and talk. My Ma wants me out of the house, lest I get in her way, and my father carps at me to get a job at the newspaper, which I don't want. Can you understand my frustration?"

"Guess so. I've got frustrations of my own."

"What are they?'

She sat back and glanced sideways, to where Flynn was playing cards, then back toward the bar where Kane stood. She wanted to talk, but said nothing for a while. There were no prospects for her, no one interested in going upstairs, nothing to occupy her time, so she started talking.

"Ingrid said you and her talked for quite a while one day. She said you were part of the reason she decided to strike west."

"Did she?"

"She and I were friendly, more than with the other girls. We talked a lot when business was slow. I knew her the best of anyone, 'cept Kane. He was her guardian."

"I know about Kane."

"Sometimes I wish I had a man like that, someone who'd watch over me." She looked directly at Devon. "Would you like the job?"

"I couldn't even if I wanted to. I'm betrothed."

"She told me you were."

"Word sure gets around."

"Secrets are hard to keep in a place like this. Mouths work faster than dancing feet. Words flow like whiskey. Everyone's got something to say, and someone to say it to, except when they're pleasuring."

Devon looked at her, saw the disillusionment in her eyes, the downcast expression, the faded opportunities, the same expressions he had seen in Ingrid's eyes. The past was there alright, hidden behind the powder and the lip rouge and the fancy curls. He wondered what went on in her mind, what thoughts she held, what secrets she retained.

"Where are you from, Sissy?"

"Now you're gettin' personal."

"Ingrid told me about her background, and I'm a right fine listener."

"Not much to tell."

"Well, I'm, listening. We have plenty of time on our hands."

"You're one for punishment," she cajoled.

Casually, she took a deep breath, smoothed out an imaginary wrinkle on her dress, and relaxed against the chair back. He could practically see her thoughts working while she rummaged for past visions.

"I can't remember much of my early years," she said straight out. "My father was German, born in a place called Mecklenberg, wherever that is. He and my Ma settled in Ohio, near a river where I grew up. I took schooling only until eighth grade. Then we moved west to take advantage of the free land. We built a sod house and had to live on the land for six months in order to get a grant. We didn't have any money. My father had to earn some, so he walked sixteen miles where he found work in the mines. He would come home on weekends to see his family, me and my two sisters, and my mother, who cried most of the time."

Sissy turned her head, took a deep breath, and then grinned at Devon as if to say, that's not the worst of it, there's more, so be patient with me. He looked into her eyes and saw anguish, hurtful memories, and lost dreams, the same as he'd seen in Ingrid's eyes.

"You don't want to hear about me," she said.

He shrugged. "I would, if you don't mind telling."

"It's a frightful story I'd just soon forget."

"Do as you please."

She sighed, glanced again at the bar, then at the floor, again at Devon. Her voice came gentle and soft.

"We had timber wolves howlin' in the mountains. On weekends, when Pa was home we'd walk with clubs in our hands just in case they'd come after us. Pa worked in the mines for a full year until he had enough money to buy a team of horses, a wagon and a hand plow. Then he started farming his land."

She paused, shrugged, and then tapped Devon's knee. "My story's like a thousand others. Sometimes it's like bringing up vomit."

"I'll listen, if you'll talk. Please, go on."

She picked at her fingernails. "I'm just a worthless woman, Devon."

"No you're not. Neither was Ingrid. Go on. I'm listening."

She tapped the back of his hand with her fingertips.

"Just when Pa started farming, the drought came. I don't remember much about it, 'cept my mother's tears. She cried so much I thought she'd end the drought. But we just kept on baking in the sun. Then came the sandstorm, almost covering our little sod house. Then it was the year of the locusts. They came like a storm, darkening the sky and they ate everything, even the coat my Pa had left outside on a peg. All was ate to the bare earth. The rattlesnakes were plentiful. We had no glass in the windows, only shutters. One day, when I was alone in the house, a rattler came in and bit my mother. By the time I ran out to get Pa, she was dead. It's all like a bad dream now, but after we buried her, it wasn't a month later that the snakes got my two sisters. There were three graves then, and I was alone with my Pa. I was fourteen, and we were penniless. Pa just gave up, so one day I just lit out on my own, and left him with the ghosts."

Devon reached over and lightly tapped her hand. She smiled, then rubbed at a scratch on the table top and looked away for a moment. The lamplight caught her eyes. She dampened her lips. "I walked east, then north, begged food, stole some, found work in an orchard where they raised apples, plum and cherry trees, black raspberries, currants, and strawberries. I put on some weight." She paused, withdrew her hands, and clasped them in her lap. "This is where I come to the present."

Devon waited.

"Never told this to anyone before, 'cept the girls."

"Your life story is safe with me."

"I've heard promises before."

"Well, I mean what I say."

Sissy nodded. "There came this boy one day, a handsome thing with a carefree attitude, big, strong arms, and a smile like sunrise. He took to me, and I was pleased to accept his kindness. He asked me one day if I wanted to go to paradise. I asked him what he meant, and he said he'd show me, all I had to do was go with him. Well, we found a place where we could be alone, and I learned all about paradise, how you could get there when a man and a woman's senses exploded during the act of pokin'. Well, he broke me. Then we did everything a man and woman could do to one another with a passion that nearly melted the ground under us. Never knew love like that before. It was paradise, for sure. Well, when he'd had enough of me, he took me to town and introduced me to his Aunt Belinda, only she wasn't his Aunt, she was a madam in a whorehouse, which I knew nothing about. I was young and dumb, and poked into numbness by then. He left me with her, then went off saying he'd be back in three days. Well, he never came back, so she put me to work doin' for men, whatever they wanted. And they wanted everything. Then I had a baby, a boy. He became a downright burden to me, so I gave him away. After a while, Belinda started hitting on me, so I went off again, found myself on the river, worked my way to St. Paul doin' favors for the boat men. When I got here, I found Mildred. Whores can always find work in a town like this."

"You've been wronged, all along the way," Devon said.

"Don't like men much. They're beasts, most of 'em. But every once in a while someone like you comes along, and I can't help but think that there's hope for us"

"Not all men are bad."

"They're few."

"You've got your share here. Kane is good. I'm good. Flynn, over there, is good. That's three."

She shook her head. "Only two are good."

"Two?"

"That gambler, Flynn, he ain't what he appears to be."

A catlike look formed on her face, that ferocity a cat gets just before it's ready to strike with its claws extended. His attention suddenly heightened. "I've spoken to Flynn. He just likes to play cards."

"He likes to batter women, too."

The statement nearly jolted Devon, but he held his amazement in check. "That's hard to believe," he said.

"Everything I've told you is true, even that."
"He doesn't seem the type."
"Can't tell you the things he does with a woman."
"Has he ever mistreated you?"
"Can't say, and won't say."
"Did he ever mistreat Ingrid?"
"You're searchin' now, ain't ya? Well, you just go right on searchin'. Sissy ain't gonna tell you nothin, 'cept that he's a two-faced polecat with a mean streak wide as this river."
"I never would have guessed it."

They sat quietly for a while, until Sissy became nervous enough to stand up. He didn't want her to leave. Not when his curiosity was soaring.

"What's the most beautiful thing you've ever seen?" he asked her.

"What kind of question is that?'

"It's simple enough. What's the most beautiful thing you've ever seen? Not a rainbow, or flowers, or a sunset, but something that convinces you that living is worthwhile."

"You're putting me on."

"No. Tell me what it is that makes you feel good?"

As she thought, he could almost see her mind working. Her expression was delicate, fixed on answering plainly and honestly. "I guess it's when a child smiles."

He sat back, and during a moment of silence he knew Sissy had feelings much like his own.

"Did my answer surprise you?" she asked

"Yes, it did."

"You didn't expect a woman like me to have feelings, did you?"

"I knew you did. The same feelings Ingrid had, deep down."

"Why do you keep mentioning her?"

"Because she had something good in her, like there is in you."

She laughed, tossed her head back, and then brushed him away with a wave of her hand. "You're a charmer for sure. Now tell me, what is your name?"

"It's Finch. Devon Finch."

"Like the bird."

"Yes, like the bird."

She glanced at Flynn again, who was shouting at one of his opponents, something about an improper bet. His voice was sharp, high-rising. He slammed his hand on the table, rattling the coins. The man he had shouted at sat back and said nothing, then reached over and tossed another coin onto the table, and said something about just making a mistake. Flynn settled back, his eyes burning with anger. Something about him raised concern again.

"Tell me more about Flynn," he said.

"Can't."

"Why not."

"Cuz it might mark me."

"Mark you as what?"

"Never mind."

"I don't repeat what I hear."

"It ain't that. I know there's devils marchin' across this land. If I tell you about him, one of 'em's certain to get me."

"I think you're wrong."

"No! Look at this." She held out her hand, folded her fingers inward and showed him the tip of her thumb. "I had a reading once, by a teller of fortunes. This teller rubbed charcoal onto my thumb and then pressed it against some paper. It showed the lines on my thumb, lines that he could read. He said the lines were the entire story of my life, and of all things yet to be. I never paid attention to my thumbs before, but there they were, the prints right in front of me. And he was pretty well accurate about what they said. One thing he told me was that he could see the future, and in it he cautioned me not to speak bad about anyone, no matter how serious it was. He said that if I did, the devils would come to get me, and carry me away into some dark place where I'd spend the rest of my life wishing I'd stayed quiet. No, can't speak badly of someone, no matter what they've done."

"What has Flynn done?"

She waved a finger at him." Didn't you listen? I said I couldn't tell you anything, only about myself. I don't want a devil overpowering me."

"Have you ever gone to church?"
"Who'd have me?"
"Those who believe."
"You're smokin' ground up leaves, Devon Finch. Why if I ever set foot inside one of those churches, they'd run me out. They'd never consort with a whore."
"Why don't you try."
She sat up straight, haughtily. "Are you some kind of preacher?"
"No."
"Then why are you talkin' about church?"
"Because it could change your life."
She stood up then, planted her hands right on her hips, and looked at him like someone who'd just been profaned. "That's all," she said. "Enough talkin'. Now if you don't want to come upstairs and take that trip to paradise, then go outside and talk to the river, because Sissy's all done talking. Good day, Mr. Finch."

She turned as he arose politely from his chair. She paused, then looked back at him and said, "Now ain't that nice, you standin' up for a whore. You're a priceless treasure, Mr. Finch, indeed you are."

She walked away, scattering sawdust with her shoes, past the bar, to the stairs where she turned. Then, with one foot on the step she smiled quaintly, grasped the handrail and went up.

He left the saloon and walked straight to the police station where he sat down with Western. They talked for about a half hour. He told Western about the things Sissy had said. Western told him to continue on, in exactly the same manner. Then he went home for a lunch of barley and corn chowder. He spent much of the afternoon reading and resting. The pain in his arm was steadily subsiding.

For supper that night they had frizzled beef, stewed red cabbage and Apple Charlotte for desert. They didn't speak much during dinner, except to mention the latest letter from Randolph, wherein he spoke of camp life and lonely nights and days of waiting for battle. Leastwise, he wasn't fighting, which made mother happier. When supper was over Harold belched, much to her displeasure. Then he sat back and began to talk about the newspaper.

"We're going to be hiring another pressman soon," he said. "More and more news is pouring in. There's talk about expanding the editions."

"That's good news," Devon said.

"There's plenty of opportunity at the Pioneer, if you just take hold of it. Why, the mission of the newspaper is becoming the vitalizer of society, the world's great informer, the earth's high censor, and the circulating blood of the human mind. At least that's what Samuel Bowels said about it. He's the editor of the Springfield Republican. We got his words hanging right in the front office for everyone to read. He said the newspaper is destined to mold the nations of the world into one great brotherhood."

Devon nodded. "Could be that the Confederates never heard of the newspaper then, the way they started this war."

"Think what you will, but the newspaper is becoming the greatest organ of social life in this country. The newspaper can send more souls to heaven, and save more from Hell than all the churches in New York, besides making money at the same time. And it was all started by just one man who borrowed five hundred dollars to rent a basement office, wherein he invented the most modern newspaper, the New York Herald. From that meager beginning he set a course for the rest of us to follow."

"He was a visionary," Devon said.

"Indeed he was. And now we got the telegraph, a fifty-thousand mile network going across the country, Kansas to the Atlantic, San Francisco to New York. It's one of man's greatest achievements. It's also unfortunate that the insulation failed in the trans-Atlantic cable. If it hadn't, we wouldn't have to rely on news being carried by packet boats. And now we got telegrams, those short, spicy messages that can be inserted into our newspapers"

Devon listened. He didn't say anything in return.

"You've got to get aboard, Devon. No use waiting until Christmas. Now's the time. I can't impress on you the urgency of the matter. Why, literacy among the Northern whites is now about eighty-percent, thanks to the newspapers that quadrupled between 1825 and 1860. On the eve of the war there were over two thousand papers, twice as many in the north as in the south. Are you interested yet, Devon?"

"Yes, I am father. But I must carry out my pledge. Then I'll think about another career. Working for a newspaper might be one of them."

"I'd be proud to have you follow in my footsteps."

"I might."

"Listen now. I'm going to tell you about progress. First we had the Hoe Lightening rotary steam-powered printing press, thirty-four feet high, fed by eight sheet-handlers, which could spit out twenty-thousand impressions an hour. Now the Tribune has developed a technique for casting lead printing cylinders from a papier-mâché mold of type. Presses will run faster. Why, duplicate cylinders can be quickly made and mounted to other presses to increase the run for special editions. Some have already mastered the process. It will only take time before we have it here in Minnesota."

Devon had gone through his father's plant, had seen the newspapers being set up and printed, and had thought it amazing. He remembered how the pressman would lay a single sheet of paper on top of an inked type-form locked into the bed of the press, then lower the pressure platen, then carefully release it and lift the paper away. The impressions on two pages would be left on the sheet and, when the ink had dried, it would be flipped over and placed back in the press to print two pages on the other side. When folded it produced a four-page newspaper. The work was tedious and time-consuming, and it left the smell of ink imbedded so deep into a man that someone standing next to him would certainly know he was a printer.

"There'll come a day when we'll be able to print photographs and not just drawings" Harold said, bringing his talk to an end.

"I might well be a printer." Devon said casually.

"Soon, I hope. The opportunity is endless. I think Caroline would like you to settle down into a reliable position. As for the pay, why a New York staffer for the Tribune is already earning as much as a Captain in the Union Army, roughly twenty-seven dollars a week, far better than policeman or firemen are earning while putting their lives on the line. And the executive office of the

Herald is already making more money than members of President Lincoln's cabinet who are earning eight-thousand dollars a year. Now that's good compensation."

"It might be, for a New York staffer, but not for a common pressman."

"One doesn't have to stop at being a pressman."

"Few rise to the top."

"Aye, but it could be you. It could happen to anyone with gumption enough."

"I'll give it serious consideration."

Harold beamed. "I would like nothing better than to have my son working alongside me. Why the Tribune now has over two hundred employees, twenty-eight of whom are editors. This city will continue to grow, Devon. In the years to come we'll be as large as the Tribune, of that I am sure."

As Nona began clearing the dishes, Harold asked, "Did you have an eventful day down by the levee?"

To that, Devon shrugged. "The day was boring enough to forget."

✯ ✯ ✯

Toward the end of August the rivers dropped to disturbingly low levels, the Minnesota River being the lowest. The lightest draught boats could barely make their runs. Crops continued to fail in the south, despite many cloudy days. All the rain fell elsewhere.

In Saint Paul, the grass crackled underfoot when walked upon.

CHAPTER TWENTY-FIVE

Railroad a'comin'

September brought cooler weather. The month began with temperature readings in the mid-seventies. An early hint of autumn set in after the first week, bringing a chill, reminding the citizens of what lay ahead. Soon afterwards, people began talking about a locomotive named William Crooks coming up river on a barge towed by a steamer. With the river level so low, most everyone thought the barge might get grounded on a sand bar, or, if it did arrive, the water at the levee would be so low that workers would be unable to move the locomotive ashore.

For some time, talk had been circulating about a railroad line between St. Paul and Chicago, a four-hundred mile run intended to replace much of the river traffic. Goods and equipment would arrive faster and more frequent than on riverboats, especially during winter months when the waters were frozen. Hopes were high that a railroad would bring further prosperity to the city.

Early in the second week rain began falling across the state. The Mississippi began rising as it gathered water from its many tributaries. Within two days the fears about offloading the locomotive began to wane. Word had it that the barge was already in Lake

Pepin. When it docked at Lambert's Landing, Saint Paul would certainly envision the future.

Riverboat traffic became less frequent than in previous months, diminishing business at the LaBelle. Devon had not spoken to Sissy since the day they had sat together. Kane was gone. Flynn was idle on some nights, so he just sat alone, shuffling cards and drinking. Devon began noticing his frustration, the way his lips pursed, the way his hands fisted, the way he mumbled to himself, and swore under his breath. Devon tried twice to engage him in a conversation, but each time Flynn just shook his head and told him to go away.

The women spent less and less time on the floor. During the day they went shopping, and at night they often appeared on the streets, silently taunting the men. They kept busy with personal things. When someone asked them for a poke, they willingly obliged. Devon assumed they were thankful to give their bodies a rest.

He was on his way home on the night before the William Crooks was scheduled to arrive. A light rain had fallen earlier and the streets were glistening wet, as muddy as river bottom. Even the lamplights appeared dreary.

✡ ✡ ✡

On the following morning, September 9th, he was awakened by the sound of a riverboat, the clanging of bells, and the screaming of whistles. He knew at once that the William Crooks had arrived.

He ate his breakfast hurriedly, and ran halfway toward the landing when he heard the fife and drum band playing a rousing march. The city appeared to be in a gay mood. Flags flew from nearly every store. Crowds had formed before he reached Bench Street. Groups of people, businessmen, and ladies dressed in bright frocks, stood close together, their children among them. Devon couldn't get closer than where Perkins and Company had their Grocers and Commissions Market. Then he saw the steamer *Alhambra,* pulling a cadre of three barges, two with handcars and fifty tons of tracks aboard, and another bearing the stately locomotive, William Crooks.

At first he just stood in awe of its size and grandeur, its color and majesty, while studying its massive maroon drive wheels, the round headlamp ahead of the chimney, its bright red lead wheels, and its gold-leafed name-board, with the designation, *Wm Crooks,* on its side.

He wormed his way closer, through the crowd, excusing himself.

Ahead, on a raised platform, a group of politicians attired in black suits and waistcoats, top hats, and ties with jewelled cravats waited patiently. Likely, Mr. Page was there, or at least located somewhere near them. At the edge of the landing, three Daguerreotype photographers had set up their cameras. He recognized the Mayor and Chief Western, who stood close to a small cadre of musicians. Other officials were gathered near the edge of the landing close to the wooden platform. There would be a speech for sure. Someone would surely talk about the magnificent machine, soon to become part of the Saint Paul scene. Minutes later a man ascended the stage and tipped his hat to the crowd. Devon could hear most of his words, except those carried away by the wind.

The man spoke of land that became available after the Louisiana Purchase, and the desire to build a transcontinental railroad following the discovery of gold in California, and how a faster route was needed in order to bring people and freight into the area east of the Pacific Ocean. He spoke of government sponsored crews that had been dispatched to survey four possible routes through the wilderness; routes that would bring the promise of economic riches to all parts of the country. He explained, that no single route had won Congressional backing, and that, in 1853, Congress appropriated sufficient funds to undertake additional surveys. As a result, four main expeditions fanned out across the west at various parallels to survey and gather information on the general nature of the country. The information gathered by surveyors, scientists and over a dozen artists, was presented to Congress between 1855 and 1856, and, as a result, hundreds of prints and maps were produced and thousands of reports were published. The effort created the most extensive source of knowledge on Western geography and history ever compiled. Now the railroad had arrived, and Saint Paul would become an important hub within the grand design. The William Crooks, built for the Saint Paul and Pacific Railways by the New Jersey Locomotive and Machine Company, would initially run between Minneapolis and Saint Paul, and eventually to the west coast port of Seattle. Saint Paul would become a vital city, lending its talent and resources to provide a road to the future on rails of steel.

When Devon heard it all, he nearly shivered in his shoes. The imagination of a railroad running all the way to the Pacific Ocean tingled every inch of his body. Now that was something he could get his fingers into. Railroading! The sound of it was enough to make him want to charge forward and shout out his desire. But his zeal was premature. His arm still needed healing. Tracks still had to be laid. Stations would have to be built. The cliff face below the Indian Mounds would have to be removed to allow for a roadbed, and on, and on; thousands of miles to be covered. The task seemed too immense to comprehend. Perhaps next year when the run into Minneapolis was complete, then the time would be right. The railroad would open up an office somewhere in Uppertown, and eventually they would begin their search for just the right people. What would Caroline think about that?

He spent the remainder of the hour reviewing the engine, observing its silver steam chests above the boiler, its eighty-six inch drivers, its red Tender imprinted with the abbreviation, *1st Divn. St. P & P.R.R.*. Indeed, Saint Paul had come of age.

Yes, he thought, railroading might easily capture his future.

✯ ✯ ✯

He saw Caroline three nights that week, two of which were spent inside her house, another up behind the Capitol until a chill hustled them home. He spoke to her about the railroad. She had already heard her father talk about the grand opportunities that would open up for those interested in giving of their time and talent. Her father had even mentioned Devon's name during the conversation. In the end she was not opposed to something of the kind. Her only worry was that the railroad would take him away for weeks on end, to far reaches of the country, some of which still teemed with savages.

✯ ✯ ✯

The river continued to rise, though slowly, and the William Crooks sat on the barge waiting for the time when it could be moved off onto its own tracks and into the large shed, recently constructed. It would be off-loaded by winter, of that they were certain. The laying of track had already begun between Saint Paul and Minneapolis,

They received another letter from Randolph. He was feeling better, eating more nourishing food, and was learning more about the army and its methods, its huge amount of resources, and how broad the country was, at least the part he was in. Again, he didn't write of conflict, only of routines, and his desire to be home again. He said he was learning to play the Jaw Harp, one of the oldest instruments in the world, a device made of a bamboo reed attached to a frame that one placed in the mouth between the parted front teeth. Music was made by plucking the reed, and pitch was attained by altering the amount of air held within the mouth. Devon had heard Jaw Harps down on the levee. They made strange music for sure. Randolph mentioned that they were about to move to an unknown location, and he told them to offer prayers for his safety.

About a week passed before Devon returned to LaBelle's. He went in, not intending to stay, but Sissy caught his eyes and came over. She sat down, leaning toward him so he could delight on her fine breasts, and she told him a thing or two.

"See that man over there," she said, pointing to a lonely figure far back in the room, who was sitting with another of the girls. He was a sad looking man with gray hair and an unkempt beard. He held a pipe tightly between his teeth where it gave off a flicker of smoke when puffed.

"Who is he?" Devon asked.

"Don't know his name, but I know that his wife and kids up and left him about three weeks ago. They just packed up and walked out. Nobody knows where they went."

"Why?"

"Because he lost his home to Flynn, in a poker game."

"Lost his house?"

"Yep, the whole of it, furniture, beds, pictures on the walls, everything, even the outhouse. A lot of money was layin' on the table, and the man thought he had a winning hand, but not enough to stay, so he bet his house."

"And he lost."

"To a straight flush. Now ain't it strange that Flynn would have a straight flush against a full house, aces high. Don't make sense."

"Poor fella."

"So his wife and kids up and left, and now he ain't got nothin' but misery. He just sits around feelin' sorry for himself, does odd jobs about town. He lost his job at the saddler because he stayed home trying to convince his wife not to go. But she pulled out anyway, despite his pleading, searchin' for something different, or someone more sound of mind who wouldn't bet his house on a poker hand."

"It's a sad thing."

Sissy pulled in closer in order to whisper. "Worse yet, Flynn wouldn't allow him to live in that house after he won it. I heard that he gave the family three days to pack up and get out. Then he took it over. Strange thing is, he just left the house sittin' there empty, with nobody in it. Now that's a devil if I ever saw one. I don't know what that poor man is going to do when winter comes. Maybe by then he'll just walk over the hill and disappear."

"I didn't think Flynn would be that heartless."

"He ain't got a heart."

"What makes you say that?"

"Because I know him."

"Tell me about him then."

"I ain't sayin'."

"Are you afraid the devil will get you?"

"Something of the sort." She kicked at his chair with her shoe and gave off a weak smile. "Maybe someday I'll get up enough nerve to strike out like Ingrid was wantin' to do. Maybe someday I'll go back east before I get too old. There must be someone back there lookin' for a woman like me."

"Why would you leave?"

She looked down at the floor, scribbled a path through the sawdust with the toe of her shoe. "Because if I don't the devil's gonna get me."

"I wouldn't put much faith in what a man said about your thumb print."

"It ain't just that."

"What is it, then?'

She kicked at him, struck him on the ankle. He flinched. "Don't keep on questioning me. Talkin' is one thing. Prying into my life is another. I'll tell you what I want to tell you, and that's all." She shook a finger at him. "If I got things to say, I'll say' em, otherwise I just keep my mouth shut. I gotta go now. I see someone who's anxious to go traveling around the world. He likes trips like that."

She left him and paraded right over to the bar and took hold of a man dressed in buckskin, whose face was half covered with hair. He gave her a kiss on the hand, and pinched her lightly on the rear, then concentrated long and hard on her breasts so generously displayed. After he tossed down his remaining whiskey, he slapped her on the rump and walked off toward the staircase holding her hand.

Why was Sissy so fearful? Was it in some way connected to Flynn? Certainly it didn't have anything to do with the murder. Flynn had been playing cards that night, sitting right there at the table while Ingrid's throat was being cut. Or maybe she just wanted to tell him about the other man inside his skin, the man few others knew, the man who just sat dealing cards, a man with a veiled personality, visible only to whores.

Devon was certain of one thing. He would continue talking to Sissy for as long as she was able to give of her time. Maybe something deep down in her conscience was waiting to come out, something fear had prevented her from telling.

He left LaBelle's soon afterwards, more confused than when he entered.

CHAPTER TWENTY-SIX

Tears, trauma, and truth

Saint Paul remained warm as September neared its end. Indian summer had been glorious, unmarked by violence, except for a fight at the National Hall Saloon when a drayman and a cigar maker mixed it up. The drayman was struck with a stone, his head dreadfully cut, his face laid open down through his upper lip. Devon had accompanied the man to the hospital.

On the hillsides, the trees erupted with blazes of yellow, gatherings of red, brilliant greens and rustic browns, mixed and arranged with nature's patient hand to make of them a pallet rich with tints and shades and blushes that, when looked upon, took a persons' breath away. Autumn was Devon's favorite time of year, not only for its beauty, but also for the memories it contained, for there had been times through the years when he and Randolph had taken long walks along the river and had played in the caves, and had lain on the hillsides to talk, to reveal secrets, to discuss the world as they knew it, and to toss stones for distance. Devon could remember it all especially on balmy days when the sun was bright. He imagined Randolph at his side then, especially when looking across the river at the blazing hillsides rich with summer's ending.

Color appeared on the streets as well. Ladies were dressed in bell-shaped day dresses with wide pagoda sleeves and high necklines adorned with lace, tatted collars or chemisettes, a common sight when the sun vanished early and night came on with a slight chill.

Devon and Caroline enjoyed an evening of dancing at Market Hall. By then he was exercising his arm frequently, strengthening it, hoping to have the cast removed by the middle of October.

Frost came on October first, and within days the leaves began dropping in number. Tinkers were seen frequently as they darted through the streets with stove pipes under their arms. Glaziers were busy with putty and glass. The cost of oak wood had risen to $4.50 a cord. Wood came into the city, wagon load after wagon load, to be stacked along the streets in preparation for the long winter. The melancholy days of autumn were nearly over, and in the public market, butchers were cutting up a five-hundred pound bear that had been killed just beyond the city near Phalen Lake. The bear meat was gone within a single day.

Nothing of note happened at the LaBelle saloon those first weeks in October. The steamers came and went daily. At times three or four lay side by side at the landing. The William Crook had been off-loaded and was nestled within its shelter, awaiting tracks that would take it to Minneapolis come spring.

Sissy was busy day and night, accepting customers at a steady pace. Flynn was always engaged at the table, winning or losing, but always coming out ahead when the last card was played. His opponents, the ones who walked away from the table with money, considered it a grand conquest, for he was a difficult man to beat in a card game. Flynn displayed his anger only once during that time, following the loss of a pot. He just sat in his chair, still as a stone, his face reddened with rage, his breathing hard and steady, his lips tightened like the snarl of a cur dog. The other men just waited for him to calm his demons, for they knew his moods better than others. Devon sensed bitterness in him then, a mean streak that could explode in violence if ever unleashed. But following his minutes of silent rage, Flynn went back to gambling as if the irritation had never occurred.

During the middle of October, the steamer *City Bell* was scheduled to go on a moonlight excursion down the Minnesota River to Shakopee. A band would play. Refreshments and hors de oeuvres would be served. The day temperatures were in the mid-seventies, perfect weather for an outing. Two days before the sailing, Devon had his cast removed so he and Caroline decided to celebrate. They signed on for the river cruise, paid a fee of one-dollar per couple, and at six o'clock in the evening of October 15, the *City Bell* set course into the river.

They mingled with the passengers, most of who were from Uppertown; men in jackets and ties, the women in dresses with low necklines and short sleeves, hands covered in short gloves or crocheted fingerless mitts. When dancing, they were a whirl of color, the men elegantly polite, and the women demure and laughable. Caroline and Devon stayed near the edge of the crowd, dancing on the sidelines away from the fanciful and the wealthy. They knew some of the people aboard, those older than themselves, one couple who worked with Caroline's father, another, a businessman who ran a small shop in Lowertown.

Devon felt like a new man when he was dancing with Caroline that night, his right hand in her left, his other on her waist, the two of them whirling in time with the music. Caroline was happy, smiling and gay, for it was the first time she had been alone with Devon for weeks. By some means the moonlight, and the river, and the music, and the gayety brought her close to him, perhaps closer than they should have been, and when her emotion was aroused, she took his hand and led him outside onto the deck where they stood arm in arm at the rail while looking out at the moon-streaked water. They managed to steal a brief kiss now and then when others weren't present, when the night sky enveloped them in a coverlet of wonder.

During one such interlude she said to him, "Oh, Devon. I shall remember this night forever."

"As will I," he replied.

"It's like another world? I feel like a queen on my royal barge, afloat on a magic river that will take me to paradise."

"I feel the same."

"This night will herald the beginning of a new life for us. Soon it will be December and you will be free of your duty, and we will set a new course."

"We will."

Her eyes sparkled with moonlight. "Nothing will sway you from your promise, will it?"

"Nothing."

She held him tight. "Oh, Devon, I dream of the day when we will be together as man and wife."

"Remember when I told you how I felt that day the William Crooks came upriver on the barge, how grand it was, how filled with adventure I was."

"I remember."

"I've been giving it thought lately, and each time I become more and more convinced that my future is in railroading."

"But you know nothing about it."

"Only that it will span our continent, and grow and grow, until it is linked to the whole of our country, until it is the preferred means of transportation, to replace even the steamboats. We in Minnesota will be only days away from the ocean, a trip that now takes months to accomplish. No more wagon trains. The telegraph will be going along with every line of track, to knit the country together as a whole. I am thrilled every time it crosses my mind."

He was like a small boy whenever he talked about the railroad, for it was like a new toy to him, something that had excited his imagination, a dream that had taken him to places seen only in his mind.

Caroline, however, hoped the wonder of it would fade with time so he would be satisfied with something of less proportion, something that might not take him away for days on end, to distant places where danger lurked.

She pouted a bit, and then spoke her mind. "But the railroad will take you away from me, for who knows how long."

"I will get a post here in Saint Paul, or somewhere nearby, close to you and our children."

"A boy and two girls."

"Two boys and a girl."

They laughed and held tight to one another, and when no one was about they kissed briefly lest someone would see them. She wanted so much to be alone with him in a room together, in a place where he could remove her dress and stroke her body, and lay her down softly, and make love to her. And whenever he was in her arms for a brief moment or more, he felt the same driving need to strip away her clothing and look upon her naked body and immerse himself in her embrace, to feel the joy of entering her, to thrill to the sound of passion.

They went ashore at Shakopee, near a place still housing members of the Dakota tribe. The town had been named after the Indian chief Sakpe (Shock-pay) and was now being developed as one of the many stops on the trade route. At midnight, the place was quiet, its houses and businesses shadowed by moonlight.

They had docked at a pier near a flat stretch of land bordering the river, and there they walked a while, gazing out across the immense body of water to the looming hills in the distance, the moon shaded by a light haze. They could not be alone because many others were near them, so they strolled slowly and took in the nostalgia of the place before boarding about a half hour later to begin the return trip to the city. They danced again, and ate bread and cheeses, and small cookies garnished with a meat paste made of liver. By three o'clock they were tired, so with a shawl around her shoulders they stood at the rail until cool air sent them inside. By four the boat was quiet. Most had found seating. Some played cards in the lounge. Others who had brought warmer wraps strolled silently along the decks. Caroline and Devon were fortunate enough to find an unoccupied bench near the bow. There, she found comfort in his arms.

They arrived at the Page house just as Edmund was going off to work.

That day they slept until mid-afternoon.

✯ ✯ ✯

The news report was brief, not much more than a few lines in the newspaper, hardly enough to raise interest. The article stated that on October twenty-first, the Minnesota Volunteer Regiment had made a crossing at Goose Creek, and were lightly engaged at a place called Edward's Ferry near a point of land called Ball's Bluff. The report went on to say that the Regiment was removed from the main fighting by several miles. Although it was a rather insignificant piece of news, it would shake the Finch family to the core.

Ten days later, on a bright and pleasant day, Nona Finch received a letter in the mail from a private in the Regiment. The envelope was addressed to the family of Randolph Finch.

The letter read:

Family Finch,
I have been acquainted with your son but a short time, and have tended and messed with him. I can say for a fact that he is the most true-hearted, free-spirited man I have ever met. He neither quarreled with anyone, always helped those in need, nor never shirked his duty. I am saddened to say that he fell at Ball's Bluff during a light skirmish. Those of us who survive mourn his loss. I do not say this from any feelings of adulation because you are his mother, but from the firm conviction of my mind and sentiment.
Of his personal effects, I do not know. He had no value on his person, and no money, save for a lock of hair in a packet over his heart, which I return to you now.
I believe he might have some pay due him, his bounty and some on clothing account. In order to receive what was due to him, you will have to inquire of Mr. Fred Olmstead, Agent for the Sanitary Commission in Washington D.C. who will inform you graciously, and obtain settlement for you, free from all costs.
Please accept my sorrow for your loss. Randolph Finch was the best of men. God bless his soul. I remain with respect, yours truly,
Private, enlisted, Corry Yardham of St. Anthony, Minnesota
October 23, 1861

Devon came home early in the afternoon that day after completing his morning watch. When he entered the house he found his mother sitting alone in the parlor, her head to one side, her hands clutched to a piece of paper. She looked up, sighing deeply, tears tracking her face from eyes filled with anguish. He went to her, knelt down, and took her hand. As she raised the letter to him, he knew exactly what it was. He didn't have to read it..

"Randolph is gone," Nona sobbed.

Devon felt the impact deep inside his body, where his heart was, an avalanche of sadness so gut-wrenching that he could hardly move. He clutched her as a child would when seeking comfort. His tears came, matching hers, and together they wept, feeling anguish like a fire inside their bodies. Sometime later, he pulled away from her and stood up. He took the letter in hand and read it line for line, unable to contain his sobs.

"I want you to get Harold," Nona said, wiping her face. Her voice was amazingly coherent. "He should be home with us now. Please get him for me?"

Devon straightened, scrubbed the sorrow from his face. "I'll get him, mother." he said. "Will you be alright?"

"I will be fine," she muttered. "The worst of it is over. Now go."

Devon left the house. Outside, even the sun scowled. The gray sky above stretched away as far as he could see, a solemn blanket filled with nothing but gloom. Randolph, dead? God, no! The news was beyond belief. His brother, gone!

He hardly knew he was walking, so deep were his thoughts. He recalled clearly the last day he had seen him, before he departed on the steamer. They were face to face that day, and it seemed as if Randolph had acquired a new personality. He said he had learned a thing or two, and that he had made contact with a new guidance that calmed his fear. And he had said he would be ready if death came to take him.

The words had sounded unrealistic then, coming from Randolph, because he had always been a kindly and laughable boy who never seemed ready to look beyond the daylight. But there had been a well of depth in his expression that day. The glint in his eyes had vanished, as if he were possessed with a new command, a captivating power that had taken away his youth, his exuberance, and his personality. His final words had been: *'Don't worry.*

The Lord will march with me.' Devon imagined that the boys in uniform talked about dying when seated around the campfire, what it would be like in battle, and how they would face the enemy. Or did they laugh and sing, while trying to escape the oncoming horror? Randolph would have wanted to laugh. Laughter had always been Randolph's companion.

When he reached the large, wooden building housing the *Pioneer and Democrat,* he went directly inside. The Editor, Mr. Pothen, was seated at his desk, working on copy. He grinned when he saw Devon. But the smile diminished quickly when he saw the grief on Devon's face.

"I have come to get my father," Devon said straight out.

Mr. Pothen arose from his chair and reached for Devon's hand. "What's wrong, son?"

"It's my brother, sir. He's perished."

Pothen wobbled slightly, and then stepped back. "Oh, praise the Lord, no."

"It's true, sir."

"I'll get him, lad. Sit down. Sit down."

Devon took a chair next to the desk where the unmistakable scent of paper and ink lingered, the same scent that came home with his father each night, as would a cowman or a boiler tender, or a druggist carry on their clothes. Each had a distinctive scent.

His father came, wiping his hands on a cloth. Devon stood to meet him. It took only a second for Harold to identify the pain on Devon's face. He knew Devon would not have come unless something was amiss.

"What is wrong?" Harold asked.

"It's Randolph. He's gone to heaven."

Harold dropped the towel. His face went ashen. Then, as his arms wrapped Devon in a strong embrace, his breath stuttered. Emotion quivered inside his body. Then he issued an awful moan, an interrupted sob, and then a gasp of sorrow as the dreaded reality struck his heart.

"We got a letter." Devon sobbed. "He fell at a place called Ball's Bluff."

Harold moaned. "I remember setting the type."

Tears, trauma, and truth

"Mother wants you to come home."

Mr. Pothen's voice came instantly. "Go home, Harold. Someone else can finish. Go home."

Harold removed his apron and placed it on the chair, said goodbye to Mr. Pothen and walked out the door with Devon. They had taken only a few steps when Harold asked, "How is mother doing?"

"She's as good as can be expected. She's mighty sad."

"She well should be. I expect she'll be caught up in memories for a while. You'll have to be understanding about her grief. Mother's carry a much heavier burden than men do. I can only imagine what it must be like for her."

"She seemed to be alright when I left."

"She will seem so. That is her way. But I know how she's hurting inside. She lost a daughter right after its birth when you were only three years old. The child didn't make it through the second day."

"I didn't know that."

"Her name was Lillith. She was spoken of when you were younger. You probably forgot. It's something one doesn't cling to."

They walked on through the streets, muddying their shoes. Devon was amazed at how stalwart Harold appeared, showing little sadness, though he felt it deep in his bones. Harold wiped his eyes twice, cleared his throat another, spoke in short sentences about their place in life, things like respecting Nona's silence, helping whenever necessary, avoiding arguments even though she might shout at them from time to time to release the misery. As men, they'd have to help her along through the mournful period when she'd be wearing black, through the bitter days, as he called them.

"I've been burying people since I was nine, first my Uncle, then my father, then my mother and my sister Verna. Some shot, some dead with influenza, my sister from an angry bull that ran her down. Always someone you love, so it seems."

"I didn't know."

"Things like that are better left unspoken."

"I'll do my best, father."

"I know you will. But things like dyin', especially when it's kin, can scar a woman for life, scars nobody can see because they're on the inside."

They were silent again, each with their own thoughts and memories, the good outweighing the bad.

Devon remembered the day he and Randolph had dug a dirt cave into the side of a hill, deep enough for them to crawl into. They had dug it with their hands, and with an old shovel they had found near one of the wood piles, prying out stones and rolling them downhill into the small stream below. When the cave was finished they crawled inside and laid side by side on their stomachs while peering into the valley below, where the stream meandered south into the city. When it began raining they thought it best to stay inside until the storm ended. But the storm prevailed, with fierce lightening and a growling sky. Then, just as the sun made an appearance they began crawling out of the hole. As they did, the roof collapsed. Randolph stepped out safely. Devon was less fortunate. The mud pinned him from the chest down. He recalled the weight on him, that horrible feeling of entrapment. He had shouted instantly for help. He remembered Randolph turning around, his face ashen with fright. And he remembered how Randolph had clawed away at the dirt, like a man gone mad, digging and throwing mud and crying all at the same time. And he remembered being pulled out, and being swept into Randolph's arms, and he remembered his brother saying, "*I gotcha. Good Lord, I gotcha. You'll be alright now.*" Randolph had hugged him for a full five minutes after he was freed. Oh, good Lord, could anyone have had a better brother than he? The memory was so strong that he broke down just as they reached the house. He stood for a while beneath his father's arm and cried it out. Then the two of them went inside to where Nona sat.

She was still in the chair where Devon had left her, the letter in her lap. She looked up when they came in and held her arms out to them, and while Harold knelt at her side, cradling her head on his shoulder Devon stood behind them and cried.

Devon didn't know how long they remained there, crying out their misery, but when the tears ebbed, Harold said, "It's time to

Tears, trauma, and truth

get back to living now," and with that simple statement, he and Nona arose and went about their business.

However, the misery was not enough for Devon. He still had one duty to perform, something perhaps his brother would deem unnecessary. But it was necessary to Devon's way of thinking. The letter was already stained with tears, some of its ink smudged. The lock of Pricilla Udahl's hair lay beside it, still wrapped in cloth.

He picked up the hair lock and turned to his father. "I have to take this back to Pricilla," he said.

"Why?"

"She has to know. I'll take the letter as well."

Harold nodded. "Then go."

As Nona prepared the evening meal, Devon left the house. The rain had ceased. The city appeared sullen and dirty, as if color or sunshine would never again brighten its grimness. The mud made walking difficult. He slipped twice going downhill but didn't fall. With every step he took, his anger increased. Ever since the day he had seen Pricilla with that man he thought she had wronged Randolph. Instead of standing true, to support him through the war, she had taken another hand. Now he was out to lay his anger at her doorstep, with Randolph's death as the guiding force.

When he arrived at Pricilla's doorway he paused momentarily, to calm himself, and to gather his thoughts. He didn't know what he would say, even though his anger had reached an explosive state.

Going on courage alone, he knocked on the door.

Pricilla's mother answered. He had never met her before, but had seen her once from a distance, on a day when she and Pricilla had been shopping.

"I am Devon Finch," he said. "Randolph Finch's brother."

She smiled, courteously. "Yes, Mr. Finch. How can I help you?"

"I would like to speak to Pricilla, please."

"She is in. Would you like to step inside?"

He shook his head. "No, ma'm. I would prefer to talk to her here, outdoors."

Mrs. Udahl cocked her head, questioningly. "I will get her."

He waited patiently, his head turned aside. He gazed at the side of a building a half block away, hoping the proper words would come the minute she stepped outside.

"Hello, Devon. What a surprise?"

Pricilla's greeting moved him a step backwards. She came outside and closed the door behind her, and for a moment he couldn't bring himself to look at her. His gaze skipped past her as the letter trembled in his hands.

"I have a letter, I . . ." His statement faltered.

"Is it from Randolph?"

He turned on her then, his eyes fiery. His appearance brought a flash of concern to her face and she stepped backwards as if confused.

He went on. "No, it is from one of his fellow soldiers. He wrote to us . . . to tell us that . . . Randolph . . . has been killed."

Pricilla's hand swept to her mouth, capturing a sigh. Instantly, her eyes moistened. "Oh, dear Lord," she mumbled. "Not Randolph."

Devon's words gathered then, and he issued them like a gunshot. "He was carrying this lock of hair when he died." He held out the cloth containing the clip. "The soldier said he had it right over his heart when he went down. I don't know what his last thought was, but it might have been of you, the woman who had forsaken him for another."

Pricilla reached out for him, but he backed away. A tear rolled down her cheek.

"Oh! You don't understand, Devon. My being with that other man was not what you think it was."

"Then tell me. What was it? I saw you with him, hand in hand. You and Randolph were . . . he told me he wanted to marry you . . . that day he left on the steamer."

"Listen to me, Devon."

"No. Listen to me. Here is your lock of hair. He doesn't need it any more. Take it, as his last gift to you."

"Listen to me, Devon," she said again as she removed the cloth from his hand. "I loved your brother, of that I am sure. But he . . ."

"He what?"

"There are some things you must know. Things only he and I knew about. Personal things. On the day before he signed up to fight, we talked about marriage, and children, and a future together. We were happy and confident, and we knew where we were going."

"And?"

"On the next day he told me he had enlisted in the Union Army. On the following day, Devon, without so much as a mention of it to me, without any thought for my feelings, as if we had never talked about marriage. He just up and signed his name and went off to war without a care about my concerns."

Devon stepped back as his anger subsided.

Pricilla continued, "On the day he left, he knew I was resentful of his decision. I tried to tell him how much I loved him, but my words didn't seem to matter anymore. He told me he had a new commitment, to fight for his country, to help save it from ruin, for me and for others, for his parents, and for you. I understood his zeal, but he appeared to abandon me as if I didn't exist. Is that what patriotism does to a man?"

"I didn't know."

She wiped her tear away. "Of course you didn't. Would you like to read one of his letters? I'll get one for you. He never mentioned how he missed me, never told me he loved me, and never expressed any words of a future with me. He wrote as if I were a stranger, telling me only about his drills and his campfires and his regiment, as if they were all that mattered to him. He wrote nothing about love. It seemed as if our past had vanished, as if a future with me was . . . unimportant."

Devon's anger faded with the last of her words. "I didn't know," he said.

"I believe he wanted me to search for another life, for someone to give me what he could not. The more I thought about it, the more I agonized over it, the more I knew he was not planning to survive. I believed he would die. And he knew it also."

"I don't believe you."

"Think what you want. But I know it to be true."

He wouldn't . . . . ."

"In one of his letters he told me of a place where fallen soldiers go, a place of comfort and peace. He said if the Lord called him, he would go willingly."

"No," Devon replied, shaking his head.

"I will get the letter for you. He wrote it before the battle of Bull Run. I speak the truth. I have them all."

"He wouldn't . . ."

"He did."

Devon turned away from her. His eyes drifted skyward, into the low clouds that hung like bleeding hearts above the river. He felt utterly exhausted, freed from anger, but enmeshed in a confusion he could not understand. He thought back to the day Randolph had left, and he remembered the distinct expression in his eyes, a far-away look he had never seen before, like someone staring out at a new destination afar off. He thought then that it must have been a look all soldiers acquired, not knowing what was ahead, fearing the worst, hoping for the best, knowing death was waiting for just the right moment to snatch him away.

He looked back at Pricilla. She stood silently, her eyes upon him, her face solemn and forgiving.

"The man you saw me with, Mr. Mallory, is a long-time friend of our family. He is a banker of high esteem, and we had invited him for dinner that evening. We were merely strolling that day you saw us. We are not lovers, Devon."

The truth stung Devon. He hung his head. "But, I was rude."

"Yes," she nodded. "You see, I am in love with no one, and I am broken to hear that Randolph has been taken away. But my feelings for him have faded. He indicated in his letters that we must each go our own way. He was not expecting to come back, as strange as it might seem to you. I will give you his letters if you want to read them. They are discomforting to me. My tears have all dried."

Devon remembered some of Randolph's final words to him then. Randolph had said that he was clothed in a new spirit, and that he was ready to go if the time came. And he remembered him saying that it didn't matter where he fell, only that when he did, he'd have reached the shining river, and that his heart would quiver with the melody of peace.

Devon took Pricilla's hand then and stroked the back of it. "I'm sorry," he said. "I hope you will forgive me."

She smiled at him. "There is nothing to forgive, Devon. You had no way of knowing."

"I should have . . . ."

"Don't," she said. "Just go. We know he is in good hands now."

Devon nodded, and then turned. He heard the door open and close behind him, and as he walked away he began crying again. He paused, smearing his face with the dampness of his tears.

His thoughts went back to that day in the cave, when they were waiting for the rain to cease. He and Randolph had been looking out toward the woods beyond the stream when they saw a small deer loping along on three legs, it's fourth tucked under its flank, half gone. Someone had shot it away. Now, for no apparent reason, he remembered it all, as if it were happening again right before his eyes.

"Look at the poor thing," Randolph had said. "It's just gettin' by. It'll probably never last the winter."

"Someone should put it out of its misery."

"If I was the deer I wouldn't want to live without my leg."

"Why not."

"Don't know why. Without a leg, or an arm, I'd just be a nuisance to someone else, a burden. No, I think I'd just as soon be dead, so's I could start over."

"You mean we can all start over once we're gone?'

"Some say we can. Preacher Granger does. There's a place we go."

"Where?"

"They call it heaven."

"Where is it?"

"Somewhere. Nobody knows where for sure."

"How does one get there?'

"You just go. When the breath goes out of you, you're there, simple as that."

"Gee."

Devon was unsure of why he remembered that day, and those particular words, perhaps because the time was right, perhaps because Randolph was in heaven, wanting Devon to know that he was fine, and that he had both his legs.

He walked another block before he turned off the road to rest atop a wood pile, and as the world around him faded, he seemed closer to Randolph than he ever had before. He felt as if Randolph were standing right at his side.

That night the sky turned red.

Beyond the river, the land near Kaposia erupted in fire. The glow of its seething flames licked at the sky through most of the night, a bright rolling pattern of fire clouds alive with anger and destruction. Devon watched its fury from the upstairs window for a while, remembering the blaze of the past year that had threatened to take the entire city.

He slept later, amid thoughts of Randolph, and he dreamed of them down by the river, throwing stones into the water to see who had the best arm.

CHAPTER TWENTY-SEVEN

Fury, and love

November saw a decline in rainfall. Most of the early days were bright and pleasant, giving of sunshine and a healthy breeze, fragrant with the crispness of autumn. Still bearing grief over the loss of his brother, Devon was nonetheless pleased to have his cast removed, and for a time he exercised his newly mended arm with high spirits. On the fifth of November the steamer *Key City* left for Prairie du Chene, and the *Northern Belle* to La Crosse. The season for river travel was nearly over. Before the month was gone, the river would ice up and the city would burrow in for the long winter, hoping that supplies would last until springtime when the cycle would be repeated.

The routine at the Finch house returned to normal rather quickly. Nona and Harold ended their grieving after packing up all of Randolph's belongings and donating them to the poor. They kept a picture of him, a Daguerreotype they had taken at his graduation day; the photo of a stern-faced young man who seemed unwilling to smile, just the opposite of the real Randolph Finch. But solemnity was the custom then. Nona dressed in black for the entire month.

On a night of the second week Harold informed Devon that printers were needed at the *Pioneer*. Several men had left to enlist, and two had decided to strike out for Kansas City.

"Here is your chance, Devon," he said. "We're hurting for manpower. It is difficult for the remainder of us to barely publish the newspaper now. There's a lifetime of work just waiting for you. Come now. Take advantage of this opportunity."

Devon told him he would think hard about it, and he did. At night, in the shadows, he envisioned himself inside the *Pioneer*, with all its noise and clanking, smells and deadlines. And then, as opposite as daylight was from darkness, he would imagine himself on the railroad, where giant engines and strings of coaches lined the tracks, where smoke billowed high, and where the smells and noises were of a different kind, hot work in the summer and freezing cold in the winter. He knew more about printing than he did about railroading, but the lure of the outdoors and the promise of adventure with steel and power always drew him away from the known confines of the *Pioneer* and its endless monotony. In the end, he told his father that he would make a decision near the close of the year, before leaving the Alliance. Though railroading still beckoned, he most certainly would end up working alongside his father in the dimness of the old building, with the smell of printer's ink in his nostrils, and in his clothes, and on his skin.

Toward the middle of the month Harold and Nona made plans to take a coach to Saint Anthony, to visit the parents of Private, Enlisted, Corry Yardham, the young soldier who had written to them about Randolph's demise. They would travel before the month was gone and not chance on the weather becoming miserable. They had written the Yardham's and had received a reply. They had made reservations on the coach line. Devon would be left alone for the day.

✵ ✵ ✵

So it was that Devon entered the LaBelle saloon after a two week absence, only to find it half filled with people he did not recognize. The usual boisterous crowd was far fewer, the noise diminished to mere chatter. Only a few men stood at the bar. The poker table showed less activity than normal. The bartender lifted his head only long enough to nod at him. The others paid him little attention.

He waved to several familiar figures, then drifted off to a table near where Flynn sat, playing poker with two other men Devon had never seen before, one thickly bearded, the other bearing mutton chops. They appeared to be trappers, judging from the weathered look of them. They had probably delivered skins to the American Fur Company and were now warming up before heading back into the woods to set their traps on winter runways. They'd take a bottle or more of whiskey with them for sure, to keep their blood warm when the freeze came.

Sissy came down about a half hour later. She stood momentarily at the bottom of the stairs to look over the offering, seemingly unimpressed with the gathering. Still, she went from man to man, teasing them, asking if they were eager enough to take a ride to paradise. She had no takers.

Eventually, she passed Flynn's table and looked the other way, purposely avoiding his eyes. Devon thought he saw her grimace, as if a chill had passed through her body. She came to Devon's table and sat down in one of the chairs. She looked tired, not from lack of sleep, but from life itself. Her face was dreary, her eyes sad.

"Haven't seen you for a while," she stated.

Devon smiled. "I got my cast off. Look. I've got a new arm."

She reached over and wrapped her hand around his wrist. "It's as strong as ever. How'd you like to wrap it around me?"

He sat back and smiled. "Now you know that I can't go to paradise with you, not today, not tomorrow, not ever. I'm betrothed."

"Same old story you always tell me. So are half the men here, but that don't stop them from being entertained now and then."

Devon squeezed her hand, and then looked at her forehead where frown lines had formed. "You look tired, Sissy."

She breathed heavily for a moment, and then gazed at the ceiling rafters where spider webs had formed. "I am. Too much goin' on. But with winter comin' I'll get a rest. Only the regulars come by when snow's on the ground, none of those river rats, or trappers, or those just passin' through. I've been thinkin' though."

Her words dropped off and she heaved a pensive sigh.

"Thinking about what?" Devon asked.

"Same thing Ingrid thought about. Leavin'. Maybe goin' down to New Orleans. I hear there's one more boat coming. It's warm down there."

Devon was only mildly surprised. "What would you do down there?"

"Huh, I'd be providing the same service, over and over, day after day, one dollar, two dollars. The more money I get, the better service I gives. Besides, men smell better down in New Orleans. Some up here smell like animals."

"Don't you wash 'em?"

"If they pay me what's due. I scrub the mean out of some of 'em'."

Devon laughed. The men at the poker table looked his way, and then concentrated on their cards.

"Flynn will be heading out, too." Devon said.

Sissy tightened, as if a chill had crossed her body. "He can't leave soon enough for me."

"Why is that?"

"Because he's a devil man."

Devon leaned forward in his chair. "What makes you keep saying that?'

"Cuz he is. He's got a black heart."

"Well then, I hope he doesn't go down to New Orleans."

Sissy was quick to answer. "He goes to Kansas City. He makes a lot of money there during the winter time."

Silence came then, as if the room had been vacated. Then Sissy sighed and turned in her chair. She made a move to get up, but Devon held her down. "Has Kane been here lately?" he asked.

"He was here yesterday. He'll be leavin' too."

"Where does he go?"

"He's got interests out west, somewhere."

"What interests?"

"Don't know for sure. Gold, I think."

"Gold?"

"He had a mining claim out there. Still does, I think."

So Kane got his money from gold, not from trapping or lumbering. It explained why he spent so much time at LaBelle's with Ingrid. He probably had money stashed away in one or more of the local banks, took some out whenever he needed cash. He most likely went into the wilderness because he was free there, nothing to encumber him, just him and nature. What was it he said once . . . that he enjoyed listening to the language of the wild places?

"Last chance," Sissy said, rising to her feet. "You comin' up?"

Devon shook his head. "No, Sissy."

"You're a stubborn one."

She walked away then, went up to two men who had just entered the bar. Neither of them seemed eager to follow her.

He sat for a while, reviewing the things that had transpired during the summer, the killings, the fights, the friendships, the concerns, until his thoughts expired. He was truly comforted by the pledge he had made to Caroline, that come Christmas he'd give up the Alliance to start a new job at the *Pioneer*. He knew some men who worked with their fathers. Most of them said it wasn't the best place for a son to be.

He sat still and silent for another half hour, sipping sarsaparilla, thinking of Caroline, hoping his parents had met the stage without incident. Sissy had finally made a connection. A man at the piano tinkered with a tune called *Early in the Morning*. Music lightened the place.

Devon was about to leave, to patrol the streets, when Flynn shot up out of his chair and pounded the table with his fist.

"You're cheating," He had yelled directly at the man dealing cards.

The dealer reacted with surprise. "You're a liar." he shouted.

"You slipped that card off the bottom of the deck. I saw it clearly."

The dealer eased out of his chair. His eyes glared. "Nobody's gonna call me a cheat. Now you take them words back, or you'll wish you weren't born."

Flynn's hand moved like lightening to his right side. In a flash, he had a knife in his hand, drawn from a scabbard hidden beneath his top coat. The dealer backed away, his hands flexing.

"You want this?" Flynn shouted. "You want a fight?"

The other man's jaw tightened. The third man at the table jumped up and fled to one side. The dealer shouted "You come slashing' at me and I'll break your goddam neck. Knifes don't scare me. The sight of a blade only makes me meaner."

"Nobody cheats Simeon Flynn."

"I didn't cheat you. You got blind eyes, or else you're itchin' to die."

Flynn gestured with the knife. The other man tightened his fists as he took a defensive stance. Flynn held the knife firmly, as if he was ready to slash. The other man crouched wolf-like, his eyes glaring, his mouth squeezed to a snarl. A second later Flynn lunged. He was on the man before he could react, his knife hand wavering just above his face. Flynn's lunge had been swift, powerful enough to drive his antagonist backwards, causing him to slip on the saw-dust floor. The two of them sprawled, Flynn on top of the other, his knife hand restrained by sheer strength.

Devon sprang to his feet instantly, nightstick in hand, calling to some of the men at the bar. "Help me before he kills the man."

One of the men laughed. "Let 'em go at it."

The second man, a brutish sort with bull-like shoulders, responded immediately, and as the two men wrestled in the saw-dust, they pulled Flynn away from the dealer, who sprang immediately to his feet, clutching his arm where he had been cut.

"Stand back, the two of you," Devon shouted. "It's over." He swung the nightstick hard against Flynn's arm. The knife came loose and clattered to the floor.

"You bastard," the dealer seethed. "I'll get the best of you yet."

Flynn was raging. "You were going to cheat me. Nobody cheats Simeon Flynn."

"I wasn't cheating you, you buzzard. I was dealin' fair."

"I saw it," Flynn seethed.

"You saw nothin' but what you wanted to see."

Devon yelled. "It's over. Get out!"

Fury, and love

The dealer leaned toward Flynn, rage dripping from his mouth. "Someday you'll pay for this, Flynn. Someday I'll cut your fingers off so you can't deal any more. It'll be the way you'll remember ol' Peder Olmsted, by lookin' at the stump of your hand."

"You're nothin' but a cheatin' weasel."

"Go!" Devon shouted again. He realized he could not fend Olmsted off if he charged in again. He could only hope that good sense would prevail, that he would back off to tend his wound. If revenge was needed, it could be played out another way, when there were no witnesses, alone on a dark street, where revenge usually occurred.

"This isn't worth gettin' cut up for," Devon shouted. "The game is over. Now go!"

Olmsted pressed his hand tightly over the slash. Blood seeped through his fingers.

"I'm goin' Flynn. But you'd better watch your back."

"And you watch yours."

Olmsted started toward the door. When he was halfway there he turned and gave Flynn his final words. "When you least expect it, Flynn, that's when I'll be there."

"You don't frighten me!" Flynn screamed.

Then Olmsted left the bar and quiet returned.

Following Olmsted's departure, Flynn swept his knife from the sawdust and returned to his chair. He leaned back, breathing hard, his mouth drawn tight like an unopened bud. When Devon went to sit beside him, Flynn turned, his eyes blazing.

"You better go, Devon Finch. You're no longer a friend."

"What?'

"You should have let me have him."

"I couldn't."

"He was cheating me. Nothing I hate worse than cheats and whores."

The rage on Flynn's face was obvious. Devon stood up and stepped away from the table. Flynn's unexpected remark about his hatred for whores set him back a bit.

"You better calm down. Have a whiskey and rest a bit. It's over and done."

"It's not over 'til I'm satisfied."

"Leave it be," Devon pleaded. "You made your point."

"Get out of here, and take that nightstick with you. And don't you ever step in the way of Simeon Flynn again. Do you hear me, boy?"

Devon nodded. "I hear you."

"Then get out of my sight, before I forget who you are."

One of the men at the bar shouted. "Better go, sonny. He's got a hate for ya."

Laughter filled the room, enough to drench the place.

Devin turned and left instantly. He stood outside where daylight came down on him like a blessed angel. Enough of LaBelle's, he thought. It held nothing but hate and drunks and no-goods who thought only of gambling, drinking and whoring. He pondered Flynn's remarks, remembering his statement about hating whores. Could he have been involved in Ingrid's death? No. He had been at the poker table that night, except for the time he took to relieve himself.

My God, he thought . . . I was so wrong about him. Was Sissy the only one who knew about his volatile side? She had said he was a devil, and rightly so. Deviltry had indeed appeared when he had that knife in his hand.

He figured it was about ten o'clock by the position of the sun. By this time his parents had boarded the coach and were on their way to Saint Anthony where they would partake of tea, and fancy cookies, and talk, and reminisce. The men would go into another room and review the past and present while the women sipped from little porcelain cups. He would have the afternoon alone, except for the time he would spend with Caroline. She wanted him to accompany her to a Millinery store to purchase a new bonnet. After the altercation inside LaBelle's, he was all too anxious to be with her. He would find shopping both boring and exciting. Just being with her was enough to quicken his steps. His parents wouldn't return until nightfall.

Thank God for winter. With the steamboats gone, and with Flynn gone, and with Kane somewhere out there in the great beyond, he could spend Christmas in relative peace.

Then he would say farewell to Lowertown and concentrate on printing a newspaper . . . and dream of railroading.

✫ ✫ ✫

Devon had been invited for lunch at the Page house, despite the absence of Mr. Page who was busy with government work at the state house. The light talk between he and the three women lasted longer than Devon would have liked, but he enjoyed their company and the presence of Caroline's eyes on him whenever he looked at her. The food left him filled and satisfied.

Soon afterwards he and Caroline began their walk toward the Millinery store, hand in hand, she as bright as the day, he as proud as any man would be, having such a beautiful woman at his side. Only a few clouds appeared over the western hills where gaunt and leafless trees awaited the winter snows.

They walked directly to the store where she picked through a blizzard of hats. He felt conspicuously out of place amid the lace and the frills as she tried on several bonnets, while seeking his opinion, which he gave freely, even though his opinion didn't matter. After sampling a dozen or so, she selected one, a blue bonnet with a short brim and a back curtain made of gathered net. It framed her face elegantly. She purchased it, and browsed a bit more. By the time they went outside the sky had turned gray.

"It looks like it might rain," he said.

"And I didn't bring my parasol. What if we don't make it home beforehand?"

"Then we'll get wet. Hurry!"

Caroline felt awkward and ungraceful, running in a hoop skirt, but she tried her best, giving way to exhaustion just as rain began falling, lightly at first, then heavier. As they reached Fourth Street, only a block from Devon's home, he shouted. "Keep running, we're almost there."

"We won't make it," she panted. "Oh my! Oh my!"

By the time they reached the house they were wet to the skin. The corset and crinoline she wore beneath the dress were soaked.

They entered in a breathless state, shaking off the rain, brushing water from their faces, laughing at the incident,

Caroline pretended to be horrified. "Just look at me. I'm a mess."

He laughed and took her in his arms. "You are beautiful," he said.

"I am ruined. Look at my hair, my clothes."

"Nothing could ruin you," he said, taking her hand, leading her inside.

"I will drip all over the floor."

"Stand here on this rug. It has accepted rain much worse than this. I'll get some towels. We'll dry off. I'll put some wood on the fire. I'll change clothes. We'll warm ourselves. When the rain stops, I'll take you home."

She stood quietly while he stoked the fire. Before long, the heat was radiating. Caroline's chill slowly ebbed away. She dried herself as best she could, first her hair, then the rest of her, brushing the damp skirt with towels, feeling uncomfortable inside the chilled clothing.

Devon had gone upstairs to change clothes. When he came down he was attired in a clean shirt and trousers, and slippers on his feet. He carried another pair in his hands.

"These belong to my mother," he said. "She will not mind if you wear them. Take off those shoes and slip these on."

She sat on the chair and unbuttoned the shoes while trying to manage the hoop skirt. Then he eased her shoes off and began massaging warmth into her feet with slow and deliberate movements. He had never touched her feet with his hands, and it was surprising to him, that in those few magic moments he could actually feel something akin to wonder. As he caressed them, he looked directly into her eyes. He felt then, like a man who had just found a treasure he had spent an entire life searching for.

Their eyes met tenderly, as if sharing words heard only in their hearts. Then her hands came toward him and took his face, and

Fury, and love

with a gentleness born of need, she eased him upward and met his lips. An instant later he was tight to her body, sealed in a kiss so passionate that the world around them disappeared.

He fumbled then, to touch her breasts, nestled within her clothing, and in doing so he drifted into a breathless world where haste was born by the movement of their hands and the greed of their lips and the soul of their desire.

He drifted away from her and spoke softly, hoping she would not reject his plea.

"Come upstairs with me," he said.

Her eyes glazed with desire. "I want to. Oh, how I want to. But we cannot. Not here in your house."

"It's early," he pleaded. "My parents won't be home until dark. We have hours left . . . hours. This . . . this is our time. Come with me, Caroline."

She leaned into him, her breasts crushing against his chest. "I want you so," she breathed.

"Come with me," he whispered.

The need for him was great. Within moments she banished all reason. The nights they had lain on the hillside behind the capitol and had wished for love, all the times they had touched, all the times they had kissed, now coalesced. For the first time, they were alone in a place where time was but a lingering thought.

"Go upstairs," she whispered, her voice urgent and insistent. "I'll take off this gown and place it beside the stove. Then I'll come up. Meet me, if you will, beneath the covers of your bed."

He kissed her lightly on the lips and then said breathlessly. "I love you so."

He dashed upstairs to his room and removed his clothing, and when naked he slid beneath the cover and waited. Aroused to the fullest, his body throbbed with an urgency that consumed every inch of his body. What if she changed her mind? What if she thought this too reckless, or too wicked, or too premature? What if she left? What if his parents had taken an earlier stage? What would happen if they came in and found them in bed? What would happen if . . .

Then she was there, in the doorway, dressed only in a corset and a light chemise. She came directly to the bed and stood above him. The gentle smile on her face eased him immediately.

"Will you unlace me, please," she asked

He eased out of bed as she turned, and nervously unfastened the ties on the back of her corset. When it was loose, she removed it. Before he re-entered the bed she took the towel and laid it down and whispered, "There could be blood. I am a virgin still." As he drifted down onto it, she stepped out of the underclothes.

Then, in the dim light of day, and as thunder rolled across the top of the house, and as rain fell against the window, he saw her naked for the first time, her full body appearing like a goddess in his sight, like something made of dreams, like the vision he had always imagined but had never seen. He reached out for her and took her hand. Deftly, she lifted her leg, and in that moment before she drifted to his side, she saw him exposed, as she had always imagined him to be, ready to receive her. Then they embraced, side by side, leg to leg, breast to breast, thigh to thigh, and in doing so their bodies fused with an intensity neither of them had experienced, creating a desire that nearly stripped their breaths away.

She drifted onto her back and he rode up over her, and moments later she guided him to the appropriate position and urged him forward. With his heart pounding, and with her sigh whispering in his ear, he met that sheath of skin denoting a virgin. As she drew a startled breath, her hands grasped his buttocks, urging him forward. Then, as she gasped, he slipped into her.

"Don't release inside me," she breathed.

"I won't," he said, easing himself slowly into passion.

He knew the feeling of ejaculation. He had masturbated before, so he knew how much time was available to him before he had to withdraw. He slowed his thrusts then, to feel the intensity of each slow movement, to experience the ecstasy that came with each conforming urge. Then, so soon, at just the right moment, he withdrew and drained his passion.

They remained embraced for a while, until the emotion subsided. Then, with great care, he lifted away. While standing, he watched her take up the towel that bore only a small stain of blood.

Fury, and love

She wiped herself, knowing he was watching her, as if they had done this a hundred times before. When finished, she turned and kissed him with a passion that nearly exploded his heart.

"I'll dress now," she said in a comforting voice. "You do the same. And wash the towel."

He took her in his arms and held her tight for a moment. "I love you," he breathed. "I love you."

"And I you," she replied. "Go now. There will be other nights."

She dressed while he straightened the bed and afterwards, when he was dressed, he washed the towel outside in the rain, wrung it out, and placed it on the kitchen line above the sink.

They sat in the parlor until the rain subsided, until the gown was nearly dry. The rain stopped sometime around four o'clock. The stage from Saint Anthony would not arrive at the American House until five, perhaps later because of the miserable weather. Time was still on their side.

The clouds passed over about four-thirty, and the sun re-appeared. Then he walked her home.

Before they arrived at her house, she said to him, "Well, my love, there is no turning back for you now."

"I would never turn back."

"We have done it," she winked. "We have waited and waited, and now we have done it." Her eyes twinkled. "Did you like it, Devon Finch?

"More than you will ever know."

"You'll be my husband then?"

"Yes, forever."

She tweaked his chin. "Then go home, and remember your pledge. Only one more month, and then you'll bid the Alliance goodbye."

"One more month, I promise."

He nodded and kissed her hand at the doorway, and as she re-entered the house he turned around and started back home, knowing his bed would never be the same.

CHAPTER TWENTY-EIGHT

Departure

"I never saw him so bestial. He was like an animal. I believe he would have killed the man had I not intruded."

Devon was telling Western about the confrontation at LaBelle's, the way Flynn had lunged at the gambler he had accused of cheating.

"He was like a different man then?"

"Yes, much to my surprise. I didn't expect such a reaction from Flynn."

"So, tell me now. Might he have killed Ingrid Lorgren?"

"He could have, especially when he indicated his hatred for cheaters and whores. But he was situated at the poker table at the time of the murder . . . or was he?"

Western nodded, stroked his beard. "It is an unanswerable question. No one has implicated him. Only he knows what happened during those few minutes. And we cannot arrest him based on an angry spurt of temper, or because he left the table to relieve himself. So he carries a knife. That in itself doesn't prove anything. Half the people in this town carry knives. Some carry guns. Others batter with their fists. But his being downstairs when another is murdered upstairs, well, therein lays his alibi if we were ever to question him about it."

"He'll be leaving soon."

"Aye, the river will close up near the end of the month."

"Is there anything we can do to keep him here?"

"Why would we? We'd all be better off if he left this city."

"But if he remained, he might tip his hand."

"Sure, he might."

"Can you restrict him from boarding?"

"On what grounds?"

"That he could be a suspect, or at least a witness who's involved in her death."

Western nodded. "A witness, you say?"

"We could tell him we have a suspect in jail, and that he might go to trial. We could say that we have need of his testimony since he was a friend of Ingrid. Anyone at LaBelle's could be a witness. There's always talk, and actions, and fights over the ladies. He need not know that we're considering him as the possible killer."

Western snickered. "You've thought this out, haven't you?"

"When one sits in LaBelle's and sips Sarsaparilla for hours, and sees what goes on there, one gets suggestions."

"Suggestions, is it?"

"Like when Flynn gets up to relieve himself. He had to go to the back of the saloon to where the commode is situated. It's just steps away from the back door. Who is to say that he didn't have to relieve himself that night, that he went up the outside stairs instead, that he entered Ingrid's room and . . ."

"Why would he want to kill her?"

"For money, though I am merely speculating."

"You have a curious mind, Devon Finch."

"My mother would agree."

The two men looked at one another with fixed expressions, each harboring their own thoughts about the matter. Devon had spoken his piece, and now he waited for a reply. Whatever Western decided would be final. If Flynn left, then it would be over. He could come back the next spring and take his place at the table, and begin shuffling cards, as if nothing had happened. By then

Departure

Ingrid's murder would be mostly forgotten, and life would go on the same as it always had. Whoever killed Ingrid would go free.

Western broke the silence. "We must remember that one of the other women might have done the killing. They were up there, away from everyone else. Surely the girls were jealous of one another, or they held a hatred of some kind. Jealously has been responsible for more than one murder."

"Then we will let him go?"

Western waved the question away with a stroke of his hand. "I will think about this. You have given me new information about Flynn's temper, and his haste to take another life. I will discuss it with others. Perhaps we'll come to a decision within a day or two. Perhaps it will be considered wise to prevent Flynn from leaving this city. If he's angered enough by his restriction, perhaps he'll say something that might strengthen a case against him. I will delve into this. For now, just go your way. Talk to the others as you have been. Continue to notice Flynn's actions when you are inside LaBelle's, and by all means, stay out of trouble. I don't want a dead Alliance member on my hands."

"I was just reporting what I had witnessed, sir."

"And a bit more."

"It is part of my job to notice things."

"Aye, it is. But you are not yet a policeman."

"But I have eyes, and a sense about things."

"That you have."

Devon left and spent the next two hours walking the streets while trying to ignore the cold wind sweeping down from the northern forests, reminding him that winter was only days away. Snow would come soon. Logging was in full swing up on the Saint Croix. Maybe Kane would make an appearance before he headed west to spend a month or two with the Sioux, among those he respected for their love of the land. Kane didn't ascribe to eliminating the Indians from territory they revered. He thought they should live in harmony with the whites. Kane was a right good man when it came right down to it.

✡ ✡ ✡

Two days later he learned that Sissy was packing up to take the last steamer to New Orleans, so he went to see her, to say his farewell. She came down at his request and sat with him for a while.

"So you're going," he stated directly.

"I made up my mind."

"Then I wish you God's speed and protection on the river, and a good home in the south."

She touched his hand lovingly. "My home, I expect, will be something like this. The same type of men, the same problems, the same wish to be somewhere else. But at least I'll be warm during the winter."

"It's likely to snow here before long."

"I can already smell snow in the wind."

She leaned toward him with her back to Flynn. "I want you to accompany me on the day I go down to the steamer. I want you to be with me when I set my feet on the deck. Will you do that for me?"

"Certainly, but why me?"

"Because I need to tell you something."

He shifted closer, toward her. "Tell me now, in case I can't get to the landing."

"Can't, and won't."

"Why not?"

"It's got to be when I leave, and not before.

Devon tapped the table nervously. "I'll be there, unless something serious happens."

"Like what?'

He snickered. "Well, maybe the army will sweep me up."

She slapped at his hand. "Don't humor me. Right now there's two eyes boring right into the back of my neck."

Devon turned slightly. Flynn was looking their way, his eyes set directly on them. As soon as Devon looked at him, he turned back to his cards.

"How did you know he was lookin' at you?" Devon asked.

"I could feel him, damn his hide."

"Is it about Flynn you want to talk to me about?"

Sissy arose then. As she reached up to fluff her hair, she replied. "Good day, Mr. Finch. It surely was nice talkin' to you."

Departure

She went off then, strutting across the floor like a peacock,

Surely she wants to talk about Flynn, and nothing else. She's scared of the man, so scared she can't even speak about it. Maybe it has something to do with Ingrid, or Kane, or just about her. For certain, he would be on the landing when she boarded. Nothing would prevent him from hearing what she had to say.

✯ ✯ ✯

Unknown to Devon, Western had spoken to Flynn. Devon learned about the exchange the following day when Western called him into his office. When Devon sat down facing him, Western spoke straight out.

"We brought Mr. Flynn in yesterday."

Devon could not conceal his surprise. He leaned into Western's statement with the intentness of a fox. "Why?"

Western eased into his chair. "We went down to LaBelle's and asked him to come with us. He asked us why, and we told him it was something related to Ingrid Lorgren's murder. He didn't say a word, just got up out of his chair and came along like a hound would follow its master. He didn't offer any resistance. He was a gentleman all the way. We sat him down right where you're sittin' and asked him full out if he knew anything about the murder. Of course, he said he was gambling all night, that her death came as a great surprise to him. He mentioned that Kane was the most talked about, that many considered him guilty."

Western stroked his mustache several times before continuing. "When we told him we might not let him go south on one of the last steamers, he didn't say a word. He just looked at us like we were intent on interfering into his life. After that we couldn't get a word out of him. He was angry, for sure, even though he kept it hidden as best he could. When told we were finished with him, he just got up and walked out without saying another word. We've informed the Harbor Master down at the landing to deny him passage should he choose to leave."

Devon took a deep breath, held it for a moment, and then exhaled through his mouth. "I didn't think you'd do it," he said.

"The staff and I talked it over. Then I went up to the State House and brought it to the attention of some lawyers, and a judge. They said we were within our rights to retain the man if we thought he had any connection with the murder, even though he wasn't a suspect. There's nothin' in the law that said we couldn't. So we went ahead with it."

Devon's brow creased. "I better stay away from LaBelle's for a while."

"No need to. He'll just go on playin' cards to quell his anger. We think he'll just settle in for a spell and wait to see what happens."

✯ ✯ ✯

Devon returned to the bar the following day. Flynn was at his usual place, with three others. He didn't look up when Devon came in. Sissy spoke briefly with Devon, in which she said, "The *Highland Mary* is coming in on Friday. She'll be leaving the following morning just before sunup, her last trip of the year. I'll be on board when she goes."

"I'll see you on Friday night then, about seven o'clock, right after my dinner."

"I'd be much obliged."

"It's the end of an era for you then?"

"And the beginning of another. The same life but in a different place. Come aboard so's we can sit for a spell."

"Yes, ma'm."

She straightened proudly, her eyes set directly on him. "I ain't no ma'm."

Devon grinned and said, "I think you are."

Departure

She didn't reply, just stood there, unmoved. He was quick to notice a slight tremble on her lips, the kind one gets when trying to hold back a sob. Then she lifted her hand and placed her fingers on his chest and gave him a slight shove.

"Goodnight, Mr. Finch," she said.

Devon would not see her again until she boarded the *Highland Mary*.

✯ ✯ ✯

Flynn was absent from his chair for the next three days, but no one knew why. He just up and vanished. Devon didn't learn about his absence until he and Western met on the afternoon of the second day.

"Well, Flynn's gone," Western said simply. "We learned that he took the stage to Saint Anthony, and from there he disappeared. I guess we're free of him at last. If he did have any connection with Ingrid's murder he took the secret with him."

Devon's brow furrowed. "How can you be sure?"

"When we discovered him gone, we checked at the American House. We learned that he'd purchased passage, and then went on his way from there. Nothin' further we can do. I never thought of him taking a stage."

"Well then," Devon remarked. "He's a worry gone. I guess it will be a rather dull winter at LaBelle's, at least until Christmas."

"What's happening at Christmas?"

"Well, I'll be leaving the Alliance then, Mr. Western, to honor a pledge I made to my Caroline. She wants me free of this, and I promised her such. You can take that as my resignation, sir."

"Well now," he said, moving closer to Devon. He stood silently for a moment, with his body erect, and his hands on his hips. "I'll be losing a fine young man then. I thought you would stay on to become a police officer when this war is over."

"I'll be taking work at the *Pioneer*, sir. My father works there."

"Good. Good. You'll have work that's lasting, and important as well. Newspapers are just coming of age. They'll have a long life, until something better comes along."

"It'll be my Christmas present to Caroline," he stated.

"And a right fine one at that. Keeping your word is a precious thing."

"Thank you for being considerate, sir."

Western threw back his head and laughed. "Considerate, hah. If it wasn't for you Alliance men my job would have been impossible. I owe you all a debt I'll never be able to repay. All I can say is, thank you. As for me, I'll be able to fill your boots, even though it may take three or four men to do it."

"You are kind, sir."

"Go now. Continue to fulfill your duty until the year is over. Then you can take up newsprint and type and feel safe when you go to work. No more walkin' streets, and takin' blows, or breakin' your arm for the sake of honor, and being outdoors in the rain and the snow and the dark of night."

They shook hands then, and as Devon left the building he felt uneasy, not because he would leave the Alliance, but because he would miss the man he had learned to respect and admire. Howard H. Western was one of the finest men he'd ever met.

✳ ✳ ✳

On the twenty-third of November, driven by a brisk north wind, snow came roaring into Saint Paul with a fury only nature could provide. Devon put on heavier clothing then, and boots rubbed with oil, a wool scarf around his neck, and a knit cap on his head.

At seven o'clock, on the night of November twenty-fifth he approached the *Highland Mary*. Sissy had already boarded, and was standing inside close to a window when he first saw her. He

Departure

went up the swing bridge and met her with a broad smile. She appeared comfortable in her surroundings, and anxious to get on with life. She led him to a table away from others where they sat facing one another.

"You look like a gaily colored bird ready to fly south," he said.

She snickered. "Let me tell you, this bird is ready to fly."

He gazed into her eyes and saw calmness, as if she was taking a first step onto a sun-drenched path. "You deserve a new life," he said.

She tapped his hand. "Well, I made it this far, better than Ingrid done."

He eased back into his chair, content with her well-being. "So what is it?" he asked. "What secret are you holding?"

"I heard that Flynn has left the city. Is that true?"

"Yes, it is. He took a stage to Saint Anthony, and from there we have no idea where he went."

"Is there a chance that he'll return?"

"I don't think so. We believe he's gone for good. He'll definitely not be aboard this steamer, if that's what you are afraid of."

Sissy took a deep breath, and then released it as if expelling all her collected fears.

"He's the one who killed Ingrid."

"What?" Devon was astonished. "Why? Are you certain?"

Sissy lowered her voice. "He left the poker table that night because he was losing. He had run out of money. Instead of quitting he did something horrible."

Sissy paused. Her fingers trembled, so he took them between his hands and tried to calm her. "Go on," he said.

"He knew Ingrid was leaving. He knew she would have money with her. He went outside, through the back door, right after he saw Kane carry her baggage down to the steamer. He went up the stairs to the hallway and entered her room. It is my belief, that when he tried to take the money, she refused, and so he killed her. When he was leaving her room, I came out of my own, into the hallway. I saw him just as he was wipin' blood from his knife. He grabbed hold of me and put the knife to my throat, and said he would kill me if I ever spoke a word of it to anyone."

Her hand trembled as he sought to comfort her. "It's all right now. There's nothing to fear. Go on."

"He's a devil for sure. Every time I looked at him I was frightened. When I was alone I would cry. I was scared, Devon, so scared that I couldn't breathe sometimes. And sometimes when I looked at him he'd hiss at me and run his finger across his neck, notifying me what would happen if I ever opened my mouth against him. And he would. He'd slit me dead soon as look at me."

"It's okay," Devon said. "He's gone, and you're heading for New Orleans. It's over, Sissy."

"What if he finds out where I've gone? He knows where I'll be, in some saloon, givin' myself to men, same as here. He'll find me for sure."

"Then get off at some other place, Memphis, Natchez, or somewhere down river. Go to Texas, or east, or take passage to the west. There is a way, Sissy. Take it. Take it."

"You make it sound so easy."

"It's a huge country."

"But he's a devil, I know he is. He'll hunt me 'till the day he dies."

"No, he won't. He'll find the nearest poker table and that's where he'll stay. He's a gambler, Sissy. It's in his blood. He can't, and won't, do anything else unless he's starving to death."

"Are you sure?"

"Sure as I'll ever be. Now strengthen up, and smile, and use that charm of yours to capture some needy, young man who'll be more than willing to take you for a wife."

"You got all the answers, ain't ya'?"

"Not all of 'em. Sometimes I can't figure out how to solve my own problems."

They talked on for a while, watched the snow come down outside the window as the wind howled across the railings. Devon stayed about a half hour, then left. He went straight home. There'd be nobody on the streets this night.

✻ ✻ ✻

Departure

When he arose the following morning the steamer was already well on its way to Lake Pepin and from there to ports in Iowa.

He sensed a relief of sorts, the kind one feels when life has reached a point of calmness, when doubts have been resolved, when fears have subsided. Flynn was gone. Sissy had escaped her devil. Soon it would be Christmas, perhaps the best one he had ever had. The New Year would find him working next to his father. With money in his pocket, and a career ahead of him, he and Caroline could get married. Why, within a year they might have a young one to steal away their sleep.

If only he could avoid the army.

CHAPTER TWENTY-NINE

Dellwood Greene

Before the month ended the river iced up. Riverboat traffic ceased.

Saint Paul buttoned up for the winter. LaBelle's suffered a scarcity of customers for the lack of river men. Devon didn't frequent it much during those early days of December. The weather turned colder. The snow kept coming. On one day, late in the afternoon, when the thermometers fell to just above zero, and after four inches of snow had fallen, a brilliant Parhelia, with circles and arcs displaying all the color of a rainbow, was seen in the sky. Even winter had its beauty.

Another snowstorm followed, and before long the streets were nearly impassable. The temperatures dipped well below zero. Only those needing to venture outdoors did so.

Well after the stroke of ten, on a night when the snow was heavy and driven by wind, Devon left the LaBelle. He wrapped the wool scarf tight around his neck, hunched his shoulders, and with sheer determination he stepped into the lacing wind. The only thought occupying his mind was a certainty that he wouldn't return to the saloon again, not the next day, or the next, or on those following.

He was finished with it. He would wait out the month doing only what was required during the daylight hours, and when January dawned he'd begin his new life.

Dang, he felt good about that.

He walked about four blocks with the wind in his face. Snow swirled in eddies around his head. He bundled his arms as his white breath twisted away like smoke. Cold to the bone and thinking only about a warm fire and Caroline's arms around him, he stumbled over something half buried beneath the snow. He pulled up short, grasped hold of a lamp post, and turned to see what had nearly tripped him. He thought it was probably a large, dead dog, until he saw a shoe extending from beneath the snow. Looking closer, he saw an arm, and then a head, nearly covered. Surely, it was a man. The sight of him brought Devon to full attention.

He knelt beside the body, and brushed away the snow. The man was bearded, attired in a long-coat, one arm stretched wide, the other beneath him. A patch of dried blood lay across his forehead above his left eye. The man was near frozen. Devon raised the man's arm. His pulse was barely detectable. He was a large man, a hundred eighty pounds, maybe more, big about the middle. Devon turned him over, wiped the snow from his face. His eyes were closed. Snow had crystallized on his eyelids. His face was near blue in the wan light.

He panicked then as uncertainty clouded his mind. The only place he could take him was to the hospital, five blocks distant. The businesses were all closed. There were few houses between, and they would not have the resources needed to bring him around. If he could lug him to the hospital, they could help him. He knew he had to take the chance. Without care, the man would certainly freeze to death.

With great effort, he hoisted him out of the snow, raised him to his feet against the lamp post and leaned him across one shoulder. Lord, he was heavy, dead weight, like lifting a small cow. No matter. He had to get him to the hospital. Five block wasn't that far. Carefully, he eased the man's lifeless body across his shoulders as he had been taught in Alliance training. Then he took a deep breath and mumbled, "God willing."

Doggedly, he shuffled through the drifting snow, making headway against the angry wind. The first block was easy. The burden didn't move but an inch on his shoulders. Confidence kept him going until the middle of the next block, when the man's total weight began to bear on him. His pace slowed. The calves of his legs began aching. Breath steamed out ahead of him like blasts from a steamer pipe. His eyes, nearly blinded by snow, blinked with increasing rapidity. He willed himself on through the block and halfway through the next.

He wondered how long the man had been laying in the snow. Who was he, dressed so fine? If he hadn't clothed himself in that heavy woolen coat he'd surely be froze by now. If he did live, he hoped he wouldn't lose his fingers or toes to frost bite. What could a person accomplish without his fingers? The thought made him walk faster, although his pace had slowed, one foot barely passing the other. The lights of the hospital were visible, just a ways farther. Another block and a half, then he'd be safe. At that point the man slipped off his shoulders.

Devon couldn't stop his descent. The man slid off his back like a landslide and dropped into the snow. Devon spun around as his breath heaved. He knew he couldn't lift him again. Only two decisions remained, leave him and go for assistance, or drag him the remainder of the way. If the man remained outdoors much longer, he would freeze to death. Time was running out for him.

Without further thought, Devon grasped his arms and turned him over. Carefully, he gripped his wrists and began dragging him. With the burden eased from his shoulders, and with the snow acting as a slide, he found it easier to drag than carry him. The only concern was his left arm, where the break had occurred. He prayed the effort would not separate the healed bone.

Within five minutes he was at the hospital. He dropped the man just outside the door and rushed inside, shouting. "Anyone. Help. I need help. Hurry!"

Within seconds two people came rushing his way.

"I have a man outside. He's frozen. Get him in here, now!"

"Orderly!" the attendant screamed. "Bring a stretcher."

Devon collapsed into a chair, shivering uncontrollably. He blew warm breath into his hands, and rubbed his legs briskly while an orderly rushed past him with a stretcher. Devon removed his coat. The warm air flowed over him like a comforting breeze. He rubbed himself vigorously as they carried the man away.

Within moments, a nurse came up to him with several woolen blankets. She smiled. "Here, put these around you. I'll get you some warm tea."

The next five minutes were hazy, until the nurse returned with tea.

He had barely sipped the drink when a doctor arrived. "I am Doctor Clayton Johnson. What is your name?" he asked.

"I am Devon Finch, a member of the Alliance Committee."

"Ah, yes. Now I realize why you took the effort to bring this man in. Someone else might have left him to freeze to death."

"Who is he?" Devon asked.

"We found only a business card in his vest pocket. If it is his, he is Mr. Dellwood Greene, an executive of the St. Paul and Pacific Railroad. He has not spoken yet. The wound on his head was perhaps more significant than his being found in the snow. He may have been assaulted. He had no money on his person."

So, he was a railroad man.

"When you brought him in, his body temperature was ninety-four degrees, just above the point where he would have suffered profound hypothermia. Fortunately, his fingers will be alright, as will his toes. We'll bring him back slowly. He's conscious now, but still confused. It will be a day or two before you can see him, if you wish to do so."

"I wouldn't want to intrude on him."

"If that is your choice, so be it. Let me thank you then for being concerned enough to carry him in. Had you passed him by we'd have another corpse on our hands come morning."

"I was just doing my duty."

The doctor nodded with a smile. "Duty alone didn't bring him here, Mr. Finch."

The doctor left, leaving Devon alone for a while to sip his hot tea, to warm him inside where shivers still roamed. So he may have saved a railroad man. Imagine that. It would be nice to talk to Mr. Dellwood Greene at some time in the future, but he was certain that such a meeting would never happen. Silently, he wished him a good recovery and then placed his empty teacup on a table

Dang, he didn't want to go back outdoors into that miserable Minnesota blizzard. But his house wasn't any further than the distance he'd carried Mr. Greene. He'd make it alright. Then he'd sit by the wood fire for an hour before going to bed, hoping his room would be warm enough so he wouldn't chill up again.

✡ ✡ ✡

Three days later Devon was summoned to Saint Joseph's hospital at the direct request of Mr. Dellwood Greene. Devon had just finished his breakfast and was talking to his father, when a knock interrupted them. When Devon answered, a young boy handed him an envelope and then left abruptly. The note inside was an invitation of sorts, hand written in neat and precise penmanship.

It read:

Mr. Dellwood Greene requests the honor of your presence at bedside within St. Joseph's Hospital, before the date of December 12, at which time I will be released from treatment. I look forward to your arrival.

D. Greene

"What is it?" Nona asked when he returned to the table.

"A message from the gentleman I took to the hospital the night it was snowing so hard."

"He probably wants to thank you in person. Right nice of him."

Harold grumbled. "Don't go thinkin' about railroading again. Remember, you're going to start with the *Pioneer* just as soon as the holidays are over."

"I haven't forgotten. Besides, what would he want with me? I don't know anything about railroads."

"Anybody can be taught anything. Just takes time. I never knew anything about newspapers until I got into it."

Devon folded the paper and tucked it into his pocket. "I'll stop by and honor his request, soon as we clean up here."

"You go right now," Nona replied. "Visiting this man is more important than taking up space in the kitchen."

Devon scanned his attire, a wool shirt, un-creased trousers baggy at the knees, knitted sweater, common winter wear. He would wear his wool coat over it, a heavy scarf around his neck, and a cap.

"He isn't going to care about how you look," Nona remarked.

Harold grunted. "Just go and get it over with."

✼ ✼ ✼

Saint Joseph's hospital was a three story structure built of stone, with galleries and balconies on each floor, several large commodious wards, and a number of well ventilated private rooms, each having a commanding view of the city or the river. The building also contained facilities for hot and cold baths, and a dispensary. The cost of internment was five dollars per week in the public wards, and eight dollars per week in the private rooms.

Devon was directed to Dellwood Green's private room, one of those with a fine view. When Devon entered, Mr. Green was sitting up in bed, cradled within a fleet of pillows. As soon as he saw Devon, his eyes brightened.

Devon spoke first, "Good morning, Mr. Greene. I am Devon Finch."

Dellwood leaned forward, shifting his body to a more erect position. "Ah, the young man who found me. Come in. Come in." He extended a hand with two fingers still bandaged. Devon found it to be firm and strong, as he expected a railroaders' hand would be.

Nervous in the company of such an important man, Devon was at a loss for words. Then, gathering his courage, he said, "First of all, I must thank you for inviting me here. I was curious about you."

Dellwood released his hand and smoothed the sheet covering his lap. "As I am about you. But I expect my curiosity is greater than yours. It affords me much pleasure to meet the man who saved my life. I knew you would be a strong lad, given the distance you carried me. Come, stand closer so I can get a good look at you."

Devon stepped forward until his legs touched the side of the bed.

Dellwood's face gleamed with pleasure. "I hoped you would be here before tomorrow, when they will release me. Already I feel like dancing a whirligig. I am a man of the outdoors and I hate being confined, especially to a bed." He reached out and took Devon's arm in a strong grip, shook it gently as he continued talking. "I am sure that finding me buried beneath snow makes you wonder why I was there, alone, and in such a state. The truth is, I was struck from behind. I never saw my assailant. I know only that whoever robbed me, also left me to freeze. Until you came along, that is."

"I was fortunate to have found you. Had I taken another route, well, you might have perished."

Dellwood relaxed, releasing his arm. "I was visiting a businessman, a furrier actually, talking about the advantages he would have when our railroad begins service to the Pacific Ocean. Our line of track will open an entirely new world to those who wish to use it to their advantage."

Devon tingled. "I expect it will, sir."

Dellwood leaned back into the comfort of his pillows. "Bear with me. I talk too much, especially upon such short acquaintance. Now tell me about yourself. I am curious to know who you are. Feel at liberty to sit down. Pull up that chair." He motioned to a wooden chair close to the bed.

Devon reached over and pulled it closer, then sat down so they were face to face. How did one tell a stranger about himself, especially someone so important, so finely educated? What was there to say about Devon Finch, who was just a common boy with a limited education?

Nervously, he cleared his throat. "I have nothing much to tell about myself except that I am seventeen, just out of school, and am presently enrolled as a member of the Alliance Committee. I was on duty when I found you merely by accident."

Dellwood shifted toward him, his eyes bearing sharply. "Sometimes futures begin by accident. This is an interesting circumstance, you and I brought together by fate. Strange isn't it, how lives come together."

"Yes, sir, it is."

Dellwood scratched his head. "You did, however, leave some important and useful information out of your introduction. You did not mention the reason you picked me up out of the snow. I expect it was because you had compassion. Nor did you tell me why you carried me block after block in a blizzard to deposit me at this hospital. I expect that was because of duty. And you did not tell me that you came here to visit me simply out of curiosity. No, I expect you came here because of a need to respond to my request, which was an act of courtesy. Am I correct, Mr. Finch?"

"I expect so, sir."

"And you are humble. I admire that in a person."

"Thank you, sir."

Dellwood reached over to the opposite side of the bed, picked up a glass of water and drank four swallows. After replacing the glass, he wiped his mustache and turned back to Devon. "For your knowledge, I have a definite purpose for being in Saint Paul at this time. Let me ask you this. Were you on the levee when the William Crooks came to town?"

"Yes, sir, I was."

"And did you hear what was said that day?"

Devon reacted with surprise. "I did, sir."

"I was there also, although I did not speak."

"I was far back."

Dellwood looked directly at him. "You wouldn't recognize me for the man I was that day, all dressed up fit and proper. Look at me now, in a hospital gown and bare headed. Why, I doubt if my mother would recognize me."

He leaned over slightly and tapped Devon's arm. "As I was saying, I have a definite purpose for being here, and that is to extend a rail line all the way to the Pacific Ocean. Responsibility to a railroad is not the same as a drover leading his sheep. It can be daunting at times."

"I expect so, sir."

Dellwood nodded as if agreeing with his own statement. "So, let's get to the facts. You are the man who saved my life. You went out of your way to bring me here. Others might have just walked on and left me to freeze. I believe something so worthy should be rewarded." He looked straight into Devon's eyes with all the power and influence his gaze commanded and then nodded. "I am looking for men with determination as their main tenet, men who can shoulder responsibility with a firm conviction, to succeed at their endeavor against whatever the odds, specifically a man who understands the purpose behind his work, someone who will not turn away from challenges. I believe you are that sort of person, Devon Finch."

Devon swallowed. He was unaware that his mouth had opened. Then, realizing the seriousness of the moment, he said convincingly. "Yes sir. I believe you have described me quite well, sir."

"Do you take strong drink?'

"No sir."

"Are you honest and trustworthy?"

"You can inquire about that from Mr. Western, who is the Chief of Police. He is responsible for the functioning of the Alliance Committee. He will give you a proper reply."

"And what is your occupational aspiration, after your time with the Alliance is finished?

"I was going to leave the Alliance forthwith, to work with my father at the *Pioneer and Democrat*, our newspaper."

Dellwood brushed his mustache. "Was that your career of choice?"

"No sir."

"What was it then?"

"If I am at liberty to say so, without sounding untruthful, it was railroading. Ever since the day the William Crooks arrived, and when I heard that speech about a rail line westward, I have been enticed."

"Is that it, then?"

Devon nodded. "Unless the Union Army comes lookin' for me. They may be asking for more men."

"Would you go if you were asked?"

Devon's body straightened proudly. "I expect I would. My brother died at Ball's Bluff just weeks ago. If I could avenge his death, yes, I would, sir."

Dellwood folded his arms "And if I could save you from that terrible war, would you accept my help?"

"Sir?"

Dellwood leaned closer. "This railroad of ours is of vital interest to our country. The government will not interfere with us in our effort to expand. In fact, they will support us in every way possible, including manpower."

Devon's thoughts raced as if hurrying to meet a deadline. Had he heard Dellwood correctly? Was he, in fact, tantalizing him with an opportunity to work with the railroad? His mouth went dry as he replied. "Are you offering me a position, sir?"

Dellwood nodded. "I am. I believe you are just the type of individual we are searching for, if you are willing to accept,"

"I am, sir."

"Then I expect we will be seeing much more of one another come the first of the year. I will be putting together my work force soon. If you accept my offer, you will be working with me in whatever category I chose for you, to further our reach to the ocean."

Devon was not a loss for words. "Sir, I don't know what to say?"

"Well, if you wish to go railroading, then say, Aye, sir."

Devon grinned. Every nerve in his body pulsed, as if he were on fire inside. "Aye, sir," he replied with great conviction.

Dellwood extended his hand. Devon took it in as strong a grip as possible. "Then we have a deal."

Devon nodded. "I can't wait to tell Caroline."

"And who is Caroline?'

"She will be my future wife. We plan to marry as soon as I am established in a career."

Dellwood snickered "Then tell her you will be a railroader. Tell her that within five years you will take her to see the Pacific Ocean."

"She will be pleased, sir."

"And, like any curious woman, she will want to know what you will be earning."

Devon's curiosity increased his intended restraint. "If so, what should I tell her?"

"Two-hundred-and-ten dollars a month, guaranteed. It is anyone's guess as to where it will go."

Devon could not withhold the startled expression that brought a smile to Dellwood's face. The salary was twice that of a policeman, and also of a printer. He could never earn that amount of money in a common job. This was the opportunity of a lifetime, an offer he could not dismiss.

Dellwood continued talking. "You may work in weather as cold as the Arctic, or as hot as the Sahara, but you will earn good money. You will be able to educate your children, and provide well for your wife, and live better than most."

Devon did not hesitate. "I will accept your offer, sir."

Dellwood's smile broadened. "Ah, I was hoping you would. Go now. I have to get ready to walk out of here. My job awaits me. I will be in contact with you, Mr. Finch, and bid you welcome to the St. Paul and Pacific Railroad."

"I will give you my best, sir."

"Of that I am certain. Good day now."

Devon left the hospital on winged feet. He stood in the snow, momentarily ignoring the wind, as he reviewed the conversation with Dellwood Greene. Their verbal exchange had grown from seed into a magnificent bloom, and, God willing, he would be working on the railroad at a wage he thought unattainable only an hour before. Fate had worked its magic again.

Snow was being cleared with shovel and horse plow. Above, the sun gave promise to a better day. He would not see Caroline until evening, nor would he see his father until supper time. His good news would have to remain silent until then.

He thought to inform Western about his good fortune, but just as quickly he changed his mind. Perhaps a trip to LaBelle's would be in order. If Kane was there, he would bid him a final farewell.

As he walked toward home, he thought about clearing ground, and laying track, and working in bitter cold and on hot days as Mr. Greene had implied. But they might not assign him to a track crew. He expected his work would be less physical, perhaps that of a foreman, or someone who directed the laborers. Time would tell. He could always back out if the work was overly demanding, or dangerous, or laborious. But as the thought crossed his mind, he knew he would accept whatever challenge came his way, regardless of its nature.

✯ ✯ ✯

When told of Devon's good fortune that night, Harold Finch sat back in his chair and said nothing for a while, just puffed on his pipe while sharing a silent conversation with Nona, leaving Devon to imagine what his response might be. He had seen his father in contemplative moods before, but nothing quite like then, with his eyes fixed in hard observation, his lips tight against his teeth. Nona said nothing. She awaited Harold's reply, as a dutiful wife would, with her hands folded gracefully in her lap, her gaze fixed pensively on Harold. Her fleeting glance toward Devon neither approved nor disapproved of the possibility that he might soon be working for the railroad, which was frightening to her, given its power and majesty.

"Well now," Harold finally said. "It is quite a surprise you have given us. It seems that your good deed has reaped a reward. I don't know who this Dellwood Greene is, except what is written about him in the newspaper. He seems to be a visionary of sorts, someone with a goal and a steadfast understanding of how to make things happen. You might have done worse, Devon."

Devon sighed, "Then you approve?"

"I need not approve. This is your choice, not mine. But I will say that opportunity is rare in a lifetime, and one must snatch it up before it fades. I believe you will make the right choice."

"I have already accepted Mr. Greene's offer."

Harold nodded, though he appeared to be doleful. "I was hoping you would work alongside me on the newspaper. I hoped that someday that you might become an editor, or a copywriter, or a reporter. You have talent for all three. But I also know that you are adventurous, and would accept that occupation only as a last resort."

Devon waited patiently for the remainder of his father's statement, knowing there would be more.

"My pride would have been satisfied, working with you. But this, this, railroading would keep you out of the army, and that in itself is a blessing. Your duty to country can be served by running a line all the way to the Pacific. It's a grand undertaking. I'm proud of you, son."

Nona gasped, thankful that Harold's statement had ended positively. "And I am too, Devon. God willing you will make a grand addition to the *Saint Paul and Pacific Railroad.*"

Devon nodded. His gratitude was nearly expressed in tears, but he held them back in preference to words. "Thank you for being so understanding. A son has never had such wonderful parents. I will make you proud of me."

They talked on, mentioning Randolph only once, of how pleased he would have been if told of Devon's decision. Then Devon asked to be excused. He had to tell Caroline of his good fortune, and announce to her parents his choice of occupation.

✭ ✭ ✭

Tea and cookies were served at the Page house. Then, afterwards, when told the news about Devon's good fortune, Caroline embraced him fondly for the first time in the company of her parents.

At one point during the conversation, Devon said. "And we will live on the bluff above the city in a grand home, from where we can look down on Lowertown and have pride in the fact that I have contributed to its growth. Think of how we will feel then."

At which point, Mr. Page said, "Bring out the wine, Lillian. We must drink to Devon's new opportunity. I personally know Mr. Greene. He is determined to bring this railroad to the west coast, and he will, of that I am sure. Devon is fortunate to have a part in this grand venture. Let us wish him well."

Wine was served to all, even to Bethany, though in a smaller amount. The night was grand. Devon was so filled with pride that he thought he might burst. Every time he looked at Caroline her eyes were upon him. If she were an angel she could not have looked more beautiful. He sensed love strongly then, and he vowed to build his dream around her, to make her remember and cherish the first day she had taken hold of his hand.

When the brief party was over, and Bethany had sung, Devon said goodnight, but not before kissing Caroline outside, where the only warmth was that of their embrace.

"I must make one last stop at LaBelle's," he said. "I must tell Willius Kane of my good fortune. If he is not there, then that is the last of it."

"Don't go, Devon," she pleaded.

"It will only take a short time. Then I will plan our future."

"Be careful."

"I will. There is nothing to fear."

They embraced, and he kissed her. Then, as she entered the house, he began his walk toward LaBelle's, a walk that would signal the end of his duty to the Alliance and to the culture of river men and gamblers, trappers and lumbermen, whores and drunkards.

Thankfully, his obligation was over. Now he could concentrate on his future, and a marriage to the woman he loved.

Moonlight blanketed the hillsides with a ghostly shroud, turning them silver-gray beneath its glow. The still silence gave the city an illusory quality; a sense of peace. He was at ease with himself and the hush of night, content with the lingering memory of Caroline's lips upon his own. Flighty with the portent of his future, he had the impression of floating above the street, above the frozen clay, as if he were traveling into the night sky winking with a billion stars.

CHAPTER THIRTY

Bill Kirkman

Devon arrived at LaBelle's well after dark. Only eight patrons occupied the place, four at the bar, three at one table, and another in the back, he being the lonely man who had lost his house to Flynn. As long as he kept buying booze, they would keep him around. He slept beneath the stairs at night, amid the crates and boxes. A poor sight he was, lost and confused, with nothing on his person but what he earned by picking up horse droppings from the streets.

Devon motioned the bartender his way. "This will be my last visit. I'm leaving the Alliance."

The bartender nodded, setting aside the glass he was wiping. He took Devon's hand in a rather soft grip. "You've seen the best and the worst of us," he replied.

"Sometimes both in one night."

The bartender laughed. "I'll keep the worst, bein' what they are. They pay my keep."

"Have you seen anything of Kane recently?"

"Yesterday."

"He was here?"

"For an hour or so. He had two whiskeys, and then left. He wasn't sociable, given the time of day. He looked like he'd just walked through a blizzard."

"He likely did."

"Looked sullen, he did."

Devon said goodbye and then wandered slowly through the place. None of the women were present. With Sissy gone, none were likely to speak to him anyway.

One man sitting at a table motioned him over. He was dressed in a heavy woolen coat that had seldom seen soap or brush. "I overheard that you're leavin' this blessed place," he said.

"I am."

"No more a need to watch your back."

"Guess not."

"Where's your stick tonight?"

"I left it home. I'm finished with it."

"Well, be gone with you then."

"I'll soon be working on the railroad."

The three of them laughed. One of them said. "Carryin' coal?"

"Could be," Devon said, moving away.

A slight yelp from the back captured his attention. The man who had lost his house to Flynn had stood up and was howling like a dog.

"What's wrong with him?" Devon asked.

"The old coot's been sittin' there all day drinkin'. Hasn't had a bite to eat. About every hour he just orders another shot, sips it, and hoots once in a while. It's a wonder he's still on his feet. Hope he falls asleep soon."

"What's his name?"

"Kirkman, Bill Kirkman. Strange one, he is."

"Isn't he the one that lost his house to Flynn?"

The man laughed, as did the others. "Lock, stock and key, he did. Dumb son-of-a-bitch."

"Then why is he so happy?"

"Drunk happy is what he is. Right now he don't know the time of day. If he don't sober up soon he might even lose his job pickin' up shit."

The heavy-set man opposite the table roared with laughter at the statement.

Devon walked away. He took one last look around the place, while remembering the day he and Flynn had first met, and the day Kane came into his life. He also remembered Ingrid, her features, her emotions, her mannerisms, her beauty. Damn her killer, he thought. And he remembered Sissy, delightful little Sissy, who was now on her way to a new life somewhere along the Mississippi.

Then a laugh came from the man named Kirkman. He was a sorry sight, hooting like an owl for no reason at all. Devon thought it impossible that someone who had nothing but the clothes on his back, and the worse job in the city, could be aroused about anything. Or was he just drunk-happy. Once again, curiosity got the best of Devon and he walked back toward the staircase. Bill Kirkman was still snickering when Devon sat down opposite him, close enough so he could smell the horse dung on his clothing.

He eased back as Kirkman sat up. "Hello, I'm Devon Finch," he said.

Kirkman swayed a bit. His half-closed eyes swam as if immersed in swamp water. His face, a mass of whiskers, was mostly black, but grey in places. His brown tongue came through his lips like a small turd, moving with the slowness of a turtle. He blinked, leveled what remained of his sight, and coughed up whatever was interfering with his voice. "Who's Devon Finch?' he asked in a raspy voice.

Before answering, Devon wondered why he had ever walked back to the table. He had no interest in Mr. Kirkman, other than being curious. He assured himself that his visit would be brief. "I'm a member of the Alliance. You've probably seen me in here before."

Kirkman rubbed his nose, wiped whatever came out onto his sleeve. He squinted, trying to remember. Then his eyes widened. "Damned if I haven't. You're the one . . . nearly got cut up . . . a while back."

Devon grinned. "Call it what you will."

A laugh gurgled in Kirkman's throat. "Hell . . . if Kane hadn't pulled him away, you'd have lost an ear, or maybe . . . your nose. Men like him, or Flynn, don't fool around."

"You know Flynn then?"

Kirkman leaned a bit, and then steadied himself with his hand. He scratched his beard as if it was full of lice. "Know him. Why he's the man . . . took my house."

"You don't say."

"Fair and . . . square it was. He beat me with a . . . better poker hand." He slammed the table hard enough to make Devon jump.

Devon suppressed his grin. "Must have been devastating, losing your house."

Kirkman lifted his shot glass, looked into it and grimaced when he found it empty. He slammed the glass down and then worked his chin side to side as if to unloosen it. His voice came out raspy. "Lost my family, too. They left . . . soon as I told 'em about my bad luck. Went south they did . . . to live with her brother in Missouri. Hope they're happy there. I thought after . . . they was gone that I'd . . . be better off killin' myself. But common sense prevailed."

Poor devil, Devon reasoned, lost everything, even hope. He'd never seen a worse specimen of a man. He wondered why he was wasting his time even talking to him. But his curiosity prevailed. "I've seen you here just about every time I've come in."

Kirkman waved toward the bar. "Old' Hank Pauls . . . he owns this place. He felt sorry for me. As long as I buy his . . . whiskey . . . he puts me up."

"That's nice of him."

Kirkman huffed. "Without him I'd be layin' out . . . in the goddam snow."

Devon watched as he twirled the empty shot glass around and around with his fingers. Then Kirkman mumbled. "I gotta piss."

"Tell you what," Devon said. "You go take care of your problem and when you come back I'll have another shot of whisky waiting for you."

"Why?" he asked, his eyes glazing.

"Because I think you need one. It will be my last gesture of good will inside this den of iniquity."

"Gotta piss," Kirkman mumbled, rising from his chair. He stood up straight as if rearranging his bones, then stepped off, and muttered. "One more's . . . about all I can take."

As he disappeared through the door at the bottom of the staircase, Devon went to the bar and ordered another whiskey. When the bartender put the glass down, he said, "What do you want with that sorry son-of-a-bitch?"

Devon shrugged. "Actually, I don't know. I guess I was just curious about him."

"I've wanted to throw him out a half dozen times, but I can't be brutal. Poor bastard's lost everything, thanks to Flynn."

"Well, I'll say my goodbye with this." Devon hoisted the shot glass and was about to lay down a coin when Hank Pauls said. "Forget it, this one's on the house."

Disturbed by his incessant curiosity, Devon returned to the table. Why was he waiting for Kirkman to return? Why didn't he just leave, and forget about LaBelle's once and for all. He was just about to do so when Kirkman stumbled back to the table. Without saying a word, he picked up the shot glass and emptied it with one swallow.

"Got to go out and . . . walk the streets pretty soon. I'm a goddam . . .shit picker."

"You clean up after the horses."

"Yep," he coughed. "And believe, me . . . there's lots of horses."

"Does the city pay you?"

"By the cartful."

"It takes strong legs to walk the streets all day."

Kirkman puffed out his chest. "Huh, got three things . . . that's strong . . . my legs, my arms, and my back. Hell, walkin' . . . ain't nothin'. Why I walked all the way back . . . from Saint Anthony just over . . . a week ago. T'was nothin' to it."

The sudden mention of Saint Anthony brought Devon to full attention. What was a man like Kirkman doing in Saint Anthony? Why would he seek passage on the stage? And why would he walk back when he could have returned the same way? Besides, where did a down-and-out loser get the money? Suddenly, Devon looked at the drunken man in an entirely new light. Cautiously, he framed his reply.

"What were you doing in Saint Anthony?"

Kirkman's eyes narrowed. "That's my business."

"I guess it is. I've never been there."

"T'ain't much there. Bunch of houses . . . lots of prairie, a goddam waterfall."

Go easy now, Devon thought. Don't lose the opportunity to a bunch of stupid questions. He leaned back in his chair, casual like, and stretched his arms. "My future wife and I thought about moving there when we get married. She happens to like Saint Anthony, especially after she'd seen the waterfall."

Kirkman became pensive then. "Maybe when I get my . . . house back, I can send for my wife again. Don't know if she'd . . . come. She hates winter."

"When will you get your house back?'

"In . . . two days."

Kirkman seemed to have lost his frenzy since mentioning his wife. Devon was confident that another question would receive a proper reply. "Why in two days?"

"You're a nosey kid . . . for knowin' me only a few minutes."

"I'm the curious kind."

"You . . . sure as hell . . . are."

Hold it, Devon thought. His father had always said, that when the going gets tough, take another course, or brace up to the present. Well, now was the time to toughen. He would steer the conversation by switching track. "I'm leaving the Alliance," he said. "This will be my last day in LaBelle's. I'm going to be working on the railroad come the first of the year."

Kirkman's eyes flowed his way. "You don't say."

"I saved a man's life the other day. He promised me a job. Maybe when I get hired on I can get you a job on the railroad too."

Kirkman sat up straighter in his chair. His shuttered eyes brightened. "Might you do that?"

"Well, it all depends."

"Depends . . . on what?"

"On how much you want the job."

Kirkman confusion became obvious. His eyes nearly closed, and for a while he appeared to be deep in thought. Then he bit hard on his teeth as he put words to his thought. "It might just make the difference . . . to gettin' my kids back. What job would I have . . . on the railroad?"

Devon knew he had him again. "Well, you'd have a choice. You could be a switchman, a Tender, or a Station keeper, or maybe someday an Engineer."

Kirkman sighed. "No more . . . shit pickin'."

"No more shit pickin' for sure. Why once you get a new job and your house back, you could be on your feet in no time."

Kirkman's nostrils flared as he righted himself in the chair. His tongue moved to clear away the scum inside his mouth. "I'd be . . . interested . . . sure as hell."

Take it easy now, Devon thought. Put that hook right where he'll see it, and juggle it a bit. "But this is my last day here. Come January I won't know where to find you."

"I'll be home, in my . . . house."

"I thought you lost your house to Flynn."

Kirkman was eager, ready to bite. He spoke freely. "Flynn gave it . . . back to me. He just up and said I could . . . have it back, that he wouldn't be . . . needing it anymore."

"Why aren't you in it now?"

"Because I ain't got . . . the key yet. He said he'd give me the key in two days."

Oh, my God, Devon thought. If Kirkman was to get a key in two days, then Flynn had not taken the stage to Saint Anthony. Kirkman had gone in his place. Flynn had never left the city. He was here, somewhere, perhaps in Kirkman's house. Suddenly his mind swarmed with thoughts. "But he's gone," Devon said.

At that moment Kirkman appeared confused. He's playing with the bait, Devon thought. He hasn't swallowed it yet, but he will. Go easy now. Every word you say might send him swimming away. "Tell you what. Regardless of when you get the house back, just tell me where it is and I'll contact you when I start working for the railroad."

The question seemed to suit Kirkman just find. "It's on . . . Fourth Street, one block east of the Western Hotel, first house . . . on the corner."

Devon smiled. "That's not far from my home."

"It's one of the few that was spared . . . from the fire . What a helluva thing . . . that was."

"Sure was. I remember watching it from my window."

Kirkman peered at his empty glass again, and licked his lips. "Can you buy me another . . . whiskey? I'm a bit short . . . on money."

He had swallowed the bait. Now, just jerk the line and reel him in. Devon knew where Flynn was staying. As soon as he informed Western they'd go and roust him out, and charge him with Ingrid's murder. What if he hadn't come over to the table? What if he hadn't spoken to Kirkman? A flood of emotion ran through him as he pushed his chair away from the table.

"Look, Mr. Kirkman. I have to go now. I've got to get back to work. But I'll be in touch with you soon."

Kirkman worked a hand through his beard. "I'll be waitin'."

"Now you have a good holiday. And if I were you, I'd stop drinkin' so much. Anyone I hire onto the railroad has got to be sober. No whiskey. You understand?"

"This is my . . . last one, for sure."

"I hope so. If you keep drinkin', then I'm afraid my offer's got to be withdrawn, safety first and sobriety being two main rules of the railroad."

"I . . . understand."

Although he had made Kirkman an offer, and had given him a stipulation, he knew Kirkman would never stop drinking, not now, not ever. He would be a shit-picker for the rest of his life.

Devon was emphatic. "Now I don't want you goin' back to that house until you get the key. I don't want any trouble between you and Mr. Flynn."

"No . . . trouble"

"Alright. Now you stay out of trouble. One more thing, you wash those clothes and take a bath, and clean yourself up. I don't want you workin' for the railroad when you smell like horse shit."

Kirkman wiped his hands across the front of his shirt. "I . . . promise."

"Good day then, Mr. Kirkman. I'll see you after the first of the year, provided you're clean and sober."

Devon could hardly wait to get out of the saloon. When the door closed behind him he stood for a full minute, reviewing what had happened. He was euphoric; the way he had been the night he and Caroline had made love in his bedroom, but in a different way.

He couldn't wait to tell Western. But the hour was late. Western would be in bed. The good news would have to wait until morning.

He stepped onto the street, wanting to shout. Dang, if he hadn't done a good piece of detective work. He had found out where Flynn might be. Kirkman hadn't come right out and said it, but all the pieces of the puzzle fit so well together that Devon could hardly believe his own thoughts. By tomorrow night, Flynn would be behind bars, and he would be a hero.

He started toward home, up Robert Street toward the Western Hotel. His body tingled when he passed Bench, then Third. He would go straight up to Fifth Street before turning for home. He was exhilarated. Even the cold didn't hinder him. Were it not for his encounter with Mr. Greene just a few days before, this would never have happened.

He came upon Fourth Street, convinced he would go straight on for one more block before turning toward home. But by then his curiosity had peaked, and without further thought he turned and began walking toward Court House Square. The street would take him directly past Kirkman's house.

He stopped soon enough. There it was, a small a-frame house with blistered paint still showing from the fire. He looked at it, wondering if Flynn was inside, wondering why he had chosen to stay in town, obviously realizing that he was a suspect in Ingrid's murder. It didn't seem right that he'd gone to all this trouble, when all he'd needed was to get on that stage to Saint Anthony.

He looked at the chimney. No smoke rising. The windows were covered from the inside. The place appeared to be empty. No tracks in the snow leading to the door. Maybe Flynn wasn't there. Maybe Kirkman had just been weaving a story while laughing inside, to fool the dumb kid working for the Alliance.

He shrugged. At that moment he heard footsteps behind him. He turned as something struck him on the head.

CHAPTER THIRTY-ONE

The Devil

Devon's eyes opened to absolute darkness. Still groggy from the blow on his head, and from the throbbing pain above his right ear, his eyes searched through the room in which he lay.

He saw nothing, just darkness, and no sense of place.

He was aware of life, of breathing, of his ability to swallow, but movements were restricted. Something tight held his hands together, and his feet as well. When he attempted to move forward his body failed to respond. Then reasoning came, although slowly, but definite enough to allow for thought. Of course . . . he was bound by a restraint of some kind across his body, his legs, and his neck. Something dry and bitter tasting had been stuffed into his mouth, a wad of cloth held in place by a length of rag fastened tight at the back of his neck. He made an effort to scream but his voice came as nothing but a dull and unintelligible grunt. Fear followed, gnawing at him like an insatiable creature, chewing at his mind, his sanity, his ability to reason.

He began trembling then, not so much from the cold, but from the fear that invaded him. Calm yourself, he thought. Get through it. You'll need a clear head and a clear mind in order to function properly, in order to think, and to act promptly if time or opportunity presents itself. Without them the chance for survival is limited. Think now! Think!

He breathed deeply, drew cold air into his lungs as his chest heaved. Then, through sheer willpower, he stilled his trembling hands, his legs, and his body, and slowly began to replace fear with reason.

He remembered standing in the street, alone, looking at the house, the one Flynn had won from . . . oh, what was his name? . . . . the drunk . . . the shit-picker. . . think, damn it . . . think! Someone had struck him just above his ear on the right side of his head where most of the pain was centered. Could it have been Flynn? Or someone else . . . the same way Dellwood had been struck . . . but no . . . it had to have been Flynn . . . could have been no one else. He had been looking at the house when the blow came, and now reason told him that he was inside the house, tied to something . . . the stove perhaps, for he could feel the rounded part of a metal object positioned against his spine.

Panic swarmed through his body. He sensed danger like an oncoming wave. He tried to scream, but his muffled voice merely groaned in his throat. His thoughts flowed away, pushed aside by wave after wave of compressing fear. He began trembling as tears welled in his eyes.

Come out of it, he thought. Come back to reality. Think! You'll have to concentrate . . . despite the pain, despite the fear.

He willed himself to calmness again, and then shifted, to test the tightness of his bonds, to seek a weakness . . . but the binding that held him would not move. He was tied tightly, with a stout rope. There appeared to be no way to shift it, or cut it, or snake through it. His assailant had done a masterful job.

His fingers had numbed, which meant he had been tied for some time. His hands were barely moveable. And the cold! Oh, good Lord, the cold . . . no heat in the room . . . only darkness, a deep, clutching darkness revealing nothing. He calmed himself through sheer willpower, while urging his breathing back to normal. Slowly and deliberately, he moved his toes, his feet, and his

The Devil

legs, but sensed only a raw and discomforting chill, as if sealed in a room filled with ice.

Then he saw a faint sliver of light across the room. Of course, the windows were boarded. He could scarcely see them. He moved his head, looked around as best he could as shapes began forming. Yes, he was in a room . . . in Flynn's house for sure. He trembled again as panic rose inside him. The increased pounding of his heart beat like a hammer against an anvil.

Panic came again, rolling through him like a mighty wave. Nobody knew where he was! No one would be arriving the following morning to free him. He would be missed, of course, but no one, not even Western, would know of his whereabouts. He was at the mercy of a madman, and any chance at escape appeared utterly impossible.

Gradually, he took possession of his thoughts. He remembered Kirkman saying that he would take possession of the home within two days. Two days! My God, he might be dead by then. No one would find him . . . no one! Immediate questions would be raised when he failed to arrive home. Surely, his parents would notify Western. Then the search would begin, first the streets, then the levee, then the riverfront, then the buildings, LaBelle for sure. Eventually, they might come upon the house, or they might not, it being boarded up as it was. They knew nothing about Kirkman's loss of the home to Flynn. And even if they did put the puzzle together, would he still be alive when they broke the door down?

His life was in peril, and he knew it. Flynn could very well kill him before the sun came up. Or he could just lay there, bound up like a criminal, to die a slow death.

Where was Flynn? Was he here, in the house? Or had he left him to die of starvation, or to freeze when the temperature dropped, or to perish of fright. Questions remained unanswered, concealed amid the cold and darkness. Once again he tugged at his restraint but his remaining strength soon gave way to weakness.

Then a raspy voice came to him from the darkness. "Your efforts are useless. I tied you tight."

Devon stiffened. He recognized the voice! Flynn! He was not more than five feet away, judging by its sound, just behind his range of vision, near the side of the stove to which he was tied. Fear galloped through him.

"Came snooping, didn't ya? I suppose Kirkman opened his mouth, told you about this place. Damn his hide. I'd kill him first if I could."

Kill him first? What did he mean by, first?

"Now that I've got you, I'll do what's necessary to silence your tongue. You had to go and send that steamer away without me, didn't you? Had to interfere into my life, didn't ya? Had to go and put my name in Western's head as a suspect to Ingrid's murder, didn't ya? Why, hell, Devon Finch, if you ain't the gabbiest man I ever met, and the one I most despise. I ought to put my knife in your mouth right now and cut that venomous tongue of yours to ribbons, so's you can swallow the mess. Truth is, you just lost the final hand, Finch. All I need do now is to kill you . . . and I will."

Devon's attempted scream was thwarted by the dry cloth stuffed in his mouth. His voice came like a moan, like the sound of a steamer grinding against a pier.

He cringed against the stove as hope skittered away.

He turned his head far to the right to where he could see Flynn out of the corner of his eye, just a shadow in the darkness. As he did, Flynn moved closer, then bent down alongside him, close enough so Devon could smell his breath, a taint of onion and whiskey, and his sweaty, offensive body.

Flynn snickered. "You're gonna stay bound, my one-time friend. If you gotta piss, then piss in your pants. It'll just freeze in time. And if you're hungry, then just eat the sock. It's one of mine. It ain't been washed in a month. It should taste just fine, of dirt and sweat, and of skin that peeled off between my toes. Something for a condemned man to suck on, who's got about an hour left to live."

Flynn was frightening him, for sure. Devon's fear moved like a snake inside him, crawling up his spine, twisting around his heart, a terrible fright he couldn't control, one that ate at him like a ravenous predator.

"I thought we were friends once. Then you had to go and turn on me. Nothin' I hate worse than a turncoat. You dumb kid. You

The Devil

just don't know when to keep your mouth shut," Flynn's voice puffed with his breaths. "Maybe I'll just cut your tongue out. Or, better yet, maybe I'll just slice off your gonads. Ha, that might be better than killin' ya. Your little woman wouldn't like you much after that, now would she?"

Something hard and cold probed between his legs. He stiffened. His buttocks squeezed tight against the floor. A knife! Damn, if Kane didn't have a knife between his legs. The cold point pierced the leg of his pants, and he felt the flat blade against his skin. Fear raced through him, shivering his entire body.

He braced himself. Breath pumped through his nose with bellows force, faster and faster with the pounding of his heart.

"Got you scared, don't I?" Flynn muttered.

Devon screamed. His voice muffled behind the sock. His eyes rolled up tight beneath his clenched eyelids. His legs strained as they tried to draw back from the cold touch of the blade.

Then it withdrew.

"Not yet. You ain't suffered enough."

Devon collapsed in his bonds as breath rushed out of him. Every muscle in his body trembled.

Then Flynn said, "I got company for ya."

As Devon squeezed his legs together, Flynn moved away, just a shadow without features, no shape, just a swelling of darkness within darkness.

"I got Sissy in the other room."

Devon's eyes rolled, searching out, trying to see beyond the limit of his vision.

"I'll bet your curiosity is up."

Flynn was lying for sure. Sissy was on the steamer headed for New Orleans. He had seen her there, had talked to her when she was already aboard.

Kane's voice slurred a bit. "You know those river men. They'd do anything for money."

What had he done? Bribed a boatman?

The silent question was answered immediately. "Found one that owed me a favor. I gave him a little money, and a bottle of whiskey. Hell, those river men would fuck a cow for whisky. All it took was a knock on her door and a little chloroform under her nose, and she was ready to put into a sack. Who'd question a seaman carrying a sack off the boat?

Was he telling the truth? It sounded possible. But why would he bother with Sissy? Why would he take a chance on being discovered? True enough, she was the only witness standing between him and a hangman's noose, but why would he have encountered her when she was leaving the city? He'd probably never see her again, nor would she tell a single soul about his crime. Sissy had been headed for freedom. She was so scared of the devil inside Flynn, that she wouldn't have told anyone about his guilt.

"She saw me right after I cut Ingrid's throat. I needed money that night, and I knew she'd be flush when she set out for the west. But she denied me. Women shouldn't deny me like that. I hate denials. My mother used to deny me things, till I put a knife in her gut. Women are all alike. Whores is the worst of 'em. They're nothin' but sin walkin' on two legs, out to devastate men's minds."

Devon strained, trying to see across the room.

"No need lookin'. She's in the parlor, tied down hands and feet, spread-eagled. She ain't dressed. Not a stitch on her, just a blanket. Damn, she's pretty that way. I have my way with her, two, three times a day, and she can't do a damn thing about it. She's got my other sock in her mouth."

Flynn laughed, just a chugging in his throat.

The man was crazy, insane. Devon strained at his bonds again amid a growl of laughter.

"You're fighting a losing battle, Finch. You ain't breaking loose. I made sure of that. You'll stay tied up until I cut you up."

Devon pounded his feet against the floor. Then Flynn came at him, his hand clenched. His fist smashed against Devon's face, hard, like a stone, followed by another, and another, and another.

Devon's senses blanked then. He drifted off into darkness and pain and fear combined. He heard Flynn move away, and later, when the ringing in his ears subsided, he heard the repetitive sounds of hard breathing. He knew Flynn was having his way with Sissy, there in the parlor, a place he could not see.

It would be light soon. Then perhaps he could see something.

The Devil

Before long the sounds from the parlor ceased.
Perhaps Flynn had fallen asleep.
Maybe Sissy was dead.

Time moved with interminable slowness, stalling thought and sanity. He counted seconds into minutes, to provide assurance that time had not ceased. The darkness was a womb of death, and he its unborn fetus. Fear rode him like the devil

In time his thoughts began to take on the form of dreamscapes, lasting only long enough to form incomplete pictures of the past; he and Caroline together on his bed, laughter coming like a sad song from somewhere deep in the black interior. At times he imagined voices in the darkness, inventive sounds that provided relief from hopelessness. He prayed then, silently hoping that God would hear him. Was there a Savior in this black and putrid house? Hope seemed elusive.

Would Flynn actually kill them?
Would they be rescued?
Would they die here?

As the next few hours passed he realized that survival would depend largely on his ability to take risks. He would have to seize even the smallest opportunity when it came, on the chance that his actions might work.

Devon Finch was not prepared to die. But he would risk death in order to live. He would watch, and wait, and when the time came he would act quickly and without hesitation. Foolish or not, it was his only option. He had already determined that Flynn would kill him and Sissy when they were of no further use to him, when he had used her up, or when his blood lust was fever hot. Today, he thought, Flynn would kill them today. He couldn't want any longer. By the time twilight came Flynn would have to get out of town, on foot if necessary.

Devon stared into the darkness, squeezing tears into submission, toughening himself for the time when he would have to gamble with death.

Just before dawn he heard the door open, and in the dim rush of early morning light he saw Flynn go outside. As a current of cold air brushed against him, he heard the door close.

He and Sissy were alone.
He had to find a way to communicate with her, but how?

CHAPTER THIRTY-TWO

Beyond Concern

Nona Finch had set three places for morning breakfast when Harold came into the kitchen. He kissed her lightly on the cheek and then took his place at the table, where he asked his first question, "Where is Devon this morning?"

She turned, wiping her hands on a towel. "Why, he must still be in his room."

Harold's brow furrowed. "He is not in his room. I looked before I came down. His bed was still made. Did he leave early this morning?"

Nona's face stiffened with concern. "I did not see him."

"Did you hear him come home last night?"

Nona thought for a moment. "No. Nor did I hear a sound from his room."

"Did you sleep soundly last night?'

She drew out her chair and sat down. Concern lined her face. "I was awake during part of the night. I heard nothing."

"What hours does he have today?"

"The same as yesterday. He should have been home shortly after midnight. Yes, I am sure." She gasped. "He is long overdue."

Devon always arose before breakfast. If he needed further rest afterwards, he did so later in the day before he went off to Lowertown. He was a considerate boy, always prompt, never expecting his mother to work more than necessary. He did not like eating alone.

"Where might he be?"

Nona's hand went to her mouth. "I don't know, Harold."

"He's seldom late for breakfast."

Nona toyed nervously with her apron. "Do you think something's wrong?"

"I don't know. All I know is that Lowertown has become both a godsend and a demon to him."

Nona's hand went to her mouth, trembling. "Now you're scaring me."

"I'm sorry. I didn't mean to alarm you." His fingers rapped on the table while Nona prepared the eggs.

Harold sat still, thinking. Devon found that railroad man lying in the snow, nearly frozen. Now maybe it's Devon out there somewhere lying in the snow. God knows, there are enough thieves ready to take a man down for whatever is in his pockets. Even though the steamboats are gone, Lowertown still housed lawbreakers and ruffians and drunkards who'd sell their mothers for a drink. Helluva town it was. Worst one on the river. And Devon's right in the midst of it, for the sake of keeping peace. Thank God he'd done his share. Now was his time to concentrate on the future.

Devon's absence weighed heavily on Nona's as well. She continued watching him, having known Harold long enough to identify his moods, to see worry, and to sense hidden anguish.

When Harold was finished, he leaned forward on the table and cradled his head in his hands. "I've got to go to work now. But first I'll pay Mr. Western a visit."

Nona sighed. "Do you think something has happened to Devon?"

"No dear. He might be there just passin' time. He does that on occasion. If I leave now I'll still have time to see for myself, and make it to work on time."

He took Nona's hand and pressed it between his own. "Now don't go worrying. I don't want his absence to bother you all day."

"But it will bother me."

"Go about your work. If he's with Western I'll tell him to scurry on home for the sake of his mother."

He kissed her lightly on the cheek and then headed out.

Harold dressed warm for winter, long underwear, heavy trousers, a wool shirt, a sweater, a sheepskin coat, gloves, and a scarf under his flat-top coachman hat.

The temperature hovered near fifteen degrees. A haze covered the city like a low fog. Smoke from log fires crowded in a gray drift above the houses. Thankfully, the wind had lessened in the morning's silence. The only sound came from the crunch of Harold's boots on the snow, the puffing of his breath, and the clatter of harness down near Cramsie's Wagon Shop. Three more months of this, he thought, before the river opens up. Three more months of ice and cold and knee deep snow.

He pulled his collar tight to his neck and picked up his pace, hoping to find Devon drowsing in Western's office.

CHAPTER THIRTY-THREE

Only Prayers Remain

Devon made a mumbling sound. He couldn't form words, just noise, hardly audible enough to be heard, much less interpreted.

Daylight had begun seeping through the narrow slats where the boards met, thin streaks of light that barely eased the darkness. But it did provide Devon enough light in which to identify his surroundings.

He was in a small room, containing the wood stove to which he was tied, a chair, a slanted picture on one wall, and a small vanity to his left, a pitcher on its surface with two glasses beside it. The thought of water made him thirsty. If he turned his head far enough he could see a doorway, probably leading to the kitchen. On the other side of the room a boarded up window offered scant light to the dismal room. He saw nothing within reach of his legs.

He could make out his hands now, bound securely, tied to his ankles with a stout rope. No way of moving them.

Straight ahead, another doorway led to what must have been the parlor, a small room with . . . what looked like a mattress on the floor. He peered into the darkness, tried to make out shapes in there, saw only . . . a foot.

Sissy!

The foot protruded from what appeared to be a blanket, a woman's foot for sure, judging from the smallness of it. She was flat on her back, her toes pointing upward toward the ceiling. Flynn had probably been raping her for days. He could only imagine the agony she must be experiencing, the total hopelessness of her situation.

He screamed as loud as he could, the word straining in his throat.

"Siz...zy!"

He could not move his tongue, could barely sound out syllables behind the sock. But if he shouted loud enough, and clearly enough, maybe she would be able to understand him.

"Siz..zy!" he shouted again. The muffled word seemed legible, at least to him.

He watched her foot as he shouted again.

It moved, only slightly, but it had moved.

"Ca yo hr me?" he shouted.

Again, the foot moved. Maybe, just maybe, he might be able to communicate.

"Ths s Dvn."

Again, the foot moved, more rapidly this time. He would not be able to receive a reply, but perhaps he might be able to put her at ease, to offer hope.

"I m tyd u."

He mumbled as distinctly as he could, hoping she would understand. Again, he tried to form words by controlling his throat muscles.

Clearly, she had been here ever since the boatman had taken her from the steamer. Flynn had been abusing her for all that time, probably denying her food, water only, giving her only ice to chew. The water wagon might have passed by the house or Flynn could have melted snow.

Their situation appeared hopeless. His bonds were tight. He was in no position to move. He was sure Flynn would return soon, fearing he would be recognized in daylight. He had probably gone out to obtain food for himself. Certainly, he would not feed them.

They were doomed.

"Dnt g v up," he shouted.

He heard Sissy weep, long, sullen sobs that chugged in her throat.

As a last resort, he shouted. "We wl b svd."

Her foot wiggled a bit, and then went still.

Devin sank into despair. He hung his head and cried, pitiful tears that streamed down his cheeks, rivers of sorrow. He thought of Caroline. Her vision came clearly. Her voice whispered through the gloom . . . *I love you, Devon*. He thought he could feel her fingers against his cheek.

Then he drew a deep breath and steadied himself.

Not now, he thought. Now is not the time to give up, not when his future was about to change, he with the promise of a railroad position, Caroline filled with the anticipation of becoming his wife. What wrongdoing had he done to place himself in such a position? He had not been a bad son, or a poor brother, or a problem to others. He had always tried to be proper and well-mannered and confident. Why had he been singled out to undergo such torture? The questions, of course, remained answered.

He gazed into the bleak interior and tried once more to loosen his bonds, but to no avail. They were tight and cold and well-knotted. His body quaked. His jaw quivered rapidly despite his attempt to still it. He wanted to sleep, but fear kept him awake. His fright and the dread panic that infected him were absolute.

He looked across the room at Sissy's foot, nearly blue. Was she freezing to death?

Had she died already? Perhaps she was out of her misery. Perhaps she was in heaven now where it was warm and bright like eternal summer.

Oh, God, he prayed. Help me. Help us.

Then the door opened, and Flynn reappeared. He pounded the snow from his boots, reached into his coat pocket, removed a bottle of whiskey, snickered, twisted the cap, and drank several swallows.

"It warms me," he chortled. "My last drink before I head out of here."

Devon trembled.

Flynn glared at him, his eyes like ice. "Cold, ain't ya'?" he said. "Maybe I should just put a fire in that stove and leave you tied up there. When your back starts to steam, well, then you might just warm up a bit before you start burning." He laughed again, sucked the lip of the bottle, and then glanced over to where Sissy laid.

He sneered. "Goddam whore is all used up. Soon now, she'll be meeting the devil for sure."

He turned back to Devon and knelt down in front of him. He moved close, until his face was just inches away, so close that Devon could smell liquor on his breath. "I'm gonna take care of her pretty soon." he sneered.

He slipped his knife out from beneath his coat. "I'm gonna cut her with this, to put an end to her whoring. An appropriate ending for her, don't you think, Mr. Alliance Committee?"

Devon bit tight on the sock to prevent his jaw from chattering. He looked at Flynn with all the loathing he could muster. Hatred flashed in his eyes. His revulsion was clear and permanent.

"You can watch," Flynn said. "I'll drag her out here."

Devon strained in his bonds, but his ability to move was nearly gone. He slumped exhausted against the stove. Would Flynn actually mutilate her? He slammed his eyes shut as Flynn moved away. He would, yes he would.

Flynn crossed the room, and for a while silence prevailed. Then he heard a squeak and the shifting of a body.

He opened his eyes, expecting the worst.

Flynn had sat down in the chair and was rocking slowly back and forth. The whiskey bottle stood upright on the floor, inches away from his hand. His eyes were closed. The knife was lying in his lap. Then the chair stopped moving and his head lolled to one side.

Sleep, you son-of-a-bitch, Devon thought. *The longer you sleep, the better our chances.*

CHAPTER THIRTY-FOUR

Death a'comin'

At Western's office, Harold stomped snow from his boots, and approached the front desk, occupied by a man.

"Is Chief Western in?" he asked.

"Who's asking?"

"I'm Harold Finch, father of Devon Finch who is a member of the Alliance Committee."

"I know Devon."

Harold's voice quickened. "Might I ask if he's here?"

"If he is, I haven't seen him."

The news sent a shiver down Harold's back. He leaned forward, nervously. "Can I see Chief Western? It's important."

"He's got someone with him, but he should be finished in about fifteen minutes or so, I expect."

"It's vital that I see him. It's about Devon. He didn't come home last night."

The man motioned to a nearby chair. "Just sit down and be patient. Soon as he's done, I'll take you in."

"I'd be much obliged if you did it now."

"I was told not to interrupt."

Harold went to the chair and sat down amid a flood of questions. If Devon wasn't here, then where was he? At LaBelle's, where he often stopped? At someone's house, talking, or maybe playing cards? He wouldn't be at the Page home, not this time of morning when they were just beginning their day. And he wouldn't be out on the street as cold as it was. He had to be somewhere safe. As his worry increased, his heart began beating faster.

He held out his hand, saw it tremble. His hand never trembled. Why now?

He was afraid, that's why. He was afraid something dreadful had happened to his son.

God, he mumbled to himself, why is Western taking so long.

✡ ✡ ✡

Sissy shifted beneath the single blanket, the one Flynn had laid on her after he had tied her down. The blanket covering offered little relief from the cold. She was barely alive. Her breath came in small puffs, at long intervals. Her thoughts had passed away, leaving only brief hallucinations, occasional visions of apple trees and hayfields and an unrecognizable face. Only a hint of life remained, bestowed by a slow heartbeat that still pumped inside her.

She was so cold, so extremely cold.

Her body had abandoned the urge to warm itself. Her blood had thickened. Her kidneys were working rapidly to process fluid overload as her blood vessels constricted to squeeze fluids to the center of her body, creating a powerful urge to urinate.

She teetered on the edge of death.

She had not been fed since opening her eyes. Water had been poured down her throat at uneven intervals, whenever Flynn thought it necessary. He had raped her repeatedly, with his own fleshy instrument, with a broomstick, with his fingers, and with his bare toes. He had ejaculated on her face, her chest and her vagina, and had cursed her repeatedly when doing so.

At first she had feared him. Now she didn't care. She wanted only to die, to be received anew to wherever she would go. She thought heaven would be denied to her, being a whore and all. She would most likely go to hell, where at least it would be warm.

When her thoughts finally ceased, in the numbing silence of the room, beneath the single blanket as cold as ice, she awaited the inevitable, hoping that death would be swift in coming.

✰ ✰ ✰

As the visitor exited Western's office, Harold stood immediately. The officer at the desk arose and went inside. Muffled words came through the open door. He heard Devon's name mentioned. Then he was ushered in.

Western was quick to shake his hand. "I understand that you are concerned about Devon. I was told that he failed to return home last night? Sit. Please sit." He motioned to a chair, but Harold remained standing.

"It is unlike him not to be at breakfast." Harold replied.

"Well, I'm sure there is a perfectly good reason for his absence. He's been known to go out of his way for people, like the man he saved just a short while ago."

Harold's hat turned nervously in his fingers. "Are you a father, Mr. Western?"

"I am. I have a son and two daughters."

"Then you know how concerned a father can be when his child is hurt or absent."

Western nodded. "I can."

"Well, that is how I feel now. His absence has me worried."

"I am sure he'll be home soon."

Harold stiffened. He fixed his eyes on Western's face. "I believe he is in danger, sir. That is why I have come to see you. I need your help."

Western's brow creased with concern. "My help? Yes, of course. Tell me what I can do?"

"As you know, he has already given his resignation from the Alliance Committee. Beginning next year he will assume a position with the St. Paul and Pacific Railroad, thanks to Mr. Greene, the man whose life he saved."

"Yes, I know."

Harold words came rapidly. "When he spoke to me last, he said he was going to go to LaBelle's one last time, to say farewell to those who had helped him along the way, namely one Willius Kane. Might he have fallen into trouble there?"

"Not with Mr. Kane. They were friends."

"With anyone else, then?"

"None that I know of."

Harold pressed his demand. "Will you go with me to LaBelle's? Now, sir."

"Now?" Western replied. "I have an entire day's work ahead of me."

Harold squeezed his hat. "There is no work more important than my son, sir."

"But..."

"You have admired his contribution. He has told me so. He respects you above all others. Now he needs your help. Will you refuse him, sir?"

Western nodded, touched his mouth. His eyes mellowed with a sense of sorrow. He nodded. "Of course not, Mr. Finch. I will go with you to LaBelle's. I am not ungrateful for your son's service, nor uncaring about the possibility of his being in trouble. No, I would never deny him help. Come. Let's be about it."

The wagon was already hitched inside an adjacent shed. Within five minutes they were on their way to LaBelle's.

CHAPTER THIRTY-FIVE

An Inch of Time

Flynn shifted in the chair. His hand fell away from his lap. He stirred and opened his eyes and gazed about the room as if he were in a strange place. Then he saw Devon, and he remembered. He rubbed his eyes, coughed, leaned over to pick up the whiskey bottle, drank three consecutive swallows, and then growled as the liquid stung his throat. Grimacing, he wiped his mouth, leaned forward, and glanced into the adjacent room where Sissy lay. A short laugh grumbled in his throat.

"Ain't you froze yet?" he asked Devon.

Devon could only glance at him, hatefully.

"Damned if you ain't the silent type. Why, I remember back in the saloon your mouth was always going. Or maybe I ain't the type of company you keep. You like to consort with those whores, and with the likes of Willius Kane, ain't that right Mr. Finch?"

Devon's voice was frozen behind the sock.

"Well, the way I see it, you ain't got too much time left to talk to anybody, least to me. So if you've got anything to say, you better say it now, because I'll be leaving soon."

Devon's eyes widened with fright.

Flynn laughed. "That got your attention, didn't it? Truth is, I'm not stayin' here much more than an hour or two more. Got passage on the stage goin' to Mankato, and from there, well . . . only those in hell know? Anywhere else is better than this goddam shanty town, that's for sure."

Flynn laughed again as if remembering something humorous. "And I'll be traveling under the name of, guess who, Devon Finch, that's who. Now ain't that a good one. You'll both be here dying of the cold, or maybe a slit neck, or, oh yea, a man without gonads, and you'll also be going to Mankato. Damn, if that ain't like cuttin' you right in half."

He laughed again, with an undertone bordering on insanity.

So Flynn had it all planned out.

Devin thought: if the authorities couldn't find Flynn in Saint Paul, they would search elsewhere. And when they learned that Devon Finch had booked passage to Mankato, why, what would they think then? Weeks might pass before they'd find him tied to the stove, with Sissy dead in the other room. Damn you, Flynn. You're insane, that's what you are. Insane!

"Oh, by the way," Flynn continued. "You know that girl they found down by the river a couple of months back. Well, she and I had a little fun one night, and she just happened to slip off the top of the bluff. Damn careless of her, don't you think? Maybe she thought she was a bird or something the way she took off, with her arms spread out and her hair flying. She did soar for a while, 'till she went straight down, poor thing. But she did know how to please a man, young as she was."

So, the confession solved the murder of Wilma Huggins.

He had killed two women. The third would be Sissy. He would be the fourth.

Flynn continued to suck on his bottle of whiskey. The liquor was just about gone, as fear began consuming Devon's mind. Would he kill Sissy first? Would he then cut off his genitals, as he said he would? He strained at his bonds again, but to no avail. No amount of effort would free him.

Flynn looked over. "You can't get out of those knots. You're going to die right where you're sittin'. Nobody's going to come and help you."

An Inch of Time

About an inch of liquor remained in the bottom of the bottle. One inch of time.

One inch before Flynn would put an end to his misery.

Devon collapsed in fear. Memories came back, one after another, like dreams passing through, and with each of the memories, tears flowed silently down his cheeks.

No more their walks through twilight, to the hilltop, where dreams were born.

No more the touch of her hand and the softness of her kiss. No more the warmth of her breath against his cheek.

No more her words so softly spoken. No more her promise of love forever.

No more her tenderness. No more her voice.

No more the visions of tomorrow.

Devon Finch waited for death the only way he could . . . by remembering.

CHAPTER THIRTY-SIX

Questions answered

Only five men occupied space in LaBelle's when Western and Harold arrived, two at the poker table, one at the bar, the bartender, and another in back.

The man at the bar was Willius Kane. He turned as Western and Harold entered, and held up his glass as if saluting.

"Kane," Western said, approaching him. "What brings you here at this time of day? I thought you were somewhere out west by now."

"I was on my way. I just stopped in to say goodbye to my friends."

Western motioned Harold to his side. "This is Harold Finch, Devon's father."

Kane reached for Harold's hand. "Willius Kane, sir, a good friend of your son. Where might he be now?"

Western replied for Harold "That's what we'd like to know. He didn't return home last night, and Mr. Finch is worried that something may have happened to him."

"It's not like him to miss breakfast," Harold added.

Flynn turned to the bartender who had leaned forward, listening to the talk. "Have you seen young Finch?" he asked.

Lowertown

The bartender shook his head. "I just got here."

"Who are those men?" Western asked, motioning to the two men at the table.

"Those would be Sam Weber and Kyle . . . forgot what his last name was. They came in for their morning punch, just after I started, about six o'clock. They'll be gone soon."

"And him." Western asked, pointing to the man at the back of the room.

"Oh, that's Kirkman. He's practically a resident. He got booted out of his house after losing at cards. He's full of whiskey, and about dead on his feet. He'll die holding a bottle."

"Looks like we're at the end of the line," Western said.

Harold took a deep breath as he glanced through the room, hoping to see someone of interest. He saw only Kirkman in the back, his head on the table, the only man who had been there last night. Harold couldn't leave until he had talked to everyone, because after leaving LaBelle's they had nowhere to go.

"I'm gonna talk to that man in the back," Harold said.

"Kane laughed. "Might just as well talk to the wall. He's just shy of breathing his last."

"I have to," Harold said. "You can wait here if you want."

He started off toward the back of the place. Kane and Western fell in behind him. "Might as well join in," Western said.

Kirkman was snoring when they walked up to the table. When Harold hesitated, Western moved in and shook Kirkman's shoulder.

"Keep your hands off me," Kirkman shouted, raising his head.

"I'm Henry Western, Chief of Police. I need to talk to you."

Kirkman's bloodshot eyes glanced up. "I ain't done nothin'."

Western kicked at the chair. "I never said you did. Now sit up, otherwise I'll haul you in for drunkenness."

"Shit," Kirkman mumbled. "Don't nobody respect my privacy?"

Kirkman sat up, wiped his nose, and glared at the three men in front of him. His mouth drooled saliva. He wiped it away with his sleeve, squinted, and focused his eyes on Kane. "I know you," he mumbled.

"Willius Kane."

Questions answered

He sat up straighter in the chair. "Now you just leave me alone. I ain't done nothin' to you. I've just been sittin' here."

"I'm the one wanting to see you," Western said. "He's just taggin' along."

"Keep him away from me."

"I will, 'lest you don't cooperate with us."

Kirkman sat back wide-eyed. "I'll cooperate."

Western glared at him. "Alright, now listen closely. Were you here last night?"

"Huh! This is where I live now."

"Might you know Devon Finch?"

"Kirkman's eyes frowned. "I know who he is."

"Was he here last night?"

"Yep."

"Did you happen to talk to him?'

Kirkman snickered. "Why would he want to talk to me?"

"I don't know. Did he talk to you?"

He might have."

"Did he?"

Kirkman grinned. "Why do ya wanna know? Has he done something wrong?"

"No! Did you see him last night?"

Kirkman looked away toward the staircase as if to remember the last time he'd gone upstairs with one of the girls. The thought brought a smile to his lips. Then he saw Kane reaching for his scalping knife, and he replied quickly, "He was here alright."

"When?"

"Late on, 'bout near . . . how the hell do I know. I ain't got a timepiece."

"Was it after dark?"

"T'was that."

"Did you talk to him?"

He looked Western dead in the eye. "Might have." he said.

"Well, did you?"

"Might tell ya if you fill my glass."

Western struck the table with his fist. Kirkman jumped in the chair as if hearing a gunshot. "Hold on," he shouted. "I'll tell ya."

"Did you see Devon Finch last night?" Western replied, his voice ringing strong.

"He came over and talked to me."

"About what?"

Kirkman scratched his head. "Goddam. How'd you expect me to remember? I got a whole lot of other things to think about."

"Like what?"

"Like gettin' back into my house."

"What house?"

Kirkman sat still, looking down at the floor where sawdust had piled up. Then he folded his arms as if unprepared to say another word.

Kane spoke. "Most everyone knows that he lost his house to Simeon Flynn in a poker game."

"Lost his house?" Western repeated.

"Yea, and then his wife left him. Poor bastard has been swimming in the bottle ever since."

Western shook Kirkman hard on the shoulder. "Tell me about the house," he said sharply.

"Lost it."

"When are you gonna get back into your house?"

"Soon as I get the key?"

"Who's got the key?"

Kirkman didn't answer. Instead, he turned away and looked into the shadows behind the stairs.

Kane drew an annoyed breath. "Flynn's the only one who could have his key. He's the one that won the house."

Western shook Kirkman hard on the shoulder. "Sit up, you damned drunk, else I'll take you to the jail house."

Kirkman laughed. "Then I'd have a bed for a few days."

"Where is Flynn?"

"He took the stage out of here, same day I went to Saint Anthony."

"When was that?"

"Can't remember."

"Where is your house? Tell me where it is"

"Up behind the Western House."

Questions answered

"Which house?"

"First one. The side's all blistered from last year's fire. But I'll fix it up, soon as my wife comes back."

Western turned to face Kane and Harold. "This guy might be hiding something. Bear with me a while longer."

Western reached down to Kirkman, grasped him by the arm and raised him to his feet.

"Hold on. Hold on!" Kirkman said, spitting.

"You're gonna go to jail for five years, maybe more, for drunkenness, and for riding out of town with a known killer. You're withholding evidence, and we're going to keep you in jail 'till you can tell us where Simeon Flynn went. Do you understand that?"

"I ain't done nothing to deserve jail."

"Then where did he go?'

Kirkman snickered. "You got apple pie in prison?"

"No! Now, where did Flynn go?"

Kirkman wiped his nose. "If I tell ya, I won't get my key back."

"I'll get you a new goddam key. Now where did he go?"

Kirkman sucked a deep breath. His eyes appeared to shrink into his head. "He didn't go nowhere. I took the stage to Saint Anthony, and said I was him. He's here somewhere."

Western shoved Kirkman back into the chair. "Devon's in Kirkman's house, sure as hell."

"And he's in danger," Harold added.

Western's face hardened. "I'll need a couple more men. We have to go there, now!"

"I'm going," Harold demanded.

"And me," Kane added.

Western spoke hurriedly. "Okay. Now listen.. We're gonna go there, right now, and break that door down. He's probably got Devon in there, and all I got is this nightstick, and my fists. I'll go in first."

Kane grinned. "I got my knife."

Western turned quickly. "Mr. Finch. You stay in the background. Kane and I will handle the dirty work. If Flynn is there, he'll fight to the end. He won't be taken alive. Now let's get out of here."

They turned on their heels and ran toward the front door. From behind them came a shout.

"I thought you were gonna take me off to jail for some of that apple pie."

CHAPTER THIRTY-SEVEN

Liberation

Flynn guzzled down the last of the whiskey and then flung the bottle against the stove, smashing it. One of the pieces cut Devon across the cheek, bringing up blood.

"Now damned if that ain't something," Flynn laughed as he stood up. Forcefully, he swung his arms in wide circles to improve his circulation, then battered at his legs, did a little dance, and blew into his hands. He looked down at Devon, kicked him with his foot, and then stomped down hard on his ankle.

"You might as well have a broken leg, too. It would match your arm then."

He laughed gleefully, kicked him again, higher, near his hip. Devon barely moved.

"Time's a wastin'" he muttered. "The stage won't wait for me. I got my cards, and my knife, and my pack. Don't need anything else except a ride out of here. By the time I reach Texas you'll be resting in the cemetery. Nice place up there, lots of trees makin' shade, lots of people sleepin' forever. You'll have plenty of company. And I'll be gambling same as always, except you won't be getting in my way this time."

He looked around the room, kicked at the chair. "Who the hell would want to live here anyway? This city's as cold as high country, and it stinks like death. Poor place to be. I think I'll just hole up in a hacienda for the rest of my days and get me a portly little Senorita for a plaything. Yea, life will be good in Texas."

So this was it, Devon thought. He could begin counting the seconds. Death would be welcomed compared to this. He just hoped he could endure the pain when Flynn started cutting at him.

During the remaining minutes, Devon thought about the sadness his death would bring. Caroline would surely weep her eyes out. With both sons gone, Mother would be unable to handle her grief. Others would miss him as well, Logan Miller, and Jimmy Hasset to name just two. Western would, but only long enough to speak his name before rushing to attend his duties.

He closed his eyes.

He and Randolph were running down the road, on a bright, sunny afternoon, toward the river, with their fishing poles across their shoulders, shouting as to who would be there first, he trying hard to outdistance Randolph, while Randolph implored him to run faster. His forward momentum was faster than his feet, and he remembered falling. His fishing pole flew out ahead of him as if it had invisible wings. He went down on the road, scuffing his knee, scraping it open on a half-buried stone. Randolph came back and nudged him with his foot. 'Why did you have to fall', he said. 'We got a ways to go yet.' Then Randolph knelt and brushed off his knee and wiped the blood away with the palm of his hand and held it there for a while, talking to him about the big fish they'd catch. Devon didn't cry. He would never cry in front of Randolph, never in a million years. He wanted to be as strong, and as brave as Randolph. When the knee had stopped bleeding, they stood up and walked the rest of the way, and he listened to Randolph's voice, strong and distinct as he talked about someday going west to see the Indians before they were gone. Devon had caught the first fish that day. Randolph had danced around him like a Sioux warrior, hooting and hollering.

Tears came to Devon's eyes then, as he remembered other days. Then he whispered. "I'll be seeing you soon, Randolph. I hope we can go fishing again. Take my hand at the end of the road."

※ ※ ※

The three men approached the house cautiously, Western leading the way. He stopped abruptly at road's edge and looked toward the door.

"There's some tracks," he said quietly. "Some point outward, others point in. By the looks of them, I'd say someone went in. See there, some of the footprints coming out are crushed down by others. I'd say he was inside."

"Windows are boarded," Kane replied. "We'll have to go in through the door."

"It don't look durable. If we put our shoulders to it we should be able to break it down."

Harold could identify with the seriousness of the moment. If Devon was inside, he was in extreme danger. He had overheard Western and Kane say that Flynn could be a downright madman, responsible for the murder of the woman at LaBelle's. He shuddered, thinking that perhaps they were already too late.

"You better stay here, Mr. Finch. There could be trouble inside."

"Not on your life. I'm comin' in behind you. If my son is in there I want to be the first at his side."

Western nodded. "Alright, then. Kane, you and I'll go in together, shoulder first. We have to hit the door at exactly the same time. If we don't take it down on the first try, who knows what will happen before we hit it again. Watch your footing. Snow's a bit deep there right in front. Don't go slipping. Are you ready?"

"I'm ready."

"Then let's go."

Harold Finch held his breath as the two men braced for impact.

Lowertown

✲ ✲ ✲

Flynn was kneeling between Sissy's legs, just about ready to cut her when the door came down. Devon had closed his eyes, gripping onto the last thread of hope when an unexpected noise shattered his concentration. At the sound of the crash his eyes flared open. He saw two men charging into the room, dark shapes, forms like giants.

Flynn reacted quickly, though he was just out of view. He knew instantly that he was in danger. Instinctively, he shifted positions, and poised his knife blade across Sissy's throat.

Devon recognized Western first off as he arose from the floor. He saw Kane next. Twisting in his bonds, he screamed behind his gag.

It took only a second or two for the two men to regain their footing. Western's head shifted rapidly to take in the dim scene. Bursting in from bright snow to a dark interior had blinded him temporarily. At the moment Kane drew his scalping knife, he caught sight of Flynn in the other room.

As hope surged in Devon's heart, a third person entered the room. He could only utter muffled sobs behind his gag, and as he slumped in his bonds, Harold rushed to his side.

Western and Kane stood aghast at the scene in the adjacent room. Sissy was laid out naked in front of them. Flynn had taken up a position behind her head, the blade of his knife poised directly beneath her chin.

"You come another step closer and I'll slit her." Flynn shouted.

Western shouted back. "You're as good as dead, Flynn. Let her be and take your punishment like a man. You'll not get out of this."

Flynn again. "She's still alive. If you come at me, her death will be on your hands."

"Let her be," Western shouted.

As Harold pulled the sock from Devon's mouth, he gasped three large breaths, and then mumbled, "Father, thank God." Then he called out to Western. "It's Sissy he's got."

Western turned his head quickly. "I thought she was on the steamer."

"He paid . . . a boatman . . . to take her off."

Western turned back to Flynn, who had cut Sissy's bonds and pulled her up tight to his own body, using her as a shield. "Get back, I say, or I'll cut her." Flynn's voice was frantic, desperate. He realized he was in a losing situation from which there was no escape, but he had to try. He shouted frantically. "The three of you . . . back off, out of the house, NOW!" The knife pressed tight against Sissy's throat, bringing up blood. "NOW! And leave the boy where he is. DAMN IT! NOW! Or this whore dies."

Western looked frantically at Devon and Harold. Devon's feet had been freed, as had the binding that held him to the stove. Harold helped him to his feet, holding him up. He was so weak he could hardly stand.

Flynn shouted again "LET THE BOY GO. NOW!"

Western turned immediately to Harold. He realized he had to go along with Flynn, to pacify him, to wait for just the exact moment to react. "Do as he says," Western ordered.

Harold's face blanked. "What are you sayin'?"

"Obey his command. We're backing out of here."

"But my boy?"

"Don't worry. He'll be okay. Trust me. You've got to trust me."

Devon quivered. Harold saw the determination in his eyes, "Mind what he says, father."

"But..."

"MIND WHAT HE SAY'S. Western knows what he's doing."

"Do you trust him?'

Devon sighed. "I trust him with my life."

As Harold released Devon, Flynn shouted. "Wait! You men . . . get into the kitchen. DEVON! OVER HERE! . . . NOW! We're going to the wagon."

Western held up his hand, hoping to calm Flynn down. "We're backing out. But if you make one move to harm the boy, we'll be on you. There's three of us and only one of you."

"MOVE!" Flynn shouted

As the trio shuffled past the stove, toward the kitchen, Devon stumbled slowly toward Flynn. As he entered the portal, Flynn dropped Sissy to the ground and took Devon around the neck. Devon could smell fear in Flynn's breath, could see it in his eyes. Flynn's voice was anxious, demanding. "Now we're goin' outside, just you and me. We're going to get into that wagon. All the while I'll have this knife at your throat. One wrong move, or if you fail to heed my directions, you'll die where you stand."

"And so will you," Devon wheezed.

"Then we need each other, don't we? Do you understand that?"

"Yes"

"Then let's move out of here."

They walked slowly toward the collapsed door, where snow had drifted in on the wind, and together they backed out.

Before Flynn turned him around, Devon saw a flash of light in the kitchen. His heart raced. Someone had gone outside.

Flynn drew back slowly, his breath hot on Devon's neck.

As Devon looked toward the street, to where the horses stood, he felt the knife at his throat, the blade pressing in. He stumbled a bit as Flynn dragged him along. "Don't fall now," Flynn warned. "Make one wrong move, you're dead."

Then, Devon saw his father and Western in the doorway. Immediately his father shouted. "Don't take my boy. Please. I beg you, don't take my boy! Take me. Take me!"

Harold's plea drifted away with the wind.

Western shouted. "We'll get you Flynn."

Their shouts distracted Flynn for just a moment. As he approached the horses, he turned his head toward the wagon.

At that precise moment, Kane appeared at the side of the house, running full out toward them. His voice cut through the crisp morning air. "GET DOWN, DEVIN. GET DOWN!"

Devon had only a second in which to react. He turned his head, saw the skinning knife raised in Kane's hand, saw him racing through the snow as his arm shot forward.

Immediately, Devon bent his knees and slid toward the ground. As his feet skidded away beneath him, the sharp blade of Flynn's knife sliced across the edge of his jawbone. Then his head struck the wagon's iron wheel and he tumbled face down into the snow.

Flynn's voice sounded with a gasp instead of words, and then a yelp, like a dog would give off when kicked.

Something heavy came down on top of him. It could only be Flynn's body.

Kane's knife had found its mark.

Frantic shouts came from the direction of the house. Boots pounded toward him. Flynn was being lifted away, amid the snorting horses and the thudding of their hoofs, only inches from his face.

Someone lifted him up. His father voice came clearly. "Thank God. Thank God. Here, take my shirt. Press it on that wound."

Devon heard the tearing of cloth, then the press of a pad tight against his jaw.

"You threw well," Western said, breathing hard. "I never saw a throw like that."

"It had to be perfect," Kane replied.

Devon drifted away into semi-consciousness amid a flurry of activity. Muted voices sounded all around him. His eyes flashed open as his father lifted him into the wagon. Words and sounds were muffled. He heard them talking about the woman, Sissy. Through eyes blurred by pain, he saw them carry her out of the house, wrapped in a blanket.

Devon settled into his father's arms, seeking comfort. Then the wagon moved forward and he experienced euphoria for the first time. Occasionally his eyes fluttered open. He saw the sky above him, a silent covering of white, and he knew he would be alright.

"Lay still," his father said. "You have the rest of your life ahead of you."

They brought Devon and Sissy to the hospital. Devon was placed in the same room and the same bed Dellwood Greene had occupied only a few days earlier.

The wound on his cheek was not severe. The knife had slashed across his jaw bone, preventing the skin from opening further. They closed the wound tight and bathed it beneath a poultice that had been dampened in hot lye. Then they gave him some spirits of turpentine to prevent lockjaw from setting in.

He slept most of the day, exhausted from his ordeal.

That evening, when he awoke, the moonlight lay across his bed like a warm sheepskin, and in the stillness of the room he remembered most of what had happened. Later, they had told him that Sissy would live, and that Flynn was dead.

Just before he fell asleep, he thought he heard Randolph's voice as if he were seated right alongside him.

"*I'll keep watch over you,*" the voice had said. "*Now you rest some.*"

CHAPTER THIRTY-EIGHT

The Heart of a Man

Devon was eating breakfast when Harold and Nona came into the hospital room, a smile on his father's face, tears in his mother's eyes, their arms out to him. They embraced and spoke comforting words. Nona mumbled a brief prayer, thanking God for his survival. Harold looked at him with pride on his face.

"So now it's over," Harold said at last.

"It is," Devon said. "I'm a free man, ready to take on the future."

"Providing Mister Greene keeps his promise."

"He will. Of that, I have no doubt." Despite his injury, Devon's eyes glistened.

"And I will continue on at the newspaper," Harold said with a smile.

Devon's euphoria faded just then. "I don't know how I will ever repay Kane and Mr. Western, and you." He glanced at his mother, and saw her nod.

Nona patted his hand. "You can thank us by being successful at whatever occupation you choose."

Then Devon remembered Sissy and he became anxious. "How is Sissy?"

"She's in bad shape. She was nearly frozen. They're bringing her back. I was told that she'll live. Her remaining wounds will be mental ones."

Nona turned aside, not wanting to hear the details. She had heard enough from Harold. With Randolph gone, and now this, she did not want to hear anything more about suffering and dying.

They did not mention Sissy again.

Devon had yet to see her. He was told that she was able to speak, although slightly. But her fears would linger. As a terrified woman, she would be unable to shed the horror quickly.

"Is Kane still about?" Devon asked.

Harold's eyebrows lifted. "Yes. He said he wouldn't leave until he had spoken to you. He should be here later today. He is quite unlike the man I thought him to be."

Devon swallowed a sob. "He saved my life."

"Yes, he did."

They talked for near a half hour before parting. Then Devon slept for a while.

❊ ❊ ❊

Caroline and her family arrived later. Devon was sitting in a chair when they entered his room. Caroline went directly his side and knelt beside him. She took him in her arms as if never to let go.

Her first words were. "What am I ever going to do with you, Devon Finch?"

Her words brought laughter, then a more serious statement. "If you ever think to try anything like this again, well, I'll just have to put my foot down."

He had tugged his robe up tight around his neck, to make his injury appear less frightening, but Caroline eased it away to have a good look at where he had been cut.

The Heart of a Man

"It will be your badge of honor," she said. "Something you'll carry with you for the rest of your life, to remind us of your foolhearty eight months with the Alliance Committee."

"I will wear it with pride," Devon said.

"And you will never go back to that sort of work, or else I will find a new man with some common sense in his head."

Although her threats brought a snickering of laughter, Devon knew, deep down, that she must never be pressed to prove her point. He had heard her pledges before, and had lived through the results. He knew that her words had the weight of steel in them.

They talked for about an hour until Dellwood Greene entered the room. Devon introduced him to the others, and was proud to say, "This is Caroline Page, the woman I will soon marry."

Then, with business-like composure, Dellwood seized command of the conversation.

"I have seen bravery many times over," he said. "But this man here, Devon Finch, has risen to the top of my list. He not only saved my life, but now, only days later, he has saved the life of a poor woman who was held prisoner by a madman. Even though I have known him for only a short time, I am proud of him, as proud as I've ever been to be associated with another man."

He looked at Devon much the same way his father used to look at him and Randolph whenever praise was given.

"I have a job ready for you, Devon. As soon as you can walk out of this hospital I want you to report to my office. Your duties await you. And if you approach them with the same zeal you have shown the Alliance Committee, I will boast to everyone that I have found the best man for the job. I congratulate you for a most remarkable and brave undertaking. I can say right here, right now, that your future is secure. The Saint Paul and Pacific Railroad is honored to have you as part of its staff."

They shook hands. Devon beamed. Caroline nearly burst with pride. Bethany was gleeful. Edmund and Lillian Page knew their daughter would have a wonderful future.

✫ ✫ ✫

When Devon was alone later that afternoon, after they had changed his dressing and given him nourishment, he walked down the hallway to where Sissy was bedded. He was given permission to enter her room, which he did silently.

She was awake, staring at the ceiling when he came up next to her. She began crying the moment she saw him.

He held her for a while in a comforting embrace. Words were not needed. Love was essential, and she accepted all he had to give.

After her tears had abated she whispered what remained of her voice. "I love you, Devon Finch. Were it not for you I would be dead now."

"You just rest, Sissy, just rest."

"Don't go."

"I'll stay a while. But I'll be back tomorrow, and the day after that, until you walk out of here."

He sat beside her. They didn't speak more at that time. They just held on to one another as if letting go would lead them to a more desolate place, or destroy their will to go on. Her eyes closed easily and she slept for a while, but he remained with her, watching her breathe, wishing she were down in New Orleans with a new life awaiting her, finding peace among friends, and perhaps a man willing to take her to his heart. He thought about them all, her and Ingrid, and the others. He knew them to be much more than they appeared to be. He knew them to be proud and honorable, and not the refuse of the world. Her hand was soft in his, limpid and colorless. He prayed for her then, and cried a bit while holding her hand.

When he returned to his room, Willius Kane was waiting for him in one of the chairs. He arose when Devon entered.

"They have taken good care of you," Kane said, extending his hand.

"It will be a small scar," Devon replied.

"But a good one. Some men wear scars badly. You'll wear yours proudly.

"I have just seen Sissy."

"How is she?"

The Heart of a Man

"She's recovering. She'll be all right, physically. Mentally, I am not sure."

"She'll come through. She's a strong woman."

"That she is."

"I can't stay long," Kane said. He reached into his pocket and withdrew a small box tied with string.

"I've known many men in my day," he said slowly. "Most of them were bad, or crooked, or idiotic, some just plain useless. Others were good, loyal, and brave. I can say firmly that you're among the best of them."

Devon's emotions began to stir. "Thank you. That means a lot to me."

"I'll be heading out as soon as I leave this building. There's another man waiting for me."

"Where will you be headed?"

"Out there." His head nodded westward."

"To where?"

"I have a claim, where the mountains are."

"Good luck to you."

Then Kane lifted the small box and placed it in Devon's hand. "This is for you, and for all you did for Ingrid."

"Mr. Kane, you . . ."

"Don't interrupt me. You should know by now, that when I got something to say, I got to say it."

Devon nodded.

"I know you have a sweetheart, and I know you'll be married soon and making a good living for the two of you on the railroad. I've spoken to Mr. Greene. I've told him what a fine man you are, and how fortunate he was to take you on."

"You didn't . . ."

"Now you listen. I'm in charge of this conversation."

Again, Devon fell silent.

"Now in this box is something you need right now, and something I want you to remember me by. You'll figure out which is which."

Kane stood up then and took Devon's hand firmly in his own. "This is perhaps the last time we'll shake," he said. "So put your muscle into it."

The handshake was extremely firm. As it ended Devon looked deeply into Kane's eyes, and there he saw the sort of kindness he had never expected from a man who carried a scalping knife, the knife that had saved his life. Devon looked him straight in the eye and nodded. Then Kane let go of him.

"You loved Miss Lorgren, didn't you?" Devon asked.

The big man sighed, and looked away as if to see a memory. "That's for me to know."

Then, as Kane turned and walked away, Devon knew that a part of himself would go along with him. The wild man with a big heart was leaving for good. His absence would be bittersweet.

When Kane was gone, Devon opened the small box and lifted the lid. Inside he found a note and a small cowhide pouch tied with string. He gasped, then uncurled the note and read it.

Marriage is something I'll never have, but always wanted. Be kind, and the sun will shine on you forever. Your friend. Willius Kane

He removed the cowhide pouch, untied the string, emptied the pouch onto the blanket, and gasped. The packet contained four gold nuggets, each about the size of his thumb. With them was another piece of paper, tightly folded. He unfolded it and read.

These were meant for Ingrid but she refused them, saying I had done enough for her. She also said I should give them to someone worthy of their value.

They are yours, on her word. Kane

He thought, Kane, you rascal, always crude, and never predictable. Placing the items back in the box, he slipped them into his trouser pocket.

"Thank you, Willius Kane, my friend." he mumbled.

✻ ✻ ✻

Devon slept uneasily that night, amid dreams of railroads, and visions of Carolyn, and the many nights with her. Eventually he

The Heart of a Man

drifted into a magnificent contentment amid the stillness and the silence, punctuated only by the whistling wind outside the window. He awoke as the sun began rising, aware of the stillness and the scent of the room, and for a long time he just looked at the ceiling while clutching the box Kane had given him. What now, he thought. I've gold in my hand, and a future awaiting me, with nothing but dreams and ambition to move me along. It was a frightening thing at times, to peer into the future where nothing familiar could be seen, where doubt and confusion lingered just beyond thought. Randolph had always said, *'When something comes your way you gotta look at it right off, to judge it for good or bad, and if it's bad you gotta throw it away, but if its good you gotta clutch it tight so it don't get away. You'll know which is which when the time comes.'* Randolph was always right. So he'd give railroading the best he had to offer, and he'd give Carolyn the best of himself, staying happy when hard times came along, remaining firm in the face of difficulty, holding steadfast when his children seemed to waver, and thankin' God for all the things they had.

Soon he became aware of footsteps outside his door, muted voices in the hallway, the sound of coughing from another room, then a groan, someone in pain. The window framed a grey sky slated with snow clouds. He touched his bandage. The wound was still tender. Lying still, he awaited the hour, while watching the shadows move across the opposite wall.

He ate breakfast, porridge and slices of apple, a small glass of milk. Later, the doctor came and examined his wound, and told him he would be released the following day, which led him to concentrate on his next course of action, that of proposing to Carolyn, right here in the hospital, away from others, and interferences that would continue throughout the day and night. No going out to the top of the hill. No being alone outdoors in winter, with the cold prevalent, and the wind howling. He wanted to propose when they were by themselves, and not amid family. He prayed she would arrive alone this day. The clock on the wall had just turned nine when she entered the room.

She came to him like a goddess, sweeping through the door on winged feet, her smile radiant, her face aglow with happiness.

She drifted toward him and nestled beside his bed with arms wide, encircling him, to kiss him firmly. Nothing could have been more rewarding. He glowed inside, thankful for his good fortune, for a woman who would honor him through life. When he lengthy embrace ended he spoke.

"I have something to show you."

Her face lost a bit of its lustre. "What, may I ask?"

He beamed. "It is nothing bad. Here, it is a package Mr. Kane left me."

"He was here?"

"Last night. We spoke for a while and then he slipped this into my hand."

"What is it?"

"Open it and see for yourself. It is ours." He patted the blanket. "Empty the bag here."

She untied the draw string and tilted the bag. Her eyes widened as the gold nuggets spilled onto the blanket. Her hands fluttered to her mouth, stifling a sigh. "It is gold," she muttered.

"Yes, they are ours, with which to start our new life."

She picked up the paper. "There is a note."

"Yes, read it."

Her brow furrowed as she read the note. When finished, she wiped a tear from her eye. "What am I to say?" she sighed.

He had practiced the words over and over during the night, and again as the sun arose. But then, in that tense and bewildering moment, he spoke from his heart. "Say that you will marry me. I ask for your hand, now and forever, through bad times and good, through whatever comes our way. With God at our side, we can endure through the difficulties of life, and give to our children a life built on the foundation of our love. Marry me Carolyn, and make me the happiest man on this fair earth."

She embraced him carefully, so as not to disturb his wound, sobbing, clutching him tightly in arms that expressed her love. Her voice, muffled though it was, came clearly to him. "Oh, Devin, I love you so. Yes, yes, I will marry you, and stay by your side through whatever difficulties come our way. You will be my husband forever, through the dark of night and the light of day."

They embraced, and kissed again, and wiped each other's tears, and kissed some more.

"I know a jeweler," he said. "I will take one of these nuggets to him and have him melt it down, and make of it two rings, one for your finger, and another for mine. And when the preacher asks for them, I will put one of them your finger, and you will put another on mine, and we will become husband and wife forever."

"Yes, forever," she sighed.

"But first, your father must give permission for us to wed."

"You know he will. He will, just as sure as my name is Carolyn Page."

She sank into his embrace and remained there until a nurse came to change his dressings. Afterwards, they spoke of the tomorrows, as if they were already there, and something else.

Devon took her hand, tightly in his own, as his eyes took on a new expression.

"There is the matter of Sissy," he said

Carolyn backed away just a bit, still holding his hand while awaiting his words.

"I must be given permission to see her through her recovery. She has no one. The women from LaBelle's won't come to see her. She's alone, and without hope. You know the whole of it. Were it not for me, and Western, my father, and Kane, she would be dead now. Please, my love, let me be the one to restore hope to her life, without prejudice, without disgust, until she is at least able to walk again, to see the light of a new day."

She took his hand and nodded. "Do what you must. I will understand."

"Thank you, my love. You have helped make a wretched life whole again."

Devon was released the following day.

On that same evening, three days before Christmas, Devon made a short visit to the Page household, and asked Mr. Page for Caroline's hand in marriage. He was, of course, given permission to marry her. He returned home, an extremely happy man.

✬ ✬ ✬

Christmas was celebrated at the Page house, with Devon and his parents.

They dined on roast goose and all the trimmings, and Mock Cherry pie for desert.

Afterwards gifts were opened, among them a gold ring for Caroline. She accepted it with a smile, and tears of happiness.

✫ ✫ ✫

Devon was put to work with the railroad on the second day of the New Year. During the month of January, he saw Sissy weekly, in the recovery ward, and after that at the home of a friend. By March she was fit enough to take passage on the steamer *Time and Tide* to Natchez. Both Devon and Carolyn were there to bit her farewell.

Spring came as usual. The river opened up in March with the arrival of three steamboats and hordes of supplies.

On June 28, the track between St. Paul and St. Anthony was officially dedicated. A speech was given. Ribbon was cut. Cheers erupted into a beautiful, blue sky as if to herald a bright and promising future. A gala crowd, including the Finch's, the Page's, Devon and Mr. Greene, boarded the passenger cars for a trip to St. Anthony Falls. The Saint Paul Daily press issued a statement that day that read, in part:

On this day the first link in the great chain of railroads which will spread all over this state from the valley of the Mississippi to the Red River of the North, and from Lake Superior to the Iowa boundary line, was completed, and a passenger train started from St. Paul in the direction of Puget Sound.

The sun was high up. The air was filled with wisps of cottonwood. Squadrons of birds crossed the sky. Brightly dressed people arrived, their faces bright with anticipation, their hopes alive with the promise of a rich future.

The Heart of a Man

Three steamers were tied up at the levee. Steam and smoke and the sound of their piercing whistles came from black stacks that rose like exclamation marks beneath the cloud tufted sky. A ferry passed by, its passengers shouting, waving, adding clamor to the festivities.

Within the city itself, Devon saw church steeples and domes where none had been the year before. Great warehouses stood in places once vacant. The streets were busy and clamorous. A row of new homes had appeared on the Uppertown bluffs, and down in Lowertown, flags and bunting fluttered in the breeze. Saint Paul was coming out of the darkness, heading toward a bright future. Soon it would be linked by steel to all the rising cities west of the river, all the way to the ocean.

Devon grasped Caroline tightly in his arms as the William Crooks moved slowly out of the city along the great stone corridor toward Saint Anthony. With her head on his shoulder, and her hand in his, he no longer had to envision his future as something vague and indistinct. With each click of the huge steel wheels, and as the train gained speed, he experienced a surge of determination, and the promise of success like a fire inside him.

Caroline turned to him then, and gazed into his eyes, and with it came that delicately engaging smile that had always sent a shiver of delight down his spine.

"I love you," she said, melting his heart with each of the words.

"And I you," he replied, the way he always had, the way he always would.

Then, without hesitation, and not caring if the entire world watched, they embraced, and as the whistle of the William Crooks sounded off the tree-lined bluffs, they kissed, sealing their future with the click, click, click of its mighty wheels, and the glory of love beating in their hearts.

✯ ✯ ✯

Finis

    Devon never saw Willius Kane again, although he heard that he had found gold in the Dakotas, in a town named Deadwood.
    As for Sissy, she healed just fine and within the year she wrote one letter to Devon. In it she told him she had met a widower named Joseph Lorraine, a strong man with a heart of gold, a man just like him. They were headed west to stake their claim in the wilderness, hoping she could bear him a child or two. In closing, she thanked him for her life. Enclosed in the letter was a lock of her hair . . . to scare away the demons.
    Devon and Caroline Finch settled down in Great Falls, Montana as the rails passed by the cataracts of the mighty Missouri River. There, he became a civic leader. Caroline bore him four children, three boys whose names were Randolph, Willius, and Justin, and one girl named Marie.
    When his railroading years were over in 1908, they settled down on a ranch in Wyoming.
    Their love never waned. Through sickness, drought, sorrow and death, they remained steadfast to one another . . . . till the end.

                            The end . . . .

Research Sources

Twin Cities: A Pictorial history of Saint Paul and Minneapolis. Authors: Lucile M, Kane and Alan Ominsky

Saint Paul, The first 150 years. by Virginia Brainard Kunz

Making Minnesota Territory, 1849-1858. Anne R. Kaplan and Marilyn Ziebarth, editors

Bring Warm Clothes. Letters and Photos from Minnesota's Past, Collected by Peg Meier of the Minneapolis Tribune.

History of the police and fire departments of the Twin Cities; their origin in early village days and progress to 1900. Alex J. Muller and Frank J. Mead

Steamboat Times, A History of navigation on the Mississippi River System

Pig's Eye Notepad, an historical Encyclopedia of St. Paul, Minnesota 1830-1850

First Minnesota Volunteer Infantry Regiment, Internet

Early History of the Saint Paul Police Department, Internet

Online Encyclopedia of Minnesota State History

Saint Paul Police Historical Society, A Book of the Saint Paul Police, 1836-1912

Minnesota Weather for the year 1861, Internet

Poetry and Music of the War Between the States, Dean Fowler of ReWEP Associates, Internet

The Story of Minnesota's past, Rhoda A. Gilman

Minnesota History Quarterly, various issues

The Minnesota Pioneer and Democrat newspaper, Issues June 1861 thru December 1861

Blue and Grey in Black and White (Newspapers in the Civil War) by Brayton Harris

Life on the Mississippi, Samuel Clemens, Internet

Twin Cities album, a visual history, by Dave Kenney

The Philadelphia Print Shop, Ltd. , Pacific Railway Surveys, 1855-1861, Internet

Hot Air Balloons during the Civil War, by Christopher Zuniga, Internet

1860's in fashion, Wikipedia encyclopedia, Internet